Warriors of Westopolis

The Bigger Man

Drew Bale

For Tom.
The man who inspired this story with everything that he is.

And for Renee.
The friend who offered me the insight and support to tell it.

The following acknowledgement pays respect to the traditional custodians and ancestors of this country, and the continuation of their cultural, spiritual and religious practices. I wish to involve awareness and recognition of Australia's First Nation people and their cultures. People, language, culture and events have been researched in preparation for this book from multiple sources. To the best of my knowledge they have been used correctly, and at all times in a manner with a purpose of being respectful, to assist in the telling of this story.

cover illustration by Andrew McDonald.

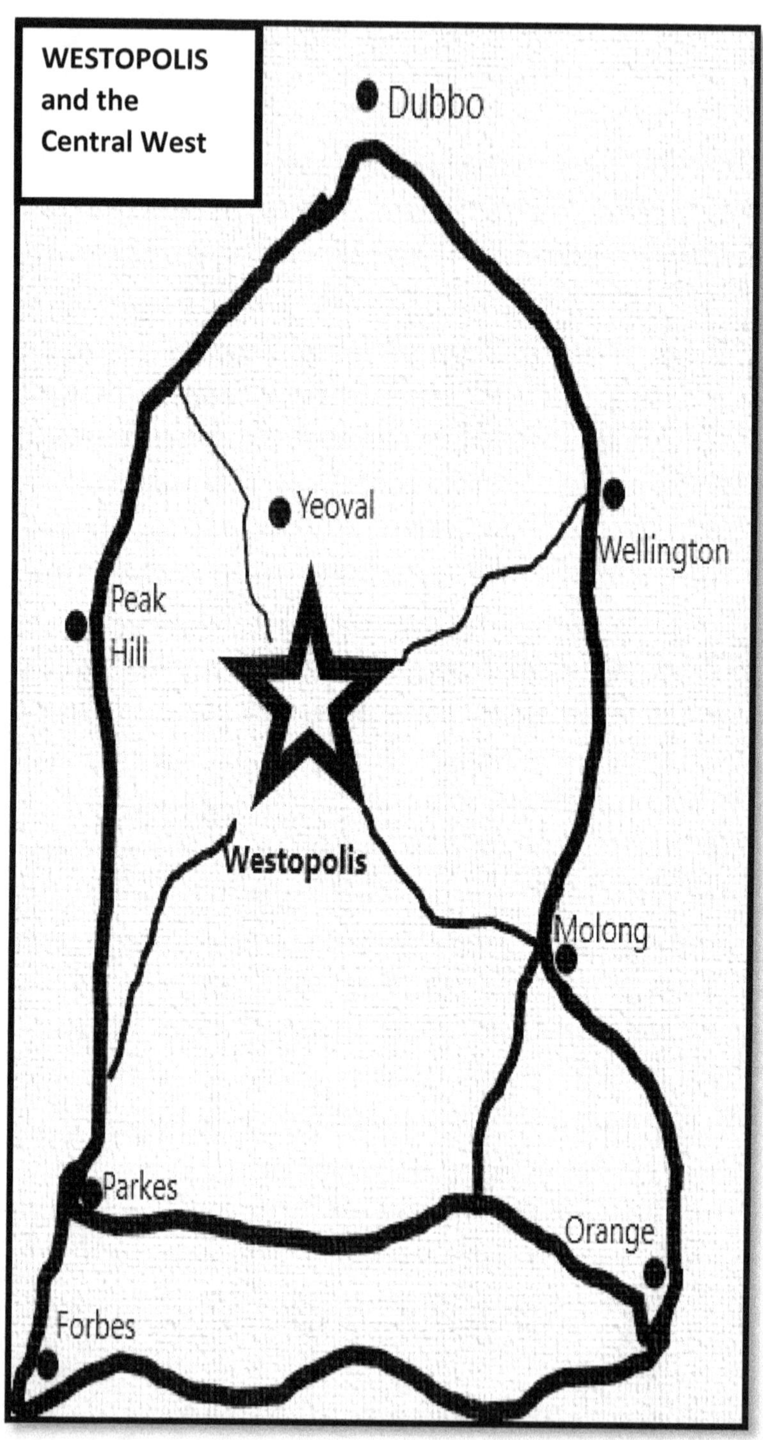

WESTOPOLIS
and the
Central West
Dubbo
Yeoval
Wellington
Peak
Hill
Westopolis
Molong
Parkes
Orange
Forbes

Chapter 1 - A walk and a swim

Jiemba simply did nothing. He had received one of the worst verbal assaults anyone had ever had to endure, ranking in his own top three, and he had done nothing. An assault which attacked his character, his race, his beliefs, the very core of who he was. He didn't fight back. He didn't reply. He didn't yell or cry or smile or shrug it off. He didn't laugh it away as if it was some weak joke like he might have normally done.

He just turned and walked away.

Jiemba could sense that some of his team mates were following him as he left, others were calling his name and urging him to return but he didn't turn to respond. It wasn't long before none of them pursued him anymore, choosing to leave him be for the moment, which was frequently the better option for everybody.

Jiemba knew that most of the people present had quickly jumped to his defence, either in spirit or physically, showing their disgust; willing to hurt the person who had made him feel this way. It usually mattered to Jiemba to know that he had friends like that, who respected who he was and what he believed in, and that made all the difference. It even made him stronger in the knowledge.

But not tonight.

Jiemba felt the air shift from the warmth that had been created by the lingering fire, towards a slight chill which he knew would gradually eat away at his body heat and leave him freezing. He was still mostly naked; wearing only the ceremonial garb that he had worn to assist in a smoking ritual alongside Uncle Lou, who was one of his closest relatives. Goosebumps started to appear, rising up upon his dark skin, the hairs on his arms stretching their length and more, forcing his skin to tighten. The Ochre, that had been carefully painted onto his body and he had been so proud of, now flaking in parts, became almost luminous the more he walked away from the light and headed towards the darkness. The outline of a goanna on his chest still appeared fierce to him, but it seemed to glare at him as if disappointed by his previous inaction. The smell of smoke which had soaked into his beard no longer the smell of country and pride, replaced with the burned out husk smelling of nothing but shame.

Jiemba felt like autopilot mode had been activated as he walked further into the dark. He wasn't actively deciding to go anywhere, or in any particular direction, he was just walking. In fact he paid no attention to his body as he was firmly present in his own mind, jumping between thoughts which were mostly negative. He was fighting hard against these thoughts, but the positive images were pushed into a cage in a corner of his head, locked there with the key thrown away.

It was far darker inside his head tonight.

"What are you doing?" he asked himself within the confines of his mind. No one would hear this conversation, despite how loud he felt it sounded.

"It doesn't matter," Jiemba responded to the voice without saying a single word out loud, knowing that he was speaking to himself.

"It has always mattered," the voice said reproachfully. "It matters not only for you, but for everyone who has to endure that sort of abuse."

"I'm tired of fighting," Jiemba replied, noticing his inner voice almost appeared to sob. "I seem to be the only one who does it."

"But by not doing so you allow someone who is obnoxious to share a view of the world that is wrong. And by doing this you allow others to think that he is right," the voice seemed to be fighting him.

"No one there thinks that he is right," Jiemba snapped back, "and I have trust that my friends will not stand by and let it slide. They can fight this time. But just because he isn't right doesn't mean that bits of what he said about me aren't true."

"Everything he said was only meant to hurt you, and he knew it was going to annoy your friends as well. That action alone, one of hate, can only be wrong."

"I am just tired of being a target of people because of my skin and my culture," Jiemba was even worn out by this fight. "And the more I find out about where I come from, and the history that lingers in my shadow, the more I realise how little I know about it."

"That has never been a problem before, because that is part of who you are. You have always been immensely proud of that, and you have always strived to learn more and be the best version of yourself regardless," the voice seemed disappointed. "He may have targeted you because of that, but it is because he is jealous of everything else that you have. You are better than him and he is trying to bring you down however he can. Besides, you don't fight alone. You are one of the lucky ones, one who has friends who will stand up for you, fight for you and beside you. They believe in you, nothing else matters."

"They shouldn't have to fight at all," Jiemba could feel his frustration rising. "Why should my friends be put out because of who I am? I never have to come to their defence like they have to come to mine. It isn't fair, for any of us. I am just so sick and tired. I am more weary of this than I am from anything else that has happened today, and all I have done is hours upon hours of training. I am just . . . so sick and tired."

"I don't think they are put out, besides, it is their choice to do so. The world is changing, even if it is slowly. That boy's words are those of the ignorant, not of the majority. Your friends stand up for what is right, regardless of who those words are said to. They fight harder because they love you," the voice spoke soothingly. He was convincing himself like he always did. He knew that he was surrounded by proper mates. Those that didn't see skin colour, or income, status, or education as a barrier towards being friendly. He was loved and that was why he fought so hard.

Usually.

Tonight the fight was gone from him.

He had lost his job, and the money that it provided. His last relationship, which he had invested so much in, had deteriorated before his eyes despite his best intentions. Jiemba's friends were moving on with their lives; getting married, relocating to different cities, and having children. The time that they had once spent together had been reduced drastically. He was happy for them, genuinely happy, so happy that he would take none of that away from them, and he would never ask them to do something which would take them away from that happiness.

But that just meant that Jiemba was completely alone.

The awareness had been slowly gnawing away at him for the last few months, so that all he felt like he was doing was holding on tight to the ropes that contained the last aspects of his life that kept him sain. He felt like his hands were slippery, the rope ripped at his fingers, and he was losing his grip.

As a result Jiemba had taken on more than he ever had before. He had become the guy who would have the difficult conversation with people and take on the problems of his friends. He would smile and laugh to cheer them up, hiding how he was feeling behind the loudness of his fake cheer. They say that a problem shared is a problem halved, which Jiemba thought definitely to be true. It would be a relief to reduce someone's burden like that. It felt nice to be involved, to be needed and wanted, to be a support to others and make them happy as well as himself. But, Jiemba was taking on the other half for everybody he spoke to. Everyone's problems had become his. He had more ropes in his hands, and he maintained a firm grip so that he wouldn't let them down. But all that meant was that he was now being dragged along with them.

His focus was broken as a glimmer of violet light was reflected in the water which lapped lazily at his feet. Jiemba glanced up and over the immense volume of water which was known as Lake Burrendong immediately to his right. The light had gone by the time he had looked up, yet another disappointment.

His ears seemed to pick out a commotion happening nearby. Too far away from where he had started walking, the campsite left far behind him, the noise was coming from somewhere else. He glanced up a small hillside which joined the lake with a steep cliff face and saw two or three young ladies fighting outside a cabin that was mostly hidden from his sight. Normally he may try to intervene, or even be a little nosey to see what was going on, but tonight he didn't want any more problems. His shoulders and his heart couldn't take it. He walked a little further, until he reached a point where the shoreline had disappeared into a sticky sludge like mud, and all the confrontations and commotions were left well behind him; leaving him surrounded by silence. He glanced into the water at his side and crouched down into the muck, allowing his feet to slide a little and the mud to seep between his toes. He could see the night sky sparkling above him in the reflection of the water, but sadly he saw none of its beauty.

Jiemba's eyes squinted and frowned until he found the outline and figure of his own shape. The features of his face slowly became clearer. No longer was there the smile of a cheery happy-go-lucky young man who could solve the problems of the world with a laugh and a smile. Instead it was replaced by a mask of disappointment and defeat.

A tear rolled down his cheek and he quickly swept it away with a sneer of disgust. He may have caught the first drop but the next evaded him, falling heavily into the water to disturb the surface by rippling further than he would have guessed. Eventually the disturbance faded and after wiping at his fluid filled eyes he could see clearly again. The calm reflection revealed that he had smudged the Ochre paint which had rested on his cheeks. He angrily dove his hands into the water and dragged the liquid up to his face. He scrubbed at his forehead, nose and bare skin, before scratching through his beard ferociously willing it all from his face. When he had finished he panted heavily and was astonished to hear his breathing so loud in the air. The ripples subsided and he could see himself again. The glow that had been reflected by the Ochre was gone and his appearance was almost indistinguishable from the night sky above him.

He was usually full of ideas or cheeky schemes that would allow others to be happy and have a good time, but now he was at a loss and could not seem to do the same for himself. He saw no solutions, and even though his feet had made heavy footprints on the dirty beach he could see no way how he could return back to the camp. Eventually the others would follow the tracks to him, as he knew they would, but what would he say to them? How would they look upon him in this state, what would he reveal in reply? He sobbed uncontrollably. It appeared like there was no way out.

Suddenly he came up with what he considered, in that moment, to be a fantastic idea. They couldn't follow his footprints if there were none left behind. He stood up, realizing for the first time that he was shaking quite aggressively. He couldn't decide if it was because he was cold or for other reasons.

"This is a terrible idea," his mind told him. Jiemba ignored the statement. He took a step out into the water and found it quite cool, he instantly felt his skin tighten as bumps appeared all over his chest and arms, and the hair on his body stood tall trying to escape the chill. He decided that the temperature was irrelevant and took another step, followed by another. A moment later he had walked almost silently out into the water until it had come up to his chest. Jiemba had taken several short breaths as his skin reacted to the reduction of warmth but he persevered anyway.

"What now?" his brain asked him.

"You know," Jiemba replied as if it was obvious. He looked down into the shimmering water and could just make out the goanna on his chest which seemed to be swimming all on its own beneath the surface.

"No I don't," his mind growled back. "You can't swim well, so the only way is back."

"It doesn't matter if I can swim," Jiemba snarled back, and then whispered as if he could hide the following thought from his own mind, "it probably helps a little anyway, besides, goannas can swim without lessons. If I go out further the others won't look for me, and if I am under the water they won't be able to see me at all." Jiemba slipped down into the water until everything apart from his face was submerged. His breath quickened as the rest of his body overcame the shock of the cold water. Jiemba felt like the water had been warmer near the camp, but that was irrelevant now. He paddled a few strokes out into deeper water until he was convinced that he could no longer touch the bottom. Then he counted to three, took a long breath, and disappeared into the depths.

Jiemba shot out his arms as he started to stroke. A chill surrounded him but he continued despite his whole body shivering. Whether his eyes were open or shut he could see nothing. He glanced up to where the sky would be, ignoring the small pop as his ears swivelled awkwardly in the water. He wondered if he could see the stars penetrating through the water to where he swam but he saw nothing. He crammed his eyelids together to avoid the muck from getting into them and he continued to swim. He kicked his legs hard to push him towards the bottom as he sought out the mud and weeds with his outstretched fingers.

"It has to be close, it isn't that deep yet," Jiemba told himself. He was groping heavily for any sign that his thinking was correct, but instead continued drifting with calm alarm through the water. He didn't care particularly where he was in the water, he knew he was getting deeper, he just wanted a source of reference. Bubbles snuck out from his seeled lips every few strokes as he took in what he was feeling. His problems seemed to be fading. Despite Jiemba being a poor swimmer he felt as if all of his concerns couldn't infiltrate below the surface of the water and he had left them behind. Therefore, the further he swam and the deeper he went down the longer he would be without them. He found himself to be almost at peace, he had left his negative views above the still water and he was allowing himself to be set free once again. The water seemed to be trying to lift him back up, when his problems always tried to pull him down.

The seconds passed almost as if time had slowed completely, allowing him a moment to become one with the water. He wondered if it was in these moments he could reconnect deeper with his spirit, but even that thought seemed like an unwanted concern at the moment and he let it float off to join the others.

"You are running out of air," his mind invaded his quiet.

"Leave me alone," he replied angrily, annoyed that he had interrupted his own solitude. The voice in his head vanished and he once more escaped into the serene darkness.

Jiemba heard a distinct sound from far away. A throbbing thud, accompanied by a flash which glowed behind his still closed eyelids, disappearing almost as quickly as it had come. He felt a small flicker through the water as if something had moved through it nearby.

"You can't keep holding your breath," his voice reminded him again. This time bringing back the old sensation as if there was pressure building up from inside. The sensation made him feel like his brain was frowning, the feeling intensifying as he felt more pain.

"Go away," he swiped out an invisible hand in his head, again the voice vanished, but the pressure lingered. Calmness surrounded him. He was no longer swimming or searching for the bottom. Jiemba had no idea how far he was from the lakefloor or from the surface. He just hung there motionless as the water caressed him. He had gotten used to the water and it had started to feel warmer to him, like a hug. Jiemba felt like this is what he had wanted and desperately wanted to stay there.

"You are going to drown," the voice in his head said calmly, "or maybe even freeze to death. The water isn't warm, despite what you think. Your nerves are frozen and that's why you can't feel them anymore." But Jiemba didn't respond this time. He was happy in the moment. A whistling sound started to grow in his ears, which sounded like a painful screech in his waterlogged eardrums. It was muffled by the water surrounding him, but that didn't mean it wasn't loud. The sound began to grow, the water began to tremble, a purplish light started to flicker more luminous every second.

His chest started to hurt incredibly.

His head was throbbing painfully.

"What are you doing?" the voice in his head roared. It was no longer one that resembled his own, but was someone else's entirely.

"Get out of the water mate," Dennis' voice appealed to him from inside his own thoughts. "You are the strongest person I know." The pain grew tighter, whistling sounds echoed around him.

"Come on you idiot," JT's voice said next, "you are bigger than this, get up." His chest was pounding, the water seemed to be surging.

"Jiemba, swim up," the words of his mum and sister cried out. "We love you." The agony had extended into his throat. He started pumping his arms and legs, hoping he was swimming in the right direction. He was sure he was, the light had become overwhelming above him, as if day had taken over the night and forced a radiant purple instead of a vibrant deep blue.

"Uncle Jim, we need you," his younger relatives squealed in sadness.

"It's all for you my boy," his Uncle Lou reminded him. "The world is yours." His arms and legs flailed wildly. He realised that he had swum too far down and he wasn't sure how much more his lungs could take. Beams of light were refracting through the surface, stronger down towards him; he knew he must be getting close. He felt relieved and savoured the thought of his next breath of fresh air.

The ever growing whistling stopped, replaced by the sound of an impact of something heavy striking the ground. The water quivered as Jiemba fought to the surface, but almost as soon as he became within reach it sucked him backwards towards the bottom. His arms reached out to grab hold of anything as if the air was something he could grasp and pull himself up upon. He was thrust further down as if grappled by some hungry whirlpool, the current overcoming him like a prize fighter stalking a downed opponent. The further down he went the more he knew that his hopes of resurfacing were disappearing. When he felt that it was hopeless and this was a fight he would lose, as outstretched hands reached for the surface but pulled him nowhere, there was another twist. The water, just as quickly as it had pulled him down, was now propelling him back up towards the surface. Upwards and upwards it surged, driving him towards the stars that twinkled above them.

Jiemba broke through the surface finally, but found no air. He was trapped in a powerful vortex of water that spun relentlessly out of control. He tried to fight but couldn't resist the authority it possessed as it twisted him violently. He became viciously nauseous as his horizon constantly shifted. The purple light was left behind him and Jiemba knew that he was somewhere high up in the air. He couldn't stop it. He had no fight left. Even though he was surrounded by water he could still feel tears that swept from his eyes as he clenched them tight. His lungs no longer sought air as they resolved they weren't going to get any. He felt like he was vomiting but water met water as his lungs and stomach evacuated everything that was left inside them. And then his organs simply shut down. He screamed at how stupid he had been, being greeted with a mouthful of disgusting, grime filled water, and how unlucky it was that during his lowest moment one more thing had transpired to bring him down. Despite the confusion of what was happening, and having no idea what that was, he was not surprised it had happened to him.

"No," Jiemba said to himself. "No more self-hating. I am not about that."

"I knew you were too strong to stay down," his inner voice replied back to him.

Jiemba focused his attention on all the other voices in his head, ignoring the feeling of his body about to be ripped apart by the never-ending force of the water surrounding and jerking him around in every direction. "I was stupid, I shouldn't have been thinking like that, it isn't fair on any of you." He knew that their voices were just tricks that his mind was playing on him, but he felt responsible for letting them down despite the fact that they would never hear his internal conversations, and may never see him again.

"You are strong we will get through this," his own mind replied. "Nothing has taken us down before." Despite the positive will his mind had shown, so quickly after being fought against so harshly, and regardless of how hard his spirit could fight, his body was arguing heavily with him. The surge of water was never going to end. He couldn't fight anymore.

"I'm sorry," he replied to everybody at once.

There were no more conversations.

Everything went black.

Chapter 2 – The Awakening

Jiemba smiled.

His eyes flickered as small beads of light pattered gently down upon him. He could hear the shifting of leaves as the wind softly stroked the branches above him. The song of a magpie warbling and the reply of a cockatoo screeching welcomed him back to his senses. His eyes, although hidden behind his still shut eyelids, searched the surroundings, through different shades of warm light, for the location of the sounds' origins.

His smile broadened. He had never felt so relaxed. Jiemba had no idea exactly where he was, or if this was all part of a dream, but he didn't care. He didn't want to open his eyes to find out the truth of what was happening around him. It seemed like he was a lifetime away from the thoughts that had plagued and consumed him before, and he wanted more fuel, more positive energy to keep them away. He didn't feel the responsibility to anybody, or anything; like a job, event or prior commitment. He knew that as soon as he started to move he would feel it all come rushing back. He held out for as long as he could. Devouring and trying to savour as much of the moment while it lasted.

It didn't last. It never does.

He eventually shifted, uncomfortably, realising that although his face was dry that wasn't the case for the rest of his body.

His pants were wet.

Jiemba's original thought was, 'Oh, no. How embarrassing. I hope no one is around.' He resisted the urge to say out loud, 'not again,' which was something he would have commonly said, more as a joke than an actual trend. He slowly opened his eyes as he pushed down on his elbows, forcing himself to sit up. His arms sunk a little as he discovered he lay not on grass, nor concrete or even something comfortable like a bed. He was lying on a floor of granite and fine rocks. The top naked half of his body lay exposed in the sunlight, while the area from his waist down to his toes was submerged beneath the gently flowing river that stretched out in front of him.

Steam was rising from the water where spears of sunlight were striking down upon it. Jiemba had been awake early enough, several times before, to know that this happened when the night had been cold and the dawn and early morning was hard at work to warm it up. If that was the case though, then why wasn't he feeling the cold or freezing, or, worse still, suffering the effects of hypothermia after being exposed to icy conditions for so long?

Or perhaps he did have hypothermia which was why he couldn't feel anything.

How long had he been exposed for? Did he need to get help immediately or was it already too late?

As he rubbed his hair, ruffling away all the grit and small pebbles which had been hiding there, he searched his immediate surroundings through blurry water filled eyes, spitting remnants of sludge and vegetation along with the rest of the river which had claimed occupancy inside his mouth. He appeared to be sitting on a point of land where the river flowed almost noiselessly around. The bank on the far side was steep and covered in grass, but a path, although overgrown, seemed to weave its way up through the old gums which hung down towards the water. The ancient trees towered above the river and seemed to thicken up the further he gazed between them.

Hidden above the upper branches the bell-like chime of a rosella echoed, only to be drowned out by the returning screech of the cockatoos which clumsily knocked gum nuts and berries down from the canopy above. The action seemed almost deliberate the more Jiemba watched, with several other birds falling victim to the falling projectiles. Jiemba could see in the water that it was shallow enough to walk a fair way out without getting in too deep. He suspected you could make it all the way across without getting anything else wet apart from your shins and maybe your knees, if you walked in the right spot. The small rocks he sat upon seemed to form a shoreline which got wider where he sat. The trees which stood on the far bank were mirrored behind him. There was only one thing which looked out of place. Many of the trees which had stood at the edge of the river had either been pushed into a lean or completely knocked over. Judging by the debris present at the base of these massive timbers, or crushed halfway up the tree's neighbour, whatever had done this had only happened recently.

"Finally awake, I see," a deep voice said from nearby, startling Jiemba to the fact he had been paying absolutely no attention to anything but the nature that surrounded him. He quickly turned and found the voice. An older man of medium build was watching him, leaning on a long thick detached branch which would have been as big as any juvenile tree. The man had a completely bald head, large overhanging belly, and a gigantic grey moustache set below gleaming mischievous eyes and above a crooked grin. "I have never seen someone sleep off the effects as long as you have," he continued, "to be honest for a while there I thought you were dead."

"The effects?" Jiemba managed to croak with confusion.

"Yeah, you know," the man replied, pretending to hold a cup while guzzling the contents down in an overly dramatic fashion.

"That wasn't what happened," Jiemba replied, suddenly seaming to reason with this man to show that he was not what he thought he was. Like it mattered.

"They all say that," the man nodded back at him. His smile had become marginally larger.

"All?" Jiemba replied suddenly interested. "You mean you find more people asleep on the river?"

The man nodded. "From time to time. They try to cross the shallows of the river further along that way." He pointed back up the river in the direction that the water was flowing from. "There is a point way up there where the river narrows and the current gets stronger in the middle. The young kids love playing about in that spot. When it is summer time it is a must do activity to pass the time. A lot of kids have made a lot of memories that way. The kids sometimes float downstream on their backs or on some sort of floatie, before making the trip on foot all the way back to do it all again. The kids know what they are doing. The adults however, that can be a different story. You see, if you are clever enough you can walk across the fallen logs and makeshift bridges over the river to cross to the other side where there is a tiny group of houses and an old mission on the far bank. But adults usually make that trek later on the evening or really early in the morning. It's hard enough in the daylight, but when the light goes and you are influenced." The old man gestured a walking man with his fingers. The figure walked across, accompanied by the old man swaying and pretending to be cross eyed, before falling in to be swept away, floundering all the while. "Eventually they give up and float down here, where they are found by me, or worse, their partners come down to find them, and let's just say that the bush isn't quite so calm on those mornings." The old man chuckled to himself before looking rather solemn.

"So yes, sometimes I find people asleep. But other times they aren't found in that condition," he shook his head. "Or any condition ever again."

"I am not in any condition," Jiemba finally replied with a low growl. He had been somewhat interested in the story, and it had brought back several fond memories of his own youth when he had spent days exploring various outback rivers with his friends, but he was not going to sit by and let some old man suggest that he was under the influence of anything.

"Okay," the old man said, "try and stand up then." Jiemba frowned at him as if the challenge was the easiest in the world to accomplish. He pushed himself up onto his feet, still glaring fiercely. He felt taller than he had before, and although assuming that the man was of similar height to him Jiemba found himself towering over him.

The sense of height and feeling of glee at finally being taller than someone passed quickly. Jiemba started swaying as he discovered his full height. His chest lunged forward as his hips shot back, his body doubling over as his arms scrambled out in front trying to maintain his balance. He felt as if he was standing on stilts and his inexperience meant he was definitely going to fall. His arms flung wildly and his feet staggered to find a grip. It was no good.

Splash!

Now every part of him was wet, though surprisingly he didn't feel the coldness of the water on his previously dry skin. The hypothermia must have really sunk in. The old man laughed loudly as he clung onto his branch in an effort to stop himself from falling over as well.

"I just slipped," Jiemba yelled through his embarrassment.

"Sure you did," the man replied, chuckling more as he turned to walk along the beaten path which lay behind him. Jiemba growled but was only greeted by more laughter.

"It's true," Jiemba argued back, "I may even have hypothermia. I need a doctor immediately."

"Hypothermia you say. Well in that case you are certainly done for, an ambulance won't help you. However, If you eventually do find your feet you can follow this track up to where my place is," the man suggested without looking back at Jiemba's scowling dripping form. "I will put a feed on, I will even make it hot to help you with your hypothermia. No doubt someone as big as you are must have an appetite to match. And I know if I had been asleep for as long as you have been I would be starving. I have gone without food for long periods, mind you, but three days is supposed to be the length of time a man can last without food or water. So you must be famished after four."

Jiemba took a moment longer than normal to fully comprehend what had just been said. "I was asleep for four days?" he eventually yelled to the empty bush. The man had already left. He heard another loud cackle from the undergrowth at his outburst.

As much as Jiemba wanted to stampede up through the bush in pursuit of the old man the task proved far trickier than it should have been. For some reason he had a great deal of difficulty in standing up. It reminded him of that time he had suffered a concussion and for several days he had lost the ability to sit in a chair, having to stand on it first before twisting himself around to lower his whole body. That, much like this, was such an easy task that he was suddenly unable to achieve. After several failed attempts to stand, he found himself pulling his whole body inch over inch in a shore long crawl to find something to prop himself up. A small boulder at the edge of the space provided fruitful and the most likely to assist him, so he fixed that as his target and set about his task. What he felt was going to be a real chore turned out to be almost nothing at all. His fingers dug into the soil below the rocks easily, clamping down with a vice like grip, before pulling him along as if he was swimming along on a conveyer belt.

He reached his target before long and looked back at the trench he had formed with his hanging stomach. As he rested a moment, sitting comfortably before reattempting the task of standing once more, he glanced down and analysed his body. The goanna which had been etched with Ochre remained, glaring up at him. He was sure that after being exposed and torn at by so much flowing water that his markings would have vanished. But the design, just like the rest of him, had somehow found a way to endure and survive. His chest was not as round as it had been before, and it felt like he had lost some size in his legs as well, they didn't look as wide and somehow they looked leaner. Perhaps that was a result of not eating for the four days that the old man had suggested. If that was true then why did it look like the goanna had gotten bigger? Longer in design and stronger in appearance? It made no sense to him. He chuckled briefly as he looked back down on the path he had made through the stones. He had left his own goanna trail. He laughed out loud as he thought of the next animal that came along to find the tracks. Both predator and prey would be horrified by what they saw, and the consequences that would arise should they come into contact with such a creature.

The smile faded as memories of him being in the water trickled back to him, slowly, as well as the reasons he had been swimming in the lake to begin with. The recollections consisted of parts which he would like to repress, parts that he was not proud of, and he knew that eventually they would flood back to haunt him.

He was not ready to deal with that yet.

Despite this, there was no denying what his body had gone through. Jiemba could remember the physical pain he had endured as he had fought to resurface at Lake Burrendong. He grimaced at the memory of losing air and then refilling that space with a torrent of surging water, which ripped at his windpipe and tore through his insides. His skin shivered as if it too was reliving the trauma. He had therefore assumed that his inability to stand was due to some injury he had sustained during the event. Looking down upon himself though, after twisting to check out his back and feeling behind all of his limbs, he found that there was no sign of a cut, abrasion or even heavy bruising suggesting an internal injury. He even tested his breathing but found that there was no pain present, even when he tried his best to cough.

The next thought that came to him was that he was suffering either from some form of mental strain which was disabling him, or, that as a result of intense consumption of water, he had suffered some form of brain or nerve damage. This, if it wasn't hypothermia, would definitely explain the lack of pain sensation, inability to feel temperature, and lack of gross and fine motor ability.

He had been in his head far too much, a habit which was making him nervous. He needed to get out of there. It was a concern he would have to deal with later, but now it was time for distraction.

The old man was nowhere in sight and Jiemba could no longer hear him as the birds returned to their early morning singing. Clutching at the rock for support, Jiemba slowly pushed himself up onto both feet. The wobbling returned, Jiemba staggering back to rest against the reliable boulder scaffolding which kept him upright. After a few attempts Jiemba could finally stand in the one place, with no confidence in his ability to walk. He felt like he was holding a bowl on his head, with a large marble that he was trying very hard to contain and stop from falling. The feeling passed by quickly enough, being replaced with the acute awareness of the muscles in his legs contracting and focusing on the job of holding him up. It was amazing how he could track the progress from wobbly mush to solid reinforcement. Several minutes passed where Jiemba didn't move at all, an onlooker could be excused for thinking he was doing his best to appear like a statue, until finally, as if given the green light by some part of his mind, he took his first confident steps.

There was no wobble, there was no face down in the rocks moment, no panic to grab hold of something to keep him upright. He was just walking. He had never imagined that he might lose the ability to do something as simple as walking, nor the fear that the loss would be permanent. He had been aware of his inability for only minutes and he was still relieved beyond words to have that power back.

His toes dug into the granite as he walked, taking big divots with each stride. He could see many jagged pieces sticking up to stab at him; he either missed stepping on them, or, if he had stepped on them, his eyes had sold him a lie on how much they would hurt him, as he felt no pain.

Jiemba trod gingerly as he took his first steps along the path the old man had taken. He was not new to the idea of going barefoot, spending much of his childhood wearing either thongs or nothing on the base of his feet, however, whenever he had the option of shoes he would wear them with visions of stubbed toes and cutting glass burned as warning signs into his mind. There was probably some ancestor looking down on him shaking their head, but his feet had become sensitive, he felt like he was being a bit precious, and he knew he would react to a rouge gumnut or root the same way any normal person would react to standing on a discarded and unseen Lego piece. He tiptoed carefully for the first twenty metres or so, coming to the conclusion that he was finding the soft spots easily and there were few burrs and thorns to impede his journey. It wasn't long until he was confident that the path would not harm him and returned to walking normally.

Jiemba didn't chase down the old man who had clearly made his escape long before. Instead he slowed his pace and took in the view. He was walking slowly uphill on a slight incline, following the path which traced the outside of the slope. The path went back on itself on occasion but for the most part it was an easy straight trail to follow. He came upon a clearing every few flights, and suspected that even though most of the native plants had grown naturally there were a handful of spots where someone, perhaps the old man, had placed trees or vegetation strategically to act as a wind break or to provide resources such as wood or food.

Eventually he found what he assumed was the dwelling of the old man. It wasn't because it was far away from the river that made it a task to locate, Jiemba looked back over his shoulder and he could see the spot where he had been lying down near the river, but rather it was due to how dense the bushland was so close to the building.

The house was nestled snuggly amongst the trees, hidden as best as it could be from trespassers arriving from the river. It was medium sized, sitting on several levels, and was somewhere between being considered cute or creepy. A small wooden fence bordered the land within the dwelling's immediate vicinity. Jiemba reached out for the small iron gate which was rusting on its hinges underneath an equally rustic, and once white, archway. He felt like he was only pushing lightly to open the gate, as he looked into the garden beyond, when he heard a small crumbling noise and looked down to see the gate had broken away from its brick restraints. The latch had been bolted and locked shut, but Jiemba had pushed through the restriction as if it was nothing. The gate hung from his hand as he felt his face flush red with embarrassment.

"You're fixing that," the recently familiar voice of the old man called out from the veranda above him.

"I'm so sorry," Jiemba replied quickly, placing the gate down to lean against the small brick post it had been removed from.

"It was old, so I will let it slide this once," the man yelled down again. "But you are still fixing it."

"I will, I promise," Jiemba confirmed, a couple of his many occupations had been in bricklaying and carpentry so he figured it wouldn't be too hard. He started to walk up towards the house.

"Stop," yelled the old man again. Jiemba stopped dead in his tracks, unsure if he had or if he was about to step on or break something else. "I may seem like a nice guy, but I promise that if you destroy any of my flowers I am going to have to kill you."

"Okay, righto," Jiemba laughed off the comment.

"I am serious mate," the old man said in a commanding voice, his smile returned but faded just as quickly. "The flowers remain unharmed, or who knows when the police will find your body."

Jiemba stood still. He was completely shocked and like the old man he shifted between an uncomfortable smile, hoping that he was joking, and a look of fear. "Seriously?" Jiemba asked.

"I have a reputation," the old man responded. The threat seemed almost sinister.

"No problem I won't touch your flowers," Jiemba acknowledged.

"Fantastic," the old man beamed, "now hurry up and get up here. Grub's almost done and it won't do to get cold." Jiemba carefully stepped through the mass of flowers, some of which had clearly received more care than others. He smiled as he thought of the old man gardening, but Jiemba was still deeply concerned by the threat he had made.

"Sit."

Jiemba didn't hesitate. A spread had been laid out on a coffee table rather than the dining table which sat abandoned near the kitchen with piles of papers and mountains of books discarded all over it. Jiemba occupied an old, yet comfortable, lounge which groaned under his weight. Upon entering the house he found that he was occupying more space within doorways than he had before, while he didn't have to stoop he also no longer had to step on the tips of his toes to look up high. Either that or the house was just smaller than he was used to. It had a cottage feel so that could have been the case, and was the most reasonable conclusion. However, he could also see higher up on shelves which is what he had been doing when he was called into the front room. There had been several pictures turned down on the shelves among other things he had no time to inspect.

"Expecting someone else?" Jiemba asked as he saw the copious amount of food.

"Nah, just meaning to cook a lot of this stuff up before it went off," the old man replied looking down at his handiwork. Plates of sausages, steaks (t-bone and rump), bacon, curly tailed loin chops, mushrooms, chicken and lamb kebabs, baked beans, a different looking sausage, some cooked tomato and pineapple, eggs, some cheese and a big chunk of steaming bread. "Figured you were near dead anyway so it wouldn't be a waste if you carked it anyway." The old man laughed as he shuffled around collecting cutlery to be used. "I would offer you a drink but I am pretty sure you have had enough."

Jiemba ignored the jibe as he picked up a fork. He noticed that his plate was bigger than the one the old man possessed, who sat in a recliner on the other side of the table. Jiemba didn't actually feel hungry, suggesting that his insides still hadn't recovered from what had happened, or the old man had lied about how long he had been down there.

"How long did you say I was asleep for?" Jiemba asked

"Four days," he replied, "eat up, it is already going cold."

"That makes no sense," Jiemba stuck a fork in a sausage and examined it. "I would have died in that time."

"You almost did," the old man said. "When I found you it was like you had a fountain stuck inside your mouth. The amount of water which was dribbling or spirting out was incredible. Eat." Jiemba chomped the end off of the sausage, chewed a few times (deciding that it wasn't too bad and definitely edible), before swallowing and searching for another.

"If you found me like that then why didn't you help me?" he asked.

"I did try," the old man confirmed, smearing tomato sauce onto a slice of bacon and shoving it in his mouth. He continued to speak through the mouthful as he chewed. "I tried to put you on your side in the recovery position, to help get rid of the water from your mouth. It was like you weighed a ton. I couldn't move you. My intention was to put you in a wheelbarrow and drag you up to the house. But that didn't work either. I then figured you weren't going to last very long and eventually the river would take you away."

"You left me to die?" Jiemba took another bite, filling his mouth. The negative thoughts started to creep back.

"No, I didn't leave you, I stayed," the old man confirmed. "I actually had bets with myself how long you would last. It is poor taste I know, but I figured you wouldn't mind as you would probably be dead soon. Boy was my face red when you sat up." He chuckled through another mouthful of food and Jiemba couldn't help but smile as well.

"What is with the flowers?" Jiemba gestured towards the outside garden. "You don't look the type."

"I would assume that you more than anyone would know better than to judge people based on appearance," the old man replied. Jiemba half choked, spluttering to explain that he meant no offense. "Don't worry about it," the old man smiled. "I understand better than most. I look like a hard nut, and in truth my history would probably agree with that. But sometimes taking your mind off things by doing something that is completely the opposite helps. That feeling is something I cherish, flowers and solitude do that for me. Do you know what I am talking about?"

Jiemba nodded. He knew the sensation, he just had to find his own thing which made him feel the same, in a safe way. Usually football and friends gave him the satisfaction he needed, but he knew that soon he could rely on neither being present in his life. He was embarrassed and ate quietly, waiting for a few minutes to pass. "Did you really think I had consumed enough to knock me out for four days?" Jiemba shook his head.

"Not for four," the old man shook his head. "Definitely for one at least. That is the usual time spent out down that river, if they live to tell about it. It's the normal with your kind."

"My kind?" Jiemba repeated almost with a growl.

"Young men like yourself," the old man answered with a smile. "Assumptions are not good for you, especially if you go assuming the worst. I set you up for that one as a test. My pale bald head has various shades sprinkled throughout, some are seen and others invisible, but somehow I expect more from you. I simply meant the young men around here are a bit excessive in their past time. I can't really blame them though with what has been going on around here lately. Anything to take their minds off the bad stuff may seem like a good idea, in the short term at least." Jiemba must have had the look that revealed that he wanted to find out more, but the old man shook his head. "A tale for another time perhaps. I am sure you have something you want to tell me about that purple light which lit up the sky the other night though." Jiemba subconsciously, but rather obviously, shoved a large piece of steak into his mouth, tearing it apart ravenously. A clear indication that it was not a topic that he wanted to indulge in, not that he knew much about the light anyway.

"Maybe later," Jiemba suggested to break the silence that followed. "I'm sorry for getting offended before. I usually brush that off, it doesn't usually matter."

"I understand, better than most," the old man nodded his head. "There will be a time where that sort of thing will never be said, to anybody. Hopefully I will see that in my time."

"Maybe," Jiemba said doubtfully.

"Maybe," the old man repeated. "Do you need me to make a phone call for you, so someone can pick you up? I am happy to drive you somewhere if it is nearby. I am going to assume that you aren't hiding a phone somewhere on your limited apparel, or if you do that thing is no good." Jiemba smiled at the thought, but didn't answer immediately. He really had nothing that he had to return to immediately, and he also really didn't want to. For the first time in a while he felt like he wasn't tied down, and looking out the window at the natural wilderness that surrounded them he felt like there was nowhere that he would rather be. However, he also didn't have any other possessions, like his wallet or car keys, which could help sustain him for a long stay.

"Not really," Jiemba shook his head. He didn't know what he was going to do.

"It is hard work staying out here," the old man interrupted his thoughts.

"I can imagine," Jiemba replied, eyes down.

"I don't allow strangers to stay here either," the old man said, his fingers were entwined as his hands rested on his large stomach.

"I understand," Jiemba said back, trying to hide his disappointment. After what seemed like the longest of moments the recliner creaked and the old man leaned forward.

"My friends call me JayDee," the old man said.

"What do I call you then?" Jiemba replied with a dry smile.

"I only have friends or enemies," JayDee said with his moustache twitching, "and my enemies don't call me anything after I have finished dealing with them."

"I don't want to be your enemy JayDee," Jiemba replied. He still smiled but he was actually terrified. He was pretty sure there was a backstory behind that moustache which would be both interesting and scary at the same time. JayDee leaned back in his chair upon hearing his name. "My name is Jiemba."

"Good," JayDee returned to his calm and cool natured manner. "As long as you work you can stay here for a little while. So that I can get some information out of you, and you can clear your head. You can tell me a bit about yourself, maybe discover some things along the way too."

"Thanks," Jiemba said with appreciation, though a little sceptical about JayDee delving too deep. He realised that he hadn't actually asked for this to happen but he was very grateful that it had. He felt bad that he was purposely choosing a path that would make his friends and family not know where he was, and knew eventually when he told them he would be reprimanded for being selfish for making everyone else worried. But for once he wanted to be selfish. For once he wanted to worry about nobody else apart from himself. He felt that after the recent events it was what had to be done. He didn't know if any good would come from it, or if he was even capable of thinking only about himself, but it was worth a try. Jiemba would be selfish to help himself. "I promise I won't stay long."

JayDee nodded for a moment then pointed to the food. "Hurry up and eat. Then we will see if I can find you some clothes to wear. I am sure I have something around here somewhere."

"Thanks mate," Jiemba said, stripping the meat from a chicken kebab from its stick in seconds. JayDee picked up a few of the cleared platters and moved off towards the kitchen.

"Oh and Jiemba," JayDee interrupted the young man's eating. "In regard to how long you can stay, however long it will take to clear your head."

"Yeah," Jiemba replied.

"And sometimes it just has to take as long as it takes," JayDee replied. "No rush."

Chapter 3 – Freshen up

"Read these, while you wait."

Those were the words on the note.

Jiemba had polished off more than his fair share of the spread that had been laid out for him. It had hardly touched the sides as he engulfed it. He only stopped because he felt like he had definitely eaten enough, in no way did he feel full.

Straight afterwards he had been whisked away to a back room to look for some clothes that may fit him. JayDee had told him that the room was full of old bits and pieces that belonged either to him or his eldest son. Jiemba's assumption that his body shape had been altered was bang on. Luckily some of the clothes accommodated the change. He was longer in the leg but had slimmed down at his upper thigh and waistline. His chest was tighter and his characteristic podge that he carried around his middle had also slimmed down. Only slightly, he was glad he still carried something there. The shoulder's which carried most of his load appeared wider and his neck thicker. He still looked like he was carrying a bit of puppy fat, but a simple prod of various parts of his skin revealed a thick layer of muscle lurking below the surface.

Jiemba selected a pair of jeans, a white shirt, a leather belt, and some underwear. The jeans could fit although the leg was slightly shorter, only just reaching to the top of his ankle. The shirt would shape to fit though there were some parts of it which had already been stretched by the previous user. The underwear he was told were most likely clean. Jiemba knew that he should be grateful, but he still only just managed to suppress a look of disgust. There are some things that you don't compromise on.

"The bathroom is down there," JayDee instructed with a crooked smile, pointing down a dimly lit hallway towards a room at the very end. "The water tank is old and needs replacing, so it takes a bit for the hot water to come." Jiemba replied his thanks while accepting a towel, scrubbing brush and a bar of soap before marching off down the hall. The bathroom was of a medium size consisting of a bath, toilet and shower. A large opaque plastic panel was allowing some light through from the ceiling. Silhouettes of leaves and sticks were outlined suggesting it hadn't been cleaned in some time. A large bulbous shape also suggested something else may be up there, he suspected that whatever it had been was now dead. Jiemba slid the door shut and placed the lock into the latch.

Looking into the mirror he saw himself for the first time. He had to bend slightly as the mirror stood lower than his eye line. Once more he prodded at himself, trying to convince himself that it was actually him. He even pinched his arm at one point to make sure he wasn't dreaming, but because he couldn't feel the pain he was no more reassured afterwards than he was before. His beard appeared a little thicker, his hair was slightly longer than he remembered dribbling down the back of his neck, and his eyebrows a little thicker. He smiled as well. The smile was definitely his, as were the eyes and the cheeks which tried to cover his eyes when he laughed.

Jiemba grabbed the scrubbing brush wanting to remove any filth before he jumped in the shower. His face was clean, as he remembered wiping away the Ochre as he looked upon himself with disappointment on the edge of Lake Burrendong. His forearms were equally bare as he had swept away the markings there as well. His chest still showed the goanna which had been painted upon it, as well as some rubbings below his neck and handprints on his stomach and upper thigh. Sliding a hand over the markings he was surprised that it didn't come off in his hand. He had expected it to be hardened and cracking, waiting for the slightest touch to easily cause it to flake and peel from his body. There was no such feeling, nor any indication that there was anything resting against his skin.

Jiemba started brushing below his neck with the heavy wet bristles. He flinched slightly expecting the rough scratching of the brush to irritate his skin. Once again there was no such feeling, and, as the marks were not coming off, he pushed harder to see if that helped. There came a point after at least two minutes of harsh friction that he pulled away. There were no scratch marks nor big red patches displaying what he had just done. The Ochre patterns remained. The only thing that had changed due to his vicious scrubbing was that the bristles on the brush were crumpled and mangled. Jiemba knew the brush was now unusable. Regardless, through gritted teeth he went even harder on the other marks, bending the handle and destroying what was left of the brush, pushing all of his strength into the tiny tip of the goanna's tail hoping that at the very least it would be removed.

No success. The markings were staying.

Perhaps they were stained onto his skin, or perhaps it was the result of sunburn forcing the outline onto him, much like a tan would do to worn clothing. If that was the case it would take time rather than strength to remove it all. The brush had been almost completely bent back on itself, bristles lay scattered on the bathroom floor. It appeared like his skin had been scrubbing it instead of the other way round. Not only was the goanna still present, but the skin around it showed no sign of redness or irritation at all. Shaking his head he stripped off the rest of his clothes and stepped into the shower.

Slam! Crack!

Jiemba felt his neck disappear into his shoulders as he cringed. Maybe he had been thinking too hard about his markings that he wasn't focusing on what he was doing. The sliding shower door smashed into the wall and the glass pane shattered under the force. He waited for an angry knock at the door, the old man out for blood as if Jiemba had destroyed a precious flower. When none came he proceeded to wash. Placing the broken glass carefully to one side, as most bits had smashed into large pieces, he delicately turned the taps of the shower not wanting to break those as well. As much as he felt like he could help with some obvious things around the house Jiemba was no plumber.

He waited several minutes for the water to get hot but became impatient. With his hand being used as a gauge to determine when he should get in he found no increase in heat at all, but nor did he feel the cold when the water started to run either. He jumped in, washed quickly allowing his hands to rediscover the new shape of his body, dried and got changed.

Upon returning to the front lounge room, in search of JayDee, he found the note. It appeared that JayDee had gone off somewhere and had left Jiemba, who was still considering himself a complete stranger, alone in his house with all of his possessions.

"Read these," Jiemba said out loud with a smirk, "Rightio." A quick glance around showed that the remains of lunch were still sitting on the bench and the pans were still filthy in the sink. He would glance at the books in a moment but he would start earning his keep with the easier tasks. A quick search of the immediate vicinity revealed other hidden plates and a landslide of coffee mugs. The odd bottle was lying around but apart from a generally worn look the place was relatively clean.

Once the dishes were washed and dried, Jiemba grabbed the small pile of books and found his way out onto the wooden decked veranda that JayDee had yelled from earlier. There was a collection of deck chairs of various sizes all over the place. Jiemba found one that looked down the hillside towards the river. The chair looked as though it could take his weight, but Jiemba still took care as he slowly slumped down into it. With a mighty groan which was more from habit than exhaustion, Jiemba flicked through the titles in front of him. He wasn't much of a reader but had found himself doing so more often due to projects or prompting from his friends. That being said, he could definitely read if he was interested or if he had the time where he could sit undisturbed without any interruption or distraction. When did that ever happen though? *The Long Walk to Freedom* was the first title. He had heard about Nelson Mandela and knew some of his history, but as much as he wanted to know more, a 700 page tome seemed like an ambitious choice for a reluctant reader to knock over in the short time that Jiemba was expecting to stay at the house. Maybe JayDee was going to be gone for a bit longer than he suggested, perhaps a month even. Jiemba flicked through the book, stopped at the pictures strewn throughout before looking at the next few remaining books. *Last stand of Leonidas, Battles of the Peninsula War,* and *Following the Leader* were some of the other selections, but the choices were many. Jiemba smiled when he got to a children's book. A note had been left on the front.

'Too advanced, don't attempt without an adult'.

Jiemba's trademark laugh returned though he was alone. A kookaburra sitting upon a burned out stump jumped in, adding his own laughing chorus as if it had been an invitation. Jiemba flicked through all the books one by one, finding a picture or sentence that he liked before putting them down. Last of all was the children's book. A few pages in and he turned his head to the side.

"Some big words in here," he said to himself, "maybe the old man was right."

"I knew you couldn't read that one," JayDee agreed as his heavy boots thumped on the timber floor as he returned unexpectedly. Jiemba shifted in his seat showing his surprise, but laughed loudly in reply.

"Didn't even get past the cover," Jiemba countered, his cheeks had covered his eyes as he smiled. "And there is only one word on it." Jiemba was clearly joking and he laughed heartily at his own joke. He was happy in the knowledge that he had returned somewhat back to normal. Even after just a short time in solitude and despite being with a complete stranger, Jiemba felt far more at ease.

"I just popped down to the mailbox," JayDee explained his absence. "You never know when someone wants to send you something. The only problem is that it is a hundred metre walk to the road, there and back that is, and when you return it's all back uphill."

"Plus all the bills," Jiemba added.

"Those too," JayDee replied. "Nothing today, which is always nice. What did you think of the books?"

"I didn't really have time to go through them," Jiemba admitted. "Some interesting and varied content. Are you a big reader?"

"I never used to be," he admitted, squinting out into the bush. "But I got tired of feeling like I was missing something important so I have been reading more and more. I picked those out because I think you could find them interesting."

"Any quick points?" Jiemba asked, smiling as he pointed to the size of some of them.

"It's better to find your own meaning," JayDee answered with a small nod. "I think if you do that it means more to you, you can make connections and learn more that way. But, to paraphrase some of those. I learned from Nelson that struggles are called struggles for a reason, they test your willpower and try to force you away from what you want to be, and try and make you something that are not. From Leonidas it was that in your darkest moments you can accept your fate, or challenge it, and in the process inspire many around you. For the children's book I just wanted to see if you could read." They both laughed vigorously.

"I just, didn't peg you as someone who reads," Jiemba said, shooting the man a sideways glance waiting for another conversation about assumptions. JayDee just gave him a knowing look before pointing out over the edge of the veranda towards the river. Every few moments the sun, as it shifted position in the sky, would cast a different pattern using the leaves as a stencil. It made some parts of the brush glow while others became covered in shadows.

"It looks like another one of your mates has arrived," JayDee smirked at his return shot but continued looking down at the river. There was movement down where Jiemba had been found.

"Maybe it's a kid?" Jiemba suggested.

"Maybe," JayDee agreed. "They usually don't hang around very long. Whoever that is has sprawled out on the ground down there. Which means if it was a kid then all the more reason to go and check it out."

"Do you just sit up here all day waiting to help people who come floating down the river?" Jiemba asked.

"Sometimes," JayDee replied. "Sometimes I have other things to do and don't help at all. Other times I just can't be bothered, there is only so many times that an old fella like me can walk back and forward on these hills. Got to have a break every now and then," he smiled again. Jiemba was finding it very concerning how he didn't know when the old man was joking or not.

"Come on," JayDee said pushing onto his feet with a groan. "Time to earn your keep."

Blurgh!

"How many is that?" JayDee asked.

"Four big ones," Jiemba replied, his nose upturned. "I am not counting that little one, or the dry retching he did before."

"What is it?" JayDee followed. He was sitting several metres away on the boulder that Jiemba had used as a prop earlier. He had been right in his assumption that the person had been an adult. The young man had staggered and fallen in the ditch that had been created by Jiemba's stomach as he had crawled along the beach. Now he was laying on his side with a trail of fluid trying to flow towards the river, but managing to seep through the rocks instead.

"Some chunks still, but at least the liquid isn't colourful anymore," Jiemba stated, grossed out that he was analysing someone else's vomit.

"Good, is he conscious?"

"No, but he is breathing," Jiemba answered.

"After he brings up again we will take him back up the river."

"And by take you mean . . ?" asked Jiemba.

"You are carrying him," confirmed JayDee. 'Great,' thought Jiemba. They waited until the next spasm from the young man surged forward, then Jiemba showing very little concern threw him over one shoulder. It took no trouble at all to place him there, and even less to keep him balanced. It was as if there was nothing there at all, and Jiemba was just weirdly holding onto his own shoulder for some reason. JayDee led the way through the small scrub along a path which had been made from years of use.

"It seems a bit early in the day to be drinking and falling in the river, don't you think?" Jiemba asked.

"It depends on what time you started," JayDee replied, but he didn't seem too interested in the man hanging over Jiemba's shoulder. "Do you see here, and also there?" JayDee pointed to several spots on the ground. Jiemba looked and saw that there was debris and plants that had been crushed next to the path. "And check out that tree. That is where the water came up the other night." Jiemba could see that there was part of a log stuck in the fork of the tree in question, which seemed to be at least five metres higher than the water level that was currently flowing in the river.

"I don't know much about it," Jiemba responded, knowing that the question was going to be asked eventually.

"Nothing at all?" JayDee didn't seem convinced. "Nothing about the light or the massive surge of water? Not even where you were?" The old man seemed mildly shocked. After turning a few more corners in the path Jiemba decided he would tell him a watered down version, but even if he hadn't Jiemba didn't actually have much to reveal.

"I was swimming at Lake Burrendong," Jiemba admitted, "I was there with some mates for a rugby training weekend."

"That is interesting," JayDee seemed very intrigued. "But before I get into details, do your mates know that you are missing or had you already left them?"

"I didn't say goodbye, we still had another day together," Jiemba explained. "But I go for long walks sometimes to clear my head."

"But surely they would be worried if you don't come back?" JayDee stated as he pushed part of a fallen bush out of the way.

"Sure, maybe?" even Jiemba didn't seem convinced. He knew they would be, but he had already sold himself the lie and decided to stick with it before doubling down. "Sometimes I don't come back. I catch up with them eventually. Some of them may be concerned but it is not out of the ordinary."

"Does that seem healthy to you?" JayDee asked as he stomped flat a fallen branch.

"Probably not, but I have done it for so long," he stopped, he was getting in deeper than he would have liked. "Anyway I was swimming and decided to duck down below the surface. I remember seeing a bright purple light in the sky. I don't know what it was though, as it was hard to see below the water. Whatever it was I thought I saw it earlier too. Maybe. Anyway I was swimming and it was getting bigger. I heard a whistling sound and then something hit the water. Hard. It could have been whatever the light was but I can't be sure. The next thing I knew I was hurled up into the air, but still in the water. I was thrown about for a bit. I'm not sure what happened. Next thing I knew I was waking up on your stone covered beach." He had come to the end of his tale and a small silence followed.

Blurgh, BLURGH!

"Well it sounds like he is still alive," JayDee called back, "just."

"Maybe," Jiemba confirmed, scrunching his nose. "Remind me not to step there when we go back. That sounded wet and I am pretty sure I have got chunks attached to my back."

"I'll try, but no promises," JayDee laughed. "Even though you don't think so there was a lot of information in your story. I saw the light. I knew it came from somewhere near Burrendong. I heard the bang, as well as saw the light start heading toward the ground. But I had no idea what had happened after that. To hear that it hit the lake and that amount of water was because of a surge, or a wave, over the wall. It makes some sense, but still leaves more questions. I apologise for assuming you were like the guy you're carrying. You really are lucky to be alive."

"If I was dead I wouldn't feel chunks sticking to my back though," Jiemba replied with a laugh, while actually hating what was touching him. As the man dried off more from the river water his smell actually got worse. "I can't believe you thought I was like this guy."

"I'm sorry to say that around here it is actually a safe bet," JayDee shuffled a little slower as they walked up a small rocky slope; the river was still in view beside them and the small trickle of a waterfall could be heard as well. "The mission and the other houses on the far side of the river have been abandoned for years. Usually this area is empty and only the odd vandal will travel out to tag a wall that no one even knows to exist. But when Westopolis shot up in the middle of the Central West the whole area sort of took off. Wellington was already a nice little place, with some issues like everywhere else, but you would drive through it or stay overnight and everything was fine. Developers saw opportunity at the foot of the mountains on the west side and started throwing money and projects that would both boost tourism but raise the local economy. High-rise motels, classy restaurants, entertainment venues and expensive residential areas shot up almost overnight. It divided the town into what they now call New Wellington, everything near the foot of the mountains, and Old Wellington, everything that existed before."

"Apart from the divide it sounds good for the area," Jiemba admitted, knowing that he was probably admitting his ignorance in the matter.

"Sounds great," JayDee agreed. "Especially for people in and around the water. Farmers and grazers around the area are loving the infrastructure being put in place. The river here is always flowing at a constant rate because of the pipes they put into Burrendong to pump the water in and out, to keep it at the same level. It never floods anymore, neither does the Bell and that was what had been cutting off the town for so long. The new residents even poured some of their own money to bring up some of the old establishments in the town. New things started coming in. All the renewable stuff sounds good, the stadium seemed like a waste at the start but it has put Wellington back on the map again. It was all looking like the town was thriving, except, it forced up prices for rentals, the caravan park was pushed further out of town away from resources, everyday items became more expensive. It started to displace whole households, families and communities. Before you knew it, good people were living on the streets through no fault of their own. The police and some of the locals were doing their best to help them, to house them, feed them, trying to employ them. All matter of people were in dire need of support. Not limited to a race or group, almost everyone who lived in the town before immediately fell below the poverty line and found themselves in trouble."

"It is good to think that people were helping them," Jiemba added, the tale was a rollercoaster of ups and downs. It was clear that JayDee didn't mind to have a conversation either, but Jiemba was happy the old man was leading the conversation. "I knew of problems but never imagined that was happening so close to where I live."

"I guarantee it is happening where you live, but not on this level," JayDee had a head of steam and was being far more informative than Jiemba thought was possible. "People are struggling everywhere. Some don't care, no matter how much you help them. If they were drowning you could hold out a stick to save them and they would break it. Some would even blame you for helping them, as if it was your fault to begin with. It's a shame. But most people, even the angry ones, just need someone to give them a chance. They need a hero to go out of their way to defend them because they can't do it themselves, and usually drive away anyone who would actually try." Jiemba heard a sniffle and saw JayDee swat something away from his face, he continued a moment later. "The help wasn't happening quickly enough for the new residents though. A short time after they put money into a privately run prison, and a security company to assist the local authorities. They pay for everything there. The

premises, the food, the employees, and they even employ them to
scour the streets looking for more people to put in there.”

“How do they afford it?”

“Easily,” JayDee explained, “they own most of the rental market
now, and as the homeless are removed from the streets the safer the
place looks. Rental prices go up, other expenses rise and people pay
them to have a part of this inland paradise. There are some pretty
bad rumours as to what goes on in that prison. They don’t answer to
anybody so how would you know. But because of that people have
fled. They have been pushed out of town, hiding wherever they can.
Places just like the old mission where there is a roof and not much
else. This place used to be a chore to get to, but not anymore. They
can hardly afford food so they spend it on whatever gets them
through the day. There are some who still fight in town; a mix of
people, some who just want to cause a fuss while others are just
trying to make a difference. Wellington is definitely a place you want
to go to now, I was fine with it before though. But you always wonder
if it was worth the cost.”

“My experience says the answer is always no,” Jiemba stated,
thinking back to past events and atrocities in Australian and world
history.

“The answer is always no,” JayDee agreed. “Another little test, he
he.” He was wheezing heavily. The hill had been long and he had
been talking a lot, plus he was vastly overweight. Jiemba suspected
that the old man also had trouble with at least one of his knees, but
probably both, as he struggled to the top with an obvious limp.
“Despite how dark that sounds, light usually shines brighter in such
conditions. You will see what I mean over this hill.”

“I am sorry I have been misjudging you JayDee,” Jiemba said
patting the old man on the shoulder. “You are far smarter than I
would have imagined.”

“I have some real gems too,” JayDee beamed at the praise. “One
day you should ask me about when the monarchy falls. New anthem,

new flag, new date, new people, new outlook. It will blow your mind."

"No doubt," Jiemba replied with a smile. The guy on his shoulder was starting to stir, and in doing so reminded Jiemba that he was even there in the first place. He was more interested in the laughter and cheer he could hear coming from down below him. In the far distance he could see the dam wall of Lake Burrendong, and he realised for the first time just how far he had been flung or how far he had been dragged in what he suspected was a raging river. Jiemba instantly saw the many attempts of a bridge that went through the shallows, particularly in sections where the river bottled up for a portion of its length. He could see where the current sped up; created by pressing a massive amount of water into a small space. It didn't look too difficult to cross, but Jiemba could imagine that when staggering the task could be more challenging.

"What is that thing?" Jiemba asked. "And what are they doing with it?" He was almost skipping down the small slope leaving JayDee in his wake as he charged toward it. There was a large pontoon which was floating in a much wider section of the river. It appeared to be about thirty metres wide and long, with ropes extending from each corner to be wrapped around a tree on the bank. There were two teams playing on its flat surface. One of the players carried a footy and was stepping wildly to avoid his opponents. The pontoon wobbled around his feet under his weight, and the force of those who pursued him. He stepped wide avoiding one attacker but hadn't seen another that was following in his blindside. The kid with the ball was wrapped up, but rather than being tackled to the ground he was pushed fiercely towards the edge; where he was promptly thrown off to squeals of delight from onlookers and competitors alike. A moment later the boy resurfaced with the biggest grin on his face. Jiemba supposed that in this game if you didn't score you were equally worthy if you simply got drenched.

He smiled at how much they were having fun, but realised that there was a vast contrast at play. Most of the youths were busy enjoying themselves by being involved in the game, or by swinging from a nearby rope swing or simply relaxing on the banks. However, on the adjacent bank, not so far away from so much positive energy and laughter, a group of people both old and not so much older showed no signs of happiness as they wandered aimlessly or sat helplessly near the makeshift bridge; emotions varying from that of rage and anger, to sadness and depression. The range of backgrounds present resembled what JayDee had suggested during the walk. If you had ten guesses to what sort of people were there you were right, plus there were more. A rainbow of colour and languages sitting sadly in the beauty of nature.

Jiemba felt bad as his attention turned away from the forlorn sight and back towards the laughter and excitement of the sport being played. He was so interested in the sport, however, that he wasn't watching where he was going. He slipped on some lose gravel at the same time he trod awkwardly on an exposed root. He tripped into a half gallop and was instantly travelling too fast down the slope. The young man bounced savagely on Jiemba's shoulder, should he fall he would be severely hurt. The awareness of the problem didn't help Jiemba much. He seemed to be running completely out of control. There was a small corner on the hill ahead of him, and on that corner stood an enormous old pine tree. Going at the speed he was travelling there was no way he could avoid it; he couldn't find a foot hold and there was nothing to grab onto. In a last ditch effort to save the guy he was carrying Jiemba turned to face away from the tree and hoped that in the inevitable impact he didn't hurt himself too much.

One moment he was sliding. The next moment he had stopped.

He opened one of his eyes, as he had scrunched them together just before the impact. He could see JayDee slowly walking down the hill after him, his mouth appearing for the longest time in a look of sheer shock. He was staring at the tree which Jiemba had run into. Jiemba's ears started to twitch as he heard a crunching and ripping sound. He turned to look at the tree he had just hit and saw that instead of the tree severely injuring Jiemba and throwing him to the ground, instead it was the tree that was on a severe lean and at risk of toppling entirely. The sound of the roots clinging to the ground as the dirt was torn from the base of its grassy trunk reminded him of the sound of skin tearing underneath your fingernails as they are ripped away and the nerves separated.

Not a pleasant thought.

"Are you okay?" JayDee asked in astonishment as he arrived at Jiemba's side.

"I think I am okay," Jiemba replied, feeling at himself with his free hand.

"I wasn't talking to you," JayDee grunted back, "I meant this poor tree. What have you done to it?"

"I was sliding toward it pretty fast," Jiemba explained, "I am honestly surprised that I am not the one on the ground." JayDee placed his hands on the trunk as if to sooth the pain in the falling tree. He then turned and looked straight at Jiemba.

"Fix it," he demanded.

"Fix it?" Jiemba replied. "What do you mean fix it?"

"I mean you knocked it down, so you pick it up," JayDee replied sharply. "Didn't your mum ever teach you not to break things, and if you did then you had to take responsibility?"

"She sure did," Jiemba almost yelled back. "My mum was the best, and if I didn't listen then I was in a whole heap of trouble."

"Then fix it," JayDee bellowed back.

"Fine," Jiemba dumped the guy he had been carrying heavily on the ground. For the first time he seemed to realise that it was no time to sleep, looking terrified at both of the men before staggering quickly away and falling harmfully down the hill and tumbling to its base. Jiemba then moved over to where the tree was leaning. He glared at JayDee as if trying to reinforce that the task was impossible. The tree was ancient. There was no reason as to why it had toppled in the first place, possibly rotting timber and roots at its base; just waiting for the next person to come along and touch it no doubt. And Jiemba had been the unlucky person who just happened to come by. But even if that was true there was no way that anyone could expect Jiemba to be able to push the thing back into position. The tree was over thirty metres tall, and whatever the weight of that wood was. "Are you ready?" Jiemba roared.

"Stop wasting time," JayDee yelled back, "just fix it."

"Fine," Jiemba snarled back. He placed his hands against the tree and pushed. Walking his feet through the displaced dirt and grass as he pushed. "There, are you happy?" JayDee was looking straight up in the air when Jiemba cast his eyes upon him.

"Well, yes," JayDee replied, there was no malice or volume in his voice anymore. "Happy is one of the things I am feeling at the moment." Jiemba, who was still holding the tree with the assumption that it hadn't moved at all, followed his gaze. The tree was once more standing perfectly erect as if nothing had ever happened, apart from the ground being disturbed around its base.

"How did that happen?" Jiemba said in complete shock.

"You," replied JayDee in equal bewilderment, "you is how that happened. How did you just lift that tree? That thing must weigh a couple of tonnes."

"Maybe it doesn't?" suggested Jiemba.

"And you pushed it up hill," JayDee continued. It took him several moments to place some parts of the jigsaw in his head together. "I believe you," he finally said, "you said your body has changed, you survived a tsunami like catastrophe, you can't feel temperature, or pain, and now you just casually lifted a tree. Did it hurt?"

"Not at all," Jiemba's voice was sounding quite high pitched.

"None of this makes sense," JayDee stood wide-eyed and gawping at Jiemba who had nothing to say to dispute those facts. After a while, desperately trying to say anything else to change the subject, Jiemba spoke.

"At least the tree is standing," he said. "I might go down and check out that game down there."

"Yes I am happy now," JayDee replied, "it sounds like a great idea."

Jiemba turned and started walking away. It appeared like no one had really taken any notice of what had occurred. That was a relief as he had no way to explain it away.

The crunching sound returned.

Jiemba grimaced as he turned.

The tree seemed to make noise long enough for Jiemba to turn back around; before twisting on the spot, screeching as it broke the last threads that were holding it in place and diving head long down the grassy bank which flung it directly down towards the river. Jiemba held his breath as it bounced and crashed its way noisily down the remaining slope before coming to a deafening halt metres away from the water. Jiemba exhaled and looked straight at JayDee.

No words were spoken.

"Hey mate," a young male voice called from behind him. Jiemba turned to look at him, avoiding the gaze of the older man. "What happened to that tree?"

"I have no idea," Jiemba replied, laughing loudly as if that would help cover what happened.

"That's so weird," the boy replied, he must have been in his mid-teens and had darker skin than Jiemba did. "You look like you could play footy, do you want to come and play some Aqua Rugby with us?"

"Is that what that is? Sounds great. I would love to. Let me at it," Jiemba nodded back, genuinely pumped to find out more, as well as liking the fact he could remove himself from the current situation.

"Cool, my name is Jonah," the boy introduced himself, "and I am going to smash you."

"I am Jiemba," came the reply with a laugh, "and you can certainly try." Jiemba turned to look at JayDee who was following slowly behind.

"Don't hurt the boy," JayDee demanded.

"I won't," Jiemba replied, knowing exactly what JayDee meant.

"I'm serious. We are going to talk later," JayDee said, eyes still wide with confusion. "At length."

"I look forward to it," Jiemba replied with a laugh.

He really wasn't looking forward to it.

44

Chapter 4 – Taking your medicine

"Nice tattoo," Jonah nodded with appreciation. "The white on black is a bold choice, and the goanna is completely sick."

"Firstly, it's not a tattoo," Jiemba corrected the young man. He had taken his shirt off to rinse it in the shallows of the river. The specks of vomit which had dribbled down his back were removed easily, but the smell lingered, causing his lip to curl. He left the shirt to dry on a small rock which seemed warmer than the others around it. "Second, I am not that dark, most of you guys are darker than I am."

"Well whatever it is it looks deadly, I wish I had one just like that," Jonah admitted, his enthusiastic gaze was both excited and off putting.

"Thanks," Jiemba started walking through the shallows towards the pontoon. "How do you play this game? And where did you get the matting from?"

"The game is easy, no different to normal footy really," Jonah explained. The boy was skinny and tall, covered in lean muscle and showing the beginnings of a disgusting moustache and a greasy mullet. He wore glasses and seemed keen to impress, showing some sort of education in how he spoke. In front of them, no one seemed to care who was playing, with skin colour ranging from dark as night to tan or white, as well as one really unfortunate ginger kid who had chosen to ignore his sunscreen as his skin was deep red. "The pontoon was a gift," Jonah continued with a big smile. "We found it near the bridge a couple of days ago, after the big flood. We think it was thrown over the dam wall from the lake up there. There are also a few others, as well as some small boats and canoes, but they are either broken or floating in bits all along the river. We are going to have as much fun as we can with this one though, until someone starts missing it and they come and take it away.”

The stones in the water provided good steps to get up onto the mat. A hand was extended down to help Jiemba.

“Thanks,” he said, noticing that his hand engulfed that of the one assisting him. “Girls are playing this too?”

“Sure are, you have a problem with that?” the girl replied with a restrained fury in her big brown eyes. She looked to be about the same age as Jonah, skinny and not overly tall but definitely fit. There was no doubt that in a foot race she would destroy Jiemba.

“Not at all,” Jiemba answered. “Just wanted to make sure I could tackle everyone who is on the field.”

“Not likely,” the girl stepped back, arms crossed and still staring up at him. “Although you are probably the biggest one up here, you also look like you’re the slowest. You have no chance of catching anyone. You don’t look like you belong here.” She squinted at him as if daring him to challenge her assumption. Jiemba rubbed his hands together, almost twiddling his thumbs as he waited for anything to happen to get him out of this situation.

“She is just joking Jiemba,” Jonah pushed between them. “This is my cousin, Joanna, and she knows that anybody can play in this part of the river.”

“No exclusion here cuz,” she laughed, revealing a beautiful smile. “Unless you have it coming, that is.”

“Well that’s good news,” Jiemba laughed, still unsure as to where he stood with the girl.

“Sport is the great equaliser,” Jonah walked into the middle as he explained. “There should be no reason why everyone can’t play.”

“That’s nice to hear,” Jiemba said.

“It’s how it should be. Your skin, your religion and your country have no idea how to play. Individuals do, so the only thing you have to do is beat others. You are a big guy, you look like you could do some damage," Jonah said with a smile on his face. Jiemba remembered his previous encounter with the tree, knocking it out of place before returning it to the soil with his bare hands. It hadn't hurt anyone when it eventually toppled down the hill, but Jiemba agreed that he could absolutely do some damage if that wasn't a one off. He laughed anxiously but several others accompanied him. As he smiled at all the faces he realised that while most of the players were young there were a couple who could easily be as old as him if not older, both male and female. "But Joanna was right, size and strength doesn't matter if you can't catch us." Jonah beamed.

"I'm probably not gunna catch ya," Jiemba agreed, he was laughing so much that he felt like his jaw was flapping in the wind. "But you better not get caught by me either. How do you play?"

"This is a very simple game," Joanna added as she had followed them. "You have to carry the ball over the far end of the mat. The edges are the outlines and if you go over them and into the water, or if you knock on or throw the ball forward you hand it over. You can tackle anywhere, not in the head, but when the person carrying hits the ground you just let them play it from the ground. Offside is only a couple of steps. No penalties or other things like scrums. If you do the wrong thing we will throw you off the pontoon."

"Seems fair," Jiemba said as he followed along and understood all of the rules. It sounded like a stripped back version of any game of football, which also included water. He was keen.

"Great," Joanna said with her intense smile. "I am on this team, so you can go on that one. Don't think that we are going to go easy on you either."

"Wouldn't dream of it," Jiemba said as he moved over to his new teammates. He shook hands with a few, trying to recall many of the names, failing at most. He decided that just like normal he would call their name in the game if he knew it, otherwise it would be a combination of either, mate, sis, cuz or bruv. Names that he would slip in and out using whenever he felt like it.

Jiemba noticed that JayDee had made his way down to the river's edge; sitting on an old fallen log while already appearing deeply engaged in conversation with several people.

"Game on," one of the players called out, and the ball which had been sitting in the pontoon's centre was set upon by all within proximity to it. Jiemba could see from the outset that all participants were engaged in the game to some degree, several players were just wrestling with one another on the fringes in an attempt to throw the opposition into the water, but those who were focused were playing to win.

A big guy on the opposing team jumped on the ball and flicked it back to a much smaller and younger boy. The kid stepped past a couple, ducking and weaving with a huge smile on his face. He stepped one too many times and was clobbered by Jonah who rushed upon him as if launched from a cannon. The boy went to ground with the ball flying free, where it was passed to Joanna with a bunch of speed behind her. She angled straight at Jiemba who was yet to move. As she got closer Jiemba failed to see a man with a big belly sneaking up behind him. The big man jumped toward Jiemba as Joanna came closer, but instead of running into him he slammed into the ground at Jiemba's feet. The pontoon shook, and as Jiemba tried to step forward to capture her his feet wobbled along with the pontoon and he fell awkwardly to the ground; causing the surface to move like a wave under the pressure of his weight. Joanna stuck her tongue out at him as she sprinted past and away, jumping into the end zone with a graceful forward somersault and crying out with the following splash.

"Still trying to find your feet mate?" JayDee called out amid a chorus of cheers and laughter. Jiemba shook his head with a smile as he watched the old man once more imitate a drinking action.

"Come on, you can do better than that," Jonah called out, clapping Jiemba on the back as he returned to his feet. "Tell you what, I will give you the ball early so that you at least feel like you are contributing."

"Is that all you got big guy?" Joanna crowed as she pulled herself out of the river; dripping wet and pouring water out onto the pontoon as it leaked from her hair. "I told you that you couldn't catch me." She dropped the ball on the ground as everyone got reorganised. The competitive part of Jiemba had been sparked. He would not hurt anybody, or at least he would try very hard not to, but he was going to show these kids that he was better than what they thought he was.

"That belongs to me," Jiemba declared as Jonah picked up the ball.

"Play starts as soon as I pass it to you," Jonah informed him, "are you ready?" Jiemba flexed his toes and dug them into the plastic as best he could. He could feel his calves and achilles pulse as he activated them. He shifted his weight through the ground and was surprised when the whole pontoon started wobbling from his movement, sending many players on both teams staggering to retain balance. Jiemba smiled.

"Ready," Jiemba declared.

"Game on," a player shouted out in a weird voice, as Jonah passed the ball.

Jiemba clasped it in his hands like it was his most prized possession. The opposition set upon him almost immediately. Jiemba stepped hard to one side. He almost knocked himself over as the pontoon jerked from the force of his foot, several other players sprawled to the ground clearing the way. The players shared groans and cheers as Jiemba found space. In a moment the opposition were clambering back to their feet to stop him. Several of the smaller, zippier, kids leapt onto him trying to bring him down. Jiemba didn't even notice, continuing to run in the straight line that he had adopted without alteration. An older, stronger looking, youth dove down at Jiemba's legs and upon making contact slid to the ground clutching at his shoulder. Others tried to drag him backwards from behind refusing to end up with injuries like their team mate had received. The big guy that had caused the pontoon to wobble, enabling Joanna to score unopposed, charged at Jiemba. Jiemba watched him launch all of his girth in his direction. Out of sheer reaction Jiemba swept a hand up towards the man in an attempt to stop him from taking him down. Jiemba made contact, but felt no mass upon him as a consequence of the big man making contact. Jiemba looked around and couldn't see him anywhere, but heard a loud splash coming from a distance down the river. Looking in that direction he could see the clutter that was being used as a bridge, but then beyond the bridge a wet flapping could be seen as someone broke back up through the water.

"Oops," Jiemba whispered as he realised that it was the same guy. He was at least fifty metres downstream, with just a swat of Jiemba's hand. The bunch of players that were trying their best to stop him immediately stopped after seeing what had happened. A few tried even harder digging their feet into the wet surface only to slide along behind Jiemba, while others abandoned the task entirely, some jumping clear of the pontoon and into the water deciding it was a better option.

"Who's next, who's next?" Jonah called out in excitement as cheers and laughter surrounded them. Jiemba could still see opponents flowing towards him while at the same time hearing the splashes of those who were abandoning the pontoon to avoid him.

After a few heavy steps Jiemba lumbered past Joanna who had decided not to stand in his way in spite of her earlier bravado. Jiemba smiled at her and leapt into the air. It wasn't an amazing jump but in Jiemba's head he felt like it was momentous.

"Game on," he bellowed as he fell towards the water, the bodies of those he had carried all the way splashing into the river around him. He hit with a mighty wave rising up in his aftermath. When he resurfaced with the ball he started dancing embarrassingly, not particularly caring who was watching.

"Who is next?" he called out, mimicking what Jonah had been shouting only moments before, looking to see who was going to take up the call.

"Jiemba," JayDee called out from the shore. Jiemba felt like he was being scolded by his grandfather. He turned slowly around as everyone laughed at him. With gritted teeth he looked straight at JayDee who was still sitting comfortably on his log. "What did we talk about?"

Jiemba smiled. The splashing sound of a person wading through water appeared beside him, accompanied by the slapping of wet feet on the stones of the shore. Jiemba looked up to see the big guy that he had swatted casually down the river standing there with a look of confusion.

"Why?" the big guy asked, with big sad pleading eyes. Jiemba's heart sank.

"I'm sorry," he offered his apology to the big guy. "I will be good. I will play nicer now."

The chorus of laughter that erupted was emphasised by the sound of bodies hitting the pontoon in fits of hysteria, and amplified by those who simply jumped into the river to ease their hurting sides. Jiemba looked over to JayDee.

"Sorry," he whispered, as JayDee shook his head.

The laughter somehow got louder.

Jiemba lay on his back amongst the towering gums. The afternoon had been fun and he was appreciative that he had been given something to take his mind off of things. Everyone that had been involved with the game had left not so long ago; with big smiles and memories of great times. Jiemba laughed as he heard one of them get scolded for bragging about an event that couldn't possibly have happened.

"And then I caught the ball on the line, stepped through everyone and scored," a male youth had stated, his recount of events seemingly accurate until he opened his mouth again. "It was at least a fifty metre run, and no-one could lay a finger on me."

"It's only a thirty metre field," one of the girls argued straight back. "And you had just jumped out of the water, you are already slippery like an eel so it just made it harder to hold you down."

"Yeah, well I jumped like twenty metres when I scored," the youth disputed relentlessly, but even he couldn't hide the smile revealing how absurd it sounded. As a consequence of his lie he got his hair ruffled wildly and laughed the loudest amongst the chorus of those who fell onto the pitch or into the water. Jiemba smiled at the memory.

The game hadn't lasted the whole afternoon. While it had been fun it had also been just as nice to sit around and do nothing afterwards. The conversations flowed but there was a good length of time where everyone just relaxed. There was an open spot where a fireplace sat unlit. It was obvious that it was frequently used as there was a large amount of soot lingering around it, nearby there were also several piles of discarded wood which had been gathered. Some rocks were used as seats, as were small logs and trunks, but there was a clearing of a couple of metres between the fire and any fixed object. An acoustic guitar was pulled from somewhere and simple tunes were played by many of the young would be musicians. Despite the banter flowing heavily during the game before, the air surrounding them was calm. Some laughed but most just listened or sung along. There were a couple of songs, one called *Under the Same Sky* and another called *I'm Free*, both song by some local artist, where the group sang along together, the guitar only being used sporadically as the young singers carried the melody fine without it.

Jiemba wasn't a good singer, and it was made evident later that he was also not a good dancer. After some relaxing and guitar playing a dance circle was cleared and many of the boys and girls started to dance. Many were well equipped to show some break dancing or amazing flips, others pulled out some abstract hip hop which drew laughter and cheers from everyone. Jiemba was lucky not to be booed for his poor attempt. The biggest pops came when two groups, engaged in a cultural dance off. A young group of Aboriginal boys stepped up delivering some of their best moves from what their families had taught them, and this was reinforced by the girls who shared their own knowledge. On the flip though, a group of tall

African boys showed their best jumps and bounces mixed with a combination of moves exaggerated by the use of their long powerful limbs shooting out in all directions. After a tense standoff at the end, both groups shared broad smiles and congratulated the others with a hug.

"They didn't always get along," Jonah told Jiemba, "they were basically rival gangs. Times have changed for everyone though. Although it is tough there is always something positive that comes from a negative." Jiemba nodded in agreement before sharing in the laughter and applause that the crowd showered on the dancers. Shortly after, the game of Aqua Rugby resumed as the energy they possessed could not be held in forever.

Eventually, after a long time playing, they had all left, leaving Jiemba to compare the afternoon with memories from his youth; with a hope that he could enjoy another time just like it again soon. The only people who hung around apart from Jiemba and JayDee, who was going to great lengths to finish a conversation that had lingered on for far too long, were the zombie like remnants of older forlorn looking people. Most, as Jiemba had found out during small breaks throughout the afternoon, were victims of exactly what JayDee had explained on the walk over. Jiemba looked upon them with sympathy, trying to hide any pity he felt towards them, while wishing that there was something that he could do for them. The task seemed far too big on the surface, but he told himself that it was something he would give more thought to; immediately admonishing himself as unable to give himself the time he needed to heal before trying to help someone else. The other's he looked upon with some contempt, as they were not victims but rather predators of a similar circumstance who preyed upon those with nothing. Many of the later group had become violent throughout the afternoon, yelling and screaming of mistreatment to those that would not give out what little they had; no matter how many times they were reminded that all of these people were facing similar situations.

Jiemba pushed aside the feeling of guilt he had. Here he was enjoying himself, without a wallet or a dollar to his name, and healthy despite the possibility of serious injury, dealing with issues that were deeply personal, when some of these people would probably kill for those problems to be their own. He pushed that thought aside as well, knowing that train of thought was probably part of the reason why he was here, he would resist negativity from invading his solitude, at least for a time.

Jiemba closed his eyes as if the action would help. He focused beyond his mind and focused on enhancing his senses. His feeling of touch was obscured, and he had gotten used to that idea over the afternoon. Constant trips into the river should have given him cuts and bruises by how many times he struck the bottom or snagged himself on a hidden object concealed beneath the water, but his skin remained completely unscathed. In each occasion he grabbed the cloaked item, pulled it free, before launching it with a loud crash into the unoccupied areas of the bush. The youths had marvelled at his strength the more he tested it, but after a few occasions they would simply point out a problem with the expectation that he would deal with it. Jiemba was happy to do so, and it wasn't long before the novelty wore off and they just treated him like anybody else. Albeit someone who could lift heavy things, but he was secretly hoping that they would seek his help out all the same.

He felt no weariness or cold, and, despite having multiple visits into the water, his hands and feet showed no signs of pruning or shrivelling up. The other players had no problem displaying the drop in temperature, almost all of them wrapping their arms around their torsos with teeth chattering as they shook uncontrollably. When only the big guy that Jiemba had hurled into the far reaches, apart from Jiemba himself, was devoid of signs reflecting the freezing temperatures the game was promptly called off with the promise of resuming another day. The approaching night and the content calls, as well as angry ones, from parents to return home caused a quick dispersal from the area. There were still a few of the kids who took one last dip via the use of a long rope swing, but it wasn't long until they were all gone; some disappearing into the scrub on the other side of the river, heading to the old previously abandoned mission, while others made their way in the other direction to where there was a hidden road that reached back towards town.

The light was fading but showed outlines of shapes as they jumped into the twilight. Frogs started to croak and chant as they returned to the safety of the river's edge. Crickets chirped amongst the tall grass, amid the screeches of families of cockatoos returning home. There seemed to be a sing off as Jiemba listened to the warble of magpies in the upper boughs of the eucalypt, sounding off against the gargle and crying of the catastrophe of currawongs which occupied the smaller wattle trees below. The rustling of grass revealed smaller animals of either birds or lizards who were trying desperately to avoid the gaze of the larger predator birds whilst they were momentarily distracted. The much heavier crush of tall grass suggested that a kangaroo or wallaby was making its way down to visit the water for a drink or a wash now that it had been abandoned.

Then there was a splash.

Jiemba sat up and watched as one of the slow moving adults floundered in the shallow water that lead to the bottleneck in the river, which surged with an almost artificial, yet powerful, current. The man's attempts to swim were quite sad, but Jiemba noticed that this man was one of those who had probably been deprived of lessons or the opportunity to learn how to swim. He also may have been incapable of doing so in his present state. Jiemba turned with a groan to JayDee, who, now removed from his conversation, had been watching on, flicking his hand to make the suggestion to Jiemba to set about helping the man. He rose to his feet and walked slowly to the water's edge, his jeans only just showing signs of drying while still clinging to his enormous calves.

The man spluttered and spat water as he flailed miserably about. Jiemba walked to the edge before the bottleneck and as the man approached he leaned over and plucked him effortlessly out. The man looked at Jiemba with disgust as if the small non-event had been entirely his fault before stumbling away. Jiemba imagined that the man was showcasing how Jiemba himself had looked when JayDee had found him earlier in the day and had no problem in understanding why JayDee had suggested he was being heavily influenced by something else.

"Time to call it a day?" JayDee asked as he approached from behind. Jiemba nodded, watching to make sure that he didn't have to help the man another time.

"Someone should fix the bridge," Jiemba suggested as the man made it safely over the makeshift passage.

"Yeah someone should," JayDee agreed, before seeming to dismiss the notion entirely. "So, you are insanely strong."

"It appears that way," Jiemba turned to look at the old man. JayDee walked over to where the tree that Jiemba had knocked over was. He sat down upon it and patted it thoughtfully, motioning for Jiemba to come and sit with him.

"This could make a good bridge," JayDee suggested.

"Some of these people can't walk straight," Jiemba said shaking his head, "they would fall off and you would have even more visitors down your end of the river." JayDee shrugged. Nothing was said and they sat in silence. That silence persisted until the last of the adults staggered away from sight.

"You seemed to be enjoying yourself," JayDee suggested motioning to the pontoon and the abandoned fire pit. They looked strange now that the pontoon floated alone with no activity on its surface, and there was no laughter or sounds coming from the surrounds of the fire pit.

"Sport is my safe place," Jiemba replied, "I have always been good at it, so I am happy to do it. It helps when everyone else is simply trying to have fun and not treat it like a world championship."

"That is as close as some of those kids are going to get to a world championship, either participating or watching it," JayDee remarked.

"And that is a real shame," Jiemba responded sadly. "A lot of those kids have real potential, they could really make a go of it if they had the chance."

"I agree," JayDee nodded, "but it is not so much about chance. The opportunities come up all the time. I think it has more to do with their role models. You spent a lot of the afternoon watching the older people here. If they don't care about sport, or anything else for that matter, then what message is that sending? It won't be long until some of these youths give up on that dream, and others, because no one is going to tell them otherwise." Jiemba shook his head.

"Jonah and Joanna seem different," he replied, not wanting to believe what he was hearing; especially as he feared it to be true. "They are full of energy, they could make something of themselves."

"They are different, despite having it worse than most," JayDee nodded his head in agreement and shrugged.

"What is their story?" Jiemba asked with intrigue.

"It is not mine to tell," JayDee answered quickly. "Let's just say their upbringing has been filled with sadness, but, nice people have stepped in to help them. They have potential, they could be great, but they lack direction. They don't have answers and those that could give them, wallow their lives away, although it is no fault of their own. They are in need of a mentor, a role model and a leader, someone who they can look up to."

"Good luck finding that person," Jiemba scoffed at the thought, "here or anywhere else."

"They look up to you," JayDee told him, "they spent most of the afternoon trying their best to get involved with whatever you were doing."

"I was a novelty," Jiemba laughed off the notion. "I am not a role model, you wouldn't want to look up to someone who is broken." A silence echoed, but JayDee shivered and disturbed it. It was clearly getting cooler regardless if you were wet or not.

"That is the best thing about things that are broken," JayDee said soothingly, "given time they can always be fixed."

"Sometimes they don't want to be fixed," Jiemba almost growled back.

"Even damaged ideas can be mended," JayDee continued. "That can remove the necessity of a safe place." Jiemba curled his fingers into balls, scraping chunks and splinters of wood out as he did so. There was no pain. He breathed heavily through his nose, and then released his fists so that they sat calmly against the fallen tree's surface.

"I know where you are going with this JayDee," Jiemba said as calmly as he could manage, "but despite getting to know you a bit, despite your chat about only having enemies or friends, you are still only a stranger to me."

"Sometimes talking to a stranger is easier," JayDee suggested, "but talking to anyone is better than not talking at all."

"There is nothing to say," Jiemba warned the old man softly, feeling immediately guilty for it, knowing that neither of them believed the lie. He moved quickly to his feet but surprisingly JayDee was quicker, the older man standing up to block Jiemba's path. "You know I can move you old man, I don't need my new strength to get you out of my way."

"I know that," JayDee replied, again without any malice in his voice despite how Jiemba was talking to him.

"And I am not going to talk to you about what may or may not be going on," Jiemba was surprised at how angry he sounded. "Don't stick your nose where it doesn't belong."

"There will be time for that," JayDee said simply, stepping out of Jiemba's way as he stormed past.

"Then what do you want from me?" Jiemba didn't expect an answer. He knew it was disrespectful to turn his back on a man who had shown him nothing but kindness.

Yet he did it anyway.

"Jiemba," JayDee called out.

"What?" Jiemba boomed back. The happiness and joy he had felt only minutes before evaporating in an instant. His rage was unjustified and had boiled over with no reasonable explanation. The signs clear to him that despite how he had been feeling he was not okay. This awareness didn't hold Jiemba in check, he was still following through with his display of outrage. JayDee took a moment, making Jiemba wait longer and listen to the heaviness of his breathing. Jiemba felt awful. How quickly he had transformed from his moment of positive feelings of contentment and relief, and then into a monster showcasing nothing but utter negative and deplorable behaviour. "What do you want old man?"

"When you get back, your room is the last one on the right," came JayDee's answer.

Jiemba said nothing. It was the worst he had ever felt. He turned and trudged away, appalled at his actions he still could not bring himself to apologise to JayDee. He fought with himself the entire way back to the house.

He punched the middle of a tree, and promptly exploded a giant hole straight through its centre.

He kicked out at a boulder as he rounded a corner, not watching as it crumbled loudly down a small ledge.

He vomited several times along the way.

He couldn't hold back the tears which flowed so freely.

He was disgusted with himself.

Chapter 5 – The labours of Jiemba

Jiemba did not sleep.

He had found his bed without any trouble. A giant king sized mattress that sat upon a heavy wood and stone frame. Inside a room which heralded that its former occupant was someone who lived life to the fullest. Musical instruments, trophies, plaques, large pieces of antique and exotic furniture filled the room. Photos of concerts, get-togethers with some celebrities and other people that Jiemba didn't know, existing to showcase memories of moments never to be forgotten. Each of them out of place in comparison to the rest of the house. Each of them staring down hatred towards him for how he had treated the old man.

Jiemba did not sleep.

The mattress was so soft under his weight that it took him an age to roll over and face the other way, every time he did it, each position lasting only minutes. Normally Jiemba had no problem in sleeping. He put so much energy into what he did physically every single day that his body was exhausted. His mind, likewise, was equally fatigued from the constant chatter from within, as well as hiding himself away and putting on a mask for others to see. He knew that his day had consisted of more stress and strain that he had ever had to deal with before. On days faced with less stress than this he had had no problem sleeping.

Jiemba did not sleep.

There was nothing wrong with the support given to him by the pillow, and the blankets did not disturb or annoy him. His eyes jumped from one thing to another, perhaps the room was stimulating him too much. He made a mental attempt to switch off his senses. He wasn't straining to listen. He wasn't searching for a smell. He saw nothing behind his closed eyes. Jiemba felt like he was becoming less restless.

Jiemba did not sleep.

"Hello Jiemba," a voice called to him. He didn't have to open his eyes nor turn on the light to acknowledge where the voice had come from.

"Not you," replied Jiemba to the voice inside his head.

"Trouble sleeping?" the voice suggested as if it didn't know. "I can help you."

"I don't want your help," Jiemba tossed and turned as he fought to remove it. If he was so strong why couldn't he get rid of the voice?

"I have never tried to harm you, in resisting me you only hurt yourself. I am only here to help."

"I said I don't want your help," Jiemba blasted, but no one would hear him but himself. "Leave me alone."

"I will never do that," the voice said, "I will always be here, hoping that you will listen. Before I am quiet I will leave you with an ultimatum. You can stay up all night, with no sleep, every instance that you try to think of something else I will bounce back up even worse. It will be like trying not to notice that little thing in your eye once you glance at it once. No matter where you look it is there. Or, you can listen and I will put you to sleep."

The voice left him alone to decide.

Jiemba did not sleep.

Jiemba fought to go to sleep. He counted sheep, sung himself a lullaby, stared at one point on the roof in an attempt to become completely bored. Nothing worked, and each time he could almost hear a small snigger from a corner of his thoughts. He became accustomed to the sound of the sheets as they rubbed against his skin, time after time that he rolled over.

"Fine," he said out loud, without intending to.

"Are you willing to listen?"

"Speak," Jiemba ordered. Again the conversation was firmly held within the constraints of his mind. He hoped he hadn't woken up the old man with the first outburst though.

"You are feeling guilty."

"I know what I did," Jiemba barked.

"You are hiding away again."

"Don't tell me what I am doing," Jiemba roared.

"How did that work out last time?" The voice asked. "What happened?"

"I don't want to talk about it," Jiemba said, repressing his memories as they returned to greet him.

"You must," the voice replied. "You must do two things if you want to sleep well. First, you must make amends."

"I was going to apologise in the morning," Jiemba said much calmer. "What I did was wrong and I am not proud of it. It is not me and not something I would usually do."

"Good start," the voice agreed, "but not just amends with the old man, but with yourself as well."

"That's a little bit harder," Jiemba said softly, trying to hide his discomfort from himself.

"The second thing can help you."

"Which is?" Jiemba asked.

"Talk to the old man about it," the voice said. It made the task seem like it was the simplest thing in the world.

"I don't know if I can," Jiemba told himself.

"You must promise to do these two things," the voice said.

"And then I can go to sleep?" Jiemba asked sarcastically.

"Yes," replied the voice, "but there is far more at stake if you don't." There was silence everywhere for a moment.

"Okay," Jiemba finally gave in. "I will do it at some point."

"Do you promise?"

"I promise," Jiemba declared, "and I don't break those."

"So be it," the voice said satisfied.

Jiemba closed his eyes.

Jiemba slept.

But not well.

From the moment that he woke up Jiemba was busy. He wanted to talk to the old man straight away, to clear his head and apologise for what he had said and how he had acted. He even woke up from his sleep to rehearse exactly what he would say. He expected to wander out and find the old man busy pottering, reading a newspaper, working in the garden or at work in the kitchen, however when he ventured from his room he was greeted with empty silence. Jiemba's heavy feet clomped around on the wooden floor, the thuds echoed within the walls of the old dwelling, as the floor in some spots threatened to give way.

Dissatisfied that he was alone and he would have to carry his apology over until later, Jiemba found some more clothes that fit and ventured out onto the veranda. The pile of books that he collected were still there and on top of them sat another note.

'Read the books, or earn your keep.'

Beneath the note was a list of things to do around the house. Not feeling hungry or even tired despite a terrible sleep, and not particularly feeling that sitting down and reading was the thing to do, Jiemba set about the tasks he had been given.

Before his abrupt behaviour he had already liked the idea of keeping himself busy. Having something to do with his hands usually calmed the rest of him regardless of how laborious it was. He had also been concerned, however, and was entirely convinced that JayDee would throw him out instead of letting him stay. The thought of jumping before he was pushed had occurred to him, but he would have felt even worse than he already did if he were to just leave. Besides, he still wanted his isolation and the note suggested that

JayDee didn't need him gone, so Jiemba set himself the task and started moving down the list.

The tasks were simple enough. He first had to fix the gate that he had torn from its hinges. He found a portable music player, which received no radio signal so he was limited to the handful of cds that were nearby, and shortly after he found a shed housing many of the tools he would need. As he walked around the perimeter of the house, while he headed back towards the gate, he added more things to the list of things he should do.

Each task took a short time. There was no given time limit and, as many of the repairs he had to make, apart from the gate that he broke, seemed like they had been sitting around waiting to be fixed for some time he didn't feel the urgency or stress to rush the jobs. In the background he listened to *Busby Marou* and *Red Hot Chili Peppers*, two very different approaches to music but served well to create a tranquil and soothing space, regardless of how loud the music became.

Looking up he assumed that it was close to lunch as the sun sat in the middle of the sky; not straight up but instead at an angle as every day came closer to winter. He had already finished the gate, fixed some rotten timber steps leading from the garden to the veranda, re-laid some pavers with concrete that had wobbled dangerously when stepped upon, reorganised the large garden shed so that it was workable (hoping that JayDee hadn't preferred how it sat previously), and readjusted the wire on the fence at the rear of the house which looked like it had been torn down by some animal. Jiemba was standing on a tall ladder looking up onto the roof, using a large branch as a broom as he had been unable to find a broom long enough, intending to sweep away the debris, nests and dead carcasses which had been collected there. A short time later an old 4wd ute appeared on the road before pulling into the driveway.

JayDee hopped out and took several trips to and from the vehicle as he removed more and more items from the car. Jiemba resisted the urge to call out to the older man as he was still not convinced JayDee would want to talk to him. The limb of a eucalypt that he was using should have been unbearably heavy but he found no problem in sweeping it from side to side and directing sticks and nuts away from the skylight over the bathroom and out from the gutters. There were several dead birds, and a possum had also died up there, but what he had assumed was a body near the skylight was actually a large nest. He swatted at it and missed with the few leaves at his disposal, before trying again. On the fourth attempt he hit it and watched with satisfaction as it disintegrated.

But then it moved.

Rats exploded from the broken twigs in all directions, including towards Jiemba. Jiemba panicked, throwing the branch away towards the edge of the yard. He shot backwards and away from the approaching creatures, just like any normal person would. His toes gripped at the metal step at the top of the ladder that he had been standing on. His body suddenly became aware that he was still standing in a precarious position, but by that point it was too late. The ladder which had been stable when pressed up against the gutter bounced away and the feet shifted on the uneven ground. The ladder swung clear and Jiemba was filled with a free falling sensation, his hands flinging out uselessly trying to grab something to stop him from falling. He found nothing and, as his momentum was going forwards and the ladder going back, his body flipped over the front steps until he was falling with his back down. He landed hard after falling at least four metres, the metal ladder sprawled out under his spine. Jiemba lay there embarrassed for a time, knowing that he had broken something.

"Jiemba," JayDee called out as he shifted quickly down the back steps. "Are you alright?"

"JayDee?" Jiemba said startled. He jumped to his feet with hands out and finger's sprawled in a bid to explain.

"Aren't you hurt?" JayDee broke in first with a look of complete shock. "You just fell from the roof. It looks like you owe me a ladder now too."

"What?" Jiemba seemed just as shocked. He hadn't even thought of what injuries he had as he hadn't felt anything. His main focus was to apologise to JayDee. "Um, no, I am fine. Sorry about the ladder. Listen about last night."

"I don't want to hear an apology," JayDee said with an angry look on his face. "Because you don't need to give me one. What happened last night, you just had a moment. Everyone has one, I know I have had my fair share. You were just angry, not angry at me, I know that. I also know that no matter what you say that sort of anger comes from somewhere deep. It was all secondary. But I will say that the only way to remove that is to talk about it." Unknowingly to him, Jiemba had curled his hands into a fist and then released it just as quickly. "We aren't doing that today though."

"Thanks JayDee," Jiemba replied after a moment, taking a deep breath to keep his cool. "You are better at making my apologies than I am."

"We can talk more over lunch. I got some hot chips, potato scallops and a couple of Chiko Rolls," JayDee replied, for some reason he still appeared furious, despite Jiemba smiling at the prospect of lunch. "I have had my share of practising apologies, don't you worry. Besides, I figured you could save yours for later."

Jiemba looked confused. "You seem sure that I will need them. I thought you said we shouldn't assume things about people. Yet somehow you know I will have to say sorry again. You're probably right though, but still."

"I did say that, and I know you will make more mistakes in your life, for sure. But I also know that you will need to apologise to me again later." Jiemba wanted to argue against the old man, instead he simply watched as JayDee turned to walk back up the stairs, pointing out towards where the ladder had fallen behind Jiemba. Jiemba turned and his face froze, a chill shooting down his spine. "It had better be a bloody good one too." JayDee stated as he disappeared back inside the house.

Jiemba nodded his agreement furiously despite no one seeing it. He completely agreed he would need to apologise. A quick glance back at where he had fallen confirmed what he had feared. He wasn't sure if an apology would be enough.

He had crushed JayDee's flowers.

Nothing was said again from that moment about what had happened the night before. JayDee had not pushed it and instead had still welcomed Jiemba to stay for as long as he wanted, or as long as it took to get him healthy. That of course meant mentally healthy as there was nothing physically wrong with Jiemba, when there definitely should have been.

JayDee kept providing accommodation free of charge, and, despite the fact that Jiemba was never hungry, regardless of how much energy he used, JayDee kept cooking large meals that they shared together and talked some more. Days rolled by, turning into weeks, and it wasn't long before Jiemba felt he knew JayDee more than he knew many of his lifelong friends. It sounded like he had a lot in common with JayDee's son, and he legitimately hoped that one day he would meet him.

In the time that passed Jiemba was kept busy, which he didn't mind at all. What started with Jiemba doing simple odd jobs around the house and yard quickly turned into attempting far more difficult challenges. Both of them agreed that something strange was happening to Jiemba and that he should be tested to see the limits of what he could do. These were less to do with him not being hurt and more to do with his strength.

"It is already proven that your body can withstand a great amount of abuse. Falling from a ladder unharmed and lasting days without nourishment is evidence enough. I don't think you need to complete any acts of self harm to discover your limits, especially in your current state of mind," Jaydee had stated, in which Jiemba whole heartedly agreed.

The first of these tasks was to replace all the loose nails hanging from the plasterboard and cladding which bordered the back of the house. As any person could do this JayDee forced Jiemba to try and do it without a hammer. Jiemba started by clenching a fist and hitting a nail with his closed hand. He expected to recoil in agony, but again he felt nothing. The house did though, as he punched the nail straight through the wall and into the next room and demolished a portion of the outside wall with his impact. He fixed it, though the task took longer, and from that point he simply had to press the nail with his thumb into the allocated spot. It went in securely each time and there was no pain or mark left on his thumb.

Who needs a hammer?

Jiemba could clearly do some extraordinary things since his accident. However, he didn't want to just break a building every time he leaned against it, so he spent time practising to control his strength as much as he spent using it.

JayDee gave him even more tasks to do outside of the home, which he referred to as the labours of Jiemba; an idea taken from an ancient book that JayDee had read at some point. They were varied in their execution, and Jiemba had to complete one of these every day. Jiemba would spend the morning of each day doing small jobs around the house before attempting one of the challenges during the middle of the day, and sometimes at night. But every afternoon he would walk down to where the pontoon floated in the river to spend time with those that congregated there. He had to admit that he preferred to play sport with the others. He would enjoy the songs and dances with whoever would join in, play with Jonah and Joanna whenever they came down, and spend much of that time apologising for the near misses his strength created as he still learnt to control himself. Surprisingly he found more pleasure talking with many of the older people who hung around the area. Some had great stories of past experiences or family history, both sad and remarkable, while others just wanted to vent their troubles at him. In both cases he was the best listener he could be, active in his questioning and sincere in his response. He didn't challenge their opinions (even though he knew many of these were wrong) or offer comparisons. He simply listened and when progress was needed he tried to offer solutions. He rarely shared his story but there were also only a few within that group who cared to find out either.

Jiemba remembered the first challenge, which just seemed convenient for JayDee rather than a task set to test Jiemba. He was charged with knocking over a row of trees which impeded his view of the river from his cottage. There was an axe handy as well as an old saw, but Jiemba decided to try and use his bare hands. He pushed three of them over in no time at all, forcing them in a direction which would make them fall away from the house and yard. One of them he kicked just for fun which broke it in half, leaving a stump still firmly rooted in the ground while sending the rest crashing through various parts of the bush. Jiemba was then made to dig out the stump.

Almost every other day he would look down from the house onto the river and see some individual washed up there. He would walk down to find them in a sick and sorry state and with JayDee, but sometimes without, he would walk them back to the top of the river where he would dump them back on the shore closest to the mission. He would then talk some more before heading back to do something else.

There were a few other tasks that he was working on daily, and he found that he added these to his routine and found time outside of his imaginary timetable as well. He would simply sit for hours, a fair portion just sitting there doing nothing, but another equally large time was spent just reading by himself. He hadn't been much of a reader, but he made himself do it, finding that he was interested in the choices JayDee had made for him. He didn't touch the children's book out of principal which became a running joke.

"Attempted any of the big words yet?" JayDee would ask in passing, hoping to get a rise but mostly getting either a shake of the head or a dry smile.

Jiemba was not much of a hunter, although several of his friends had asked him along on weekends to track down various feral animals on their properties. Those experiences, which he declined on most occasions but when he went he was more of a far off observer rather than a participant, would have come in handy as there were a few days when he was made to track down some animals on the old man's property and capture them.

There was a giant deer that was roaming in the upper reaches of the hills, tearing down trees and destroying the natural environments of many other native animals. Likewise there was a family of wild pigs that had been adventuring down near the river, tearing up the vegetation and churning up the water. It had taken some hard work in preparation, where he had to make some traps from fallen logs and a large net to get hold of them before he had any chance of being successful. The deer had been the harder of the two as it would scramble away, leaping up small ledges and into the higher ground. Despite his improvement in strength and durability he hadn't become much faster, though his speed and stamina definitely increased.

The deer eventually got tired of being hunted and charged Jiemba, assuming he was like every other person or animal it had ever come across. The buck lowered its head and attacked quickly with its sharp prongs angled down at Jiemba. He hadn't expected it and felt his shirt tear from the impact, but he grabbed hold of the animal and wrangled it to the ground without too much effort. After carrying it back over his shoulders, which was awkward as it was bigger than he was, he gave it to JayDee who took it away in his ute to sell for extra cash.

Jonah had heard about Jiemba's hunting expeditions and had trailed him on a couple of occasions. He suggested that when they captured the pigs they should have a gathering and cook them for everyone. Jiemba loved the idea and it was a lot easier to find the pigs than it had been to get the deer. On the day that Jiemba and Jonah caught them, Jonah scared a large group down the river. He was effectively acting like a sheep dog as he pushed them down to where

JayDee was waiting with a large net. It was all going smoothly until one of the boars did what Jiemba hoped it wouldn't. It turned and charged back towards Jonah, bearing its large dangerous tusks as it tried to gore him. Jonah ran from it but it pursued him, cutting corners through trees and demolishing small bushes. Jiemba knew of the danger and tried to head it off. Jonah was starting to run uphill in an attempt to tire out the feral pig, but it powered even stronger up the incline, closing the gap as Jonah fatigued far quicker than his pursuer. Jiemba arrived just in time, lunging onto the pig with some force and rolling it onto the ground. It screamed as Jiemba took control, before being dragged helplessly back towards JayDee.

The old man had managed to trap the others. He told Jiemba to 'leave the rest to him', before instructing him to go and set up a series of spits down near the mission. Later that night, next to several safely roaring fires, everyone at the river's edge filled their tummys with some of the gamiest and odd tasting meat that Jiemba had ever tasted. He could see that many of them squirreled away some more for later or another time, but if that is what they needed to do then he was not about to question or deny them. There was plenty to go around. Some of the other older men had captured some kangaroo that they graciously added to the pile of meat to be cooked. Jiemba saw JayDee smile as some of these men were attacked with questions from the younger generation, who hung on every word they said. All of a sudden they were full of energy as they had been given a purpose. An older skill and custom which had suddenly become relevant to the progress and culture of the group.

Jiemba smiled too.

He was starting to sleep a little better.

The morning after, Jiemba dragged the logs that he had knocked over, down to the water's edge. It took him most of the morning as he could take only one at a time. The logs were awkward and for the first time in a while he did feel some strain when carrying them, but knew that he shouldn't actually be able to carry them at all. He was fine, but he silently hoped that his new found strength wasn't already beginning to fade. Once they were all there JayDee stepped in to help. He had used the money that he had gotten from selling the deer, and spent it on some tools like wooden planes, rulers, handsaws and chisels. He gathered up anyone who was keen and taught them how to do some basic wood work. Jiemba was asked to cut the wood into lengths, which didn't take very long, and left the men to their craft.

Meanwhile Jiemba still had more work to do. He cultivated a small field at the back of the house, tilling it with a heavy iron hoe that had historically required a horse to drag it; Jiemba had no horse so he did it himself. Then he trapped a group of larger than normal emus that had been invading and scratching at his newly ploughed soil.

Afterwards he found a neighbouring farmer who was in need of some assistance. Jiemba had no idea that farms surrounded the bushland area that he was residing in, though he supposed he should have known it was possible. The procession of cattle that appeared knee deep in the river was an obvious hint that this was the case. A broken fence had led to the cows escaping and as he couldn't get a vehicle down into the gully where they splashed about the farmer was at a loss. Jiemba, with the assistance of Jonah and Joanna, as well as several other teenage helpers as it was the weekend, worked on fixing the fence before trying to get the cattle dry and safe on higher ground again. The youths worked so well together; focusing on the same goal, laughing together instead of fighting despite failing several times. Jiemba assisted them when the bank became too run down, having to push the cattle up the muddy embankment with as much care as he could.

At one point Jiemba struggled, much to the delight of all those present. A bull had not been pleased with the group returning his friends to the enclosure, and as such growled in annoyance and threatened to stampede anyone that came near. The more he bucked the deeper he got into the water, until he alone was the only remaining creature to be removed. Jiemba, although still strong, lost a bit of his patience as he struggled to find his footing in the deep water. The closer he got the angrier the bull became. Jiemba walked closer and slipped on the uneven rocks hidden below the surface. As he fell the bull came closer and bashed its skull against Jiemba's. There was a distinct crack, and when Jiemba looked up he saw the bull standing in a daze with a broken horn. Jiemba managed to push the beast out eventually, where it returned to its paddock feeling sad and sorry for itself. Jiemba on the other hand had felt nothing. There wasn't even a puncture mark or scratch. Jokes were immediately made about how his head was thicker than that of a bull's. Jiemba replied by saying that the ladies loved war wounds, which was received by more laughter as he could show none. Jiemba's own infectious laugh louder than the others.

The farmer was so grateful that he promised he would help in any way he could; offering the youths a chance at earning some money doing farm work if they wanted which he said was not an empty gesture. He also gave Jiemba a bag of seeds which he promised would grow apples of the golden variety. Jiemba spent no time at all in planting them and ensuring that nothing came to eat or remove them from his new crop.

The last task Jiemba did was to help clean out underneath the house. JayDee had left this area off his list, which led Jiemba to the assumption that he probably didn't want anyone to go down there. Nevertheless it was the only spot left to clean.

There was a large wooden beam which restricted access. Jiemba lifted it aside as if it was nothing, knowing that he could place it back exactly where he found it when he was finished. It was dark underneath but there was a fair bit of clearance so Jiemba could walk through unimpeded. He found a light switch nearby and after flicking it he marvelled at exactly how much space existed under the house, and what was contained there. Jiemba whistled, impressed and slightly surprised by what he saw. The space could only be described as a car park, but for motorcycles. There were literally dozens of them. Jiemba read the names as he walked alongside them all. Ducati 907, Honda CX500 turbo, Harley Davidson Panhead, Kawasaki Z1, and Triumph Bonneville were some that he could read. The rest were

so old the names had either worn out or not been displayed on them.
Jiemba had no idea about motorcycles so had no appreciation at what
he was looking at. His first impression was that they were just
remnants of junk from an old collection. He was still impressed all
the same.

JayDee was a mystery within himself. Jiemba had heard all sorts of
things about bikers, many of them negative, and he just didn't think
that JayDee was one of them. He did remember that JayDee said he
had a past, as well as the many times he had trailed off in their
conversations. He also remembered that he had been told not to make
assumptions, good or bad. Perhaps he was simply a collector. Would
Jiemba have thought differently of the old man, who had helped him
so much, if suddenly he found out that he had a criminal history
which could contain some terrible acts? Jiemba liked to judge people
on their merit, he hoped he could look past that if it was true.

Regardless of the condition of the bikes he knew better than to
touch or clean them, having heard somewhere that sometimes dirt
has its own value. The ground on the other hand was something he
could deal with. Weeds, decayed leaves, sticks and mounds of dirt had
been swept onto the concrete floor, either by the wind or by water
running down the hill during heavy rains. He grabbed a broom and
got started.

"Time to clean the stables," he said out loud, wondering if it was
going to be his last labour for his host.

Jiemba was reflecting on all of the tasks that he had been made to
complete as he stood waist high in the river. He reflected on the idea
that he was made to, as he had volunteered happily for the most part.
Jiemba felt like he had been making a difference, even though he had
made no money and hadn't travelled anywhere. He was somehow
richer. JayDee had also done a fantastic job in teaching most of the
older men how to use the tools at their disposal.

"All they needed was a chance," JayDee told him, nodding with
glee as they were hard at work. Not everyone had seized upon the

opportunity, with some still sitting glumly off to one side looking either disinterested or angry at the suggestion they should be made to work; but most were now placing the finishing touches on a large wooden bridge that spread the length of the river. Jiemba had helped drive wooden pillars down deep into the ground beneath the water, as well as reinforce the ends into the banks that ensured that it was secure against even the most ferocious flooding that could sweep down from the dam. The rest of the work had been done by the people, and now, finally, it was almost finished.

"That looks good from here." Jiemba called out. Several men were implementing sturdy beams to act as protective barriers, to help people from falling in the water regardless of condition. Jiemba was helping them bolt the posts to the main logs underneath the bridge to help reinforce them. In less than an hour, after taking several days prior, the actual bridge, which looked and worked like a bridge, was finally completed. There was a great cheer that erupted from everybody involved in the project, which was greeted by several loud splashes as some of the younger observers immediately used it as a diving board to propel themselves into the river. It was a very lovely day, so why not?

"More work to be done though," JayDee declared as he pointed up over the far shore towards where the mission lay. He had been helping many of them build doors and furniture from old logs that Jiemba had cleared. The community of outcasts had come together and created the best out of a bad situation, with JayDee saying on occasion that he could hopefully help them to help themselves out of the circumstances they had found themselves in. They were very appreciative to JayDee, and under his guidance of the last few weeks they had made some progress. There were even fewer that had to be dragged out of the river these days, JayDee refused to give them any tools unless they were sound of mind and not influenced by any liquid or substance.

Most of them were appreciative.

"You shouldn't be fixing that place," one man shouted out as the cheerful procession passed by, "it is a memory of a time where we weren't treated well. Have you forgotten?"

"No one will ever forget," JayDee called back.

"It is better used as a sanctuary than a relic," one of the women called out in defence of JayDee's project.

"It should be destroyed," the angry man yelled out. "You should all be ashamed to stay there, and accept help from a man who lives in luxury up on that hill. We don't need help from them. Leave the outcasts in peace."

Jiemba was making his way out of the water when a younger voice added their viewpoint. "JayDee is helping us, therefore he is one of us." Joanna yelled loudly. Her voice was shaking suggesting she wasn't confident in standing up against the man who was older than she was. "We shouldn't be talking about them and us anymore anyway."

"That is how it has always been," the man spat back.

"No it hasn't, it wasn't before, and it doesn't have to be anymore," Joanna cried out. "The more we think like that the more we move backwards, the more reason we give to get pushed back down."

"We are pushed down," he took a few steps forward, brandishing his skinny chest. "You just built a bridge and you are excited about it. It's pathetic."

"It's better than lying beside it, or hiding beneath it," Joanna bellowed back. "If we can build a bridge from nothing, we could build anything from something."

"They are still hunting us," the man seemed taken aback from Joanna's ferocity. "Have you forgotten? It won't be long until they find you out here. They will break your bridge and take you in."

"They can try," Joanna snarled, daring the man to say anything else. Instead he retreated into the trees, casting back fierce looks as he mumbled angrily under his breath. Joanna walked over to JayDee and followed him and the others up towards the mission. Jiemba watched the man slink into the shadows after they all left, before

Jiemba sat down on the edge of the bridge. He looked up at the dam wall and smiled as children still played before him. A new game of Aqua Rugby was being started, as others flipped from the rope swing or fought in the shallows.

"That guy isn't one of us," Jonah said as he sat down beside Jiemba.

"Didn't you listen to what your cousin just said?" Jiemba suggested with a smile.

"No," Jonah replied with a shake of his head. "I mean he isn't from around here. That was maybe only the second or third time I have seen him at the river ever. Who knows where he is from? I think if he lived here like some of these people do he would know better than to talk like that."

"You don't live here though, do you?" Jiemba asked. Jonah shook his head.

"No, I am lucky," Jonah smiled. "I live at a home in Wellington, what they call Old Wellington now. But my carers don't live so far from here, so they either drop us off or we ride our bikes or walk."

"JayDee said that you and your cousin have had a lot going on," Jiemba prodded gently. "He didn't tell me what, I assumed it was bad, yet you still think that you are lucky?"

"My circumstance is a little different," Jonah said. "I had some really bad stuff happen when I was little. I was there, I saw some of it, even the bad stuff." Jonah trailed off for a moment, and without Jiemba actually knowing what had happened, his mind created several likely scenarios. "It got bad, for Joanna and I. Our families lived together. The house was too big for all of us, we were never comfortable and always afraid. We were separated, and we were both angry. I was moved from school to school, house to house, carer to carer. I never felt wanted, I had no confidence, nothing good was happening. I felt like I was useless and had nothing. I acted out. I pushed some good people away, it was just easier if they cast me aside early."

"That's not the person who sits here with me," Jiemba declared, still dangling his feet lazily towards the water but listening intently. "What happened?"

"I let someone help me," Jonah said with a smile.

"Congratulations," Jiemba said with a soft smile, and no celebrations; knowing that it was something that he had failed at often. "That can be pretty hard to do."

"It was," Jonah confirmed, nodding but smiling. "I fought it the whole way. But that someone took every blow, they listened to every word, they never fought me back, they could have walked away, passed me on. But, they didn't. They just took it. It was like I was a rhinoceros charging out of control, and I was pushing as hard as I could. They just hung on, waiting for me to stop, never letting go. I stopped eventually, getting tired of having to do that every day, and in the end I marvelled at the strength that that person had. Then it changed. I finally had someone who knew where I was coming from without ever being there. Someone that I trusted and looked to for advice. Then one person became two and three. Then I got new friends who wanted me to do well. Then I realised I was good at things, lots of things, but my anger had stopped me from seeing it. The more I talked the easier it got. I can look back at who I was and see a lesson in who I don't want to be, but I can also see people who haven't done that yet, who may never be able to do that. I can't blame them."

"So yeah I am lucky," Jonah added, "because I could be in a position where I am a whole lot worse."

"You and your cousin are pretty strong," Jiemba said. "I wish I was as strong as you guys are."

"Yeah right," Jonah scoffed, his glasses popped off his face slightly so he pushed them back. "I have watched you, you could move a mountain if you wanted to."

"I doubt it," Jiemba laughed, "but even that power has only been available to me for a short time."

"Where did it come from before?" Jonah asked, happy to accept the answer.

"What do you mean?" Jiemba was confused.

"I mean, my strength comes from my friends, from my teachers, and from those who care about me," Jonah broke it down. "I learn things and draw strength from them. They make me stronger."

"But you are already strong," Jiemba replied.

"Yes I know," Jonah said with a laugh, "but they make me *stronger*."

"I see," Jiemba said understanding what he meant. He thought about it for a moment and then explained what he thought. "I think that I get my strength from four places. The first is my culture, but I am still building that area and I really want to know more."

"Me too," Jonah agreed. "I think that is why I am allowed to come out here so much. So I can play and learn from people like me. My carers are nice but there are things that they can't do for me. It isn't their fault, and I don't blame them. I want to engage more." Jiemba smiled at him.

"The second is my dad," Jiemba continued. "I think I get my outer strength from him." Jonah pretended to flex his own muscles, and he was considerably ripped, but Jiemba shook his head. "Sort of, I am sure that I have got some physique from him. But I meant that I am able to draw strength from things external to me. I can find things to make me better, find help and support when I need it and know where to find it, understand what will make me strong, have the ability to communicate with people, to build relationships. My dad used to say, 'when you meet someone get your hand out first,' because then you are introducing yourself in a positive way. He had a knack of being able to talk to anybody, about anything, regardless if he knew much about it and you would feel better and think that he was smart and strong. I try to emulate them all the time."

"The third is my mum where I get all my inner strength," Jiemba continued, smiling as he thought of many situations where both his mum and his dad had made an impact on him without even knowing.

"When I was younger, even now actually, I was impulsive, and my mum would say things that would make me think. They weren't lessons like don't do this, or don't do that, but she did those too, they were more like references to how you should hold yourself. Like how to gauge risks, and how to act when someone did something to you. I remember a time where my sister and I were getting bullied so bad on the bus and all I wanted to do was hit the person doing it, and I had to trust that what they were doing was wrong and other people would see that. I helped my sister first, and then before anything else happened my friends stood up for me. My mum said that I wouldn't have known who my friends were if I had acted out and got in trouble. There was another time when I was sad or angry and she would say the right thing, but in such a way that I remember it. She was like Lego and just kept putting bricks up and building me up, her voice was stamped on me and I never wanted to do things to let her down, because it was absolutely the worst feeling and I knew I was letting everyone else down too."

"And the fourth spot," Jonah was nodding the whole time Jiemba spoke about his mum.

"The fourth is me," Jiemba said with a bit more sadness. "And I know I can be strong. I know it. But there are times when I ignore myself and everyone else and do things that I shouldn't be doing. If I had to think about why that is, I would have to say it is because I don't know who I am, and because of that I don't know my worth to anybody."

Neither of them spoke for a while.

"Well at least that is an easy fix," Jonah said finally.

"Easy fix?" Jiemba laughed. "I have been trying to solve this issue for ages. I have laughed so hard to cover that my voice box is burned."

"Well you are doing it wrong," Jonah said as if it was the most casual thing in the world. "If you go to the shops and you want to buy something you don't laugh at the salesperson, you talk to them." Jiemba stared at Jonah as if he had just said something profoundly enlightening, that had never been thought of and was the most exciting discovery in the world, yet it had been overlooked since that point. He was shocked that he was hearing it from someone half his age.

"You just have to talk," Jonah continued, "and that's the easy part. There is still the harder part to do."

Jiemba dreaded the talking, he was trembling just thinking about the harder part. "What is the harder part?"

"I will tell you only if you promise to do it no matter what," Jonah said as he returned to his feet. "If I can do it you can do it."

Jiemba thought briefly and stared back at the younger man. After Jonah had told him so much how could he refuse when he had gone through far less? "Okay," he said finally. "I will promise to do it no matter what." Jonah smiled at him, knowing that he was telling the truth.

"Okay, you have to talk about it," he began, "but the hardest thing is not talking, but rather that you have to let someone listen. Then you have to listen too." He nodded and walked away. "Oh and one more thing," Jonah added with a look over his shoulder. Jiemba simply nodded to say he was ready for some more advice. "Make sure you thank the person who you talk to. If you are willing to open up to someone then they must mean a great deal to you. People don't tell others that they appreciate them, and they realise it too late and regret it." Jonah smiled, waved, and then left Jiemba to sit and think.

Jiemba felt like he was a complete idiot.

"I'm just not into you that way," JayDee said as he returned to the garden by his home. Jiemba laughed at the remark but understood what he meant. Jiemba had returned to the homestead, made a clearing, created a fire pit, lit a fire, and had grabbed some food and drinks. Night had fallen and the outline of the fire blazed purple and blue, with the Milky Way spreading out in the sky above.

It looked very romantic.

"Ha ha, devo," Jiemba laughed back at him. JayDee grabbed a beverage and sat down on a log that was acting like a seat. "Look I just thought I would say thank you, and this is probably the best way I know how."

"I think you have done a lot of work around here to cover that already," JayDee replied, "but I am not complaining."

"That stuff was in payment for letting me stay," Jiemba interrupted, "for which I am grateful. But I think I have got far more out of staying here and learning from you, and listening to you, than I thought I could have ever gotten. I can't tell you how appreciative I am of you, or what you mean to me."

"Thanks," JayDee said, cracking the lid of his drink and having an enormous slurp. "Still going back to separate beds though."

"Agreed," Jiemba laughed loudly again, "but before that I wanted to know if I could tell you something?"

"Anything mate," JayDee responded.

"At any point you can tell me to shut up," Jiemba continued.

"Noted," JayDee replied, "start talking."

"Okay," Jiemba said. He took a deep breath and told him the sequence of events which ended with Jiemba being found passed out on the river bank. "What do you think?" he asked afterwards. His whole body had shaken the entire time he had told his story.

"I think you have told me what happened," JayDee replied, cracking his third drink. "But you haven't told me why."

Jiemba took another long deep breath. He remembered the promise he had made to Jonah only a short time before. "Here goes," he said to himself more than anybody else. "I am known as the guy who laughs, the guy who is everybody's friend and who everybody knows. I genuinely want people to be happy but I feel like I take on every problem. It helps them which is great, but then afterwards I feel flat. I have no outlet. So that is why I play footy, to get it out of my system. But then when I play, although I have so much fun with my mates, there is always someone who says something. I don't mean in a competitive way, I can deal with that, but in a way that is meant to hurt me. I suck it up and don't let it show. Then laugh it off and hit the guy as hard as I can next time he runs the ball." Jiemba laughed uncontrollably for a moment, memories of folding people popping back into his head. "Then there is the Aboriginal thing. I love being me and what I represent more than anything else, but I hate people referring to me as the friend who is, so therefore their actions are justified. I want to be heard, but I want to be listened to just as much and valued. I have a lot to say, and a lot of ideas, and people may not like it but they should listen. But then I don't really want to annoy those people." The laughter was gone as another breath was taken.

"The thing I hate the most is letting people down," Jiemba finally stated softly. "I know without anybody having to tell me that I am a role model. I am a leader of my people, a mentor to the young and a shoulder to my friends. I don't want them to think that I am weak, and therefore someone that they can't rely upon. I want to give my all, in everything, to everybody, at all times, but it is tiring. I am now at a point where all my walls are coming down in my mind. I am talking to myself, saying the same things I usually do. In the past when I have gone looking for help at these times, something gets lost in translation. Whoever I talk to somehow turns it around and I am made to feel like it is all my fault, and, that by voicing my problems, I have inconvenienced someone and made the whole situation worse. I tell myself to stay positive, knowing what the correct course of action is, knowing that there are times in my life that I can use for reference where everything was perfect, but I am not listening to myself anymore. It is becoming dangerous. I am just so tired of all of it. Do you know what I am saying?" He looked over to JayDee, panting.

"I do know what you are saying," JayDee replied.

"I expected you to jump in and say something at some point," Jiemba said with some confusion. "To agree or say that I was wrong."

"I could have, but I was never going to," JayDee replied, climbing slowly and painfully to his feet. Jiemba looked at him with confusion. "As much as I am happy to talk more about this, and I absolutely am, that is not a job for tonight. Definitely another time though. Tonight my job was simply to listen. You have told me everything that you needed to, and you have shared your problems not just with me, but with this place, the trees and the stars. None of us are judging you and all have listened." Jiemba nodded his understanding. He had an odd feeling in his stomach, he was disappointed that he had received no feedback, but doubly relieved that he had his say and was receiving no critique on it. He inhaled and exhaled slowly, finding it odd that after weeks of carrying things far heavier than anybody had ever carried before, and having no pain or struggle in doing so, he could feel the weight on his shoulders suddenly lift after the only thing he had shifted were thoughts and words. He slumped forward on his log looking hard into the fire.

"Words are the heaviest thing sometimes. Thank you Jiemba," JayDee finally said as he had stretched out his stiffness. "Thank you for trusting me enough to talk to me. It shows more strength in doing that than knocking down any tree."

"Thank you," Jiemba replied, "and thank you for listening. Please don't tell anybody."

"I will take it to my grave," JayDee replied with a smirk, "and on that note I am going back to mine. I am totally buggered. Enjoy your sleep. It will be the best one you ever had. In your own bed, not mine."

Jiemba smiled at the waddling old man. Left all alone, with no voices in his head telling him anything, Jiemba enjoyed the serenity. He extinguished the fire and watched the stars that sparkled so beautifully above him. Before long he packed up everything with the intention of heading back up to the house and to the bed he had become so familiar with.

Jiemba never made it though.

Feeling completely at peace and content at the spot he was in at that moment he chose to not move at all. He shifted down on the log so that his back was propped up, before falling happily asleep next to a crackling fire.

And had one of the best sleeps he had ever had.

Chapter 6 – Lost contact

"Are you sure?" JayDee asked with a look of concern. He cast a hard stare into the shadows on the other side of the new bridge. Jonah nodded his head, as did Joanna beside him to add her confirmation. JayDee snuffed heavily out of his nose and down his thick moustache. He pulled an old brick like phone from his pocket and headed up towards the privacy of a small glade surrounded by juvenile trees.

"I need to make a call," the old man said.

"When do you think?" Jiemba asked with a look of concern on his face.

"Soon," Joanna replied. "We heard that guy talking about it with others who we have never seen before. They are going to try something. Either at the mission, down here at the bridge or elsewhere."

"But you don't know which or when?" Jiemba asked again. He too was standing with arms crossing his massive chest, glaring into the shadows of the trees; daring someone to come out and try something.

"No, but I am sure something bad is going to happen," she kicked a small pile of rocks which splattered into the edge of the trickling river. "Just when things start getting a little bit better, someone has to go and try to ruin it. And you just know who is going to get the blame. It always happens, one person always stuffs it for the rest of us."

"The worst thing is that no one knows who that guy is and he keeps bringing more people in, and we don't know who they are either," Jonah added.

"But no-one is going to believe that, one bad all bad, that's usually how it goes," Joanna slumped onto a rock, an angry scowl stamped on her face though her eyes quivered as if she were about to cry. "It will begin all over again. Walking into any shop or any place and being watched. People looking sideways at you, or just looking away. You know exactly what they are thinking, and what they will say when they think we aren't looking."

"Officer Gumbo was talking to me yesterday," Jonah mentioned, breaking the silence. Jiemba wondered what the conversation would be about. "I told him what was going on, and he said he would keep an eye out, but he said it would be hard if we didn't have a name."

"You shouldn't trust that guy," Joanna growled, referring to the police officer. "He is just as likely to turn on you."

"I don't think so," Jonah shook his head, a strong bond was shown in his conviction.

"How do you know him?" Jiemba asked.

"I play basketball from time to time at the PCYC," Jonah admitted. "I started doing it years ago and it really helped keep me focused. Because I was tall and quick I was pretty good. Officer Gumbo is usually there and I talk to him a lot, and I talk to some of the others as well. They are really trying to help, but their job is pretty hard. It has only gotten harder. He isn't very good at basketball. He is pretty solid and has a big forehead, but he is pretty strong and can throw the ball a long way. He has never forced a conversation either, most of the time he is just happy to listen."

"Listens, but does nothing," Joanna groaned unhappily, "he doesn't care."

"You're wrong," Jonah said back, softly, though there was some command in his words. "You shouldn't assume the worst anyway." Joanna smiled a little. She cast a sideways glance at JayDee who was still out of sight but along that direction. No doubt they had received the same advice that Jiemba had.

"It doesn't matter anyway," Joanna finally said, "nothing will happen until *he* is gone." The he that she referred to was clearly Jiemba, as he was greeted with a piercing look from her big brown eyes.

"What?" Jiemba looked shocked. He wasn't denying the fact but he hadn't advertised it yet either.

"Rumour has got around that you are leaving soon," Jonah said, dragging his long black hair out from behind his glasses. He no longer had a mullet, it was now just a mass of unkempt hair which still hung down and curled around the base of his neck. "It's okay, it had to happen at some stage, just wish you had told us. You have been fun, and if I was going to fight someone it wouldn't be you. You are like fun muscle."

"To be honest I hadn't actually decided upon doing anything yet," Jiemba said with a smile at the comment, taking his eyes away from the far trees for the first time. "I would absolutely tell you before that decision is made. But just think, that as bad as that would feel for you it would probably be a relief for others. I haven't made any contact with anyone else since I have been here. Including friends and family."

"They don't care then," Joanna stated under her breath.

"Maybe they think the same about me," Jiemba corrected. "They just don't know where to look. I have a lot of faith in my friends, which is why I feel bad that I haven't touched base. I can't stay here forever, besides you don't need me around anymore."

"That's not what the other kids are saying," Joanna admitted with a smile finally emerging.

"Yeah," Jonah chuckled, knowing that Jiemba wanted to know. "They think you are some sort of superhero. Super strong, can't get hurt, have a gnarly goanna tattoo, which is not a tattoo, etched across your chest."

"I'm no superhero," Jiemba dismissed the idea.

"They are even making names up for you," Joanna laughed even harder.

"Really?" Jiemba seemed astonished.

"Yeah," Jonah nodded, his hair bobbing down to annoy him again. "Some of them are okay, but others are just weird. You were called Goanna Man, and one of the old fellas called you Gugaa Man."

"I think it is Wiradjuri for goanna," Joanna added. "But doesn't really flow."

"But then there were some basic ones," Jonah continued, "like Mr Strong, Strong Man, the Muscle Buster, Mighty Man, and Force-of-Nature. And some really bad ones."

"Roid Man," Joanna cried out, before Jonah joined in and they each alternated shouting out a name.

"Captain Calves."

"Mediocre Man."

"Don't forget the Wombat."

"The Bulge."

"That will do," Jiemba stopped them. He had to stop himself from laughing as both of them were bent over holding their sides, as if the laughter was going to explode from deep within their stomachs. "I don't need or want a superhero name, because I am not a superhero."

"That's what JayDee said," Jonah reported once he had managed to settle down a little.

"Really?" Jiemba asked, trying to hide his disappointment that the old man had so quickly dismissed the idea. He had secretly hoped that the old man would give a suggestion that Jiemba could completely disregard, and laugh mockingly back at him. In truth, as he had built so much respect for JayDee over the last few weeks, he would probably be willing to accept his name no matter what it was.

"Yep," Joanna backed up what Jonah had just said, though she didn't smile anymore as she had gotten over her fit of the giggles. "He said that despite having the strength of a superhero you didn't need a name, because superhero names were used to protect your identity, but if you don't know who you are then you don't really have one and therefore have no need to protect it."

"Ouch," Jiemba said, wincing at the comment. "I can't argue with that, but still harsh."

"He also said that we should all take a lesson from you," Jonah added, "because as much as you have taken knocks and haven't been hurt, or even felt any pain, or cold or heat, you are still hurting as much as the rest of us."

"It is okay to be strong and weak at the same time," JayDee finished off the comment as he returned to the trio.

"Wise words," Jiemba said.

"It must be the moustache," JayDee smirked. "I made a call. I have some people who are going to come out later on, they will stop by and give us a hand if anything happens here. Then I also have someone else who is going to head out. He won't be here today, but he should be a big help to us." He then pulled Jiemba aside so the others couldn't hear him. "I have also arranged for one of them to take you back to Orange. I know that you have been wanting to make a move. It can happen this afternoon, if you want."

"You and I need to have a chat before I go, though," Jiemba whispered back.

"Happy to," JayDee smiled. "But you probably need to say goodbye to these guys first."

"I have some things to do around here before that," Jiemba said sadly. "I said I would clear the river of any more large rocks and hidden logs so it is safer for them to play. It shouldn't take too long."

"It takes as long as it takes, remember," JayDee reminded him. "I am going to make a start back up to the house. I will meet you up there." He waved his goodbyes to the young pair as well. "Stay out of trouble you two." They smiled warmly at him before JayDee shuffled slowly back up towards the crests and ridges that led to his house. As they watched the old man, Jiemba was amazed that a small wagtailed bird fluttered down to land on his shoulder. It stayed there a while, dancing from shoulder to shoulder, apparently unnoticed. A moment later it flittered away.

"That was, unique," Jiemba shared.

"But not a good sign," Joanna added, sharing a concerned look with Jonah.

Jiemba gulped down hard, not at the comment she had just made, but at the realisation that he really didn't want to say anything upsetting to these two youngsters that he had gotten so attached to, let alone uttering the hard words of what would lead to a goodbye. He looked at the pair out of the corner of his eyes. He knew that they knew the end was coming. There was an awkward shift as he walked towards and past them, a smile that was not so genuine shared between them. He said nothing, instead diverting towards the task he told JayDee he would be undertaking.

Jiemba pulled numerous fallen trees out from the river, waterlogged or hollow, placing them in a large pile so they could dry before he took them off into the scrub. He knew that he may be removing a home from a water dwelling creature, but he also knew that he was likely to create just as many for land loving animals.

He didn't remove everything from the river. Sometimes he would just rearrange fallen logs so that they could be used as seats along the edge of the water, or so they could be clambered upon to serve as diving boards into the deeper and wider parts, or positioned as a half pipe like path to enable smaller participants to access the pontoon which was still yet to be claimed by anyone from the lake.

Jiemba finally pulled, with some difficulty, a giant boulder out from one section of the river. He had left most of them in place but this one had an edge like a razor and was concealing just as many sharp ripping rocks underneath the shallow pebble covered river bed as it was above it. The boulder was the granite equivalent of an iceberg, only a small portion of the shape could be seen above the surface, and it took him a solid shoulder bump to separate its base from the ground that it had sat amongst for countless years.

"Why don't you just throw it into the bush like some of the others?" Jonah asked, seemingly taunting Jiemba's efforts. "Or maybe I should go and get that farmer down the river to bring his tractor up to help?"

"That tractor couldn't have gotten itself out of the river, let alone pull this rock out of there," Jiemba retorted as he tried to contain his strain. He was confident he could carry the multi-tonne boulder, but it was awkward to get a grip without slipping as it was still wet and quite a bit larger than Jiemba was. "Besides," he continued, "imagine you were some bush animal, sitting down to have your lunch, on what has to be one of the most glorious autumn days ever, when all of a sudden, a giant boulder comes flying into your dining room, crushing your home and your family."

"I can imagine that," Joanna said with a slight smile, clearly laughing at the action rather than the consequence.

"Maybe you need a hand?" Jonah offered jokingly, spreading his arms as if he could actually do the task.

"Sure, I would love a hand," Jiemba played along. The image of Jiemba passing the boulder over to the youth, and crushing him immediately popped warningly into his head.

"Hey, do you hear that?" Jonah suddenly called out, clutching at his ear, "someone is calling my name. I have to go, sorry I can't help." The only thing that Jiemba could hear was the sudden throb of an approaching motorcycle, accompanied by several others. Not an uncommon sound as the vehicles frequented the surrounding area on occasion; there were countless bike and bushwalking tracks littered throughout the area. The sound was definitely not someone calling out for Jonah. Jiemba smiled as Jonah walked halfway across the bridge as if in pursuit of the voice, before the young boy stopped to lean against the wooden handrail with a smile.

Jiemba carried the boulder a small distance, knowing that he still had to do a return journey to remove the piles of sticks, branches and small logs which had been drying in the sun. He didn't want to place the boulder on the nearby hill though, just in case something caused it to roll, in such an event the bridge and the people who enjoyed their time in the area would be in danger, and he couldn't have that or be responsible for it. He had to walk a fair distance away until he found a gravel and sand filled ditch. Jiemba dropped the boulder with a solid thud, resulting in a cloud of gritty dust flying into the air that covered Jiemba and the surrounding area. Though he could feel no pain he could still taste, and the sensation of small sand particles grinding and rubbing between his teeth was not pleasant. He tried to spit out as much as he could, scraping his finger nails down his tongue, between his teeth and around his gums to try and remove the feeling. The action distracted him from what he had tasked himself to do, but it also somehow masked the sounds.

The buzzing of motorcycles had returned, if they ever really left, although now they seemed to be much closer.

Another sound of an immense volume accompanied it, filled entirely of people screaming.

As the dust cleared Jiemba's senses came flooding back towards him. Smoke flared at his nostrils, alerting him to danger. He took several large steps in what was almost a jumping action to get back up out of the ditch. His breathing quickened as he glanced down and took in the scene. From his vantage point he could see the residents of the derelict mission stampeding away from it as it was engulfed in a mighty inferno. The building was mostly made of concrete walls and stone slabs, with the run down wooden shacks decaying and rotted away a long time ago. The only addition had been what JayDee had been helping to construct in the form of new doors and simple bits of furniture, but all of that was a work in progress and not of numerous quantities yet.

Jiemba had no idea how it had caught flame so suddenly and in such a immense way. The people fled down to where the river flowed, crossing the bridge and the river wherever they could. Alarmingly they were pursued by dozens of people on foot, but also by many others that were threatening from the back of dirt bikes close behind. The wasp like buzzing of the engines harassed all those that were escaping, with the riders throwing flaming bottles into the trees in all directions to cause further chaos; reducing the number of spots that those fleeing could hide within. The people, somehow, were still managing to escape from the new coming aggressors; Jiemba surprised at just how well they knew the area and the paths that they could take if they were in danger.

Jiemba hadn't moved from his position. Not because his first instinct wasn't to run down and help the people, but more because it didn't make sense. Not only the attack, but the amount of smoke surrounding him didn't match what was happening below him, especially as the wind was blowing in the other direction. He turned to look into the breeze, the smoke not harming his eyes or forcing him to protect his face.

There on the far hill he spied something equally alarming. In fact it was more so. JayDee's house was also on fire. No, it was engulfed by it.

"Help," a young voice called out, swivelling Jiemba's focus. He turned back to see Joanna being pursued by one of the bikers. There was no way Jiemba could run down there in time to help her. Instead he bent down to scoop up a bunch of small rocks which rested at his feet. He took no time to take aim, instead just launching the projectile as soon as he had a target. It screamed through the air, Jiemba did not hold back. The rock arrived mere metres and seconds before the rider could catch Joanna, crashing into the helmet with a deafening crack; splitting it into pieces as the rider was launched from the seat of his bike in a backwards motion, recoiling from the impact to the head. Joanna ran into the tree line and out of sight, never stopping to thank Jiemba or check on who else may be pursuing her; many of the others already in the process of doing the same.

Jonah, however, stood alone on the bridge. One lone figure walked towards him, their bike standing at the entrance to the bridge as if guarding it from one end. The person wore a helmet with a unique appearance, where the visor looked like the gaping mouth of a terrifying snake. They had a blood red scarf wrapped around their neck which trailed off behind to flutter wildly in the wind, building the impression that there was a serpent like creature wrapped around the upper portion of this person's body, if not in fact being a part of it. The other bikers pursued their targets into the undergrowth but Jiemba knew they would most likely be safe. Jonah on the other hand appeared to be in real danger. Jiemba could only hope that that wasn't the case with JayDee; assuming that the old man was smart enough to get away from such danger.

You should never make assumptions, the thought struck him hard.

The snake helmeted rider walked toward Jonah, igniting traces of the bridge as they walked by, turning it instantly from its fresh cream and olive colour to a stain of burnt black.

"Jonah run," Jiemba called out, hoping his voice would carry. Either Jonah didn't hear him or he completely ignored him. Instead of running away he charged towards the other person. A small explosion erupted on the pontoon just beyond the bridge, causing Jiemba to pull away as he watched Jonah approach his opponent. Jonah's arms swung out as he unleashed an energy filled barrage of fists at the intruder. It was an impressive display, if any normal person had received such a focused attack from Jonah, who was strong and deadly despite his youth and normally calm demeanour, they would have been beaten down or scared away in an instant.

But that was not the case with this person.

They swatted each blow away with ease, seeming to be content with blocking, evading or parrying each blow and allowing them to come. Jiemba noticed that none had landed on the mark, and could only watch as the intruder spun quickly around to finish with a powerful kick, sending Jonah sprawling painfully to the ground. The bridge had caught fire, its makeshift ropes that had been used to tether it together as well as the bolts and nails all starting to blister and snap. Fragments of the broken pontoon were floating down the river, with some parts still chained to the shore while others sunk to the bottom. The air shimmered with the intensity of the heat. Jonah climbed groggily to his feet but was cast back down with another brutal kick. The intruder pulled a bottle from a small bag strapped to their chest, swiftly ignited it and moved closer to Jonah. They held it aloft as Jonah miserably tried to crawl away from his opponent, the fire that he had used to fight back completely extinguished.

Jiemba couldn't hear what was being said, but couldn't wait another moment. He had been moving gradually closer at a slow rate but knew he still would not reach the pair in time. He furiously threw the few rocks that he still carried with him. He watched as the first struck the bottle, causing the liquid flame to collapse onto the intruder's hand before spreading to the rest of their body, lighting them up like a human torch. This confusion gave Jonah the time to move quickly to his feet, where he stumbled for several steps before finding his feet and leaving the bridge. He needn't have worried too much. Jiemba's second shot missed but his third struck the very tip of the helmet and propelled the shocked attacker into the water. Jiemba cast one final look, to ensure that Jonah had no more pursuers and had cleared the bridge that was now well ablaze, before sprinting the other direction towards the small cottage which was consumed by flame.

He put as much energy as he could into his effort. His speed had improved as had his fitness, but it simply meant he was charging with the power of a rhino, but not the speed of a freight train. He was making up the distance quickly, hoping that he wouldn't be too late.

Jiemba felt like someone was watching him as he ran. If they were above him towards the house he couldn't see them. A glance behind him showed the sorry state of the bridge which was burning along its length, the hopes and efforts of all those who had worked hard in its creation up in the flames along with it.

The lone figure of the snake rider stood on the far bank amongst the smoke, staring in his direction.

Jiemba promised he would deal with that person later.

He bounded into the yard as the back veranda collapsed down into the garden. Blistering timbers throwing burning embers everywhere as the iron roof creaked and groaned as it tried to resist following the veranda down. Jiemba could hear the revving of engines and throbbing of mufflers, knowing that more bikers were present and had most likely caused this damage. He ignored them for the moment as he searched desperately for a sign that the old man was clear of the flames, and hoping that he was anywhere else but inside.

"JayDee?" he screamed, when his search proved futile. He could hear no response. "Where is he?" he roared at the bikers as he rounded the front of the house. The small group were busy spinning wheels on the road at the end of the driveway, as if there was nothing else of interest happening. One of them, closer to the house, pointed with a sneer, straight at the roaring hulk of fire. Jiemba was instantly afraid. As much as he wanted to tear the person who had pointed limb from limb, and having no doubt that he could, there was no time. Jiemba ran up the front steps and exploded through the disintegrating wall.

It was not the time for doors.

"JayDee," he shouted again, unable to see much through the thick blanket of smoke. Jiemba felt no heat but his vision was entirely obscured. He worked his way through the front room and into the kitchen but found no-one.

"JayDee," he bellowed with all he had. He panted in frustration, not exhaustion, wishing he could find his old friend.

"Jiemba," he heard the faintest call back to him through the haze. He immediately charged off in the direction of the sound. One of his feet fell through the floor as the timbers gave way beneath him, the whole frame was squeaking and grinding in its final death throws. He pulled it angrily free and pushed forward, a whole section of floor collapsing because of his effort. Jiemba squinted as he moved, holding onto the walls and doorframes hoping the remaining floor would hold his weight for at least a little while longer.

"JayDee," he said in a sob as he finally found and fell to the side of the old man. He had collapsed on what was left of the outside deck, clinging on the doorframe, despite the rest falling away prior.

"Jiemba?" JayDee seemed confused by his presence.

"It's okay," Jiemba told him, although he knew tears were flowing down his face. JayDee was very badly burned, the tips of his moustache singed from grey to black, his breathing deeply rasping and pulling at his lungs. "I'm going to get you out of here." Jiemba delicately picked the old man up, cradling him in his arms as if he was a small infant. Jiemba wrapped his shoulders down around him and bent his head forward. He would protect JayDee, but Jiemba didn't need to worry about what he ran into anymore. He pushed off in a giant stride. He heard the rest of the deck collapse behind him. Jiemba powered through a wooden wall, folding the timbers around his forearm and splintering the rest in his wake. Another partition failed to remain standing after Jiemba blasted a hole straight through it. In a few more steps the window at the front of the house shattered into a shower of glass as Jiemba exploded out into the open air.

Jiemba ran forward several more metres before placing JayDee gently onto the ground. The old man was hardly breathing. Jiemba removed the shirt he wore to place it beneath the old man's head for some form of comfort; watching as the remainder of JayDee's house collapsed in on itself.

"Stay still old man," Jiemba urged JayDee, he obsessively fiddled with the shirt folded up beneath JayDee's ash smudged bald head. He forced a smile, though the tears flowed freely. "You are going to be okay."

"I knew you would save me," JayDee coughed.

"I had to," Jiemba sobbed, his eyes could see even less now than when he was immersed in the smoke filled house. Water welled in the corner of his eyes as his nostrils tried to stop the flow. "You saved me first."

JayDee smiled up at him. He must have been in serious pain, but he wouldn't show it.

"It was my absolute pleasure . . . my friend," JayDee beamed. "I don't think we will be able to have that chat though." Jiemba wanted to tell him that he was fine, that everything was going to work out.

Instead he just cried.

Jiemba held JayDee's hand tightly as he wept into the old man's chest. He could smell the flesh burning and the steam rising as the water in his skin boiled. The old man was shivering from his pain, but the trembling gradually decreased until it was gone completely.

"I'm not afraid Jiemba," JayDee smiled through shaking lips. "I have done some bad things in my life, but I know that there has been some good too." Again Jiemba found no voice to say anything.

"It has been . . . my absolute . . . pleasure in knowing you," JayDee said with great difficulty. "You were my friend, and . . . I am grateful," tears had swelled into JayDee's eyes too. "But now it is time to do something else."

"Anything JayDee," Jiemba stammered.

"Find . . .," JayDee looked up at Jiemba, but his strength was fading as his head slumped back down to the shirt it lay upon.

"Who? Find who JayDee?" Jiemba blubbered, "We can find them together." The old man shook his head.

"No," JayDee gasped. "You must find . . . yourself, and then promise to be that person. Always be, the bigger man."

"I promise," Jiemba nodded, refusing to move or release the old man's hand.

"Heh . . . heh," JayDee struggled to laugh, coughing and wheezing.

"What is it?" Jiemba asked.

"Bigger Man," JayDee smirked, "sounds like a superhero that I could follow." JayDee smiled broadly, and Jiemba forced himself to do the same.

Then there was one large breath.

Then there were no more.

JayDee was gone, with a large smile plastered upon his face.

Jiemba couldn't hold it in any longer. He collapsed onto the large belly of his one-time mentor and unleashed the depths of his soul. His whole body shuddered and convulsed as he wailed and moaned openly. He could not catch his breath, nor control his trembling as he roared like a wound was being torn open. The sound chilled him to the bone, his soul only managing to just hold on to Jiemba's traumatised frame.

Snap-hiss.

Sparks of electricity jumped excitedly overhead. The pole which supplied all the power to the house buckled on its base which had been eaten away by the firestorm that still flared up behind Jiemba. The pole stood for a moment then teetered away to topple near the road. The growl of engines revealed the bikes spring back to life and take off along the road. Jiemba could hear the squeals of laughter and delight as they sped away.

"RARGH," Jiemba roared, stumbling to his feet, spit flying in every direction. The fury that burned inside him was more intense then what had brought the house down. He stamped over towards the downed power pole, snapped off the wires, ignoring the tingling sensation that they gave him, and carried it out onto the road resting it on one shoulder. He breathed heavily like a crazed tiger, staring down the road at the fleeing bikes. Jiemba seemed to juggle the pole in one hand, before taking a dozen steps forward and launching it like it was a javelin. He watched as the almost ten metre length pole soared at speed after those that had caused him such grief.

The pole collided with the rearward biker, before continuing to slide and bounce down the road taking down several others. He had dealt a great blow to the group, but some had gotten away. Jiemba felt no pride in the throw, or triumph in striking down those who had hurt him, as they had removed from him so much more. He had no doubt that he may have just killed someone, and as heavy as that thought was, and its consequences, he just didn't care. He trudged slowly back to where JayDee lay, a hollow shell with no idea of what he should do next.

Another group of vehicles, emergency services including a fire engine and ambulance, were speeding up the road behind him. Most stopped at what was once a dwelling, while the others continued along to where the bikers had been crushed and lay dismembered on the bitumen.

He didn't care what they were doing.

He didn't care about anything.

For someone who couldn't feel pain, he was feeling the most he had ever felt in his life.

A small period of time later a single car finally arrived at the scene. The scar of smoke left on the afternoon sky was like a beacon for anyone even remotely close to the town of Wellington to see and attempt a journey to find answers.

None had done so.

The owner of the car knew what the scene would look like the moment she travelled down this abandoned stretch of road. It always looked the same. She was the sole occupant in the backseat and waited until someone came and opened her door. She then stepped out and casually walked between each vehicle present. She had no need to see what had happened for herself, and had no desire to be seen by police or emergency services; or anyone else for that matter. She stood off to one side as her driver disappeared into the throng, returning a moment later with another person trailing behind.

"Hello Mistress Green," the man greeted her with some trepidation, despite being of a much larger build than the woman he addressed. The woman looked him up and down with a look of indifference. The uniform he wore was that of one of the private security that had been hired by the people of so called 'New Wellington'. The security group tasked with bringing peace to the town and reduce unrest in the streets. They were good at their job, fantastic in fact, but of course that was why they were employed by her, and not the people of 'New Wellington', to do what she wanted. Her own special task force, rather than the simple security that they were pretending to be employed as.

"Has it been taken care of?" she asked. After a moment of hesitation the man answered.

"The mission in the area has been destroyed," he reported. It was very clear who was in charge in this conversation as every now and then the man would catch his words together. He was still strong in his character as it was hardly noticeable. But she noticed. Nothing was ever missed. "As expected the residents have escaped, but the matter of finding them will be resolved in due time. There is no concern in this matter."

"Is there concern in another matter?" she asked, sliding a finger through her dark red hair to return a loose hair back into its position. "The old man perhaps?"

"No," the security officer replied. "We intercepted the message of assistance. The house was destroyed before we got here, the old man deceased."

"A shame," she said with no show of sadness, "what of the attackers?"

"Most of those that attacked the mission have fled," the officer informed.

"Most?" the lady asked. "There was a struggle? The resident's fought back, that is interesting."

"Not the residents," the man replied, starting to shift as if he was uncomfortable. "I mean not just the residents."

"Explain," there was a hint of annoyance.

"Some of the residents fought back," he said standing taller, trying to recompose himself. "They were dealt with, but most managed to flee. But there was also something else. Some of those at the mission were struck with projectiles, rocks, among other things. The same happened with some of the assailants here."

"What happened to them?"

"The ones here, are dead," the officer confirmed.

"From projectiles?" she frowned. It didn't make sense.

"Yes, Mistress," the officer responded. "The projectile here appears to be a wooden telegraph pole."

"You're joking," she sneered at him.

"I know better than that," he said without the hint of a grin. "We believe the man in question of achieving such a feat is sitting near the house. He was found near the body of the old man." She didn't laugh at the officer. Instead pondering deeply what he had said. It wasn't the first she had heard of such things happening.

"Take care of him," she said, fixing her tight suit jacket as she turned back towards the car. "You know what to do."

"Yes Mistress," came the almost regimented response.

"I expect that I will be able to use him by the time I return." With one last brush of her vibrant red hair she was gone.

Chapter 7 - Walk of the lost

The walk from the homestead to Wellington was at least twelve kilometres, but closer to fifteen when you account for all the bends, crests and falls along the road. Jiemba had asked the youths and some of the adults how long the journey would take by foot, as so many of them made the journey daily. As they weren't ever in a hurry to get anywhere it was a safe two hour trek. Jiemba had marvelled at not only how far the walk was, but how little the people cared about making the four hour round trip. It was about a fifteen minute drive, but most couldn't afford the luxury or the comfort and wasted no breath complaining about it.

Jiemba knew it wasn't too long for him.

He had been battling within himself once again. He was too tired to take sides, instead choosing to be a spectator as the different voices of his mind argued amongst themselves. The points were all valid in their own way.

"It wasn't his fault."

"What is the point of being ridiculously strong if you can't save anybody?"

"There were so many at once what was he to do? Any one choice to save a group or person would result in the other being abandoned."

"You knew the character was shifty."

"Maybe, but you can't assume. So many do and it leads to worse things happening."

"He was your friend, close enough to be family. You didn't do enough."

"What else could I do?"

"You even let them take the body. Who were they? You did nothing."

Over and over his mind argued. He had no idea what was the correct train of thought, and in his grief he even doubted if he knew how he should be feeling, or how to show that. When faced with grief what was the correct action? Jiemba had let a dribble of tears flow down his cheek as he had left the charred remnants of JayDee's property. He had simply nodded when paramedics had informed him that the body would be removed, before being interrupted by the group in the white vans who stated they would deal with the whole situation. Jiemba didn't ask for names or look anyone in the eye. He simply went with the flow of the terrible situation as if it was easier to be led along by those who knew better; those who laughingly seemed to have more power than he did.

Jiemba could hear the rear hem of his jeans drag along the rough bitumen road; he hardly lifted his feet as he trod along wearily. He didn't look back to see how bad it was, or lift his feet to stop the damage that would be caused, knowing that by the time he arrived at his destination the bottom part of his jeans would have worn away into strings of broken fabric. He forced his head down to look at what was only metres in front of him. He wiped away a sniff every now and then though no more tears came to him. He knew that he was frowning, something that he had always tried not to do as it brought down his pronounced brow and gave him a natural intimidating gaze. He didn't want to make people feel afraid of him, but he didn't care what people thought of him at this point.

Every now and then, as he walked along the shoulder of the road, a car or van would stop nearby to offer him a lift into town. He recognised most of these vehicles as those that had been present at the house. There were very few other cars on the road anyway, and it was rare for any of them to stop to volunteer a ride. Regardless, he gave each the same short response. A quick shake of his head and a resounding 'No'. He was not being polite, he wouldn't even look over at them. Once informed that he didn't require their assistance he kept on walking and they pulled away quickly.

Jiemba focused his sense of hearing as he walked along. He trained his ears to listen for the throb of a motorcycle engine. His eyes would flick to the side of the road on occasion, where he would search for something that he could use as a projectile to make quick work of the bike when it drew near. He heard nothing of the sort. He was so focused on someone driving by, that his mind would engage in a different argument.

"Revenge is not the answer."

"I don't care."

"JayDee wouldn't want that."

"He isn't around to make the choice."

"It isn't who you are."

"Maybe it should be."

Jiemba again tried to fight off the argument and not choose a side. He would soon after become aware of what his body was doing. Hands clenched into shaking balls that felt like they were trying to tear away from his body. On occasion he couldn't control his rage.

"Raaargh," he roared as his whole body flexed. His strength appeared to even convey a louder deeper yell. His ears that had been so focused could hear the pain in his own voice. Tears flowed freely down his face and his breathing became heavy. His whole body heaved as he staggered from the road. An old gum tree was his first victim. Jiemba kicked out hard, slammed the base of his foot straight into the trunk at about chest height. The wood exploded where he had struck, his foot driving straight through. The tree screamed and groaned as the fibres snapped and crumbled. As if in retaliation it fell down towards Jiemba. Jiemba dug his bare toes into the dirt bracing for the impact but took the tree with little effort over his right shoulder. With a small grunt he used his left hand to get a firm grip on the timber, then, unleashing his rage, he bellowed even louder and launched the old tree over a nearby barbed wire fence, watching as it destroyed everything in its path. Jiemba didn't move. He allowed time for his rapid breathing to slow and the pulsing in his muscles to reduce.

Other victims included the remains of an old stone wall, which he made short work of punching through, and an abandoned burnt out car which was then flipped end over end into a tree in a nearby paddock. Each time that he had let out his anger in such a way he felt immediately disappointed in his behaviour. Shame would flood through him and the cycle would continue again.

Eventually he arrived at the outskirts of the town. It wasn't by way of the main roads but by the backroad he had walked down. He had no idea where he was going, figuring that if he didn't find a memorable land mark or person to direct him before he walked out the other side he would simply walk back in and try again.

The houses didn't look familiar. The yards within each looked as if they were thriving with neglect. The yellow strands of grass that he remembered, trying its best to find sustenance and survive, and the bowls of dirt, which would throw up dust and grit in the slightest zephyr, replaced by tall green grass blades and flowers which grew tall to the roof and trees above. But as nice as the flourishing colour was to see, most of those yards were unkempt and looked as disregarded as the dishevelled houses in which they occupied. Jiemba decided that the homes should not have looked like that. Many appeared brand new, of a solid build, or showing an exterior design which he would have said was on trend only years before. The care that he would have expected from the owners was simply not there.

At the next intersection he saw an old park that he recognised and immediately headed in that direction. Jiemba had no idea what day it was, whether it was a weekday or the weekend, but either way the park had occupants. Jiemba noticed the sign showing the name of the park, Rygate Park, was worn, missing letters (though the glue and paint stains remained), and the part of the sign which had shown the rules of use at the park was splintered and laying among the long grass at its feet.

Jiemba remembered playing at the field in his youth. Remembered his first game there, first run, first try, and first scuffle. A smile spread across his face as he skirted the occupants on the main field. He approached one of the small steel grandstands which sat alongside the field. One of the coaches, wearing red and green colouring, the same that the players wore, was busy ticking off names from a list on a clipboard as he gave instructions to players nearby and pumped up balls.

"What team is this?" Jiemba asked, realising that his mouth was parched as his lips stuck together with glue like saliva.

"Western," the coach replied without acknowledging his presence by looking at him. Jiemba didn't mind as he was clearly busy. "Primary school rugby." Jiemba observed the man who appeared only slightly older than Jiemba, with small slivers of grey starting to spread along his thick black hair. The rest of his features looked youthful and although busy he looked to be happy at what he was doing. Jiemba gazed out at the players who were warming up, and the other coach, who also looked familiar.

"Fantastic," Jiemba said. "It is great to see some life in this town, especially kids playing footy."

"You're not wrong," the coach said, fixing a needle of a pump into another ball. "Which is sad because I live here. If you look hard enough though there are some real gems to be found here. God's country in disguise is what I usually say." The coach finally looked up at Jiemba and seemed to be taken a little aback. Jiemba silently agreed that if he were the coach he would have been concerned by this newcomer. His appearance was unwelcoming, the threat he carried was real which would be of concern to the younger players. The coach seemed to look past this and hold his focus rather than away. "Hey do I know you?" the coach asked, squinting as if trying to get a better look at the massive man who stood before him. "I feel like we have met before."

"I don't recall," Jiemba replied truthfully, "perhaps we played against each other." Jiemba offered the solution was entirely reasonable.

"Nah, I think I would remember if someone your size ran at me, but then again maybe that's why I don't remember." Jiemba smiled at the coach. He watched the team being run through their paces by a coach who seemed to be entirely in control, with the players learning and having fun. Jiemba smiled again, waved goodbye to the coach nearby, before continuing on his way.

Jiemba found he was more conflicted as he continued his journey. He had decided that he would go to the police station, and now that he had his bearings he knew which direction he needed to go. The growling of his mind continued, but images of the young kids playing sport, and words which had been said by JayDee now swelled around as well. He saw almost no one on the streets as he walked along. He couldn't hear any voices, lawnmowers, youths on the street or much else. Perhaps it was just a time of the day thing where everyone was either at school, at work, or in-between. He doubted that, as it was getting quite late in the day. Without knowing the time he imagined that it would have been about four in the afternoon. Many of the local businesses he walked past were clearly closed. Not just for the day either. Several of them showing faded signs, boarded up doorways, or massive structural deformities.

Jiemba crossed the railway line and looked at a fire station which had seen better days but at least still looked operational. He made a left and walked down the street that he had driven down several times before to get a feed at the local McDonalds. There was more traffic here, but that was more likely due to the road being one of two routes along the highway going through town. There was only one building in the street which looked like it was open. It was the local RSL, but the carpark was empty. Buildings which Jiemba walked past, former pubs, motels, mechanics and small merchants had long been closed down. It still resembled what he remembered although there was far less life.

That changed when he turned the corner at the end of the street.

As he looked left he looked up at a group of cement silos which he had always remembered being there. Tall structures but mostly unimportant. When he turned to the right, where he knew the police station stood halfway down the block, he looked far beyond any of the buildings in the street towards the horizon. At the end of the block, down the slight hill before him, there was a bridge that crossed the Bell River. Jiemba's memory of this view was a small road that stretched out on the bridge's other side towards the base of a tall green and blue mountain range containing three peaks. That would remain only a memory as the reality was now quite different.

The small bridge had been replaced with something twice the width and displaying a far grander façade. The river seemed to have been made wider, no doubt as a result of the Westopolis water enterprises that JayDee had mentioned to him before, and along its bank were a string of fancy looking restaurants and boutique stores. Off to the right, where a large oval once occupied the space, there now stood a stadium to rival those of a capital city. Beyond the stadium he could see high rise buildings which all but blocked out the mountains from view. Jiemba could see that although some displayed signs from a range of successful businesses that others were actually apartment complexes consisting of eight floors or more. The view would not be lost to those who had managed to purchase a residence near the very top.

There were still beautiful trees skirting the pristine streets, but the farmland that Jiemba remembered was completely gone. He could even spy expensive looking houses built into the mountainside hanging out into the clouds that floated around them.

"Whoah," Jiemba couldn't help but release a gasp. He had created and recreated images of what this would look like but he hadn't come close. "So that is 'New Wellington'." It was clear that there was a divide amongst the town, you had to be blind not to see it.

As he progressed automatically towards the amazing sight he realised that he had arrived at the front of the police station where an actual argument was taking place. One of the security force members that had been present at the house was berating a police officer. They both stopped as Jiemba approached, neither batting an eyelid at his appearance.

"You must be Jiemba," the police officer stated, taking a step toward him and offering his hand. "You fit the description that Jonah has been giving me. My name is George Scott, Senior Constable of the Wellington Police Department, but the locals usually call me Officer Gumbo. I am so sorry to hear about what has happened today."

"It is easy to say sorry, Gumbo," the other man scowled, "but what are you going to do about it?" Jiemba recognised this man as one of those that been present to help after JayDee's death.

"As I told you already, Price, we have opened an inquiry into the matter and we will be bringing in resources to assist with the process."

"It shouldn't be a process, it should be immediate action," the security officer referred to as Price struck back. "The residents of New Wellington are concerned at your inactivity to get the job done."

"I don't serve the people of New Wellington, I serve all of Wellington and all of the people who may be living in the area, regardless if they are your clients or not. I also don't answer to a security force that is constantly overstepping what its jurisdiction demands as necessary conduct."

"We have names of those involved already and are willing to pursue matters now," Price snarled again. "Why are you so hesitant?"

"This conversation is finished," Officer Gumbo growled straight back. "And if I hear that you are interfering in this investigation I will move to have your licence and whatever authority you have removed. You are lucky I haven't done so already as your practice verges on vigilantism. You are an overpriced security force and nothing more." At this point he turned towards Jiemba. "Mark my words young man we will get to the bottom of this and deliver justice as seen by the law. I trust that we can count on you when the time is right to provide information to assist our inquiry and move towards a suitable resolution. Check back in so we can take your details, and share any information we can with you. I hope you are willing to do the same." The police officer didn't wait for a response, instead bidding farewell and returning to the station, leaving Jiemba alone with Price.

"Young man," Price repeated with a snort, "Gumbo is not too much older than you are I suspect." He leered for a moment towards the door of the police station as if daring for the policeman to return, then he turned his full attention to Jiemba.

"I'm sorry you had to see that," he said shaking his head in distaste at his actions. "As the officer said, my name is Price, Thomas Price. I am the head of the Spartan Security Force currently being employed by the residents of New Wellington." Thomas Price did not have an Australian accent. Jiemba guessed it was British, but had a slightly Americanised twang. The later was more because Price looked largely of African-American decent.

"Spartan, like Leonidas?" Jiemba asked, he had done his readings at the very least.

"The very same," Price replied with a smile. "We take on the name in spirit rather than physical attributes, we don't all possess six packs, but we do offer a service which is more proactive then reactive. Through our surveillance we can identify issues before or as they arise and deal with it thusly, allowing our employers to have a sound mind that their business and assets are protected. We therefore, with my smallish force, do a job that many larger or more established groups cannot. We do not shy away from a challenge." With the last statement he shot a look back through the doors of the police station.

"How do you take action on something that hasn't happened yet," Jiemba asked, thinking about everything he had been told prior. "Surely you would get a bad reputation for presuming someone is guilty when they are innocent, or stereotyping and profiling groups."

"I know that more than most, but we take care not to do so," Price stood straighter as if being interviewed. "Crime has a look, and I am not talking about people, and it also leaves a trail. We follow that trail and analyse our data to intervene in an appropriate manner. That may result in incarceration but mostly ends up in people being rehabilitated and relocated to best suit their needs. And in regard to reputation I would rather be seen to be doing something that helps others than sitting back and doing nothing. Wouldn't you agree?"

"It depends, I guess," Jiemba replied. His mind was everywhere and he was finding it hard to fix an opinion.

"Your small community near the river was thrown into chaos," Price snapped back, "who knows where they are now. Probably living in fear somewhere. Free to be preyed upon without protection. Finding them quickly could lead to their safety, if found by the right people. Otherwise they could still be in danger, even as we speak. And what about your friend? I am assuming that he was that, why else would you be there? He is, I am sorry to say, killed, in his own home. You might not be sure about what to do, but my conscience is clear. I could not stand by knowing that there is a killer, or killers, in our community. I could not allow someone to feel the depths of despair, grief and sadness, like I would be feeling, like I presume you are. If I could take action to ensure that that never happens again I would, and I will. Someone may not like me and my team for doing that, but countless others, as well as myself, will sleep easier knowing that there isn't someone like that out there." Jiemba could feel the agitation in his body returning. Price was saying things that one part of him agreed with entirely, and it was forcing the rest of his willpower to move aside. "Not everyone is willing to do what is right," Price had calmed down, "but someone has to do it. Someone has to be strong enough, to be brave enough, to take a stand, especially when others cannot, or will not."

"You said you have names?" Jiemba asked, restraining himself and forcing his palm flat instead of the ball it was curled up in. "Names of those who did this today?"

"I don't just give out my information to anyone," Price shook his head, "people might do something silly with it."

"What if they want to help?" Jiemba asked, he realised how obvious he was being in offering.

"You heard Officer Gumbo," Price replied, "my force is not to intervene. I can't be seen doing things to oppose the law."

"I'm not part of your force," Jiemba stated again. This time Price glanced cautiously back towards the police station as if worried he would be overheard.

"I can't ask you to do this," Price whispered.

"You aren't," Jiemba replied stubbornly. "I'm offering. I can make a difference."

Price smiled. "Yes, I believe you can."

Chapter 8 – A foul taste

Shame.

It was a word thrown around a lot. Generally, Jiemba wanted nothing to do with the word, it seemed like a word that could be used as an excuse rather than a reasonable justification. Instead he would challenge people who used it on another person, and try and support those who used it on themselves. However, in this exact moment, Shame was all he felt.

The word didn't usually refer to something that someone had done, although Jiemba did think that he definitely could have done more. Normally it was a feeling of sadness and depression about someone's predicament, appearance or situation.

Price had asked Jiemba to wait by the river nearby until nightfall. That time was not too far away and the location not too distant. Jiemba had walked down towards the bridge, still amazed at what he saw spread out on the other side, but he would not cross. Somehow he did not feel worthy of the bridge, and reflected on how shabby his own attempt had been in comparison, despite how proud he had been in building it. He walked through the small park towards where he would wait, admiring the small efforts that had been made to make the area family friendly; brand new play equipment, barbecue areas and shelters for gatherings, plus signs showing historical facts and information about First Nations people. The buildings which sat across from it were mostly derelict, and in the shade of the stadium across the river the area was not inviting.

Jiemba sat and waited. In the falling twilight he knew what he looked like. A dark skinned man, sitting in the shadows of ancient trees, head bowed down as he looked towards his shabby appearance. He wore no shoes, his jeans were in taters, his shirt that he had retrieved after JayDee's removal was dirty, the hair on his head messy and the beard on his face wild. There was no one walking nearby, but he knew if there were then all would give him a wide birth afraid of what he might do. The fact that he was sitting around waiting to search out someone who had done him wrong didn't make him feel better. He wrapped his arms around his body to ward of the cold he couldn't feel, and hide from the embarrassment that he definitely could.

Don't assume, that was what JayDee had said, but despite Jiemba hating that stereotype he wouldn't blame people for being afraid of him. For thinking that he was up to no good. After what had happened that day, and what he had been feeling for some time, he didn't feel like he was a decent person so why should anybody else.

Shame surrounded him in the darkness. He did not hide from it, did not fight it, he did not run. He let it envelop him as he felt he deserved.

Silence grew louder as the shadows grew longer. Eventually sound and light were all gone. The lamps which stood damaged throughout the park had not seen maintenance in some time. The paint had been mostly scratched or beaten away, the bulbs long since destroyed and never replaced.

Finally, a man in a hood approached. Jiemba hid a smile. He imagined that someone, somewhere, was hiding and sneaking a look at the pair in the darkness of the park; concerned, as where there was only one before there was now another to spread fear into the night. He had come so far from where he had wanted to be.

"Good, you are here," the distinct voice grew closer before the man sat down beside him.

"Yup," Jiemba replied in no mood for small talk.

"I have a name for you as promised," Price continued, "we have been searching all afternoon for him but unsurprisingly he has gone to ground."

"So, what now?" Jiemba asked. He was angry but tried to appear disinterested and bored.

"Luckily he has left a trail," Price persisted unconcerned. "We have enough data that will enable you to find him, and in doing so lead you to the gang that attacked both the river community and your friend's house." Jiemba had been busy fiddling with his fingers as Price spoke, but he hoped the man had missed the sudden tensing of his muscles as he reminded him of what happened.

"The cyclist with the snake helmet?" Jiemba asked. He had assumed that they had some role amongst the group that led the attack.

"We have our ideas about that," Price revealed. "We scoured the river after the attack and found no trace of the person you have identified. We found some others and they are being dealt with. It is our hope that one thing leads to another and we get this whole syndicate off of our streets." He paused speaking for a moment as a police paddy wagon slunk past. Jiemba knew his shape would stand out, and assumed that the two figures occupying the darkness would cause suspicion. "They won't stop," Price watched as the car drove by, "they are cowards. Them driving around the streets is all for show."

"That's your issue?" Jiemba interrupted. "The name?"

"The name is Jerome Less," Price disclosed immediately. "He has a reputation for being underhanded and bounces around providing a disservice to the community. As I said, we don't know where he is, but we know he runs in a local gang, and we know where members of that group hang out. I will give you a place, you can go in and ask some questions."

"That is all I need," Jiemba nodded. Price dragged out a small map from his pocket. "It's rare that we use these things anymore." He pulled out a small flashlight to light up the scrawl on it. "This is the place, head down this road and it is in the middle of the block, backs onto a small oval. Be careful. I would not be knocking as it would be safer for you if they were surprised. I will stay away, but I will wait here for you to return." Jiemba nodded, pocketed the map, jammed his hands into his jean pockets and walked off. He didn't need to be told how to be safe.

He headed east back towards the entrance to Wellington from the direction of Orange. Thinking of Orange brought back memories, and compounded the shame. Were people worried about him? What would they say when he returned? Would they be happy or would they be upset with him?

Thoughts for another time.

His senses were heightened as he walked along. He was not afraid for himself. He was just not used to going to someone's house unannounced, especially when he suspected that he wouldn't be welcome. He glanced shiftily over each shoulder as if he was being followed. Staring at each shadow that was being blown by the wind, annoyed at the growl of prowling cats. His breathing was loud, he was aggravated by the scraping of his soft padded feet as they trod along the footpath. The night was calm with only a few clouds covering an otherwise glimmering night sky. Jiemba arrived at the corner of the street where his destination would be. He glanced once more at the map he had taken before hiding it away. At the very least he didn't want to disturb the wrong property.

Jiemba approached the front gate. The lights were on beyond and the sound of multiple voices alerted him that there were more than a couple of people inside. The gate squeaked on rusty hinges as he pushed past it. The fibro house was unremarkable. The urge to just open the door and surge in was strong. He thought about Price's suggestion and questioned its relevance to him. Surely that would be useful for a security team, especially when they were not welcome, but, even though he was a stranger he disregarded the notion. It was not what Jiemba would do, and he needed to somehow move past his emotions to return to what he wanted to be. He imagined JayDee standing on the broken wooden deck next to him, shaking his head at the thought. Instead of dissuading him it simply reminded Jiemba again that his friend was gone. He balled his hands into fists and glared at the door knob. He fumbled at it for a moment with trembling hands; regardless if it was locked or not he would be inside in moments.

He exhaled all the air in his lungs, then waited.

Jiemba took a deep breath in. Then he knocked gently on the door and awaited a response.

A moment later a young man opened the door with a smile, revealing that he had been involved in some happy moment inside. The young man took a step back as he realised that the newcomer filled most of the doorway.

"Can I help you?" the young man asked hesitantly.

"I sure hope so," Jiemba replied soothingly, "do you mind if I come in?" The young man hung to the edge of the doorframe as if contemplating his options. It would take nothing for Jiemba to simply walk past him or move him out of his way. Jiemba waited with a smile instead.

"Sure," the young man said, "come on in. The lounge room is that way." Jiemba followed the direction that the youth was pointing, again trying to smile reassuringly. His bare feet clomped on the dusty timber floor. Jiemba walked slowly and even allowed the young man to get in front of him to guide the way. They both came into a back room, where Jiemba realised that his hands were still scrunched together as fists. He quickly released them and took another deep breath.

"Don't assume," he whispered to himself.

"What was that?" the youth said.

"Nothing," Jiemba replied. The interior was not what he expected. The space was larger than he imagined though there was barely enough furniture to fill a small portion of the space. At one end of the room they were in was a television that had several other young people sitting around, all heavily involved in the videogame they were participating in. Other rooms leading off of the hallway were visible, all with lights on and seemingly occupied. A young girl was dishing up some food in the kitchen while another young man was busy cleaning the dishes in a soap bubble filled sink.

"Whoah, you're a big fella my brother," one of the players suddenly caught sight of Jiemba standing awkwardly at the room's entrance. "Who is your friend Josh?" The young man, Josh, wasn't sure how to answer, his mouth searching unsuccessfully for the words.

"My name is Jiemba," Jiemba told them, helping Josh out in the moment. "I am simply here to ask some questions."

"Nah, uh," the same player said, shaking his head. "We're busy, and we don't do questions. Josh take him into another room and give him his answers." He turned back to the game, realised that his avatar had been killed while he was not paying attention, and started wrestling with the others in an attempt to get justice as they laughed heartily at him. Josh shrugged and pointed to another room. Upon entering Jiemba noticed that several of the walls had holes in them. Again the room was simply furnished with a small dining table and a few chairs beside it.

"Josh Northman," the youth volunteered before they begun. "Okay, Jiemba was it? What do you need from me?" Josh asked as he sat down in a chair opposite Jiemba. Josh, Jiemba suspected, was about eighteen years old. He was slim with black hair, eyes wide with expectation though his hands fidgeted on the table. He wore a slim black moustache that only a teenager could grow as it was neither impressive nor thick, and his complexion was a shade darker than Jiemba's.

"I don't want to make a fuss," Jiemba began, although a commotion was exactly what he thought he would have received upon entering the house. "But I am searching for someone. A friend of mine told me I could find some answers here."

"I will try," Josh said openly, "who are you looking for?"

"I am searching for a man named Jerome Less," Jiemba revealed the name quickly. Josh shifted uncomfortably at the name.

"What do you want with Jerome?" Josh inquired. "Is he in some sort of trouble?"

"Is he likely to be?" Jiemba asked. He wanted to know the details of the man quickly but didn't want to push too hard.

"Everyone around here is likely to be," Josh answered accusingly. "It all depends on who you ask."

"Why do you care if he is in trouble?" Jiemba pondered.

"'Cos not many people would," Josh stated simply. "It is not uncommon to be blamed for things you didn't do around here, and sometimes people assume the worst. There has got to be someone who at least asks the question."

"Is this your house?" Jiemba changed the topic slightly, seeing that Josh was starting to go on the defensive. "I admit it is not what I thought it would be."

"Yes, it is mine," Josh said calmly. He rubbed his forearm, a sign that he was still uncomfortable. "No doubt whoever told you Jerome was here told you it was some dive or slum."

"Gang house actually," Jiemba corrected, laughing loudly and uncontrollably.

"Figures," Josh said, "well it isn't. Not anymore at least. That's what it used to be, but I have been using it as a place for young people to come and hang out at night."

"Is that why you let me in?" Jiemba asked.

"I let you in because I like the door where it is and figured you would knock it down," Josh said with a half-smile. "Besides, I think that a lot more can be gained by helping each other. If I fought you then I know I would lose, and that doesn't help anybody. If I do something small then at some point something good will come of it." Jiemba glanced back into the other room and watched the food being prepared on several plates.

"Where is your family Josh?" Jiemba asked. "Who is your mob?"

"My family is not from around here," Josh explained, "I am Wiradjuri, though I don't know a lot. My parents, brothers and sisters are all better at that stuff than me. They are real leaders."

"You are a leader too Josh," Jiemba smiled and stood up. "I don't want to keep you from your dinner. It was nice to meet you." Josh nodded, unsure what to say.

"Bruh," the same player yelped as Jiemba walked through the lounge room, "where are you going? There is heaps of food for everyone."

"Not hungry, but thanks," Jiemba had no desire to be in the house anymore. He had come looking for a fight and hadn't got one. His body had energy he needed to use while he could control it. He also didn't get the information that he had wanted. He felt like he could have pushed Josh or one of the others for information, but he chose not to. Jiemba liked the boy. He would have to find another way. Jiemba waved at the rainbow of faces that appeared though each door way as he moved towards the exit.

"Have you met a kid called Jonah?" Josh called out as Jiemba walked down the few steps leading up to the house.

"Jonah and Joanna?" Jiemba acknowledged. "They are good kids. I've spent a bit of time with them lately."

"You sound like the guy they were talking about," Josh nodded. His hands were pressed firmly in his pockets as he scrunched his body to stop from shivering. The vapours from his breath turning to fog in the cold night air. "You helped those kids out a bit at the river then?"

"I tried," Jiemba nodded.

"Listen, I want to help you," Josh stated looking at the ground. "But I don't want the wrong people around here. The wrong people being anyone that gives that security mob or one of the gangs an excuse to come barging in."

"I wouldn't want that," Jiemba agreed. There was another pause.

"Listen," Josh said. "Because Jonah said you were alright I am going to say something to you. On the north edge of town, before you cross the railway line that goes out that way, there is a house hidden down a dirt road."

"Is it small?" Jiemba asked.

"You will see it," Josh countered, "it's big enough, bigger than you think. You will hear them too."

"Gang house?" Jiemba suggested.

"Naw, man," Josh shook his head. "Enough with the gangs, we aren't all bad. Jerome, is actually a concern for a bunch of reasons. There are some others around like that. I know an old guy who would beat you up if he heard you were talking about people how you are. Brushes are not as thick as they used to be, so it isn't fair to paint everyone the same."

"Did that old guy live in the hills near the river?" Jiemba enquired. He couldn't imagine there would be too many others like him around.

"You know JayDee too?" Josh threw the name out willingly. Jiemba had chosen not to use it out of respect, and slightly baulked at it being used so soon after the old man had died. "Fine, if you find that place chances are you will find who you were looking for. But you have to be careful going there."

"I was careful coming here," Jiemba replied.

"Yeah, but I ain't them," Josh shook his head with a smirk. "Those guys are up for a fight. They are good people but they are not likely to talk nice to you. Their actions do the talking. They feel disrespected and unless things change, a lot, then they are unlikely to listen. Don't tell them I sent you."

"Agreed," Jiemba promised, "thanks for your help Josh. You are just like the rest of your family."

"Do you know them?" Josh seemed hesitant with his response.

"I don't think so," Jiemba shook his head. "I would like to though. What I meant is that you are well on your way to becoming a great leader. Often enough it is actually the smallest person, rather than the biggest, who is the best to follow. I can see why others would come here." Josh smiled but looked down at his feet. Jiemba swung the noisy gate open and walked back onto the street. He was aware that Josh had followed him to the fence.

"Hey Jiemba," Josh called after him. "What did Jerome supposedly do anyway?"

"Are you friends with 'the old man'?" Jiemba asked, again not using his actual name, instead using the term that he had used frequently. Josh nodded, he looked like he was getting colder by the second. Jiemba wanted to tell the young man the truth. He thought long and hard about how he still felt at that moment and didn't want to convey that on to anybody else.

"He is a good man," Jiemba stated. He smiled warmly. Then Jiemba disappeared back into the night without revealing a thing.

Chapter 9 – Part of the team

Jiemba sat in the corner of a very large, noisy and well-lit room. It was more like a factory floor and it was just as busy.

Jiemba had not gone to the destination that the young man, Josh, had given him; instead returning to where he knew Price would be waiting, and where he eventually found him. The security officer didn't say much at the news Jiemba returned with, he glanced at Jiemba a couple of times as if deep in thought before finally beckoning him to follow him. The pair walked to a nearby street that was just as poorly lit as the park. A white van waited there in which Jiemba was told to sit in the back.

The ride hadn't been long and after sitting in the dark closed off interior of the van for a couple of minutes the side panels lit up as they approached a large warehouse. Jiemba had sat quietly as they proceeded through a heavily guarded and extensively lit check-point, nestled between tall razor wire topped fences. The van then proceeded to drive straight into the airplane hangar sized building before coming to a stop at the far end. The van door had been opened for him by people he didn't know and he was ushered off to a side area where he had been sitting ever since. At one point he was offered a bed in an adjoining area where he could rest but he had declined.

Jiemba knew what it would be like if he tried to rest. He would do nothing but toss and turn as he relived what had happened that day. Even as he sat in silence the images fought their way back to the forefront of his mind, attempting to bring him down like they always did. His emotions simmered, rather than dealing with them here in this place he chose to ignore them and focus on his surroundings.

It wasn't too hard to move towards distractions. Jiemba had chided himself about assuming what a security force in a country town would look like. He had suspected a few cameras on a feed from the town, a couple of personnel occupying a small house sized building with a few cars at their disposal. Again his assumption was wrong.

What sat before him was more military than security. The building was a hive of activity. Vehicles were constantly in motion in and out of the large hangar doors. Some were small cars being used for surveillance, Jiemba suspected, while others ranged from vans like the one he had arrived in to larger off-road vehicles. In one corner of the area, across from where Jiemba sat, there was a mechanic style station where returning vehicles would all proceed towards after arrival. Some vehicles were being washed and cleaned, which was the case with the four-wheel drives as some were covered in mud, others were receiving some sort of maintenance, while the rest were being refuelled and positioned neatly to the side ready for the next use.

Jiemba frowned as he watched them arrive. They all drove through a small shed like space hidden from his view. He knew that most stopped there, and he presumed that the contents were being removed and taken somewhere else, as a short time later they would join the rest. Although on a much larger scale of what he had expected, none of that caught his eye more than the machines. They were like forklifts on legs, large robotic like machines that were being controlled by a driver, and they were using their obvious strength to lift all manner of things into a storage area at the far end. Larger military style bushmaster vehicles were stored in the area, as well as other truck like transports which were similar to emergency vehicles used by the fire services or the NSW SES. Large shipping containers were stored there as well, what a security company needed with all the items Jiemba had no clue. It warranted the use of several of the machines that were almost constantly in use.

Each machine was at least five metres tall. They utilised a dozen large wheels per leg, six on each side of both. Jiemba noticed that despite the biped looking machines using the wheels to move mostly, on occasion they would stomp around without the use of the wheels to correct their positioning. There were two sets of arms on each side, one attached with strong looking grappling claws while the other long beams similar to that on a heavy forklift device. From above the canopy there was a crane device fitted with a hook and some chain. Jiemba could see an array of other devices and items attached to the machines but had no idea what they were used for.

"Impressed with what you see? Those Gear machines are definitely something," Price had returned in a smart suit and tie.

"Gear machines?" Jiemba replied, hardly registering the man's arrival. The first time it seemed that day he actually took in what Thomas Price looked like. He was average to tall height, still easily above six foot, his thick black hair was combed neatly with a part, thin sideburns stretched down to the bottom of his earlobes where they connected to a black yet greying slim beard. The characteristics of his face appeared handsome and strong, and the smile he wore as he spoke to Jiemba seemed like it would easily charm, while his eyes always seemed focused. He filled out the suit he had changed into and Jiemba suspected most of that would be muscle.

"Yeah, that's what we call them anyway," Price explained. "The actual name is Green Intuitive Electronic Hydrolic Robotics. The short form is G.I.E.H.R, but rather than call them that all the time we call them Gear machines, or heavy Gear machines. They are new products straight from GreenCorp. The bigger ones do the job in the central area, but we have also been given some experimental ones to do heavy lifting in smaller spaces. They have not been tested yet however."

"They look expensive," Jiemba commented, "this whole place does."

"It all is," Price nodded, glancing around as if noticing the place for the first time. "But luckily we have some wealthy sponsors that enable us to run this for the people of this town."

"For New Wellington?" Jiemba mentioned.

"For, all, Wellington," Price shot quickly back, emphasising the *all*. "It is no secret that residents and businesses in the newer developing areas have had a hand in our employment, but we seek to help all the residents so that the town, soon to be a city, will be prosperous. It is no good only having half of an area functioning. It doesn't work with the human body why should it work with a city."

"Not everyone thinks that way?" Jiemba recalled the many comments made by many of the people he had met.

"Let me ask you Jiemba, are you from the area?" Price asked receiving a small nod from Jiemba. It was a small lie, he wasn't from Wellington exactly but he had been around the area long enough. "In the past have you looked at Wellington as being a great place to be? Honestly?"

"It wouldn't be first on my list of places to visit," Jiemba answered truthfully.

"And that is fair," Price replied. "The town has made inroads in the recent past, adding infrastructure, programs, support to the residents and taking steps to make it a sought after place to live. However, a poor reputation, not helped by the fact that we have so many incarceration facilities on the town's doorstep, is hard to overcome. We are here to help these people attain the potential this place possesses." Jiemba couldn't argue, as much as he wanted the best for the place he had on occasion thought along those lines.

"Some people around the area call it God's country," Price continued, "it was supposed to be the centre of industry and the main capital city in the west of the state. Flowing mountain ranges, two rivers meeting here, land fertile for crops and pasture. Yet it has never achieved its full potential. My job is not just to provide security to those who live here, but to ensure that everyone feels secure in coming here. That way people who can help reimagine that dream will come and Wellington can be as great as was once hoped." Jiemba nodded, the idea seamed honourable. He still wasn't sure about the execution though.

"What is happening there?" Jiemba pointed to where the vehicles had been hidden by the partition.

"That is a drop off point," Price explained, extending a hand asking Jiemba to walk beside him. "My team patrols all hours of the day. If they come across activity which is deemed to be antisocial or illegal, they will apprehend those at fault and return them here."

"Isn't that the job of the police?" Jiemba asked.

"Absolutely," Price agreed, "despite what you saw earlier I have a lot of time for the local law enforcement, especially Officer Gumbo. They do the best with what they have got and have been making inroads with the community for years. But they don't do enough, they don't have the capacity in some sense to do that. We do, so we render assistance to them by either holding them in our facility, processing with the evidence we have collected, or handing them over to the police. Speak of the devil." As they walked towards a series of doors near the entrance, a prisoner escort carrier vehicle drove into the centre of the space. They exited and assisted as some of the security personel led out some of those that had been jailed. Price waved at the police officers but they did not return the gesture.

"How many people can you hold?" Jiemba asked as they approached the doors.

"As many as required?" Price replied as he turned the door handle, "but hopefully it will never come to that. Those few can be quite violent." Price pointed out, Jiemba could see the captives fighting hard against their restraints, striking out with their heads and feet as they twisted in an attempt to escape. They were swearing loudly and aggressively towards their holders, which echoed around the vast space.

They entered a medium sized hallway which Jiemba could walk through comfortably, the sound from the constant movement of vehicles disappearing almost instantly. The floor slanted downwards, twisting and turning several times. Jiemba was good with positioning himself wherever he was. The more they travelled the more he figured that they were somewhere underneath the main warehouse space, at least one floor down if not more.

"I have to admit I was surprised that you were able to get the information you needed," Price eventually filled the silence. His voice reverberated from the close white walls. "And walk out uninjured I might add. Regardless I am glad that we have made progress. I have people working on a plan as we speak."

"We couldn't have gone there now?" Jiemba replied with a hint of frustration.

"I would have liked to have sorted this for you today," Price apologised. "But the location you have given to me is a bit more complex than that. The man who occupies that house is known to us. He is also known to be violent and causes the town a lot of trouble."

"All the more reason," Jiemba responded.

"Very true," Price acknowledged. "But someone like that gains all sorts of attention. Not just from us but also from those who are like minded. You wouldn't think it, but that house is almost like a fortress. It backs onto the railway line, but there is a sharp cliff which separates the two spots. That means the only way in is the same for everyone. You are seen before you arrive. I have had some of the rasher members of my team injured as they approached. It requires more thought so that no-one gets hurt." Jiemba followed the reasoning, not that it would apply to him. He didn't know the full extent of his power so it was probably better to err on the side of caution.

"I want to be involved, whatever happens," Jiemba demanded.

"I imagined as such," Price concluded. They stopped at one door along the hallway, where Price turned to completely face him. "Jiemba," Price drew in a deep sad breath. "You aren't going to like what you see through here. But I feel like you must. I am sorry." He pushed the door open as Jiemba tried to compose himself. On the other side was a room which smelled sterile and something similar to a medical institution.

"We will hold him here for the time being. The closest medical area is either Dubbo or Orange, but our facilities are well up to the task. State of the art. We figured a family member will want to see him first though we haven't been able to get in contact with any. I just wanted to reassure you that we are looking after him as best we can. I will be just outside the door," Price told him as he walked back through, his hands already on the handle. "Call out if you need me. But take all the time you need." The doors were shut and Jiemba was alone.

Jiemba hadn't had time to take in what was in the room with him. A lone table sat in the middle; a white sheet covering whatever it was hiding. Jiemba already knew what it was. He did not rush to see it, instead slowly making his way along the room. His chest was shaking, his lips trembling, his eyes already watering. Jiemba wasn't sure if he should be in the same room as this man, whether he was disobeying some ancient ritual or cultural law by simply being present. Regardless he was drawn to him. He pulled the sheet that had been placed lightly across his face, and removed it down to his shoulders. Jiemba wept as he looked down on his friend. The bald moustachioed face of the man who had saved him slept before him. His skin was clean with no sign of pain, and his lips almost seemed to form a smile.

Once more Jiemba did not know what to do. He leaned onto the table, holding back his weight so that it didn't break anything. The face in front becoming blurry as the fog of his tears filled his eyes. He felt like his stomach and lower organs were trying to escape his body; an empty feeling from deep down inside lurching forward to fill his torso and tug at his lungs. He struggled to breath as his giant frame heaved, fighting for air and to control his emotions at the same time. He let himself slide down to his knees as if that would be a better spot to support himself. His shoulders pinched together as they flexed in confusion. He was glad he was alone, the sound he released; an exasperated gurgling choking combination, was unnatural and concerning. He stayed there for an age, feeling the moisture swell his beard and dribble down his chest. His fingers slipped on the liquid that congealed on the floor.

Eventually he crawled his way back to his feet, using his massive forearms to wipe away the trail of water from his face. Once more he looked down on JayDee's smiling face.

"I am so sorry," Jiemba whispered finally. He didn't look away this time. He forced himself to show control despite nobody being able to see him. For the first time since his accident he felt pain in his skull, his head ached and although he winced slightly he welcomed it. Jiemba felt like he was on the verge of repeating the whole scene again when a blue light above the door started to flash. He walked towards it wondering what it meant and saw Price on his phone in the hallway through the window in the doors. He turned back to where JayDee lay.

"I will come back," he promised. A shove of the door alerted Price to Jiemba's return. "What is going on?"

"The carrier that you saw earlier has crashed," Price told him. "The driver called in the accident but said that he wasn't at fault. Just before he told us what had happened the line went dead."

"What does that mean?" Jiemba asked, whipping a big hairy arm over his face one more time. He could feel the salt hardening on his cheek and he imagined his eyes were quite bloodshot.

"Trouble," Price replied as he started to jog back up the hall towards the entrance. "And luckily, or unluckily, it is our job to fix it."

"Can I help?" Jiemba asked. He was sick of sitting around uselessly. Price turned around and stopped, contemplating what to answer as he stared straight back at Jiemba.

"I wasn't lying when I said I thought you could be useful," Price told him, "you can come along, but don't get in the way. We will deal with what happens." Soon both of them were jogging down the concrete hallway, boots and bare feet slapping on the surface as they neared the end.

Price opened the door to a scene of activity. One of the fire response vehicles was in the process of being lowered to the ground from its perch up high, with the assistance of one of the large Gear machines. Some vehicles were already on the move, the rescue vehicle sped past in front of them not concerned by the two men emerging from the door.

"Get in," Price ordered Jiemba as another van squealed to a halt right in front of them. This time both men occupied the rear as the vehicle sped off as soon as the door shut. The car sped toward the destination. "We know where they were going. And the route they were taking, so it shouldn't be too hard to find." All three of them stared through the front window as the engine changed gears loudly and roared on the straight stretches. Each corner was greeted with more squealing from the tyres as they bit into the concrete.

"See the glow?" Price said aloud, pointing to the sky where a faint orange light had appeared amongst the darkness of the night sky. The clouds that hung there, which could actually have been smoke if the light was from a fire, lit up like a beacon drawing them towards where the van needed to go. They crossed a different bridge, heading out of town towards Dubbo, and turned hard right.

"That's the place there," Price nudged Jiemba as he pointed out the side window. Jiemba was confused as the glowing sky was not in that direction. "The fortress." Jiemba tried to get a better look as they sped past. He failed as the house was barely lit and was mostly a blur in the fraction of a second he had to observe. "Try and get a better look when we come back," Price said as he continued to look out the front. Jiemba tried to make a mental note to do just that. They sped around a few more corners and then the situation opened up before them.

The carrier was on its side against a rural fence off the road. It hadn't just misjudged the corner and flipped, for starters it was on the wrong side of the road for that. A pair of vehicles, one car and the other was an old ute, were ablaze. The car still sat in the centre of the road, bonnet and front section smashed in, whilst the ute was on fire alongside the carrier; on its roof and spewing toxic black smoke. The rescue vehicle was on the scene as well as a few other cars, all of which Jiemba had seen at the security premises. There was a thicket of trees littering the side of the road making it impossible to see any further into the shadows. Price opened the door and started bellowing orders.

"Secure them," he snarled, pointing and barking orders to personnel who were hurrying forwards to greet him; pointing in the direction of the people mover. The doors that opened up onto the outside of the vehicle, in which resided the prisoners in small booths, had all been forced open and the occupants were fleeing in all directions. It was obvious that there were not enough people to secure them all. A few of the officers made towards some of the escapees that were still relatively close, others apprehended those that had been injured in the crash, but Jiemba could see that a handful had already made it into the new developments of townhouses nearby and were vanishing by the second.

Swearing erupted into the night sky drawing Jiemba's attention. He looked over and saw a bunch of people causing a commotion near the cabin of the carrier. One guard was free of the vehicle and staggering outside, another was laid out on the ground whilst a third was hanging lifelessly upside down at the driver's seat; seatbelt still attached and restraining him. A small group was standing over the downed guard shouting, kicking and taunting him, before turning their attention on the one that staggered by. Jiemba identified the pursuers as the few who had been fighting the guards inside the security headquarters. Jiemba hadn't wanted to get involved here, but he could see where this would end and the odds weren't good for the guard.

"Hey," Jiemba called out as he started to jog towards them. They either hadn't heard him or had chosen to ignore him, as the swearing grew louder. One of the men lunged out and punched the guard, flattening him to the ground. "Hey," he called out again. This time he was noticed.

"Hey what?" the man who had done the punching snarled. He turned and looked at Jiemba, hesitating for only a second before regaining his composure. "You're one of us," the man continued before the rest of his group turned to stare and growl at Jiemba. "How dare you disrespect us, by siding with them. Don't you know what they have done?"

"I am not siding with anyone," Jiemba replied with his hands out in front, "I am just here to help."

"Help who?" the man yelled back. One of his accomplices kicked the guard on the ground as he started to stir. "Those fools hunt the town's people down like animals and you are helping them. My brothers and sisters are locked up because they don't obey their rules. I am not standing by and letting that happen again." He fumbled about at the guard's waist and pulled a belt toward him. In a second he held what resembled a gun and pointed it down at the guard. "Sometimes you have to fight back."

"You don't have to fight," Jiemba stated taking some steps forward. "There are other ways."

"That should be true, but that is not the case around here," the man called back. The man who had been swearing and kicking at the security premises prior to the crash pulled a similar weapon from the other downed officer and held it out toward Jiemba. He was smiling as he tried to intimidate him with it. "Others have tried to talk, to be reasonable. But they either lock 'em up or run 'em out. If they want to take me, then they will have to fight for me. Freedom is something that you have to take for yourself, I ain't waiting for someone else to give it to me."

"These men are just doing their job," Jiemba continued to tread slowly forward. "You have made your point, you could leave without anyone else getting hurt, just leave them alone, they aren't going to hurt you anymore."

"Maybe not today," the man called back, "but tomorrow will be different. I have no compassion in me for those that would crush my people, whatever colour they are, and then penalise them trying to stand up under their own strength. The time for talking is over." The man looked hard at Jiemba, then before Jiemba could say anything the other man holding a weapon jumped towards the guard on the ground.

"You want to see mercy?" this man yelled.

He pulled the trigger.

Two needles shot out and pierced the guard's skin. A moment later he could be seen twisting and writhing on the ground as powerful volts of electricity shot through his defenceless body.

"Stop," Jiemba called out, motioning forward as if to stop him.

"I'll get you as well," the man dropped his taser and grabbed at the other weapon his friend was holding. He then aimed it at Jiemba, before adding a few more expletives. Jiemba ignored him and surged forward. Jiemba saw him pull the trigger as he continued pointing in his direction. Jiemba watched as the needles shot out towards him just like they had done to the guard. But unlike the guard they didn't stick.

The needles struck and bounced harmlessly away. The swearer swore more and rushed Jiemba, lunging forward with outstretched hands and a steel poll he had resting by his side. Jiemba let him come. The poll was swung hard at him.

Jiemba caught it. He grunted stiffly from his nostrils, smoke spreading into the cold air like an angry bull. Jiemba took hold of the poll with one hand and the shirt of his attacker in the other. In one swipe he spun the man and flung him high up into a nearby tree, then watched as he struck almost every branch on the way down to lay motionless at its base.

"Get him," the leader yelled to the others before sprinting off towards that same tree line. Jiemba once more let them come. This time he caught both of them, banged their bodies together and left them in a heap at his feet. Jiemba watched as the man disappeared into the tree line, and listened as a great muffler coughed loudly as an engine was ignited. A moment later he saw a deep maroon car that had been hidden from view, shred grass from the ground as it accelerated onto the road. A second later he could see only the rear lights as it sped off into the distance.

As Jiemba returned towards the road behind him he was greeted by Price and Officer Gumbo once more going toe to toe. Multiple police and security vehicles were on the scene, some in the process of recapturing those that had escaped, others returning from unfruitful attempts to hunt down fleeing prisoners. Several turned back towards the town as they continued the attempts to regather the rest.

"This is what happens when you start playing police," Gumbo snarled, "you held citizens in your own mini-prison in an unlawful way and this is the result."

"This carrier is under your jurisdiction, constable," Price spat back. "Whatever happened here is on your watch. You are lucky we were on scene to catch so many before they made it back to the streets."

"You would do well, my friend, to stay away from this group," Gumbo shared the suggestion with Jiemba this time. "They will lead you into a bad situation."

"If we hadn't brought Jiemba along this situation would have been a whole lot worse," Price retaliated. "You can ask those guards over there. And then you can thank Jiemba that they can actually talk back and answer you." Officer Gumbo growled a warning but said no more, storming off to assist wherever he could.

"I for one am thankful you were here," Price said calmly, observing what was happening around him. "This could have been far worse." Jiemba watched as the fire crews, from both the town and the security force, put out the fires and freed drivers and passengers from where they had been trapped. The rescue service was on task as well as the paramedics which had just arrived. It was all working together for the betterment of everyone. "Unfortunately this is not over."

"What do you mean?" Jiemba asked. For the first time that day he felt drained, even though he knew it was not physical but rather mental fatigue.

"Well for starters," Price scraped his fingers through his hair with a sigh. "Many of those that have escaped were on the violent end of the crime spectrum. Car thieves, drunks, thugs and the like. It will be a task to capture them quickly without harming the community or my team."

"Until I get the answers that I need I am happy to help," Jiemba replied. "But that won't be for too long because I want those answers soon."

"Once again I am happy to hear it," Price smiled and patted Jiemba on the shoulder, "and we will get onto that as soon as we are back. That is after you get washed up and a change of clothes." Jiemba looked down at his clothing and could not disagree about how shoddy his appearance was. He nodded and scratched at his beard to remove some of the grass he could feel itching in there.

"We will need to re-evaluate first," Price continued as he led Jiemba back to the van. "Things just got a little bit more complicated."

"How do you mean?" asked Jiemba, wondering how on Earth it could be any more so.

"The place you are trying to get into," Price started.

"The one you keep calling a fortress," Jiemba added. "What about it?"

Price chuckled. "The guy in the maroon car owns it," Price answered. "And I don't think he will be too happy to see you again."

Chapter 10 – The list

Jiemba knew it was going to happen. As soon as he slipped into a satisfactory slumber the nightmares returned. This time, instead of being the person the visions revolved around, he was nothing but a spectator. His mind was restless anyway, and it needed to find calm which he wouldn't find being awake, hopefully his soul could be as resilient as his body.

In the nightmare, he sat on a hill, watching the tormented version of himself skirt around the edge of Lake Burrendong. The version he watched moved erratically, his head turned in all directions as if choosing a side; sometimes directing Jiemba this way or that. Jiemba knew that the other version was actually battling the voices inside his head, which were directing him in all directions. All around the hill he sat upon was a haze, he hadn't noticed what was going on then so why should it be present now. He did see a small group of teenage girls fighting at a small cabin nearby, his mind recalled the sounds but not what had been occurring. There seemed to be nothing but negative energy anywhere he looked. Even the lake seemed dark and foreboding.

Jiemba watched in the dream as the old Jiemba stopped, thinking about something deeply before turning and submerging himself in the water. Jiemba wished that somebody, anybody, had been there before he had taken the action. Hoped that somewhere else in the world, somebody was stopping someone else who was doing the same thing that Jiemba had done. There was a flash and a rumbling from the night sky above. When Jiemba looked up he found even in the dream he was made to squint, his arm forced up to shade his face from the overwhelming glare. He still could not make out what was happening. A moment later an explosion of water filled the sky and a giant wave emerged, spreading in all directions. Jiemba watched as the water spread out, knowing that somewhere amongst it was his own drowning form. He heard a scream nearby from the girls, and louder yells from further away, which stunned him as he had not thought he had heard them before. Then the wave hit him and the vision changed.

Now he was a bird, sitting in a tree. He was back at the edge of the river, sitting behind JayDee's shoulder as he observed Jiemba splutter after waking up on the bank. He saw JayDee smile and the vision switched. He swirled about in his nightmares. Each flash was quick and showed a time when JayDee had shown him compassion, but he had replied with contempt. There were so many moments. Jiemba felt sick with how he had treated the old man.

Flick, flick, flick, flick. He wanted them to end. Finally they did. He was back on the front lawn of JayDee's house. JayDee was deceased on the ground, but JayDee also stood beside the body looking down with disgust. A gross phantom representing an ugly version of what JayDee had been.

"My spirit is restless," the phantom told Jiemba, not the old form of Jiemba but the current one who was observing the nightmare unfold. For the first time he felt like he was relevant in the vision.

"I'm so sorry," Jiemba told him, words he had shared numerous times but had felt no better at any point after sharing them.

"You should be," JayDee replied, then swooped in close taking the form of a giant black duck. It was bigger than the house nearby, engulfing the fire that blazed and the red light that surrounded them.

"My spirit is restless, I am dead, and it is all your fault."

Jiemba woke up in a sweat. His breathing was uneven and his whole body shook. He swung his feet over the edge of his bed and sat with his head held in his hands. His fingernails felt into the depths of his beard and he felt the muck that had been resting there. He still sat in his jeans but his chest was bare, the goanna staring up at him.

The electric door, the only spot in the room that was letting light in, opened with a satisfying whoosh and the lights within the room automatically flicked on.

"No doubt you needed that," Price entered, carrying a small bag and referring to the rest that Jiemba had just finished. "I had no idea you would sleep so long though."

"Good morning to you too," Jiemba stretched, pretending to go through some sort of morning routine. His body was already tensed and ready to move. His eyes quickly adapting to the new harsh light.

"In the bag I have a selection of clothes, that should fit, as well as some shoes," Price ignored him and continued setting things down on a table nearby. "As you don't have any personal belongings I have provided you with a wallet which contains a small amount of cash if needed, and a phone so that you can contact me at any time while you are with us. The contacts are already entered in the phone. For consideration I have also placed some things in there to help you shave and return to some level of hygiene. Your choice whether you use those or not, of course." Jiemba secretly held a cupped hand up to his mouth and breathed out, taking air back into his nostrils so he could smell it. He couldn't disagree with the need for a tooth brush.

"While you were sleeping we have been very busy," Price pressed a small button on the wall and the door opened again. "I encourage you to refresh yourself as required and then promptly meet me in the conference area." Price was gone without a response.

Jiemba watched him leave but didn't get up immediately. Everything in the dream had been a memory from a different point of view. Everything except the last bit. It all remained so vivid to Jiemba. From the moment they had met the old man had been focused on helping Jiemba, while Jiemba had rarely showed that he was thankful for any of it. He had received far more than he had deserved. JayDee was now one of those cases where the world was a poorer place due to his absence. Jiemba had not saved the man despite what he owed him. The others that had relied upon JayDee would also be in a far worse situation.

Was the phantom right?

Was it all Jiemba's fault?

Jiemba could not see any way in which it wasn't. He doubted that JayDee would have ever told him that was how he felt, or that Jiemba was to blame. The memory was therefore a conjuring of guilt from his own mind. It didn't make it wrong. He dreaded if it was true that JayDee's spirit was restless. He wasn't sure if JayDee had been a believer in what would come after someone's death, but the spirit was important and it must be allowed to finish the journey it started. Jiemba could not bare to be responsible for that journey stopping in its natural course. He had no idea how to fix it though, just dark suggestions. He climbed to his feet and clutched at the bag. He had to calm JayDee's spirit, so he had to start making things right. He walked over to the bathroom, hoping that the shower was big enough for him.

The warehouse was a labyrinth. The open space where he had come through had made the place look massive, but the warren of hallways, rooms, and corridors that burrowed in every direction made it seem so much larger. Finally, after asking multiple people multiple times, he made his way into a largish room where several other people had already gathered. Price was busy at the far end setting up some presentation, that he didn't acknowledge Jiemba's arrival.

"Sleeping beauty finally arrives," one of the men sitting down announced, causing everyone to turn and face him.

"At least he scrubs up alright," a young woman added. The rest said nothing and turned back to face Price. Jiemba swept a hand down the front of his shirt as if ironing out the last crimples. He was not wearing a suit jacket or tie like everyone else in the room, but did wear the fitted white dress shirt and the black slacks and boots like everyone else. He had trimmed his beard and combed it so it flowed down his face rather than in every direction, as if a bush had been attached to his chin. He had also shortened his hair a little so it looked smarter and wasn't rolling all over the place.

"That is enough you two," Price intervened while still setting up his computer at the front of the room. He was clearly the senior member in the chamber. Almost everybody else in the room looked to be in their early or mid-twenties while Price looked to be in his forties. The screen sparked to life and everyone picked up a small booklet that sat in front of them. Jiemba took a chair at the back of the room and noticed that the young man who had spoken still smirked in his direction. Jiemba ignored him, instead focusing on the booklet.

"We have an opportunity here to do a lot of work in a short amount of time," Price started to explain. "Last night, as you are all aware, one of the prison carriers was ambushed and was run off the road."

"Ambushed?" Jiemba said with quiet alarm.

"That's right," Price confirmed. "There were two other vehicles found damaged at the scene. In analysing the crash site, evidence suggests that the ute was the cause of everything that happened afterwards. We believe that it has driven off a side road at the very moment the carrier has passed, before slamming into it deliberately. This has then caused the carrier to veer and tip off the side of the road. The lack of skid marks or tyre fragments left by the vehicle braking suggest that it never tried to slow down. The other vehicle we are not too sure about, it may have been involved but it is more likely that it was just in the wrong spot at the wrong time."

"What about the third car?" Jiemba asked. The rest of the group looked up at the newcomer with a look of confusion. When Jiemba looked down at his booklet he noticed that there was no mention of it.

"That is the focus of another investigation I will be involved with today," Price said, quickly moving on from the idea without any other explanation.

"Could we ask the driver of the car at fault?" one of the older looking security officers asked.

"Deceased at the scene," Price replied. "The body has already been moved and examined by local police and has been transported to a suitable location in Dubbo. We will get no hints from him. Now, what we are left with then is a clean-up job. The police have taken over the investigation of what happened at the crash site and have, advised us, to leave the area to them. We will honour that request as it has nothing to do with us any longer, but the escapees are of particular concern. Because the risk to the community is quite large we have, with the support of the police, alerted the community to remain indoors and have implemented a day time curfew for the next 24 hours. That will," he emphasised the *will*, "give us enough time to round up all the fugitives in the area and hold them."

"Bet Gumbo wasn't happy with that," the young man said again.

"He wasn't," Price replied bluntly, "but he is saving face and we have to be seen to be fixing the problem by those that employ us. We can't have this sort roaming around causing mayhem in Wellington or New Wellington." He flicked to a new slide on the screen, a flurry of paper answered as everyone flipped over in their booklets. "Each of you has been given a list of names and possible locations for where each person can be found. You are to move through each name until you have identified a location or have them secured. Should anyone need more support I am forming teams to do so currently."

"How many people fit on that carrier?" Jiemba asked with astonishment seeing the long list of names. He had guessed only about a dozen but there were scores of names listed. Again he was ignored.

"You all have your assignments and the teams that you have been allocated to, get to it," Price ordered. Once the rest had gone there were only four remaining. "Jiemba I have to introduce you to a couple of members of my team." Here he pointed to the young man who had announced Jiemba's arrival, who stood showing his whole frame; flexing slightly as if it would either impress or intimidate Jiemba. It did neither. His blonde hair had been slicked so that it spiked slightly on the top of his head. He was cut with an athletic figure, his jacket looking like it would pop the buttons at any moment. He had blue eyes which looked as if they were daring Jiemba to try something, and a stupid side smile with a shaved clean face. He appeared to Jiemba to be mocking him with his gaze. "This is Brett Rogers," Price explained. "He is one of the heads of my security team, and is most likely to get results. And this," he then gestured towards the female. She was smaller and slimmer. She smiled at Jiemba with fierce green eyes that felt like they could pierce straight through him.

"I am Selena Fang," she held out her hand to be taken. Jiemba shook it, trying hard not to break it. "I like a firm grip." She added.

"Jiemba," Price spoke directly to him. "Last night you demonstrated that you could handle yourself in a tough situation, and I know you are driven to get this done so we can move on. I am getting these two to work alongside you in apprehending the more dangerous individuals on this list. They will take the lead and you will support them. This should not be hard for you three, but again I have provision to assist if required. I doubt this will flush out those that we seek to help you Jiemba, but there is a chance."

"You send support after me, and I will be sending them back," Rogers remarked, pointing angrily at Price.

"That is not how it works," Price chided him unmoved. "My hope is that it will not be necessary and we can move on from this into more important matters."

"Sure, anything else, boss," Rogers replied with more than a hint of annoyance.

"No that is all," Price, again, ignored his tone. "You can both leave." Selena smiled at Jiemba as she left, while Rogers stared him down.

"Jiemba," Price stopped him, but still led him back towards the door. "I know you are not part of this company, and normally I would not just invite someone who has not been trained by me to be involved with anything like this. However, this is a very different set of circumstances and I do value your assistance as I do believe it will be useful. If at any point you are not comfortable you can stop, we will find these people eventually, although it may take longer. I do think however that there is a chance that you may identify someone that you know while the others search. You have my permission to talk to them, or even bring them in if you would prefer. Any leads will help, and I think you have a better chance of finding someone who has the information to resolve this quickly. Rest assured that I will be working on a plan to move on the property swiftly while you are helping my team, and will be able to alter the plan if you deem it necessary. I may even allow you to be part of that plan in a larger capacity if you show you can handle it."

"I have to find those who killed the old man," Jiemba added. It was his only focus to bring justice to JayDee. "As well as those who destroyed the small community out by the river."

"I want to see those responsible brought to justice just as much as you," Price nodded and gestured towards the doorway where the other two officers waited for Jiemba. "Good luck."

"How many is that now?" Rogers grumbled.

"We have found nine," Selena replied, "two others have fled town, and are no longer our immediate concern as we have already identified the area in which they have entered. Others will be on scene presently, leaving us with just three left."

"Good," Rogers complained. "I am over this."

"Isn't this your job though?" Jiemba asked mockingly. Rogers turned from his seat behind the steering wheel and snorted his disgust at the interruption.

"It wouldn't matter what the job is, Rogers would still find something to complain about," Selena added with a smile.

"All I am saying is that we are supposed to be security," Rogers mumbled, "We aren't a clean-up crew, we are above dealing with this filth. And I don't like going around doing a copper's job. I do that enough as it is." Neither Selena nor Jiemba replied this time, but that didn't stop Rogers from mumbling more under his breath. The three of them had started their assignment just before noon and had been going down the list for a couple of hours. Apart from a couple of names most had been in the location that they had been given. A clear statement to Jiemba that Price and his team knew what they were doing. Each time they entered a property or searched through an area the scenario changed but the outcome was almost always the same; with either a security support vehicle coming to take away a fugitive or, far more rarely, a Wellington police car doing the job instead.

Jiemba would enter last every time. Rogers, although constantly grinding at Jiemba's patience, and incredibly heavy handed, was competent at his job. In some of the cases the person they were searching for would try and assault them at the first instance. Rogers had been ready and hadn't taken long to turn the tables; forcibly disabling the attacker and removing them immediately. Selena was more subtle. She had a knack for finding a fugitive quietly and coaxing them out into the open with her calming nature. Sometimes she had even made family members or friends give an escapee away as she convinced them it was for the best. They had been thoroughly efficient.

Jiemba had been completely useless.

He felt like the muscle in the group, the one in most stories that would let the bully get their way simply because no one wanted to take Jiemba on. The feeling annoyed Jiemba because it gave the idea that Rogers was actually one of the smart ones when he was actually a complete brute. He hadn't found anyone that he had recognised and each face stared guilt back at him. In truth he had been overwhelmed upon entering most of the houses they entered and wouldn't have been much use anyway. On some of the visits he stayed outside as he didn't want to be inside. Like he had seen upon walking into the city, most of the houses had yards which were neglected and overgrown. Inside almost always reflected the outside.

Jiemba had gone in thinking that his mum was right to berate him when he didn't clean up areas of his house or even his room. Clothes on the floor in the bedroom, near the wardrobe or dirty clothes basket, some small stains on the tiles as he hadn't vacuumed or mopped in a couple of weeks, and some balls of dust on some of the furniture the usual things which got him in trouble. His mum would have hated these places. Plates covered in sauce left all through the houses, some with other things like books or paper stacked on top as well, cabinet doors hanging from hinges or sitting somewhere on the floor nearby, you were lucky to find the floor in some. Jiemba crinkled his nose as the smell was usually overbearing. The brown marks on the floor with the blackened ceiling and yellowing walls was enough to suggest he didn't need or want to know what was the cause of it all.

The experience had not been pleasant to say the least. Without any other information he had almost completely agreed with the apprehension of many of the people. In most of the scenarios there was an obscene amount of swearing and violence. The amount of anger was immense. Jiemba stood by with little sympathy as those people were taken away. In one case he also had to get involved as one man tried to be violent towards his own wife. She had not defended him enough and he let her hear about it, threatening her with the worst sort of actions and threats. Jiemba would not stand for it and had intervened, stopping the man in his tracks before he could say or do anything else. His actions were likely not warrented as she did not appear to be intimidated by him, sending her own spectrum of abusive language straight down the hall after him as he was led outside.

There were others where they lived in filth but he chose to believe that if given a chance they could do far more with their lives. Some houses were not too different to what he grew up in, but rather than question why those people were being taken he chose to turn a blind eye so he could avoid another confusing train of thought.

Jiemba was only happy when they were almost finished, but equally surprised at the same time. He hadn't imagined that there would have been so many people to find, especially as he had already concluded that a large portion had been accounted for either at the time of the crash or in the early hours of the next morning. And to think that there was a room full of security officers with similar lists searching other areas within Wellington. The town wasn't big but it wasn't that small either. He wasn't amazing at maths, but after doing a few sums, and even adding extra people who had been taken in simply because they were related to the fugitive, the numbers still didn't add up. There were too many names listed to be needed, and equally as many security members seeking them out. It didn't make sense to Jiemba.

"We are here," Rogers alerted them.

"Our information says that there is a chance that we will find all three remaining fugitives at the same residence," Selena told them, "which means this could be our last stop."

"Please let that be true," Rogers groaned as Selena stepped from the car first.

"Hopefully Selena can throw some kind words around and we will be done quickly," Jiemba suggested.

"Kind words?" Rogers questioned the notion. "Looks can be deceiving, she is more dangerous than she appears. If she fluttered her eyelashes in your direction you wouldn't last a minute." He laughed loudly as he pulled himself from the vehicle. "Besides, who would want to waste kind words on these sorts of people? They are lucky that we aren't just rolling through with a bulldozer. Ridding the town of another worthless hovel and its occupants is a far better use of our time." Rogers watched Jiemba intently before he drew closer to the house. Jiemba hoped that the brutish security officer was just playing with him, but there was no way he could be sure. He felt like there was a lot of intent to act in what Rogers was sharing. Jiemba flicked open his phone and made a call.

"Price here," the phone answered.

"It's Jiemba, we are at the last location. If it's anything like the last few we will need a support car to help escort the escapees away," Jiemba explained.

"Of course," Price replied, "I will send a crew out immediately, and, unless there has been any new information gathered in this search, upon your return we need to discuss the next steps in your search."

"I look forward to it," Jiemba replied, "thanks." He disconnected the call and moved towards the house.

"Get out of the way," a voice boomed, he was certain it was Rogers. The scream which followed chilled Jiemba to the core. His whole body dipped in height as if getting lower to the ground would somehow make him safer. There was more than one screamer, at least three by his reckoning. They were joined by the wail of a small child and the crying of a baby. Jiemba walked into the house and was surprised at how dark it was. There appeared to be no lights on, with either large wooden ply board or heavy curtains covering all the windows. He stomped into one room and was greeted with a crying woman clutching at her child.

"My bad," Jiemba uttered the words uninvited, apologising as if he was the one at fault. He was walking into someone else's house and he knew they didn't want him there. His attempts to soothe the woman and her child were met with a heated response. He would be pretty angry if that happened to him. There was a commotion coming from the kitchen area. A dog was barking and going off in the front lounge area. Jiemba was sure there was fighting happening but he hadn't located it yet.

A loud thump revealed a body being knocked to the thin timber floors, whose he wasn't sure.

"Coming your way," Rogers called out loudly. Before Jiemba could think the thumping of footsteps moving quickly came towards him, and the person that owned them took him completely by surprise. A man entered the small hallway, leapt into the air and punched Jiemba square in the jaw as he sailed by. The man cried out in pain, clutching at his wrist which hung limply at his side. The attacker could see that Jiemba still stood opposed to him and swiftly threw a kick towards his chest. Jiemba caught the foot before he could be struck, causing the other man to hop around clumsily as he nursed his injury. Jiemba lifted the foot as high as he could, causing the other man to flip, slam into the roof, and then slump noisily to the floor.

"That is two," Rogers stated as he entered the hallway, rubbing away some blood that was oozing down from his nose and trickling along his upper lip and jaw. He looked down at the crumbled heap and gestured further along. "Last one went that way."

"With Selena?" Jiemba asked, and received a nod in confirmation. The screams and cries became muffled as the immediate threat was gone, but Jiemba was less comfortable with the silence that surrounded him. He slunk along the dim corridor, glancing in through the few doors that he passed, knowing that the far room was his destination but still searching for any threat or information that would aid his cause.

"Selena," Jiemba called out, probing for a response.

"Don't come in," her voice replied. The door it came from was shut and on the left, although there was another at the end of the hall just opposite. Jiemba turned to look at Rogers who was close behind him. The security officer glared at him as if challenging his right to be there, before reluctantly nodding at him and gesturing with a small swing of his hand to proceed. Jiemba slowly slid forward, eyes focused on the door, not wanting to make any movement that would place her in any more danger. He stopped outside the door, pausing for a quick breath, thinking through what he was going to do one more time. A sharp squeal came from the other door opposite. Jiemba instinctively turned that way as the door he had been approaching swung open. A man holding a steel pipe jumped out swinging hard at Jiemba, striking him solidly on the side of the head. The man didn't wait for Jiemba to fall, retreating instantly back into the room and slamming the door.

Jiemba didn't move, and he didn't hit the floor. He simply stood there comprehending what just happened. He finally turned to look at Rogers who looked shocked at what had occured. Jiemba felt his nose twitch as his anger flared. A click sounded, revealing that the door had been locked from the inside.

"I don't think so," he growled. Jiemba took one step and drove his foot straight into the door, as Rogers did likewise to the other room. The hinges erupted as the door exploded inside. It was as dimly lit as the rest of the house but Jiemba still had to wait for his eyes to adjust. He heard movement, expecting it to be the man who had attacked him. There was a sudden flurry and once again a loud thump as a body hit the floor. Selena swept back her long hair as she stood over the fallen form of the last fugitive.

"Three," she whispered, smiling while she took a few sharp breaths. Jiemba stood dumbfounded at what had just happened.

"Told you," Rogers said as he entered the room after dealing with the others, smiling at the look plastered on Jiemba's face.

"Yeah," Jiemba replied in an inaudible whisper. "You did."

"That means the list is finished," Selena told them.

"Great let's get out of here," Rogers snarled. A snappy ding sounded three times in the room. Rogers pulled out his phone as they had received the same message. "Just in time too. It is happening tonight."

Chapter 11 – Meeting the boss

"You're in," Price said as he scoured over an old map he had in front of him.

"I'm in?" Jiemba repeated. In his mind there was no thought that he was ever out.

"Yes," Price ignored Jiemba's indifference. "Selena said you did well today, better than expected in fact."

"And what did Rogers say?" Jiemba asked, not accepting that he had done anything remarkable at all.

"He was less flattering," Price continued, looking towards Rogers who stood grinning across from him next to Selena, "but that isn't unusual. Let's move on though. There have been a series of developments throughout the day. We have located your man, Jerome Less, and conveniently perhaps he has been seen entering the fortress. We also know that Docker has returned there."

"Docker?" Jiemba questioned.

"Yes," Price was becoming less patient. "I thought you knew the name at least. He was the man who fled in the red car last night at the crash site. He is the owner of that property and he is a constant thorn in our side."

"How is that?" Jiemba needed to know.

"He has been an ever present voice against the development of New Wellington and the added support infrastructure," Price explained readily. "I have my suspicions that he is one of the people responsible for causing unrest in the town, leading to vandalism, destruction and antisocial activity. I also have my suspicions that he is becoming more militant. Now we have reason to go into those premises as we suspect he is harbouring Jerome, plus a number of the other escapees, men with warrants for their arrest, and other people we would like to speak to. We want to get Jerome and any other information we can to progress with your investigation, but finding those men there will allow us to take Docker as well."

"That will be better for everyone," Rogers grumbled, "then I can finally take a break."

"Everyone can at least take a breath for a moment, yes," Price agreed. "But that is not why we are trying to resolve this quickly. The town is suffering because of this constant conflict."

"What were the other developments?" Selena asked next showing more concern than Rogers had. Price stood taller, instead of remaining hunched over the desk in front of him. He appeared to be choosing his next words very carefully.

"There are reports of a biker group having infiltrated the town at some point today, we have been aware of some groups but this is something new," he said. "We have been stretched looking in other directions and did not notice them slip in as we were preoccupied." Jiemba noticed Selena flinch slightly as she listened with intent. Her face was a mask of seriousness. "The whereabouts of this group is unknown, however," he suddenly turned on Jiemba. "This could mean an opportunity to get both the man you are looking for, and the group responsible for your friend's murder without a prolonged search." Jiemba stood firm, slowly gulping down the spite he held in his throat. Price looked once more at Selena and then turned back towards the map.

"Let's get this over with," Rogers yawned with disinterest.

"We will have two groups," Price began as he swept a hand over the map. He had a large pin showing the location of what he called the fortress. "The main group will consist of just you three. Jiemba will go in alone, and if there is a concern you two can go in as support. I can't imagine Jiemba getting much push back from anybody in the main house until he is in front of Docker, which could be interesting, but if you find Jerome, Jiemba, then you drag him out of there and return to the main access point here. You two, will not go past this point unless directed."

"And the second group?" Jiemba asked. He was concerned by the plan but wanted to know it all.

"It isn't called a fortress for no reason," Price continued. "It is unlikely that you will even get in, but your presence may be enough to spook some of the other people present." At this point he placed pins all around the proximity of an imaginary circle opposite the primary entrance. "We can't spread further than this point," he said pointing to one pin in particular, "as the railway line and the ridge next to it are here. But we will form a line on the boundary of the greater exterior to the property. There is a large shed beyond the house which we know can be filled with activity, so we expect movement from there. Once we see that we will move in, get those that we need, and withdraw. The police are already observing what we do, waiting to charge us with interfering with their investigation. Despite still having a possibility of harbouring some of the fugitives this action is not being seen as necessary like our other searches today. I told Gumbo I would stay away and this is very dark shades of grey. If we have Jerome and the others, we want you to hold Docker until we arrive. Then, finally, this whole situation can be resolved."

"I don't see why we don't just grab him anyway," Rogers grunted. "If he has been running this whole operation surely that is enough. Didn't he shoot someone?" Jiemba remembered that Docker had threatened to taser one of the guards.

"No we can't," Price reprimanded him. "The locals are holding just short of a complete riot, as much as it will bring the group out it will also be a bad look to our clients. Everything we suspect of Docker is not confirmed, even the incident that you are talking about isn't official as no one has come forward to say they actually witnessed it. Heresay won't get us the support we need, and I know that Gumbo and his men will come down hard on us for that."

"What will it be like inside?" Jiemba asked, changing the topic as he shifted uncomfortably. He was genuinely interested however.

"No one in my service has ever been in, but it is usually buzzing with energy. I can imagine it will be what a magnified version of what you have seen today. It isn't unusual for the police to be called over to the place with noise complaints and people fighting on the premises, but they have never bothered going in either. The likelihood that it is filled with a small militant minded force are very high. We must be careful, if we are reckless there is a risk that many of the Spartan employees could be harmed and this whole situation could boil quickly over into the streets. If that was to happen we may not be able to contain the overflow." There was a knock at the conference room door and Price moved over to answer it. Jiemba was rolling the simple plan over in his head. He didn't really want to go through with it, but if it gave him the answers that would help him put an end to this horrible situation then he felt he had no choice.

"Sorry everyone," Price apologised after a brief conversation with one of his other officers. "Officer Gumbo has requested me." Price forced a smile and moved out of the room.

"I'm getting something to eat," Rogers wasted no time in following him out the door leaving Selena and Jiemba alone.

"What will you do when this is over?" Selena asked almost immediately. Jiemba looked up, finding the sound of her voice soothing, to be greeted with a warm smile.

"I am not sure," Jiemba answered truthfully with a frown. They had spoken many times, although only momentarily, throughout the day. Not about anything meaningful, but enough to make their conversations seem more natural. "I have been away from home for a long time. People will probably be worried about me. But . . . I have been searching for something while I have been away."

"Have you found that something yet?" Selena asked, taking a step closer to him. Jiemba shook his head.

"I don't know," he answered truthfully, "I thought I did, I thought I had found a purpose, but now I am not so sure. Everything has been so confusing."

"I can only imagine," she said placing a hand on his shoulder. Somehow he felt the warmth of her touch. "I hope you find the answers you seek, but if it takes longer and you are still hanging around, I am happy to help if I can."

"Really?" Jiemba asked, he could feel a warm blush spread onto his face. Hopefully his beard was still bushy enough to hide it.

"Absolutely," she answered sincerely. "I am stuck here with 'men' like Rogers all day long. I would be happy to get out of here and help you out."

"Don't you have other things to do though?" Jiemba asked. Why should she bother with him? Others who had known him for far longer didn't care so why should she?

"Of course," Selena replied swiftly. "But they don't take up all of my time, and soon we may have more time to spare if all this stuff gets resolved. I would have thought you would be happy for the offer and the company."

"I am, I would be," Jiemba blurted out, hoping that he hadn't offended her.

"Good," Selena's smile returned. "I sort of owe you for what you did earlier. Besides, I like your company. You make me feel safer." She smiled at him. Jiemba had no idea how to respond to her sudden attention. He did what he usually did. He opened his mouth wide and laughed so that his eyes were forced shut and the room was filled with mirth.

Price returned abruptly, forcing Jiemba to stop.

"Where is Rogers?" Price asked.

"Stuffing his face as usual," Selena replied. "You look annoyed, what was that about?" Price looked at her, perhaps more annoyed that she had called him out for his ruffled appearance. He straightened suddenly as if it would hide her spoken analysis.

"Gumbo interfering again," Price informed her. "He is demanding that all of those we apprehended today, that we are still holding, get handed over to him immediately. And he reminded me that any bodies of deceased parties need to be dealt with by the proper channels and authorities and at no point should be held by us."

"What did you say?" Selena asked.

"I agreed," Price said, finally smiling. "I said that we will transfer as many that his own office can hold in the next few hours, but those that were already designated to be delivered to the correctional facility will be held until tomorrow. I offered him the use of a convoy under my watch as the only carrier we can use was destroyed yesterday. He reluctantly agreed. I hate that man's meddling. Are you two ready to begin?"

"What about the old man's body?" Jiemba asked with concern. "Will that be moved?"

"No, his body was not asked to be moved so it will remain with us for the time being," Price answered.

"Why is his body different?" Jiemba asked with confusion. "Is it because of the circumstances?"

"No," Price took a deep breath. "He didn't ask for it because he isn't aware of it. His department has no idea that there was a death in the Wellington area, apart from the driver of the ambush car yesterday."

"He doesn't know?" Jiemba spat out, shocked at the revelation.

"Like I said," Price said quickly. "I don't like interference, and this process would be a whole lot slower and probably non-functional if they were involved." He didn't wait for Jiemba to calculate what was just said. "It is time to make a move. Let's go."

Jiemba stood in the darkness on the edge of the road. On his right was a bridge. Beneath that bridge were train tracks about ten metres below. In front of him was a long dirt driveway, which Jiemba could see for about a hundred metres before it disappeared behind thick bottlebrush and wattle bushes; hiding from the full moonlight.

The van that had dropped him off had already left, leaving him alone to listen to the sounds of the night. The glow of Wellington filled the sky behind him, he was only a street away from the busy highway and the edge of town, while the charm of the night skies guided his way in front. Jiemba could see a plume of trees which surrounded a tall building he suspected was at the end of the driveway. He started to walk towards it in the same outfit he had worn all day. Selena and Rogers had changed into a darker attire, similar to what Price had worn when he was trying to remain unnoticeable.

He could hear his footsteps as he walked, and see his breath stretch out in a quickly dissipating mist in front. Stepping down onto loose rocks of granite and disturbing clumps of dust. The smaller stones shifted beneath his feet from time to time but the small crunching was the only sound he heard.

Jiemba kept a slow pace. He glanced in behind the trees, bushes, and discarded cars and materials that littered the edge of the driveway; each time trying to build some sort of danger out of the shapes that the shadows created. He shortened his breathing as if that would reveal a hidden assailant lurking nearby. Jiemba received no such attention. Rogers had been in his ear the entire ride over, telling him stories of the house he had almost reached. He likened it almost to an outpost in a warzone. Guards manning the driveway, fences stopping anybody from entering unwanted, cameras pointing in every direction. None of that appeared before him, it sounded more like he was describing the security headquarters. Rogers also shared his version of the world, where the problems were only caused by those who complain, and those who complain have nothing to whinge about, and history is past so no one should be upset by things that have happened before, and that all of this could be controlled, with those not wanting to conform having a place to keep them warm within four concrete walls and a set of iron bars. Others should change to fit the system and not the other way around.

Jiemba did not agree, but the arrogance of the man was enough for Jiemba to refuse to argue with him. He didn't want to waste his breath though he knew he definitely wanted to and should have.

The house loomed before him. To Jiemba it looked like it could have been one of the original houses built in the area, by someone who possessed a fair amount of money back in the day. It was two storeys of ancient brick, with wooden borders and fashionable arches covering the façade. Some of these were worn out, moisture separating some of the timbers while others had been chipped away. Several of the windows were hidden away by vines and ivy that had climbed the exterior, crawling along the railing securing the outdoor decking of the veranda up above. Jiemba saw a shape move there, that was instantly hidden from sight.

The music and loud noises he expected had not appeared, and there were few lights on inside the dwelling. They were the only evidence that there may have actually been someone living in the place at all. Jiemba could see the large shed situated out the back, one single light illuminating the area. He stepped onto the slippery concrete steps leading up to the large main door. The front porch was surrounded by plants, almost creating its own dark room. Jiemba reflected on what he could see as he stood next to the doorway. It resembled something more like a haunted house rather than something owned by a militant resistance group. The occupants that he had expected, spilling out into the yard to surround and harass him, were nonexistent. He knocked on the door, received no answer, before turning the door handle. It was unlocked and he ventured inside.

Jiemba was amazed as he walked into the house. Every room showed signs of destruction, decay and disregard. Giant holes filled many of the rooms, ancient furniture lay broken and there were mould stains almost everywhere you looked. If you looked beyond the defects, and if you imagined someone walked through with a magic wand and rejuvenated every part, it was something that you would see in any older part of Sydney or even at home in some ritzy parts of

London. Remnants of a chandelier hung from the roof, oil portraits profiling important people generations ago lingered on the walls, tapestries and rugs with a million stitches lay dirty in many corners. The timber looked old and heavy but strong enough to withstand the torments of the time it lived in and the ages that had passed.

But despite how amazing it looked it lacked what he had come in to find and what he expected would have been there in abundance.

There were no people.

Jiemba took several deep breaths. He was heightened, expecting a fight which once again did not eventuate. It hadn't helped how much Rogers had been building him up. What they had said may have been true, the damage within the building could have been proof of that, but the place was empty. Jiemba was disliking Rogers the more he thought about him. Jiemba stopped looking into the side rooms, which were only lit by the lights located in the huge main foyer and hallway, and followed the trail of light which ventured up a grand staircase which sat before him.

With every step he was trying to remain silent, still expecting someone to jump out at him at any moment, but he couldn't help how heavily he stepped. Each foot clomped on the floorboards which groaned under his weight, echoing from every direction, infiltrating the soundless places of the building. Remarkably the upstairs area was in far better shape than the floor below. There was only one light on. Jiemba ignored everything else and walked towards it. He hesitated outside the door, wondering what he would see on the other side. Another man possessing a pipe or weapon, ready to jump out and attack Jiemba seemed to be coming more common place and not out of the realm of possibilities.

"Come in my brother," a hollow voice called from the inside. "I am unarmed and alone. You have no reason to fear." Jiemba obeyed, as it was the only thing he could do. There was no point lingering as he had already been discovered. He pushed open the large double doors which revealed a large dining room, with a tremendously long polished timber table spanning the length of the room. Matching chairs sat politely along its edge, and at the table's far end stood a man. The figure was not watching Jiemba, instead he looked out of large windows which filled the entire wall. During the day time Jiemba imagined that you could see a long way from that vantage point.

"You can sit if you want," the voice broke the silence filled only by the heaviness of Jiemba's breathing.

"I would rather stay standing," Jiemba replied evenly.

"Your choice," the man shrugged finally turning to face the intruder.

"Are you truly here alone?" Jiemba asked. He wasn't sure if he could trust the answer, if one was given, but he wanted to believe that no one else would join them.

"Yes," the man said, moving slowly to sit at a seat about halfway down the side of the table. The location was easier for Jiemba to reach the man if he needed, and although the same could be said about the reverse Jiemba was not afraid. "Why would I risk others? What sort of person would that make me? I am sure that you were told many stories about me." He chuckled. "Perhaps ninjas will jump out from these old drapes. Or maybe a strike team will emerge from the basement. These ideas don't belong in the real world. The only person who brings in those thoughts to this place is you."

"There is no risk from me," Jiemba said, "I am alone and all I seek is answers."

"No risk," the man chuckled again. "Sorry if I find that hard to believe, when so many people have been taken in for no reason on this day. And you were one of those people doing the taking." There was a hint of anger in his voice, but he calmed enough to continue. "But I am getting ahead of myself, my brother, we have not been introduced to each other. My name is Shane Docker, most people call me Docker or Doc, very few call me Shane."

"I am Jiemba Tomson," Jiemba replied.

"I suspected," Docker nodded. "Which I must say upsets me."

"I don't care if you are upset," Jiemba said. "I am looking for answers so that I can resolve some great wrongs."

"You should care," Docker stood up taller, raising his voice. "You should care about everything that is happening here." Jiemba's whole body tensed, reacting to the sting in the man's words. "I was told that there was a man who had come to Wellington who could help us here. And that man had helped a community set itself up in the old missions. A community that had been outcast, run out, for no reason except that they have no place in someone else's desired social ideals. That man was strong, caring, inspiring. So much so that everyone forgot what had happened to them for a moment. That the children could see sparks of a future which was always out of reach, and through the light of this man they could see the path they needed to take to turn dreams into a reality. That man was supposed to be you. But, they must have been talking about someone else. I don't see a pathfinder here. You have crushed more dreams in one day than you could have possibly created out on that mission." There was spittle coming from his mouth. "What stands before me is a child, a boy who is easily led, who follows the easy instruction despite how wrong it is, to fulfil a basic desire."

"I lost a friend," Jiemba yelled back, "and he is gone because of someone you are hiding."

"We have all lost friends, and family, today alone many people lost more than one. Taken from the simple lives they tried to lead because their name was on a list. Surely you know how many people can fit into the back of a prison transport. Less than a small bus. All the people of Wellington don't fit on that bus." Docker was not intimidated despite being smaller and slimmer. The man was commanding the room regardless of who was or was not in it. "Every day there is a fight we are losing because lies are being told, and whether or not there is a man here who has done wrong to you, there is no way I will let your group take him."

"He is important," Jiemba blasted. "That community you were speaking of was betrayed by that man. He led a group that meant to cause them harm, that group destroyed what they had been working hard to create, that dream was gone in an instant, a better man was slain because he helped those people reach for that dream. You have no idea what that meant to me, what that helped me to believe in. After what I have gone through.”

“We have all gone through it, had dark clouds spread through our minds giving us more despair than simply what rain can bring, been a part of a fight which involves no fists or punches to be thrown,” Docker shot straight back, “but you take your grief and place it in a situation where you are applying different views, where you have no idea what is going on. Without that education, or being willing to learn, you are not going to be doing anything worthwhile. You are blinded and have become something no more than a common thug. I was wrong when I said you were one of them, you are worse. At least they stand for something, despite the evil intentions that drip from it. What do you stand for? Regardless what your ideals are, right is right, and blindly walking past that, to achieve some selfish end that you believe is important, adds more to the problem.”

“I just want the name of a location,” Jiemba said calmly. He understood the man’s anger, but the overall problem was not his. It probably should have been but he didn’t accept that.

“I gave you my name,” Docker replied far more subdued. “And I thank you for yours. But your presence here is not enough to force me to give you the name of another. You are searching for a man with a name, who you were told was important. Most likely he is the same as any other you had on your lists earlier. He may not be the man you search for, but one instead that your security team want you to find for them. You are no closer now to answers than when you walked in. Your friends will find no-one else on my property, no matter how hard they look, and no matter what they told you. And, despite how big you are, my resolve is stronger, you are not going to get anything else out of me.”

“You won’t help me at all?” Jiemba was annoyed, he refused to listen to what he told him. Lies were being spun and he needed to stay on course. "That man is the key to taking down a group who have destroyed so much good."

"You may think that, and in some aspects that may be true," Docker said. "But I can say the same thing about those who you represent."

"I represent no-one but myself," Jiemba replied.

"HA," Docker spat. "You look every bit like a pawn from that Spartan group. From your shirt down to your boots. But regardless whether you think you represent them or not, you most certainly don't represent yourself. You have no idea who you are, and until you do you will get nothing out of me. When you help yourself, then I will help you." Jiemba growled, but could see that he was getting nowhere and was unlikely to get any further. He turned to walk out of the room.

"The old man would be disappointed in you," Docker said softly as Jiemba made it to the door, "and he was so proud." Jiemba didn't look back, he could barely hide the quiver covering his face surfacing from his anger.

Jiemba just left.

Chapter 12 – Another Way

There had been no exit strategy, despite the one where Spartan captured a large vigilante group which didn't exist at all, and no order to wait for a pick up.

So Jiemba just walked.

He felt hollow, and for once he could pinpoint the reason. Usually while he walked he got caught up in his own head. This time he was thinking things over for himself. The feeling inside was a sense of failure. He had gone into the raid expecting to get either the man he was looking for, or his whereabouts; maybe even some extra information about who controlled the bikers and where Jiemba could find them. Instead he had left with nothing.

Not with nothing, with something else.

Jiemba felt he now carried a burden. He already hefted around the despair in JayDee's loss, but now he carried around Docker's words. Why would the expectation of someone who was being hunted for leading a mass revolt on law and order hit him so hard? The honest truth was that he was right. Jiemba had no idea who he was, had very little context of what was happening around him, and despite being someone who usually fought for the rights of everybody he was unable to do so.

Not unable, unwilling.

The closest he had come to realising who he was had been when he had managed to relax under the guidance of JayDee. He had calmed down enough to finally quiet the voices in his head and start recreating some form of himself. He tried to bring back all those images of faces and activities that had given him such joy. The tasks that he had achieved with the help of others, who had offered nothing but their time as it was all they had left. He found himself frowning as all those images and feelings were repressed from him.

It wasn't long after he had started walking that the cars started speeding back. The obvious looking white vans sped through town one after the other. The curfew was still in place so apart from the rare travelling car venturing through town there was nobody else around to see them. Jiemba imagined that the cars seemed angry and annoyed as they returned to the base of operations. No doubt because they too had gone foraging that night, hoping to be filled, but were retreating with nothing to show for it. The sight did not concern him, apart from Jerome not being located. Jiemba was not part of the security business and did not wish to be. They were a means to an end, and that end may never arrive.

"Hop in," Selena called out as a van pulled up alongside him. Jiemba climbed into the empty rear of the vehicle, a position he had become too familiar with, and silently sat for the duration of the return trip. Nothing further was said by anyone.

Upon the vehicle returning to the well-lit hangar-like Spartan headquarters Jiemba exited slowly and glanced around. There was a ruckus occurring near the doors leading off to the conference area. Jiemba could see Rogers raging in that space, others fled before him as his anger flared. Large metal containers, bins, tool cupboards and anything he could get his hands on were hurled into the air. Loud crashes where the items had made contact with polished concrete or solid steel echoed through the area. Some security officers had been hurt in the wake of his violent outbursts.

"Nothing, we came away with nothing," he roared. He temporarily saw Jiemba, pointed a quivering finger in his direction, and started stomping his way towards him.

"You," Rogers thundered. "Think you are so big, but you couldn't hold one guy. You are nothing, you are useless." Jiemba simply blinked. He was taken aback by the outburst, but he was neither intimidated nor afraid. He would be quite happy to have a physical argument with the man, Jiemba had already had enough of his boorish attitude. Rogers was lucky that Jiemba had shown so much restraint so far. Usually he would have been flattened well before now.

"Rogers," Price emerged from behind a door nearby, his voice immediately filling the room; stopping any actions dead in their tracks. Rogers stopped in the same instant, but shook as he continued to stare down Jiemba. "I want to see you, now." A slow smile spread across Jiemba's face, which he knew was only going to taunt Rogers further. Rogers tilted his head and his eyes formed thin slits as he contemplated his next actions. "NOW," Price boomed again. Rogers appeared to hiss, but obeyed. He turned and walked towards the Spartan boss, the other employees gave him a wide berth as he passed by.

"Guy needs a hobbie," Selena whispered to Jiemba, which made his smile return.

"That bloke is so high strung," Jiemba said laughing loudly, "knitting would suit him, but I would be worried about what he would do with the needles." The laughter grew louder, Selena joining in but hid it behind a slender hand.

"Yeah," Selena agreed. "I can understand him being disappointed, but there are ways you show it and ways you don't. It just isn't professional."

"I had no idea that knocking someone out with a trash can was a bad idea," Jiemba snorted as his laughter continued. Selena continued with him, until slowly the laughter subsided. Jiemba suddenly felt sorry for the guy who had been knocked out by that trash can.

"Hey," she started, seeming to be instantly more serious, "I know the last few days have been hard for you. Did you want to debrief, discuss anything about tonight or anything else? Sometimes it is best just to get it off your chest." Jiemba's smile vanished from his face. He hadn't been prepared for that. The idea had a lot of merit. He had been encouraged to share while he was in JayDee's care, but it somehow didn't seem appropriate.

"Thanks," Jiemba replied, "I think I am just going to turn in though. Maybe another time. I would hate to drop stuff on you the very first day we meet." Selena nodded with another warm smile.

"Anytime," she replied. Jiemba smiled back, and waved awkwardly at her. Trying not to run, or appear like he was fleeing, he swiftly moved away to rest in his allocated room.

Jiemba slept soundly. He had no nightmares or visions. Nothing reminding him of what had happened or what was happening around him. There was just a void of nothingness and Jiemba welcomed it. When he awoke he was aware that it was before dawn. He had no desire to hang around for hours until told to do something. He got refreshed with a shower, got dressed in clean clothes, and went for a walk. The guards put out a hand to stop him from leaving but Jiemba snorted his amusement at the notion. He brushed past them, informing them that he would be back. He looked towards the stadium on his left, which hid the rest of the town from his view, then turned to the newer developed area on the right and walked that way.

There had been a heavy dew fall throughout the night, linked with an almost subzero temperature that had cast a silver veil over the usually green grass. Despite there being no rain the ground was moist, in some parts it was crunchy as ice had still managed to infiltrate the ground in some areas. As he looked around he realised something for what was probably the first time ever.

Wellington was a beautiful place.

Not just the new parts, but the old just as much. Jiemba looked up at the apartment high-rises which existed on every street in this part of the town. He glanced upon how pristine they appeared, with the latest in popular architectural design shining down upon the rest of the town as the early sunlight crept up at Jiemba's back. They brought a sense of class which wasn't there previously, and he wondered if that was what had been lacking in the town before. He shook his head at the idea. It created a new class, which created a comparison between what was present now to what had existed before. Like apples and oranges they shouldn't be compared as each had their own charm that the other could never have. And you couldn't turn an apple into an orange because you threw money at it.

He quickly made it to the end of the street. Jiemba, despite looking like a tourist to a big city with his eyes constantly looking skyward, did not want to linger where he suspected he wasn't wanted. He knew that the people who were early risers would be looking down from behind the tinted windows above him, and he knew that in one look they were casting judgement as to why he was there. He knew that few, if any, would be happy at his presence. He knew the feeling far better than he should.

The street was a straight one though, and it led to the edge of town. He arrived at the base of one of the mountains that bordered Wellington's western side. The development had extended almost the entire road behind him, with more land cordoned off for future construction. In the hills above him he could see more new houses hidden amongst the giant blue trees on the mountain side. He ignored these, instead choosing to focus on the natural features which stood gloriously before him. He took a deep breath, as if filling himself with this air somehow gave him more strength than the oxygen within the town.

JayDee had told Jiemba about how and why the mountains were named. He had argued at the time that it was something his friend Dennis would have found more interesting, but Jiemba did somehow take it all in. The names of the three main peaks were called Arthur, Wellesley and Duke. The peaks, alongside the town itself, were named after Lord Arthur Wellesley, Duke of Wellington, and British General of the Peninsula Wars opposing Napoleon in Portugal and Spain. The area supposedly set to be the spot where a capital city in the west of NSW was to be built. An idea that had long ago been dismissed. Jiemba walked to the road's edge and sat on a large boulder which would probably be moved in the future. He swept the leaves aside as

he perched, the natural growth still surrounding him. The boulder
was large enough for him to lay on, albeit at an inclined angle, which
is exactly what he did. The sun rose from behind, and as it did it
illuminated more of the mountains as light started from the tip and
spread to the bottom. He was watching the flow of time occur before
him and he could feel nature replenish the life force within him.

It didn't do the whole job but it was a start.

Eventually he made the journey back to the Spartan headquarters,
dodging traffic as people returned to their normal lives with the
curfew now over. The guards glared at him as he walked past them,
he had no identification and no proof that would normally allow
admittance, and Jiemba knew they had not been happy when he left.
Still, they made no move against him and said no words to reprimand
him. He looked in through the enormous hangar doors, his head
aching at how busy it looked. His eyes followed the building to its
western side where he saw a flight of stairs leading up to a balcony
that looked over towards the area designated New Wellington, and
the place he had just explored. As he climbed the stairs he glanced
down at his phone. He had placed it on silent mode the night before
and he had seen no reason to remove the function. The whole
purpose was for him to contact Price if he needed help. An unlikely
scenario except if a vehicle was needed. The home screen showed that
he had several missed call. Normally that would be cause for alarm,
but Jiemba just slipped it back into his pocket and left it unanswered.

"I was watching you walk back along the road," Selena's soothing
voice spoke to him as he reached the top.

"Just clearing my head," Jiemba replied, "sometimes a walk alone
is better than anything else." He walked over to her side, noticing
that there were many people filling the conference room behind
them.

"I understand," she said, "but sometimes it is also good to talk
about it." Jiemba nodded at her suggestion, which was the same as
the night before. He couldn't help but try and identify the faces in the
room behind him. "Price has been looking for you all morning."

"I saw that someone left me a bunch of messages," Jiemba acknowledged. "I didn't feel like being attached to a phone this morning, and I am sure he will survive. What does he want?"

"He wants to see you," Selena continued. "He has been in meetings all morning, despite it still being really early. He is talking to the leaders of his main force at the moment as he organises the transfer of prisoners over to the correctional facilities. Not an easy task as they have to be designated between the different locations. High risk to low risk." Jiemba nodded but he wasn't really interested. He did take a moment to realise just how important Price was to this whole operation. Jiemba suddenly realising that he had probably had more individual conversations with the senior officer in one day than many workers here had probably had their entire time in the job.

"You asked if I wanted to talk," Jiemba spoke to Selena without looking straight at her. He had felt something with her despite their only recent acquaintance, and he had decided that he would rather talk with her than anyone else.

"The offer still stands," Selena said in reply. She didn't turn towards him, instead focusing on the same part of the mountain range that Jiemba was. Jiemba nodded and then started.

"I am not from here," Jiemba said, "not from Wellington directly. I come from Orange but I have family everywhere. I have dabbled in many things, and although I am okay at most I am amazing at none. I enjoy footy and hanging out with my friends, but I am the most comfortable with my family. Some of my best friends are almost as close as family." As an active listener Jiemba could see Selena smile with the positive aspects, but did not interrupt. "All that sounds great, and is enough for anybody, it is enough for me. But . . . sometimes, frequently sometimes, I get stuck in my head. I argue with myself about what I should and shouldn't be doing, about what is right for me and what is good for everyone else."

"Who wins?" she asked quietly.

"Everyone else," Jiemba replied with a sigh. "I know how much of a burden my problems are for me, so why would I give that to someone else? Who am I to whinge about what is happening in my life when other people have so much going on in theirs? I think it is best to help others out, support them through their stuff, or treat everyone with a smile so that they think everything is okay, at least in that moment."

"Then they keep coming back," Selena added.

"They do," Jiemba confirmed, "and then I feel like I know so much about what is happening with people that I can't possibly make it about me, that would be selfish."

"Yet you get no help, and you get everyone else's problems," Selena was following what he was saying. He had expected her to rebuff his train of thought. "It has to come to a breaking point."

"It has," Jiemba said with a nod. "Several times, and it almost ended in a big way. I feel like a fraud, because I am the one who stands up in front of everyone, waving the flag for support, raising money for every charity, showing the face of positive energy, of Aboriginal and men's health, when I feel like garbage inside a lot of the time."

"Anxiety and depression walk hand in hand," Selena whispered. "I am no counsellor, but I am something of a fighter, and even I know that when you are attacked by more than one thing it is hard to fight off, no matter how strong you are, and even then it is almost impossible to do when you don't believe you can." She extended a hand out and grabbed at Jiemba's as it gripped the rail. Her touch was smooth and safe, yet strong and focused. "That's why even the strongest of us need a friend, need a friend to talk with. It doesn't matter if you can take a hit with a metal poll, walk alone into a warzone, or be covered in cultural tattoos."

"I'm not covered in tattoos," Jiemba corrected, "but I get where you are coming from. I never used to though. Which is why I need to get this done. For the first time in a long time I found a space where I could just be me, where I could do what I wanted, where no one had any expectations of me, and I had to earn my spot on what I did. It finally gave me the confidence to talk, to lead. Then it was all taken away. I have to think that it meant something more to me, something that I am willing to hold onto. But even now the darker thoughts are crawling back."

"You will get over it," another voice interrupted. Jiemba didn't have to turn around to know it was Rogers. "Everyone gets depressed sometimes, you just think of something happy and it's all over with. Move on. That's what I did last night."

"No, what you did was make a huge mess after throwing a massive tantrum," Selena snarled in Jiemba's defence. "And you didn't just get over it, Price threatened you with your job if you ever did it again." Rogers smirked smugly, he stayed leaning against the bricks near one of the doors leading from the conference room. "I have no idea how long you have been standing there, but you have no idea about what you are saying."

"Like hell I don't," Rogers replied. He swaggered towards the pair with a stupid smile. "Jiemba here is feeling useless because that's all he is. You would think that a guy his size, that is as frightening as he is, as strong as he pretends to be, would actually be able to do some good and be useful. But instead he gives some sob story about how hard it is to get out of bed in the morning."

"Rogers, stop," Selena continued.

"See," Rogers did not stop. "The poor little guy can't even stand up for himself. He is no different to anybody else around here, cos' he has no idea what is good for him, except when to pull his head in so that he doesn't get it knocked off. And just like them I would be happy to give him a lesson and put him in his place." Jiemba spun on his heel, finally hearing enough.

"Let's do this," Jiemba suggested.

"Jiemba," another voice called out. Price had stepped through the glass doors leading into the conference room. "I need to see you now."

"Oops," Rogers whispered. "Looks like once again you did nothing. And, it's likely, you, will, be, gone." He smiled again, as if inviting Jiemba to hit him. A soft touch wiped at his arm as Selena silently urged him to move away. Jiemba obeyed the suggestion without looking back at the woman. Rogers waved mockingly as he went.

"Jiemba, follow me," Price demanded as he entered the room. Price led him out of the door and into a small room on the next floor up. Jiemba realised it was the highest location in the entire complex. Price opened the only door along a small corridor at the top of the stairs and waited for Jiemba to enter, promptly closing and locking the door with a loud click the moment he was in. The room had no windows, the door being the only way in or out of the room, and was occupied by a desk, a few chairs for guests, and a large black leather chair behind the desk.

The chair was occupied by a striking woman, in a sharp black jacket and deep red hair.

"Hello," Jiemba said, unable to hide the confusion from his voice. He was completely calm despite wanting to throw Rogers out of the building only moments before. The woman did not reply, instead gesturing for Jiemba to sit in one of the chairs opposite her. Reminded of times when he had been called into the principal's office at school, and on very few occasions was it for a good reason, Jiemba declined and chose to stand.

"Jiemba," Price interrupted the stalemate, announcing that despite being hidden in a corner that he was also present in the room. The woman rose to her feet to sit comfortably on the edge of the desk. "This is one of the sponsors I was telling you about who gives us financial support and information vital to the success of our operations." Price paused as if the statement was supposed to impress Jiemba. It did not, and Price, despite seeing this, continued. "Last night we reached a dead end in regards to our investigation into the murder of your friend and the tracking down of those responsible. Thanks to our sponsor we have received some information that will assist us greatly." Jiemba showed the slightest hint of interest, but he was not holding his breath.

"As I told you before," Price continued, "our relationship with the local authorities is strained. So much so that they are most uncooperative with us despite our efforts to help in reducing, and removing, crime and unwanted activity in the area.”

“You have told me this,” Jiemba was more annoyed than interested. “What does that matter?”

“Because this entire time they have known the location of Jerome Less and have withheld that information,” Price reported, noting the immediate frown he received from Jiemba’s face.

“What do you mean? Where is he?” Jiemba demanded with confusion.

“The local authorities were aware of the threat that Jerome presented to the town at large and your little community, and they had him under surveillance. On the morning of the attack, they received indication that he had threatened violence and they arrested him. This would have been why he was not present during the raid on the mission. That afternoon they moved him from the holding station at the police station and straight into Wellington Star Five, the high security correctional facility just outside of Wellington. He has been there for the last few days.”

“Why didn’t they tell us?” Jiemba said with frustration. “Gumbo knew when I was standing there with both of you, yet he wouldn’t let us know that and we have been chasing ghosts all over town ever since.”

“It appears like the crash on the carrier was an attempt on Jerome’s life, except that he had already been moved earlier,” Price answered. “Gumbo has been neck deep in everything that has been going on around here and can’t be trusted. He didn’t even process Jerome, there are no leads on who his accomplices are or where they could be.”

“So that’s it then,” Jiemba finally did sit, defeat pressed heavily on him. “We found him, but he can’t help us. It was all for nothing.”

“Not quite,” Price continued. “As you are aware we are still holding many of the escapees that we captured yesterday. They are to be transported in the next few hours to all the facilities, including Wellington Star Five.”

"So we can talk to him at the same time?" Jiemba was slightly uplifted.

"No, we can't," Price brought him straight back down again. "It is called Star Five because it is a five star establishment and one of the most secure facilities that can be found in the business. That is for everyone else's safety, but also for theirs, which is definitely appropriate in this case. It doesn't help us, but it means no-one else can get to him either."

"So why are we talking about this then?" Jiemba was even more confused.

"Because there is another way," the sponsor finally spoke up. Her voice was like velvet but immediately had a vice like grip on his ears. "Price is correct in that this would normally be a dead end, however, I can assist you here."

"How?" Jiemba was not convinced.

"Usually I would not condone such action, but, the success of the Spartan security group is dependent on removing all threats to the community. If we don't know who the threats are how can they be removed? I, fortunately, have a couple of men on the inside of Wellington Star Five. One that can get you in to a point, and the other who is already looking after this Jerome creature so that he is removed from harm. I present to you an opportunity, that is all. To you it provides a means to obtain information. For Price and his company it provides evidence to show that the local authorities are not to be trusted. Very soon I will not be able to guarantee the safety of your man as I will need to ensure the safety of my own people. Therefore it needs to be done today. You will be able to speak to the man you seek, but you may also have to remove my people from the facility if they are compromised." Jiemba was calculating what it all meant.

"We are accepting the offer Jiemba," Price spoke again. "For its success we would need you to be a part of the group. It is the only chance we will have."

"So we are breaking into prison?" Jiemba asked.

"Hopefully not," Price corrected him. "We are going in with prisoners, and simply overstaying our welcome for a couple of minutes to get information. Then we leave. That's it." Jiemba kept calculating, but no matter the equation in his head he pulled out no answers. A moment before he was sunk and falling back towards his depressive cycle, now he had a chance to resolve it once and for all. The means in doing so was indeed a concern. The inner voice he heard so often filled with the mocking laughter of Docker.

"And you are sure he is there?" Jiemba asked.

"I can show you on the security cameras if you want," Price suggested, "we have access to those." Jiemba thought for another second, then he was done.

"Count me in," Jiemba declared, "let's end this." Price immediately became busy with the next step in the process. The sponsor simply smiled at him.

Chapter 13 – Two steps forward, three steps back.

Jiemba was in vehicle five. It was the last of five transports taking prisoners to Wellington Star Five, however, in the convoy there were another dozen vehicles trailing behind them going towards the other facilities. He sat in the rear of the vehicle in the guard's position, keeping watch on a dozen people who were chained to the seat in front of them. He wore no weapons, but none of them had bothered to cast an eye or a word in his direction.

Rogers was in one of the other vehicles going to Star Five, instructed to take the lead and to avoid Jiemba at all costs. Price wasn't with them, and to Jiemba's knowledge neither was Selena. She could have been amongst one of the other transports but he hadn't seen which one.

The plan was simple. Each of the transports would individually go into the correctional facility as per the guidelines that the place had set out. Each prisoner would be processed in a separate room under the watch of the facilities staff. Rogers would oversee the whole operation, ensuring the process started and finished smoothly. Both the manager of the facility and Price were making a show of making no mistakes to prove that they were both worthy of the trust of the public. Rogers would see each group on and off the base, providing an efficient face to the Spartan group's image. Jiemba laughed at the idea.

Jiemba's job was to escort the last group in. Once the group was being processed he was no longer required to be present and could wait in a guard's room. At this point he would be redirected, given a disguise to ensure that they couldn't trace him back anywhere, and then be granted time with Jerome Less. The time wouldn't be long and Jiemba needed to get what he wanted before it ran out or his chances were done. Then he would simply leave and rejoin the rest of the group, regather at Spartan headquarters, and, after acquiring the names of those involved, would immediately hunt down those who were responsible.

Simple.

Jiemba chose to ignore the simplicity of the plan and focus on other things on the small journey out. Almost as soon as they left the headquarters he was retracing the steps he had taken the night before. It was different during the daytime. The shroud of darkness was gone and everything looked far less sinister. They passed the fortress that was Docker's dwelling and just like he thought the night before, despite not being able to see big portions of it, it still looked like a rundown older style house. A renovators dream with the size of the house and the land it stood upon. They then passed the site of the carrier crash, which, apart from small hidden fragments of wreckage reflecting sunlight from the grass, had been completely cleared as if nothing had ever happened.

Jiemba couldn't help but stare at the country side all around them. What once had been endless paddocks of dry crops filled with hungry livestock, now contained glimpses of the future. That future was again the one that JayDee had told him about. Instead of wheat, barley or Lucerne the fields were filled with row upon row of solar panels. They stretched from the roadside all the way to the far hills and beyond. Jiemba tried to pick a single row to count how many panels were located in each, just so he could do some simple maths involving arrays to come to an approximate number of how many panels there were in total. He arrived at an approximation, which he knew would be an underestimation, and the number was staggering. He had no idea what each panel would produce electricity wise but he presumed it was enough to power the city of Wellington if not the entire Central West region. Added to these were the enormous wind turbines which climbed high into the sky, taller than any other building, new or old, that already existed in the town. These turbines, which were located in every other paddock, were far easier to count, but there were still dozens of these. Jiemba hadn't seen anything like this anywhere and was shocked to know that these had just popped up seemingly overnight to him, but also that the location for such a focus of renewable energy had been Wellington. Every paddock they passed was filled with even more power structures and batteries, along with countless people maintaining them. Unsurprisingly the paddocks were still multipurposed, many of them still sheltering livestock which hid beneath the large structures.

When they finally arrived at the correctional facility it required a long time sitting idle in line. Jiemba was fine with that. In fact, despite not really liking sitting around he made good use of the time. He was not worried about those that he watched, and knew that should anything happen he could deal with it. He instead sat in silence and worked on controlling his breathing. It was a technique he had practised years before, and sporadically ever since, under the guidance of his Uncle Lou, but the method enabled him to play a didgeridoo with some success. He inhaled through his nose with his cheeks inflated. He would then breathe out of his mouth while keeping his cheeks just as full. Then he would do it again, but the next time he would squeeze his lips tight before slowly pushing the air out of his mouth. He would have to tighten his jaw and cheek muscles, which he found came easier now than ever before. Every now and then he would let out a 'Ha' sound, which was not a laugh but just a sound, and he would push it out from deep inside his core. Jiemba smiled every now and then, but he found that he was so focused on what he was doing that all the voices in his head faded away. He felt truly in the moment, but also elsewhere, above it perhaps. Time flowed by but it seemed inconsequential now. He snuck a look at the prisoners who sat in the back with him. Some still avoided his eye, others were interested or confused in what he was doing; a few of them were mimicking him as they tried to do it as well. Perhaps feeling like it could help them to stay calm like it had just done for him. Jiemba decided to teach them how to do it if they were willing. Soon most of the group were trying. There was a range of backgrounds present in the background, and although the Aboriginal group were more keen initially, knowing that it could help them play a didgeridoo, some others joined in as well. There was nothing better to do. Jiemba still saw others who looked at him with contempt, as if saying how dare he show them something so sensitive to them, how dare he give hope to prisoners who sat in front of them. He was a captor, not a teacher or a colleague.

"It's our turn now," the driver piped up from the security of his barricaded front seat. "Start getting ready." Jiemba started going through the process as he had been briefly shown. The group didn't fight him, forming a line outside and individually being shown where they had to go and what they had to do. There were enough guards for two per each new inmate making Jiemba's presence almost redundant. When the last person entered the confinement area Jiemba followed and was greeted with a well-lit, yet concrete dense, hallway with several interrogation style rooms leading away from it. Within each there was a bathroom, changing station, and an opportunity to eat before they were designated a number and a room and taken to where they would remain for the foreseeable future. There were not enough for every newcomer so some were made to wait under the watchful eyes of the guards.

"Everything okay?" Rogers asked as he walked towards Jiemba. It was more of a statement as nothing was going wrong from where he stood. "You waited out there a long time. The guard's room is just down the hall there, first door on the left. There is a nice guy in there called Adam, big guy, almost the size of you. He can help you out with what you need." Rogers gave him a somewhat firm pat on the arm. It sounded like he was being civil but it was all part of the act. Both men knew how much they loathed the other, but somehow both had managed to remain professional. Jiemba nodded at him, noting the name as it was the information that he needed for the next stage. He followed the directions he had been given and entered the room only moments later. The guard's room was as you would imagine, storeroom off to one side with a combination lock on the door, television hanging on one wall, which was not on at the moment, several tables and chairs littered the space in a cluttered fashion.

"Okay, here is what you need," the only person in the room, who he had presumed was Adam and the name badge pinned to his chest confirmed it, walked over to him with a small package. "You can get changed around the corner there, no one will come in but it is a little more discreet. Once you are finished you can come back here and I will lead you to an isolated interrogation room. You will have no more than five minutes from the moment you walk in."

"Thanks," Jiemba replied.

"I would need more than your thanks if we get caught," Adam growled back at him. "This is more than my job, now hurry up. The sooner you're ready the sooner we will finish." Jiemba took the package, and the hint, swiftly moving to the designated space to gain the small amount of privacy required. It was a completely different uniform, just in case someone was to spot them he would not be identified as one of the Spartan group. Even then, if he was questioned, it would be easy enough to say that he wasn't a part of the group. He stripped down to his underwear and carefully unwrapped the package so he could hide his own clothes inside while he was gone. The dark slacks hugged at his figure but weren't restrictive, and it was a similar story for the shirt which clung to his big frame. A smart sleek jumper with an inbuilt hood which folded into the collar was the final part of the ensemble. As he pulled it over his head, shifting it so that it sat comfortably on his large physique, he noticed a single amber light start to flicker in the changing area.

"What is going on?" Jiemba asked as he returned back into the guard area.

"There has been a breach," Adam replied with alarm as he leaned over one of the computer terminals at a desk at the side of the room. "And before you ask I don't mean you."

"What does that mean?" Jiemba asked impatiently.

"It means we have a change of plan," Adam spoke what Jiemba feared. His opportunity had evaporated before he had even had the chance to take it. "In fact the plan is no longer on the table." Jiemba felt his heart drop, but at the same time his brain engaged reality. It was a highly secure facility, supposedly one of the best in the country, how could there have been a breach?

"Maybe I can help you?" Jiemba offered.

"Ha, no thanks," Adam scoffed at him as he continued to focus on the screen. "You aren't supposed to be here anyway, so I don't know how I explain that one away. It is best if you stay here, get changed, and return to your group. I promise you will be safe there."

"The breach makes it seem like an empty promise," Jiemba replied, and receiving a sneer for his efforts. Adam poked a finger at the screen then scanned the map which hung on the wall beside him. In the next second he was gone, having already secured the weapons he needed to secure the breach. There was an amber light which glowed overhead, a moment later it flicked to red. Jiemba assumed the situation had gotten worse.

The room shook as a loud blast could be heard from somewhere deeper into the complex. Lockers wobbled in reply but none tipped. A mug which sat on the edge of the kitchenette bench slipped to the ground and shattered. Jiemba would not be getting changed or following Adam's instructions. He glanced at the monitor that Adam had left open in his haste to leave. On it was a series of small screens showing a live feed from several different cameras throughout the facility. One showed the main area that he had entered, where he could see the last of the inmates he had brought in preparing to enter interrogation rooms. Another showed the vehicles waiting patiently outside for the return of Jiemba and Rogers. Other cameras showed several other spots, many of which revealed nothing untoward happening. One, the camera in the bottom left corner of the screen, was showing smoke bellowing from a building close to the outside fence. Jiemba clicked on it, which resulted in the focus being placed on it but the surrounding images were replaced by other cameras that were close by. Jiemba watched in shock as one after the other these cameras revealed more and more intruders, cutting through fences or blasting their own openings to gain access. He could see a parade of bikes being ridden around the outside of the complex. Jiemba stared at one camera in particular, pressing a finger on it again which resulted in a much larger image.

"No way," Jiemba leaned forward with more interest. The image in front of him showed many people, that he presumed were bikers as there were many taking up places in the background, but the one in the centre directing what was happening took up all of his attention. The rider was wearing a helmet like many of the others, but this one showed the image of a snake.

He had seen that image before.

In the top of the screen he could see a location for the camera. He glanced at the map beside him, just like Adam had done, and quickly found the location. Jiemba kept his finger pinned to the spot and glanced at other spots where there had been disturbances. They were all in the same area leading towards the cell blocks.

"They are going for Jerome," Jiemba said out loud. He looked at the map one more time, finding what would be the quickest route and memorising it. Then he was running out the door.

"Jiemba," Rogers called out as soon as he exited. "What is going on?"

"The biker group that we are looking for is here," Jiemba exclaimed. "There are a heap outside but some have broken through the fences and making their way towards where the inmates are kept. I think they are going for Jerome. If they get there first this will be all over." Rogers seemed perplexed at the news, but, to his credit, he acted immediately clutching at his phone and making a call.

"Yes I want a security crew here now," Rogers roared into the phone, "everyone we have got. Containment is required." He slammed it back into his pocket and started barking orders to a group of Spartan employees he had standing nearby. "All of you are with me," he shouted at them, before moving over to the information desk. "Which way do we need to go?"

"I don't know," stammered the guard. "But you aren't supposed to be in there."

"I do," interrupted Jiemba, "though all the doors are shut."

"Open the doors then," Rogers demanded. The man shook his head pleading he could not, but it didn't take much convincing that everyone in the premises were in danger to change his mind. "That man there is in your uniform, he can take us the rest of the way. We can help."

"I can only open the internal doors," the guard said after accepting that Jiemba was one of the guards stationed at the facility. He then set about pressing multiple buttons in front of him. "But they will all have to be shut again before the outside doors can be opened, and I can't open them from here."

"Whatever," Rogers snarled, "just do it." As soon as the first door was open the group was off and running. A wailing alarm rose to greet them, cheering them on as they followed the flashing red lights in the corridor. They entered chamber after chamber as the doors slowly opened in front of them until finally they had come to the last one. The doors closed automatically behind them and they stood in front of another information desk that was heavily barricaded.

"Open the door already," Rogers barked to the crew hidden behind it.

"You don't give orders around here mate," the man replied. "And you lot shouldn't be in here anyway. We are dealing with the situation and until it is resolved you lot will remain right where you are. Then we are all going to have a long hard talk."

"Is this part of your plan?" Rogers growled at Jiemba.

"No," Jiemba replied under his breath, "my plan was to get inside to secure the prisoners, get our contact to a safe place, and then go and get those responsible for my friend's death."

"Well as usual you are showing that whatever your plan may be, you are useless in executing it," Rogers stabbed at Jiemba, causing his anger to grow.

"Open the door now, or someone will get hurt," Jiemba ordered, receiving mockery and laughter in reply.

"If you aren't careful that person will be you," the person replied from behind the safety of the wall. His voice was mechanical as it came through the speakers. "I am even less likely to take orders from you than him. Now show me your passes. I think that you guys are intruders just like the others. I might get a promotion from this station if I catch you as well as the others." Jiemba glared at the man, then shared the look with Rogers. Jiemba bit down hard trying to calm himself. Everything he needed was on the other side of that door.

"Open it," Jiemba roared. The man was unintimidated.

"What are you going to do about it?" the man replied. Jiemba had had enough. He turned his back on them and walked over towards the heavy steel door which sat on sliders. He could hear laughter from the guards behind him as his intention of opening the door became apparent.

"Clearly you aren't all there," the guardsman chortled, "give up mate and we will take that into account later." Jiemba had heard enough. He grunted slightly, tensing all of his muscles as he gripped one side of the enormous door. He pulled hard on one side and found it no more difficult than opening a tin can with a ring pull attached. The door grated noisily as he shifted it, then, still under the shroud of anger he had built as they laughed at him, Jiemba pulled the door clear and slammed it into the barricade behind him, in which the guard and his crew had stood laughing. Jiemba couldn't hear them through the communication speaker anymore, and he hoped there was a back door to the room because he had destroyed the entire front of it.

"One more door," Rogers said, seemingly hiding his shock at what Jiemba had been able to do. Another far smaller electric door had been hidden behind the first. "And I bet the controls were in that room you just destroyed."

"I can open this one easier than the last one," Jiemba replied, taking a deep breath, "still think I am useless?"

"Yes," Rogers was not impressed. "You have done nothing but open a door."

"How about you open this one then?" Jiemba remarked.

"I have a different set of skills," Rogers replied, "and you are wasting our time." Jiemba snorted his derision at the security officer. He turned towards the last door. "But if you insist." Rogers pulled something from his bag and placed it along the edge of the door and along the wall beside it.

"Stand back," he instructed everyone, then smiled at Jiemba. "Anything you can do, I can do better. Because I simply am better than you." Before Jiemba could shoot back at him, or ask why in the world he would have his own explosives kit stored away, Rogers flicked open the lid on a device he carried and flicked the toggle. "This was just in case." Rogers smiled again.

"Hold your ears." Rogers pressed the only remaining button and the wall exploded in front of them. The debris exploded away from the group, causing the wall to fall into an outside area. Light filled the smoke filled chamber immediately. Jiemba noticed that this section of the prison had no alarms blaring or lights flickering to reveal that any danger was occurring elsewhere. He could see guards walking normally on upper platforms of what he could see as a multi-storey structure. There were inmates out of their containment areas and other guards keeping a closer eye on them. The squealing of alarms kicked off in the next second, and the flashing lights joined them in creating a chaotic scene. He could see the guards scramble out of the way while others found phones, or walkie talkies to report what had just happened.

Jiemba found a section of the door which had crumbled. Instead of being flat it had been rolled so that it resembled a large metal pole. He had noticed the cameras inside the room and assumed it would be useful to at least try and keep up the façade of being just like anybody else, despite him having just ripped a massive blast door away. The shape looked like a battering ram so that is what he would use it as. Rogers moved forward with his group, their black jackets pulled tight around them as the rest of the team was smeared an equally dark shade thanks to the smoke and the heat from the explosion.

Jiemba knew what Jerome looked like but had no idea what cell he was in. There had to be at least a hundred rooms in this section of the correctional facility alone. He heard a call come from one of the rooms nearby and headed in that direction.

"Over there," Rogers directed him, "knock it down." Jiemba obeyed for the time being, hefting his large chunk of solid metal in the direction of the door. It struck with a mighty clang, shattering the lock mechanism and bending the door slightly. Confusion was setting in for all the inmates who were either yelling swear words down at him or cheering for them to be released next. It wasn't a jailbreak, Jiemba reminded himself, it was just essential and the only way to secure information that he needed.

The smoke haze from the explosion had started to clear but it was still hard to see. Jiemba peered into the cell, expecting and hoping to see Jerome so that he could leave the man to Rogers and seek out the person with the snake helmet. He found that he couldn't move at all, and that the man inside was not Jerome.

"Ah, Jiemba," the inmate spoke to him softly as he casually walked out from the cell. "So nice to see you." Jiemba froze on the spot. Memories came flooding back to him that he had suppressed since his time at the lake. Images of Jiemba dancing around a smoking fire as he completed a smoking ceremony for his rugby team, only to be greeted by harsh words. The same harsh words that would send him spiralling into a state of depression that would almost kill him.

The harsh words that were spoken by the youth that stood before him.

"Jiemba," the young man yelled at him as Jiemba stood motionless. The man stepped forward and slapped him hard across the face, removing Jiemba's hood from his head in the process. Both seemed shocked at the action. For the first time in a long time Jiemba felt pain shoot into his cheek where he had been struck. The fact that he had felt it was one thing, how this young upstart had managed to hurt him, when so many other things had not been able to, was another.

"Jiemba," Rogers interrupted his thoughts. "Get to work. Show us the way." The last command was towards the young man who nodded and started casually pointing to several other cells.

"Why are you opening so many?" Jiemba questioned. "We only need Jerome."

"You only need Jerome," Rogers bit back, "we need more than just your little snitch. There is a far bigger picture here that once again you don't see. Just open the cells." Not knowing who was in which as the doors were completely obscured, Jiemba obeyed knocking down each as they were pointed out. He had knocked down more than half a dozen as he finally reached the last door. His makeshift battering ram had already disintegrated and he had been forced to knock several down with his bare hands. He did the same here and the door tumbled in effortlessly.

"That is him," Jiemba growled.

"Get them all," Rogers ordered. "Then let's get out of here."

"This way to the outside area," the youth replied, "through that door."

"You know what to do," Rogers ushered Jiemba towards the door as the rest of his team grabbed hold of those prisoners who had been released. Jiemba punched it through, listening as the pins within the hinges snapped and ricocheted down the small hallway. There was no way that all those cameras around the place didn't discover what he had been doing with his sheer might alone. Jiemba was surprised as the scene outside showed far more chaos than what had happened inside. Buildings were smoking, fences tilting dangerously from side to side, guards cowering atop towers. How didn't they know this was happening inside the cells? Surely there had been communication.

Jiemba pushed past the group and raced out onto the field.

"No," he yelled. The group that had infiltrated from the outside had gone. Some had been captured by a small group of Spartan forces that had arrived, but the rest could be heard roaring on their bikes back down along the highway which bordered the premises. Safe from the Spartan group's reach and too far away for Jiemba to pursue.

"Come on," Rogers called out, his crew already sprinting towards where some vehicles were idling in wait outside the fence line. "I don't mind leaving you here though." Jiemba growled but set off behind him. The first of the two vehicles was filled but the door was still open. The young figure hung out from within the door and smiled at Jiemba. Jiemba looked at him, eyes staring straight at and through the youth, hoping his gaze could be like bullets. The young man gave a mocking wave, before shutting the door and allowing the van to speed off. Jiemba let out a groan reminiscent of a wounded animal. He lurched into the rear of the remaining vehicle, slammed the door and felt the transport immediately speed forward. Rogers sat near the front, but apart from only a few inmates and the security personal who held them Jiemba sat alone at the back.

He had been swept along in a crazy moment that resulted in failure. He had been responsible for the break out of several inmates considered dangerous, when all he had wanted was a conversation. The bikie group were to blame, but Jiemba doubted it would be seen that way. There was no chance Jiemba would be exempt from whatever fall out there may be. The leader of that group got away, he hadn't even gotten close to them when he could have ended the whole thing. Yet somehow none of that was the worst thing.

The boy.

The boy was the worst. The focus of Jiemba's breakdown and push towards complete darkness, in which Jiemba had completely lost everything about himself, was free. Jiemba imagined what terrible thing he had done to be placed in a maximum security prison, and now Jiemba had released him along with many others. He had hurt him again, physically, and it was like he had been hit by the hammer of hell.

Rogers was right. Jiemba was useless. The day had been a failure, no matter how you looked at it.

And Jet, the torment of Jiemba's nightmares, had returned.

Chapter 14 – The meeting

"What do you mean I can't see them?" Jiemba asked the secretary who sat cowering behind his desk.

"Like I told you already," the secretary trembled in response. It had been a couple of days since the incident at Wellington Star Five and word had gotten around about the strength that Jiemba possessed. That knowledge, with the fact that Jiemba had not been allowed to leave the headquarters, as a serious investigation was taking place in which he could be implicated, and he was not in the best of moods, was enough to send Jiemba's intimidation status through the roof. "Mr Price cannot be disturbed as he is in constant meetings," the secretary continued. "And as to your other enquiries, the woman you have described has not ever been seen on the premises, and the young man matching the description you have stated may have been on site initially but has since been moved on. The inmate, as I have instructed you every time before, is under strict orders to not be approached by anyone." Jiemba flexed in frustration, but could see a dead end when he saw one. Yes he could go storming in to demand an audience with Price, he could also lay siege to the lower levels in an attempt to find Jerome Less, but Jiemba knew that he would be no closer to the answers he needed and he still needed the security chief's resources to find the rest of the bikie group. He stomped his way back out through the doors he had entered.

"Nothing?" Selena asked, not expecting a reply as she already knew the answer. "I told you. Looks like you just have to wait around here a little bit longer." She joined him from where she waited outside the room. Jiemba stormed past her, but didn't ignore her comment.

"I am tired of waiting," Jiemba replied, acknowledging her without looking at her. "I was so close to getting what I needed. Answers to who is responsible for what happened. Not only did I not get my hands on the person who was responsible for the attack at the river, but the guy who can give me the answers has been locked away. And then on top of all that, we broke out a whole bunch of inmates, and I have no idea why, and one of them is that upstart Jet."

"You knew that boy?" Selena asked, showing some interest. They had spoken numerous times since the incident at Wellington Star Five, and each time she would chip away at another layer of Jiemba until he had calmed and shared some memory or thought. Jiemba exhaled a mighty sigh as he calmed himself. He filled his cheeks, breathing in and breathing back out. He had been running through the process more and more to help relax his mood. Even falling back into older techniques like square breathing. Breath in, hold, breath out, hold, repeat, each for three seconds. He hadn't done that so much since he had left high school.

"Yeah," Jiemba answered. "I knew him, although not well. He was a young man showing a lot of potential when I met him, with a typical chip on his shoulder and a poor attitude. But I, like many others, tried to take him under our wings. We tried to help him see that his behaviour was not acceptable and that he could change and become something truly special, while at the same time trying to tolerate what he was doing. You don't expect people to change or even understand straight away."

"Sounds like a couple of other people I know. And what happened?" Selena asked coming to rest beside him. They were alone in one of the longer corridors with rooms hidden off to each side.

"What usually happens when you try to help someone?" Jiemba replied. "You get burned. And in my case that pain went deep and sent me over the edge. It wasn't just his fault, but he was the last thing in a series. The sad thing is I saw it coming."

"If you saw it coming why did you keep going?" Selena asked.

"I don't know," Jiemba said, stating the response in reflex. "It is something I have always done. I was putting so much into helping him, and some of my friends were putting in more, that we just couldn't see him fail. Every time he or someone else fought us and told us that we were useless, just like Rogers is doing with me, we knew that they were wrong and we doubled down at the expense of ourselves. It doesn't mean that it didn't already hurt. A friend of mine always tells me that if you have the power to do something you should do it, because if you don't there may be no one else who will."

"Sounds like wisdom to me," Selena stated with a nod, "does he say anything else?"

"Yeah," Jiemba continued, "sometimes he says really dumb things, such as pine cones have feelings, and that if you are recording something you can have as many takes as you like even if you are not allowed, all you have to do is swear in the take." They both giggled at the suggestion. "But he also says that it is easier to live with the failure of an action, than the regret of not taking it at all." Jiemba reflected in silence for a moment. He found that Selena had once again drawn closer to him. "I think that is why I am so focused on this. The old man got me to talk about this stuff, knowing all along that someone more professional would have been better. But he was what I needed at the time. The lessons I learned from him I will never forget. I was distraught when he died, but part of that was that we had no closure. There were things that I needed to say to him that I never got the chance to. My failure is in my inaction."

"Jiemba," Selena said as she leaned closer. "I am so sorry about what has happened to you. Most people have a story hidden behind the mask that they portray. Few ever share that story. Remember, even after you leave this place, I am here to talk to you about anything at all. You have my number in the phone in your pocket. Promise me when this is all finished, that you will keep it."

"I promise," Jiemba nodded, patting the device in his pocket to establish that it was still there. She drew closer again to him. Jiemba felt like his chest was like jelly, instead of the dense muscle it had become. She was closer to him now than anyone had been for a long time. Usually he would push people away at this point, afraid that they could hurt him or he would hurt them. Or even laugh awkwardly to change the mood entirely.

This time he let her draw closer to him. She started to lean in.

"Jiemba, Selena," a voice interrupted from down the corridor, causing Selena to shift backwards immediately. It was the secretary who had only moments before sent Jiemba on his way. "Mr Price wants to see you now." Jiemba forced a small smile at Selena, and pushed clumsily past her. Nothing was said as they moved towards where they were requested to be.

"Come in, sit down," Price ordered. The pair obeyed and sat down where Rogers was already waiting. He gave his 'charming' smirk from the side of his face before turning to watch Price. Rogers had also been restricted to headquarters, but was hidden in a different part of the facility, no doubt to keep him and Jiemba apart. "No one say a word," Price continued as he finally sat at the end of a desk situated at the front of the room. "I am going to bring all three of you up to speed with what has been happening and where we are going from here. You are all going to be allowed to resume duties as of now."

"Finally," Rogers released a sigh of relief.

"I don't do duties," Jiemba added.

"I said shut it, both of you," Price shot both of them a hard glare. "I have been in non-stop meetings ever since you returned from delivering those inmates to Wellington Star Five. The amount of scrutiny our company has received has been immense. However, there have been a couple of developments. The first is that they have dropped any investigation into Spartan personnel, there is no proof of anything untoward or otherwise occurring within that facility.”

“How can that be?” Jiemba couldn’t help himself. “There were cameras all over that place, plus the guards. . .”

“The cameras, and all communication at Star Five, were knocked out, there was no sound or images recorded. I have no idea who was behind that, the facility staff have no leads either. The guards who were hurt and on duty shared some ridiculous stories which could not be corroborated and have been given leave until further notice. The others were too busy dealing with the other insurgents. And before you ask, yes that means there is no evidence to look over in regard to tracking them down. So while you are free to resume normal duties we are no longer allowed at Star Five, or any of the others, until further notice.”

“I am getting sick of dead ends,” Jiemba muttered.

“We haven’t reached one,” Price huffed back, “but let me finish. I, personally, have been chasing up any leads from our friend Jerome Less. He has informed us that there will be a meeting with town leaders tonight.”

“That can’t be true,” Rogers was the one who interrupted this time, “otherwise we would’ve heard about it before now.”

“It was organised through the local police,” Price explained. “It seems the people still do not understand what we are trying to do here and have placed their trust in Gumbo and his crew.”

“I still don’t understand what that has to do with us,” Rogers growled, “I am sick of wasting my time with these people.” Price took a deep breath. It appeared that he was stopping himself from making an outburst. “Surely we have enough material showing their incompetence to force them to step aside.”

“Continue Price,” Selena urged him, “please.”

“It matters to us for a couple of reasons,” Price seemed deeply concerned about what he was saying, while ignoring Rogers’ outburst. “A call came over the channels not too long ago. Something big is happening at Orange. All law enforcement regardless of if they are active or on call have been actioned to move to the area. That means that all stations are skeleton crews."

"And that meeting was going to be maintained through the local police?" Selena asked.

"Correct," Price said.

"So do we go in instead?" Rogers groaned.

"No," Price responded. "The leaders of that meeting have already conveyed that they don't want Spartan assistance, in fact if we arrive then the meeting is off."

"Sounds great," Rogers nodded with satisfaction. "Win, win."

"Except Jerome has informed me that the bikie group that hit the mission, and Wellington Star Five, will be making an appearance at the meeting. They are rounding up everyone who got away from the river and don't care how they do it," Price made the point he had been trying to make the whole time. "What that means for us is this. Spartan security is already spreading through all of Wellington to cover for the lack of law enforcement. That meeting will go ahead, and we won't go. We will observe from a distance. We have to send someone in to observe. We are all too well known, and the two that I trust to do the job, Rogers and Selena, are easily recognisable. I can send others but I don't think they will be as effective and the effort will be a waste. We don't want to spook those at the meeting or it won't happen. We need them, to be put bluntly, as bait." There was silence as they all took it in. "Which leads me to you, Jiemba. I need your help to go in and supervise this meeting. You don't have to engage, but we want you there if and when something happens. I am tasking you with keeping those people safe and I give you permission to apprehend anybody who should cause trouble." Price stopped talking, again letting the information linger. Jiemba realised that all eyes were on him as if his choice made all the difference.

"First of all I don't need your permission," Jiemba stated as he got to his feet. "I am done with Spartan security and anything else that comes with that. The only reason why I am still here, despite you thinking that you can stop me from leaving, is that I want this whole situation over with. This sounds like a way where it can be done today." He walked around the room, stroking his trim beard as he comprehended what he was being asked to do. It was hardly a decision, he just didn't want to think that he was too keen. "Okay then," Jiemba finally said, "I'll do it."

"Splendid," Price said with little excitement as he jumped to his feet. "I will finish making all the arrangements. Let's get this done."

Jiemba once more walked alone. The twilight fell soon enough, but as he waited for the time to arrive he had become fidgety and agitated. He had been told off several times for pacing around Spartan headquarters and generally getting in the way. He found it hard to make himself busy, and had spent a great deal of time watching the immense Gear machines go about their tasks. But still he felt like he was watching the clock too much and taking far less notice of important aspects. The feeling was like he was going on a date, presenting at a job interview or appearing at a special occasion; except of course for opposite reasons.

As Jiemba walked along he could smell the chill in the air. He couldn't feel the cold but his nostrils could sense the sensation as vapour in the air cooled around him. Jiemba felt more like himself again. He was no longer wearing the slacks and shirt that would stain him with the same brush as the Spartan security members. He had obtained some sports shoes that were big enough for his feet and felt comfortable. He wore the same jeans he had arrived in and had insisted that apart from being cleaned that nothing else was done to repair them. Jiemba also wore a tight fitting shirt, which stretched around his muscles and pulled tight enough to see the outline and shading of the goanna on his chest.

Countless times, as he harassed those around him while he anxiously waited, he had found himself in the vicinity of Selena. Sometimes she was too busy to notice, other times she was just there as if she was waiting for him. They hardly shared a word. It may have been because they had very different roles to prepare for to help the success of the meeting's outcome, but she appeared a little distant, almost sad. Jiemba felt like he may have offended her when he went off on his rant about not wanting anything to do with the Spartan security company. He felt that she was stronger than that to let it affect her, but he also couldn't figure out what else he had done. Perhaps she was also having second thoughts about her offer to him.

Perhaps it was because she had gotten too close to him, and then had discovered it was not what she wanted. Jiemba had understood the situation, too many times. It had never been good for him. As those memories came flooding back, with faces of old girlfriends and lost loves haunting their way into his mind, he shook his head to dismiss them and resumed his focus.

Walking past the gigantic stadium after he had left, over the bridge that had become the boundary between new and old Wellington, and through the park in which Price and Jiemba had met incognito on that first night, Jiemba finally arrived at the meeting place. The old council building was the location, and it was mostly only used for important meetings as otherwise it was abandoned. At some point in the past the Wellington Council was removed, amalgamated into a council which was run by Dubbo and encompassed a much wider area. Perhaps because the focus was elsewhere was the reason why Wellington had been disregarded. Some greater focus may have improved the declining qualities and saved the town.

The meeting was on the bottom floor. At one end there was an elevated stage where the previous council chamber had sat its members, now it had a small contingent of leaders who sat patiently. The rest filled the remainder of a large hall in front of them. There were countless chairs, but as many people filled them as could fit, while others were content to stand around the edges and at the back.

Jiemba walked into the room which was filled with noise and bustle as the restless community talked to one another in anticipation of the meeting starting. All eyes fell on him as he entered, with the hubbub subsiding briefly at his expense, making him feel immediately like he wasn't welcome. He wasn't sure what to do.

"There is a spot over here my friend," a voice called down from the lectern, from a man that Jiemba didn't know, pointing to a space along a church like pew in the front row. Jiemba smiled and waved, motioning towards the location. He didn't look at who surrounded him, but did notice who sat on the stage behind the man who had reached out to him. There were several seats up there, each with their own microphone set up so they could speak when their moment came. Jiemba did not know many of these people either. Some were old, some no older than his mum, and others younger. Jiemba nodded at the young man he had met when he had first sought out Jerome. Josh Northman smiled at him, and Jiemba smiled back. The man on his right was Shane Docker. Docker did not seem either angry or happy to see Jiemba, but regardless at the moment he said nothing. Shortly after Jiemba found his seat and took it, the meeting commenced.

"Welcome everyone, and thank you for coming to this meeting which is of the gravest importance. We are missing one member from the stage who was going to welcome you all, but he is not here yet, and we must begin. I will ask Aunty Mary Ash to come and do the welcome," the man stepped aside from the lectern and allowed the older Aboriginal woman to speak. Jiemba took note on how she did it, he had been asked many times to do an acknowledgement, he was unable to do a welcome yet, and each time he had felt flustered in case he did something wrong. He would own it someday.

"Thank you, Aunty," the man resumed his position after assisting Mary back to her seat. "Firstly, if you don't know who I am, my name is Jonathan Mires. I am a Wiradjuri man from Wellington and I love this town. I have been meeting with the people you see on this stage, and others, to try and bring together a group who cares deeply for our community, and is upset and disgusted by what is happening to it. It is not enough to complain, we must take action and set a course towards solving this problem before it becomes even worse. My job out the front of you this evening, despite usually being a happy and positive man, is to outline the issues, but also to offer some solutions, of which we have many, and outline what we plan to do." Jiemba watched as the man already owned the room. There was no individual or group arguing with the point of being there, with most nodding their heads in agreeance. There had to be close to a thousand people in the room.

"The first thing we need is to reverse the amalgamation of our town. We were forced into this without any consideration as to what the consequences would be. We have an administrator who is absent, who has no idea what our qualities or our strengths are, and doesn't care about the decline that happens around us. The town has an unwarranted reputation and the man who is responsible for us, will neither defend us and bring good light towards us, or identify the concerns and address them convincingly. We were already moving forward as a community, and there is no denying that our reputation was not the same as other towns, but work was being done and progress being made. Our town is one of the greatest sources of renewable resources anywhere in New South Wales, or in fact Australia. The police presence, once non-existent and dismissive of the real concerns that we had, was bolstered and engaging with community issues and removing identified problems. Abuse of substance, violence and antisocial behaviour, are not wanted in any community and slowly they were being resolved. Then under the watchful eye of an administrator who is corrupt and turns a blind eye, development has torn our town apart. It is not that we don't want a thriving town with advances to make it desirable all over the country, but we want a thriving community to go with it. It has been a situation of a square peg and a round hole. The development is the round hole, the community of Wellington doesn't fit so we are the ones that have been removed. Spartan security seemed like a great idea, until they started acting like hired goons or bounty hunters; a private military only waging war on the citizens of this town. Anybody who held a grudge was taken down. I am surprised that they aren't here tonight, despite the fact that we asked them not to be. They don't play by anybody's rules but theirs, if they were here you could bet that you wouldn't be going home to your family tonight, you may not be going home to your family ever again. I would take care as you leave." Jiemba could feel many of the eyes fall on him, and watched as Docker made no secret of the fact. He watched Jiemba as if he was a mouse that invaded his home and needed to be removed.

"We have programs that are ready to go to support community, not rip them apart," Jonathan continued, "and we are happy to work with anybody, old or new, local or foreign, to make our dreams a reality. We want to work, we want to be educated, we want to rebuild what we know is a beautiful place, but we need the opportunity to do so. Today we have no power to do this. We are meeting here to outline this and to ensure that when the time comes we are united in getting the power back." Jonathan rose his voice to climax where he intended at the end. The room was in his hand, and as he rose so did they. Cheers and whistles filled the air, many people agreeing with what he had said, others shouting out their own problems or commenting. Some swore, some were angry, some wept openly in the room. Jiemba had taken it all in, knowing that he was supposed to be an observer but was unable to ignore the man's plea.

The room eventually settled, as Jonathan forced his hands down in a calming motion hoping to continue the meeting. Jiemba was captivated by him and could hardly wait to hear all the things he was going to try and put in place. However, as the quiet returned Jiemba could hear the singular loud clapping of one solitary person. A man walked down the main isle of the room. Middle aged with a bald head, a large belly and a larger jacket, his boots clomped loudly as he walked to the front of the room.

"That was really moving," the newcomer said. "That was a great speech, you did a great job, really. That's why it is a shame that everybody in this room is part of the problem, not the solution. This town doesn't need a rebirth, it needs an overhaul. Vermin shouldn't be allowed to have a say in how the house is run, they should only be exterminated." More people started to walk into the room from every door, many with a similar appearance, closing, locking and barring the doors as they entered. Jiemba looked around frantically. He could identify several of the intruders from the attack at the mission, and a couple he knew had been part of destroying JayDee's home. His fury grew as his eyes jumped from one person to the next, trying to decide who he would take down first, he searched for one individual more than the others. "Now we don't want anybody getting hurt," the main man continued, though there was less sincerity in the claim, "so you either all come quietly or we start taking you out one by one. If you know what I mean." The man had a wicked smile and then pointed towards the stage. "And we will start with your so called leaders, until there are none left."

Jiemba released a growl as he glanced up at the stage. Several people had appeared up there behind the leaders. Each brandished a weapon, but most carried a gun or a knife. The central figure, holding a gun to the head of the young man Josh, was the biker with the snake on their helmet. Jiemba leaped to his feet but was greeted by the interloper that had been talking.

"Now now big guy," the man smiled as he looked at Jiemba. "You wouldn't want to be responsible for anyone's death would you? Sorry, sorry, that came out wrong. What I meant to say was, you don't want to be responsible for the death of anyone else, would you? You already lost someone close to you, didn't you? It was likely even your own fault. But then again, you also took away some people that I know well. You must love hurting others. You do, don't you?" The man scowled. "We did not forget about you my friend. I may have to amend what I said before. We don't want to hurt anyone, except for maybe you." Jiemba was stuck. Move and everyone else was in trouble, don't move and they would all be taken and he would be the target of a gun fight.

"Hey, hang on a sec," another voice was added over the whispered sobs and the strain between Jiemba and the bald man. Jiemba stared at the snake helmeted rider before he searched for the owner to the voice. A guitar started to play, single notes being strummed one cord after the other. "The point of a meeting is to discuss things, with words, not violence. After all, we all live under the same sky." A figure suddenly emerged from behind the curtains at the side of the stage. He had long untamed hair, which he swept one hand through before wiggling his head a little to let it fall. He wore what looked-like a hand knitted poncho, over a buttoned shirt which was open from the neck down to the middle of his chest, revealing strong features and a collection of hair. He was slim and handsome. There was a silence as he carried a guitar to the centre of the stage. Seemingly oblivious to all that was happening around him. "Allow me to introduce myself," he continued, "ladies and gentleman, my name is Justin Rhymer."

"No one cares what your name is," the bald intruder yelled at the stage. "You don't seem to understand what is going on here."

"Please, sir, let me finish," Justin seemed hurt by the interruption. "I am more commonly known as Justice, and I am a member of a group known as Judge's Court. Before you ask, no, that is not the name of any band." Jiemba had no idea what was going on, but the bald headed intruder clearly did. The blood drained from his face as he started to shift from foot to foot, more worried about this newcomer than he had been about Jiemba. Justin tweaked his guitar for a few seconds before he started to strum. "This song is one of my favourites, it's called 'End of the Day,' and I will inform you that I don't like people interrupting me when I perform so I brought a couple of friends."

"Hell yeah he did," another voice yelled. A figure erupted from the back of the stage as if he had been pulled from the air itself. His head was covered in dreadlocks which covered half of his face and hung down between his shoulder blades. He had a deep brown moustache which was cut up in random places. His eyes were darting around in a wild fashion. In two strokes he had beaten down two of the people holding the stage members captive. Then he stood behind the last person remaining, the one with the snake helmet, and yelled at the top of his voice.

"Everybody run," he yelled. The scene erupted in chaos. The man called Justin Rhymer started playing a tune on his acoustic guitar, unphased by the noise which bellowed out as the people of Wellington leapt into a frenzy in a bid to escape from the rising threats. Two of the side doors exploded open to create a means to escape, but not before two motorcyclists rode through them into the crowded area. The man with dreadlocks had been wearing a smile, but the snake helmeted rider quickly turned against him and started to fight. Choosing to turn away from Josh and face a far more serious danger. The rider threw several strong chops and kicks which the dreadlocked man only just managed to dodge. While that fight happened many other riders emerged from outside the building on foot and immediately started beating down and chasing off those that had meant to imprison the town's people.

Jiemba was entirely confused. He discovered that where he had thought there was one bikie group in town there appeared to be two. It also didn't look as if they had much love for each other. He wasted no more time in jumping to action. He moved off to his side where another door had been locked. Jiemba grabbed the person who stood in his way and threw them whole bodied into the wooden frame. The door buckled around him, and with a sweep of his hand Jiemba removed the debris and created another exit. More people fled, some faster than others as the elderly tried their best to avoid what was happening around them.

Jiemba couldn't tell who was on whose team so did his best to just aid those who were escaping. The bald man stood above a small group, threatening them if they didn't follow his directions they would all suffer. Jiemba knew that this guy was no good and moved towards him. More fighters emerged from both sides and injected themselves into the chaos, some protecting the townspeople, while others joined in the anarchy on the stage or increased their own numbers in another area.

"Want a piece big guy?" the bald man mocked as he noticed Jiemba's approach.

"Not just a piece," Jiemba replied. The man swung a metal baton at him which Jiemba blocked with his forearm. Jiemba had no doubt that the blow would normally have broken his arm. All it did was release a dull dinging sound as a bend emerged from the solid steel frame. The man had half a second to realise what he was dealing with. Jiemba didn't give him any more than that as he grabbed him by the scruff, marched him from the group, and threw him into the rest of his people who had been barricading the main entrance. The bald man struck them with a thump, the whole group slumping to the ground. Those that weren't knocked down quickly gave up the fight and dragged the rest out with them.

The music that Justin Rhymer had been playing on the stage suddenly stopped. The stage had been rushed. Jiemba watched as Justin placed his guitar carefully at the stage side before jumping into the melee. Punches were flung wildly as members of both sides joined the group. The man with the dreadlocks had been separated from the rider with the snake helmet. Both were the clear winners in their own separate fights, a pile of downed bodies littered the floor around them. The snake helmeted rider looked as if they were about to turn and flee when a space had been available, but was stopped hard in their tracks. One of the rescuing cyclists had ditched their bike and leapt onto the stage. This fight was more of a match; punches, kicks, blocks, dodges, all happening at lightning speed. Jiemba made his way over as the other cyclist chased away everyone else who remained. The fight went on and on. Justin and his team were getting on top as more opponents either fell before them or fled.

Jiemba had arrived just in time for the snake rider to fall from the stage. Before they had time to clamber to their feet and escape he grabbed hold of them with his firm grip.

"Finally," Jiemba whispered, "I have got you, and you can help me get everyone else who is responsible for the old man's death. Now let's see who we are dealing with here." The rider struggled and squirmed but Jiemba's grip was unrelenting. He was not about to let them escape. With one hand he pinned them to the ledge at the front of the stage, as he removed the helmet with his other. He was expecting someone lean and strong, with a mangled and evil expression, as they had managed to hold themselves in a fight for so long, but also someone who commanded with their look. Either way it did not matter, regardless of what they looked like they would be of great use to Jiemba.

The helmet was removed.

Jiemba, against all instincts, let the person go. The rider jumped to their feet immediately.

"What?" Jiemba stared in shock at who stood before him.

"I'm sorry Jiemba," the figure said back.

"Selena?" Jiemba's heart sank, he was so confused.

"Grab her," the dreadlocked man cried out. Jiemba did not reach out to follow the direction. He simply watched as Selena sprinted to the edge of the meeting room and fled into the darkness. He didn't move as the rest of the area was cleared, or notice that it was happening. Eventually there was only five people remaining, including Jiemba.

"I can't believe you let her go," the dreadlocked man yelled at Jiemba. They almost saw eye to eye as he was so tall. Jiemba did not answer him back, which enraged the other man as he stormed around. Justin retrieved his guitar and sat down on the edge of the stage, attempting to retune each string. The third person had not taken off their helmet, nor spoken at all, but Jiemba could tell that they were looking at Jiemba with confusion if not contempt. They retrieved their bike and waited for the fourth.

The fourth was the other person who had ridden into the meeting on a motorcycle. They rode it right up to Jiemba, not caring about the proximity to the man nor that they were inside. As the rider parked his bike and removed himself from it Jiemba realised that the others had surrounded him, suggesting perhaps that this person was the leader. This rider removed his helmet, revealing a man in his late thirties. He was of stocky build, with straight yet ruffled dark brown hair and a cleanly shaven face. He smiled at Jiemba which was both warm and at the current moment unsettling.

"Are you Jiemba?" the man asked.

"Maybe," Jiemba replied stubbornly. He had still not come to grips with what he had just seen. He had no idea what to think about what was happening, or about Selena. For so long he had wanted to harm the rider with the snake helmet, but now they had transformed into the one person who had tried to get closer to him. It was all a mess.

"I reckon you are," the man smiled again. He even pressed a hand to Jiemba's chest, stretching the fabric slightly to reveal more of the goanna. He had a fuller face, but Jiemba would have classed him as solid, maybe even slightly chubby. Nothing worse. "Do you know who I am?"

"Should I?" Jiemba growled back.

"No I suppose not," he said, the smile hadn't faded. Jiemba noted that the man with dreadlocks stood roughly behind Jiemba, but Jiemba was still not bothered by him. "I will tell you then," the biker continued. "My name is Judge, and I am known as the Judge. I am the leader of a group of cyclists called Judge's Court. We have travelled a long way to be here. My father told me that he needed my help, but when I arrived I found that he had been killed. When I asked around I found out who the person responsible was."

"And who was that?" Jiemba asked. He was so confused he was only just getting to understand who this person was.

"I asked around a bit trying to be sure, but all answers pointed in the same direction. The person who killed him, was you," the smile vanished from Judge's face. "So, you will have to pay."

Jiemba started blurting out that there was a mistake, that they had all got it wrong, but his pleas fell too late and on deaf ears. "Do it," Judge instructed.

The dreadlock covered man had been behind Jiemba for a reason. He had pulled out a sidearm and had hidden it behind Jiemba's back. When the instruction came from his leader, he did not hesitate. He swiftly pulled the gun free, pressed it firmly to the back of Jiemba's head and pulled the trigger.

BLAM!

He didn't miss.

Chapter 15 – The Court

Jiemba lay flat on his back looking up at the darkness. His eyes were open and he could see the night sky clearly above him. The twinkling stars only obscured by the shifting of clouds or the interruption of swaying trees moving in the breeze. There was a crackling fire off to his left, which was attended to by only a few others. The gentle strumming of an acoustic guitar returned to accompany it.

"I will dedicate this next song to you, Easter, the rose in our merry band," Justin whispered into the night. The man known as Justice smiled, swung his hair over his face to let it bob there as he bounced to the sound of his own beat; mouth opened wide in a silent cheer.

"I will listen to your song," Easter replied, "but I will accept no dedication from you. If there is any mention of love you may be looking for a new guitar." The threat was real although a smile was shared between the two. Easter King was an attractive young lady. She had been the rider that had gone toe to toe with Selena and easily held her own. Easter was slim with long dark sandy brown hair, and, judging by the limited skin that she showed, was tanned. Her features were dazzling though Jiemba had noticed her face rested in a scowl. When she smiled her mouth widened and she possessed a youthful enthusiasm. In this group Easter was known as Jury.

"I call it, beautiful eyes," Justin smirked at her. Only moments before he had pretended to be hurt by her remarks. Jiemba thought that she did have beautiful eyes; of deep brown so that you couldn't distinguish between the colour and the black. She didn't smile back, instead glaring at him with murderous intent through those same eyes.

Laughter rose from a small campsite closer to the road. Jiemba didn't have to look in the direction to know where it had come from. He had lived on the property long enough to know where everything was, or at least where everything had been. The group up there were the majority of this biker group, although it appeared by status they were separated. More laughter erupted though Jiemba could not hear the joke. Since arriving back he had kept to himself. The small fire that he sat near lay outside the bottom gate to JayDee's property that he had broken and then fixed after he had first arrived.

"I still don't understand why this fire is so far down the hill?" A loud voice emerged from the darkness, heavy boots crunching sticks and sliding on loose gravel and seeds.

"Because Jiemba said he didn't want to be near the house, and refused to ruin what was left of the flower patches. Judge agreed," Easter replied.

"Well Judge is getting soft," the man replied.

"Are you going to tell him that, Gary, or shall I?" she threatened. Gary McShaun, the heavily dreadlocked tall man who also went by the name Executioner, swayed dangerously as he analysed her threat. It was clear to Jiemba that the man had been drinking heavily and that it wouldn't be long before he was unable to move under his own strength. He mumbled something under his breath before collapsing heavily in the remnants of a burnt out deck chair. There was a small groan from the timbers as he sat down but they managed to hold.

Jiemba continued to look up at the stars. He got lost amongst them as he focused away from the small pollution of light that the escaping embers created. Jiemba had said nothing to the group, and they hadn't said much to him. After he had been shot in the back of the head Jiemba had spun around and crushed the gun that had fired the bullet. All four of the group stared in wonderment as the bullet crushed itself against the back of his head to fall harmlessly to the ground without leaving a mark. Jiemba had fought back his anger at

the action, took control of his rage despite the confusion of the
moment and uttered only a few words.

"I didn't kill him," Jiemba had said. Shock surrounded all of them.
Jiemba assumed that the riders had a plan for everything, including
his death, but as the plan had failed they were lost.

"Meet me where he lived," the one called Judge had said, "we will
sort this out there." It was a command that Jiemba could have
ignored, but he obeyed. If this man was related to the old man then
Jiemba wanted to talk to him. There was so much closure that Jiemba
needed and if he didn't start finding it he was sure it would consume
him. It already was. Jiemba had then walked the distance back to
what was left of the property, ignored the camp on the front lawn
and they took no notice of him, and then set about making his own
campsite further back.

Judge had been busy with the rest of his men and apart from the
fleeting discussion that he had shared with Easter upon his arrival,
words had been sparse.

"What are you staring at up there brother?" Justin asked Jiemba.
He had finished playing his song, which Jiemba imagined was usually
a quicker tune but he had slowed it down for his female counterpart.
Justin had been Jiemba's company since his arrival. Jiemba imagined
that they could have been friends in other circumstances, and he
quite enjoyed the songs that he had played into the night, but Jiemba
had chosen to be silent for the most part.

"Try and find some constellations up there while you are ignoring
us," Gary sneered, wobbling though he sat, "it'll make you far more
interesting. You probably can't join the dots though." The
dreadlocked man chuckled at his own comment.

"Constellations aren't just about joining the dots," Justin replied
shaking his head. "That is just part of it, you need to have a bit of
creativity and imagination to see the rest. The stories would be lost
on someone like you." Justin received a warning growl from the other
man but continued. "Besides, Jiemba is an Aboriginal man, you see
stories not just in the stars but in the spaces in between."

"You mean the black bits," Gary snorted, "if I shut my eyes I can imagine lots of things too. Maybe Easter might be in there as well."

"Instead of shutting your eyes, perhaps start with your mouth," Easter replied, "and if I hear any more of that talk I will shave your head while you are sleeping." Gary was immediately quiet.

"Not just the dark," Justin continued, he was retuning his guitar again. "There are stories surrounding the star clusters, the nebulas and yes the spaces. I only know a few, but then I only know a few other constellations. The Dark Emu should be visible up there. It is one of the examples I know where it has multiple parts. It is a mix of worlds, where cultural stories mix with science. Both are present and co-exist, like we all should be." Jiemba listened. The moment Justin mentioned the creature Jiemba found it in the night sky. He looked for the Southern Cross, then his eyes scanned for the Milky Way. He found the image and held it, for some reason despite being recently shot and the man who did the act sitting only metres away Jiemba felt at peace. Apart from the light strumming of another song the small group sat in silence. The scuff of footsteps interrupted the serenity a few minutes later.

"Time to sort this out," Judge said as he emerged from the darkness. Jiemba for the first time since his arrival sat back up. Judge had made his way over to the fire and stuck his hands out to get warm. Jiemba supposed that it would have been cold. Judge rubbed his hands together as if that would speed up the process, blew into them when they were cupped, and then stood glaring into the flames.

"I think we got off on the wrong foot," Judge said finally, continuing to stare into the flames.

"I can't imagine being shot in the back of the head is usually considered to be the right foot," Jiemba replied.

"You would be surprised how often it is though," Judge replied calmly, suggesting that this wasn't the first instance of such an act. "As you have survived though I feel like we have to hear you out, sort of like if you had survived after being hung in the old days, so we know what to do with you."

"You shot me and it didn't work," Jiemba replied sharply," I don't know what else you think you can do."

"We have many options," Judge confirmed, "but I want to hear from you. You seem unable to move beyond what happened earlier. I think you need to put that behind you for the time being."

"Is that what we do?" Jiemba laughed loudly, "thanks for helping me out, as it is my first time being shot in the back of the head." Whatever response he expected he didn't get it. Judge simply smiled and looked deeper into the fire. It appeared like he was waiting for Jiemba to begin his tale.

Eventually he did. As he retold all of the events up to that point, from when he had washed up on the river bank, the other four listened silently. They listened without any interruptions, smiling at some points, shaking their heads at others, each of them allowing him to tell his tale. When he finished there was more silence as they took it all in. Eventually it was Judge who spoke first.

"Jiemba," Judge stopped, fingers resting on his chin as he decided on what to say next. "I want to start off by saying that I am sorry that we shot you."

"This is one of the only instances where that apology would work in retrospect," Jiemba replied.

"You are probably right," Judge agreed, "but I will point out that as we listened without interruption to your tale, you should extend the same courtesy."

"Is courtesy a common thing among bikies?" Jiemba asked sarcastically.

"I don't know about any other groups except this one," Judge shrugged, "but rules should be in place or anarchy will ensue."

"Anarchy? You shot me in the head. Isn't that anarchy?" Jiemba said with concern.

"Perhaps," Judge answered, "but I apologised for that." Silence followed the statement as if it was the end of the matter. Jiemba could see it was getting him nowhere.

"Fine, I will listen," he said reluctantly. Judge nodded before continuing.

"Thank you. We were wrong in executing justice as we have seen fit. But that is your fault."

"What?" Jiemba spat, "It was my fault that I got shot in the head?" Judge gave him a look as a reminder that he shouldn't talk. Jiemba obeyed but he wasn't happy.

"It is your fault," Judge continued, "and if I am to believe your story then you have been wrong in so many ways."

"First off," Gary McShaun sat up as he engaged in the conversation. "The old man's name is not JayDee. For someone who pleaded that you knew him well enough to be considered a role model you should at least know his name. JayDee is a nickname. It isn't a name, JayDee is just the letters of J and D. These are short form for 'Judge's Dad'. It isn't his name, and as he is dead I will not say his name out loud. You can keep calling him JayDee if you wish though."

"Second," Justin was next, "despite being in the old man's company for so long you didn't take in any of his lessons. He was all about others. You say that you have been acting on his behalf, but he doesn't have a behalf anymore, and he certainly wouldn't have wanted this. Everything you have been doing has only been for you."

"I'm next," Easter added, "it was your fault because you were ignoring the people you should have been helping. And in doing that you became the very thing you were trying not to be. The people are the ones who told us that it was your fault. You didn't help them, you helped the people who were harming them. Even if you weren't at fault the people aren't going to help you and would probably be quite happy to get rid of you."

"Listening is more than hearing," Judge added finally. "You came in broken, you walked out broken. You had the opportunity to be better and you weren't, not just for others but for yourself. I don't blame you for his death anymore, but I blame you for wasting his life."

"He saved me," Jiemba stated abruptly. "I am thankful. I can't admit that he wasted life when he used it to save mine."

"It is a waste if you do nothing with it," Judge looked at Jiemba for the first time. "I know the man. I have lived in his shadow and he has been disappointed in some, many, of my choices. But I also knew, eventually, that if I was trying to better myself and help others then I was doing something right and he would be proud. Despite what people would think of me I would be better than their assumptions."

"You should never assume," Jiemba whispered.

"It appears you learned something from him," Judge admitted. The leader walked over and sat down in the dirt next to Jiemba. "You need to forget about this quest you have set yourself on to find his killers. Revenge is not the answer for you, even if it is for me. His death is not your responsibility. His memory is though." The laughter from the ruins of the homestead echoed into the night sky again, interrupting the thoughtful silence.

"What do I do now then?" Jiemba asked.

"You are asking a bikie?" Judge replied. "I sensed that you thought we were beneath you."

"I am asking JayDee's son," Jiemba responded.

"The old man would say something profound like, it is your path so you must be happy to walk it where ever it may lead. Don't do what you think he would want. Do what you want. And from what you just told me you need to put yourself first." Judge nodded. "If you are asking me though, I would say that you should do what makes you happy, but, you should always leave a place better than you found it. You have made a mighty mess here. It is going to take a superhuman effort for anyone to help put this place back together. Know anyone with that sort of power?" Jiemba nodded and pulled himself to his feet. He walked over and put his hands near the flames of the fire. It was a reflex as he felt no heat, but he was deep in contemplation. For the first time in a while he felt no pressure, despite all the things he knew he still had to do.

"What will you do?" Jiemba asked.

"The Court will hold here for a little while, we still have some things to do," Judge pulled himself up, the others joined him by his side. They looked formidable together, and that was without the rest of the group that was up by the road. "If you are thinking of doing something and you think you might need our help, and you aren't embarrassed by having a bikie group as back-up, then you can call me and we will be there." Jiemba nodded with a smile. He had no idea what he would do next but he would love to have support. Hopefully he could do what was right in everyone's eyes and make things better.

"What is that?" Judge whispered, nodding at a group of bushes that were rustling nearby. Gary McShaun took the first steps forward to check it out but Judge shot an arm out to stop him. "Not you." Gary looked hurt at the comment, and snarled at Justin as he pushed past him to do the leader's bidding. A moment later Justin was back, dragging the semiconscious forms of two individuals. "I could have sent the Executioner if I wanted them dead," Judge growled at Justin.

"I'm really hurt that you would compare the two of us," Justin replied as he dumped them close to the fire. "I barely touched the rouges. They will come to in a moment."

"I know these two," Jiemba interrupted as he moved to their side. "The boy is Jonah, the girl Joanna. They have a family in town but were out here a lot when I stayed with the old man. They are good kids."

"If they have a family in town and this place is a ruin. Why would they be out here?" Gary asked.

"We can find out in a moment," Easter answered, "they are starting to stir."

Jiemba couldn't imagine how the two youths would feel when they awoke. Being roused against the backdrop of the ruined house of a former mentor amongst five hard looking individuals and the sound of a gang over the hill in the dead of the night would surely have been enough to force them into unconsciousness again. Jiemba knew these kids were made of stronger stuff, but was yet to know what they had been through since the raid. Joanna was the first to wake. She immediately jumped to her feet, hands crunched into fists as she stood guarding Jonah. She yelled his name a couple of times to try and get him up but he was still slow to rise. Jiemba walked fully into the firelight, hands open so that she could see he meant her no harm.

"Whoah, whoah, easy Joanna," Jiemba said soothingly, "you are amongst friends here."

"Jiemba," she squinted as she made out his shape. She didn't lower her guard though. It actually appeared like she strengthened it. "I thought it was you. Jonah said it couldn't be as you were standing with those people who destroyed this place."

"These are not from the same group," Jiemba said, "you have to trust me."

"I don't have to do anything," Joanna snarled at him. Jiemba was taken aback at the hostility he was receiving. "Lots of people have been saying lots of bad things about you lately. Jonah has been defending you saying all those things weren't true. He has been getting a bad name for it too."

"I'm sorry Joanna," Jiemba apologised. "A lot of those things are probably true. I was doing what I thought was right and ignoring everything else. I am lucky to have people like you and Jonah who would stand up for me. I am sorry to put you in that position." Her hands came down as she wiped tears away from her eyes, but they almost immediately shot up again. Jiemba moved in to give her a hug. She punched at his chest for a couple of seconds and then slumped into his arms.

"I saw you," she sobbed. "You were with them. They took our parents away. Our carers were good people. And you helped those people who were doing horrible things."

"Jiemba? Is that you?" Jonah had finally come to. Groggily he made his way to his feet.

"It is Jonah," Jiemba replied through Joanna's sobs. He was taking in what she was saying. "Why were you two out here?"

"We didn't really have a choice," Jonah replied. He was being supported by Justin as he swayed dangerously close to the fire. "Our carers were taken into custody a few days ago and we were forced to flee."

Jiemba's heart sank. He realised that either he had been apart of the action or he had enabled it. "Why were they taken into custody?"

"No clue," Jonah replied clutching at a lump on his head, "they said they had a warrant but I didn't see it. Our carers refused entry as they wanted to take us as well. Next thing I knew they were being dragged out and we were sprinting out the back and jumping the back fence. We have been between a few places in the last few days, then we decided to come out here. It has always felt like home out here, especially when you were around, even now though the whole place has been destroyed. We heard your voices and thought that someone had come to get us."

"You're safe here," Easter volunteered. "We have some food and we can find a mattress amongst the group for you to use. No one will harm you tonight."

"Thanks," Jonah replied, "it has been pretty scary. We were looking for you Jiemba. I knew that if anyone could help us it was you. We just had to find you first."

"You bet I will help you out," Jiemba replied. "First thing tomorrow we will start getting a plan together to see what I can do."

"I told them you would help us," Jonah collapsed back to the ground, still holding his head but with a smile. "No matter what any of them were saying about you."

"Who?" Jiemba asked with confusion. "Who did you tell?"

"We aren't going to tell you," Joanna snarled. "We were hoping that you would help us the whole time. When those people attacked us. When we fled. When those people came to take us from our home. I never thought that would happen again. We came back here and everything is gone. Everyone in town hates you. Everywhere you go everything falls apart. It is your fault." She didn't wait to be comforted, taking off once more into the undergrowth. Easter held her hands out to the remainder of the group silently urging them to say. She flicked her hair over one shoulder before delicately following Joanna into the shadows.

"There is a big group of us," Jonah continued. He also had streaks on his face where tears had hardened. As much as he was holding it together Jiemba felt that the young man was feeling the same way. "More and more come each day. They hide out during the daylight, and then at night we have a secret spot where everyone meets. Some of the grownups are planning something before it's too late. But some say that it is already too late. I keep telling them that you can help them, help all of us. You could be the difference. No one believes me, but if you can't do it then no one can."

"I think it is time to get you fed and off to bed," Justin interrupted. "If you want us to help you, you need to be able to lead the way with enough energy to finish the job. Even freedom fighters need to keep their strength up." For the first time since knowing the pair Jiemba was amazed at the strength that they actually possessed. When push came to shove they were fighting, not withdrawing like he had done. Jonah moved off after Justin as he was bidden. Jiemba hoped that Joanna would calm herself and do likewise. He felt the sting of Joanna's words because she was right. Everything had fallen down around him and he had just let it. The other's pondered as well.

"What do you think Judge?" Jiemba asked after the youngsters had left.

"I think you have been presented with an opportunity," Judge replied, "I think you have the power to make choices that will help these people. But regardless what I think, it is all about what you think. So, what do you think?"

"I think there is no choice at all," Jiemba said back.

Chapter 16 – Friendly faces

"Hey kid," Jiemba said as he slowly sat down. Joanna looked up at him but then turned away. She cuddled her legs to her chest as she sat at the edge of the river where they had met weeks before. More damage had been done to the area since Jiemba had seen it last. The destruction was mostly limited to the trees that stood on the banks of each side. Many had been cleaved in two, others burned through along with all the grass and bushland surrounding them.

It had been a week since they had arrived back at the property and this was the first time that Jiemba had wandered down to his old stomping ground. All the time in between had been used to lay low and clean up much of what remained of JayDee's property. Judge had left town with the majority of his group, leaving only Justin, Easter and a few others to help Jiemba. Most of what remained of the house could not be saved, placed onto a large bonfire for Justin to play a lonely tune next to at night times. The rest was sorted and piled so that Judge could make the final decision when he returned. When he eventually came back, most of those piles were burned as well.

The rope swing across the river had been cut and lay in a pile half submerged over a fallen log. The pontoon was fractured into too many pieces to count. The larger bits no bigger than a boogie board, the smaller chunks looked like a bag of rubber confetti had exploded everywhere. The foundations of the bridge still stood though the timbers that formed a path had been completely burned away.

"It's all gone," she mumbled.

"I'm not worried about that," Jiemba said as he made himself more comfortable. "It can be replaced."

"I'm not talking about the stuff," she shook her head weakly. "I am talking about everything else. The feeling is what I meant. The feeling is gone."

"You're right," Jiemba nodded. It was more littered than any other spot along the river now. "But that feeling will come back too, when the people come back. And they will. They will remember the feeling like you do and they will come back to feel it again. But the only person I am here to worry about is you."

Joanna looked at him briefly, her hair flowing into her eyes with the swirling breeze. She swished it away and let her head fall back in between her knees. He knew that she was still angry at him. Even though it had been a week and she had slowly been helping out, within close proximity of Easter, she had been mostly closed off to him. History suggested that whenever Jiemba tried to comfort a female when they were angry with him that he would fail. He suspected he would again, but he was willing to try.

"A few years ago a football game came to Orange. It was between the Canberra Raiders and the Newcastle Knights. It was a pre-season game and I didn't support either of those teams but it was still cool to have a game in town. Everyone was excited. So many people came out to watch the game, including heaps of kids because the teams had gone into every school in Orange. They handed out posters and hats, signed heaps of stuff and made everyone feel welcome. It was a big deal." Jiemba looked down at Joanna. She wasn't yelling at him or moving away, yet, so he decided to press on. "Everyone wanted a bit of the players. They signed autographs and took heaps of photos, they spoke to everybody about every facet of their lives as a football player. I was interested in one thing only. I had a small group of kids who I was mentoring at the time. Most of those kids were worse off than me, so I was going to do everything I could to make their lives better. I brought them all down and did the same thing as everyone else. Got them the photos, the merch and the signatures, then got them tickets to stay and watch the game. It was the best day ever. I still felt like I was an imposter though. I thought that I had no right to try and force what I thought was best onto other people. They probably thought that their lives were normal and I was the one that needed help. Anyway, one of the players was heavily involved in youth work. I really admired what he was doing. While the kids were distracted I went and found him chilling with some of the other players. I introduced myself with embarrassment. Declined all the merch and stuff they wanted to give me, and then told them I wanted something else. They looked like something suspect was going on and I was acting all weird, but then I asked them, when mentoring young people what were the things that I had to do to make sure everything was going to be okay? They laughed at me, several of them smiled and left. But the guy I was there to see looked at me and shook his head. He said it wasn't a secret, and it didn't just apply to young people, it applied to everybody."

"What was it?" Joanna asked, still hiding behind her legs. Jiemba smiled.

"He said there was only one thing that I had to do, and that was to just . . . be there. It didn't matter what we were doing, how much money we had or if we were going anywhere. It didn't matter who I was, what religion I followed or whether we believed in the same thing. I just had to be there. I took that to heart and from that moment on I made sure I was there for everybody. That anybody who needed help had me right there beside them. That was until a few weeks ago, where for the first time I wasn't there." Jiemba stopped and breathed in deeper.

"I am sorry I wasn't there when you needed me," Jiemba apologised. "And I know that it might feel like history repeating. Anything else I say would be an excuse, and that is not fair."

The two sat in silence.

Then that silence stretched.

But that silence felt okay.

"Do you really think you can rebuild this place?" Joanna eventually asked. Jiemba spied her wipe a tear away using the long sleeve of her jumper.

"No, I can't. I can only rebuild it if I have help, and to rebuild the feeling I need people," Jiemba declared. Joanna looked like she was going to say something else but she chose to remain silent for a little longer.

"It will have to wait until later," she finally said as she shuffled uncomfortably, before standing and looking away down the river so that Jiemba couldn't see her face. "There are other people that you need to apologise to first."

"And then you have to help them as well."

"Seriously, this is the place?" Jiemba said with astonishment. They had walked the entire way back into Wellington, just the three of them; Jiemba, Jonah and Joanna. Judge and his group had reminded Jiemba that they would come in like the tide if there was any trouble, but otherwise he would leave the trio alone. It was nice to know that someone else had their backs. Jiemba had told Judge that JayDee was being held at Spartan headquarters, and Judge had decided he would pay the place a visit. His phone number was entered in Jiemba's phone, but he was still warned by Justin that it was only for use in an absolute emergency. Although Jiemba could have gone in on Judge's behalf he imagined he also would not have received a warm welcome. The word would have gotten around that he had been shot, and he had been missing in action for the last week, but he also didn't want to deal with the fallout of Selena being involved with the bikie group. That would be its own fight and he didn't want any part of it.

Once the trio had entered the outskirts of Wellington Jiemba had followed the lead of the two youngsters. Not wanting to be seen by anyone they had walked between houses, down alleys, through overgrown bushland and almost entirely through shadows. They had left just after midday, arriving in the early afternoon; the shadows were already long as the seasons had changed into winter. Jiemba hadn't seen anybody as the small group slowly made their way to the secret destination. Whether that was due to the threat of a storm hanging overhead or the strangling presence of oppression in the town Jiemba couldn't guess. Probably both.

The secrecy had been necessary to ensure all the people who were hiding were kept safe, but even Jiemba was taken aback when he found out where it was.

"The old silos?" Jiemba questioned the pair again. "Are these things still in use? Is this even safe?"

"No they are not in use," Jonah answered.

"But even if they were these people are desperate," continued Joanna.

Jiemba followed the cousins around the base, watching as Jonah pointed out the many access points. Many were barricaded and could not be entered, while others, despite looking overgrown and inaccessible, were actually the only routes to enter. They climbed up a rusting iron ladder which accessed the silos a short distance from the ground. Jonah told Jiemba to stand back. Jonah knocked several times at different frequencies, with Jiemba slightly excited that they were using a secret knock. He held back showing it as the situation had become more dire by the day. The trio waited for a moment before a giant grating could be heard on the other side of the metal door and slowly it was opened inwards. The big guy that Jiemba had accidently swatted into the river during his first attempt at Aqua Rugby stood there. He gave Jiemba a piercing look, but after a nod from Jonah he allowed them all to pass. The door slammed shut almost as soon as they were through, turning the small corridor they had entered pitch black. Jiemba followed Jonah blindly for a few steps with Joanna trailing from behind. The hallway turned on itself a couple of times, each corner he took allowing the smallest extra shard of light to venture into the tunnel. A couple of minutes later he could see the exit.

The trio walked out onto a metal vantage point high up above the silo floor. Jiemba couldn't help but gasp. He looked up at the giant interior of the sandy coloured concrete silos. Whatever had existed inside had long since been stripped leaving nothing but stone on every side. Old roller doors stood at each end, as well as doors littering the exterior though at varying heights. A ladder was hanging from the ceiling leaving Jiemba to wonder how on earth someone would have ever managed to reach it. The floor was a mix of dirt and remnants of the last crop which had been held inside the building. The only thing breaking up the depressing floor were all the people who were strewn all over it.

"What is the population of Wellington?" Jiemba asked as he slowly made his way down an iron staircase that lead down to the silo floor.

"Wellington? About four thousand. There is about another thousand people across the bridge in New Wellington though," Jonah answered.

"How many people have been taken from their homes do you think?" Jiemba asked again.

"I would say at least about half that number," Joanna replied this time, scorn in her voice. "Probably even more over the last week."

"So this looks about half of what is left in the town," Jiemba whispered. There were hundreds of people all around him. There wasn't much light creeping in from outside, the only spot it could penetrate were through broken rafters looking out onto the overcast sky outside. But the light that did come in showed all sorts of people. Some huddled together near the edges of the building in small groups, others lay resting or asleep wherever they felt comfortable; covered in rags and remnants of discarded blankets or clothing. A small few were walking around trying to share small quantities of food and water to those who would take it. Very few were making any action, and nobody was yelling or fighting amongst themselves or anyone else. All seemed like they had accepted their sorry state of affairs.

"Pretty sad isn't it," a young voice asked as Jiemba arrived on the solid silo floor.

"Josh?" Jiemba identified the young man with a shake of his head. "I had no idea it was this bad."

"This has only happened recently," he volunteered. "Most of the people you saw at that meeting have no idea of this place. Up until a few weeks ago this silo was only occupied by those people who you would normally see as truly homeless, and any normal person wouldn't bat an eyelid or even look in the direction of people like that. But since then it has slowly been filling up. In the last week even more have been taken and those that escape have made it here."

"But why are you here?" Jiemba asked as his eyes still moved between different groups present. Once more he saw a rainbow of people, but where a rainbow shines separately all these people were mixed together. There was no difference between them, they were all outcast together.

"I am trying my best to help where I can," Josh replied with a sigh. "Most of the older ones don't want much to do with me, but many of the younger people will let me assist. It isn't much, just a tag team into my house where the vulnerable ones can take refuge, or spend an hour or two playing games and taking their minds away from all of this. There are too many now. The risk of being caught is getting too high."

"The risk of what," Jiemba asked, finally looking down at Josh. "You are just doing what any normal person would do at your age. Well you actually aren't, you are doing far more."

"The risk is in assisting the people here," Josh answered. "They are part of the problem, the filth that needs to be removed from the streets of Wellington. The solution is to get rid of them, and, as the old saying goes, if you aren't part of the solution you are part of the problem."

"The thinking is all messed up," Joanna added, her nose rolled up at the sides showing her displeasure.

"But the execution of the thinking is constant," Jonah added. "Spartan headquarters rolls out half a dozen vehicles at a time. They monitor the bridge and are constantly looking for people who do not fit their idea of an ideal citizen. If you are seen with a person who fits that description then you are no different than they are."

"We are all the same anyway," Josh spoke up, the calm in his voice dispelling some of the tension that Joanna and Jonah shared. "Some have just had better luck than others. The town has slowly been 'cleansed' from the east side into the centre of town. Pretty soon it will all be gone. The town will become wealthier, but all the people who have made Wellington the place it has been for so long will be gone."

"What are you going to do about it?" Jiemba asked angrily, "this is no way to live."

"This isn't living," Josh agreed, "right now hiding is surviving, but it won't be long until they find this place too. I am just trying to keep spirits up but there are others who are trying to work on a solution. I can take you to them if you would like?" Jiemba nodded. He could see as he looked around that there were other access points into the silo. A large concrete pipe, that looked big enough to drive a car through, was exposed near the centre of the building. It had exit points on both sides but while one side was barred the other had all the bars torn aside. Several roller doors, some collapsed or barricaded showing a low chance of use, also sat on the far end.

Jiemba walked awkwardly up a small pile of what looked like a combination of old wheat and clay filled dirt. It formed a small hill in the centre of the silo, which in turn was hiding away almost a third of the building.

He was more upset to see what was hidden there.

It looked like so many images that he had seen of field hospitals in warzones in multiple world conflicts. Cots and beds by the dozen were all filled with sick or injured people. Some looked worse than others but the rasping breathing of the elderly, mixed with the muffled wails from younger children and babies, was heartbreaking.

"Feel good about your efforts now?" There was a small table standing off to one side with a smaller group standing around it. The speaker was Shane Docker, but despite the mock in his tone there was nothing smug about the look on his face.

"I had no idea," Jiemba stated as he approached them.

"Finally you are right about something. You had no idea. That usually happens when you only think of yourself," Docker replied, before being interrupted by another man.

"Even if sometimes that is exactly what you need to do." The man said with a smile, walking forward with his arms spread wide. Jiemba embraced the man with tears in his eyes.

"Uncle Lou?" Jiemba whispered. He could feel the older man's skinny frame and stopped himself from holding him too tightly for fear of injuring him.

"Hello my boy it is so good to see you, especially in times like this." Uncle Lou greeted him. They embraced for what seemed like an eternity but neither tried to pull away from the other. Eventually it was Jiemba who pulled away first, after linking the eyes with Joanna who still stood frowning at him.

"I'm sorry that I haven't spoken to you," Jiemba apologised. Uncle Lou waved away the motion.

"A discussion for another time," the older man said before gesturing to another few people. "Let me first introduce Jonathan Mires."

"I remember you from the meeting, although that seems so long ago now," the man said, he seemed like he was a similar age to Uncle Lou. Though Lou was not a tall man Jonathan was shorter still. Apart from that they looked very similar.

"And I remember you as well," Jiemba replied shaking his hand. "I thought everything that you said was very interesting. It was just a shame it was so rudely interrupted. I would have very much liked to have heard more."

"I was just glad that no one was hurt," Jonathan said. Placing a hand firmly on Josh's shoulder as he joined them. Jiemba felt bad that he hadn't checked on Josh's wellbeing when he had arrived. He tried to convince himself it was because he was distracted by everything else he had seen in the silo but he knew there was no excuse.

"Josh you have met," Uncle Lou continued, "and I know you have been in contact with Docker." Shane nodded but it was not overly friendly. "The others here are Gum Majok-Prince, an outstanding football player and stand in leader of the Sudanese community in Wellington. This young man is Will Kalebson. He has been working with myself, Josh, and lately Jonah and Joanna with many of the youth in Wellington. They are irreplaceable." The two young men simply waved at Jiemba without a smile. They were both taller than six foot and were the tallest in the group apart from Jiemba. They were both slim but strong looking. Even though it was cold outside Will wore a singlet which looked old as it hung from his muscular frame. Gum wore a tracksuit with no labels.

"Joanna and Jonah have brought me along to see if there is anything that I can do to help," Jiemba was the first to talk. "I know that word has got around that a lot of this may be my fault, or at least caused by me. I want you to know that none of this was my intention. I was focused on other things, which I have been thinking about frequently, and I realise now, that while those things are important, they are not more important than what is happening here."

"I for one am happy to accept any support," Jonathan smiled encouragingly.

"I however am not so quick to share my trust," Docker declined the help. "While there were troubles in the past all of this accelerated when Jiemba arrived on the scene."

"That may just be a coincidence," Jonathan objected, "I firmly believe that there is something else that is at play here. It is simply convenient, too much so in my opinion, to just blame Jiemba."

"The mission burns down, the people of Wellington are hunted without reason or mercy, the police force disappears leaving us to the mercy of the violent biker gangs," Docker listed them.

"But surely the Spartan group would want them gone as well, the more they are present in Wellington the more likely they will be to get caught," Jiemba offered.

"Spartan don't want them gone," Docker blasted him. "They are part of the same group you fool. Ever heard of plausible deniability. Spartan employ those criminals to do their dirty work and then come in to clean up the mess."

"What?" Jiemba staggered back a step. "What are you saying?" He was starting to link a whole bunch of possibilities together.

"Oh it is becoming clearer now is it," Docker continued though the others put their hands out for him to stop. "Everything bad that has happened here is because of Spartan. The attack at the mission was by the bikie group because Spartan wanted to get their hands on the place but had no reason to do so. They burn it down and then help the people out. The crash with the inmate transporter, the night that you and I met, that was all a set up as well. They needed a reason to move into more properties, what better excuse than rounding up inmates. I asked you before how many people do you think are in one of those things. A dozen? Twenty maybe? How many homes were invaded the next day? It was probably to get you on their side as well. I couldn't believe when they ransacked their own prison. It is worse for you though, Jerome Less, the man you were searching for. Never existed. That man you saw was most likely just a plant to avoid detection."

"Their own prison? And I saw Jerome," Jiemba was watching as if his recent life had been part of a jigsaw puzzle. All the pieces had been in the wrong spots, which he had forced to suit his need. He had been chasing ghosts while doing it for someone else the whole time.

"You saw a man, who you were told was a man named Jerome Less, and you have been chasing him around town like a carrot to a horse. Blindly doing what they wanted you to do. And, Wellington

Star Five was paid for and built by the people of New Wellington. Why would you put someone in there just to break them out? How could you save face in doing so? Stage a jail break by the same criminals you employ. I make it sound like I knew all along. I didn't. I learned too late, but by that stage I had already been involved with hit and runs of Spartan vehicles and personnel, running interference for others to escape."

"While Docker was doing that Uncle Lou and Jonathan were trying to be more civilised in their approach," Josh added, seeing that Docker had become worked up and was seething at both the information and his failure. "They tried to be reasonable and a series of meetings were being put in place. The people were meeting the governing body as well as the local police to try to sort out the supposed problem. The police could see something was wrong, but understaffed and still fighting historical issues with trust of the population they were making little progress. It didn't help that the people of New Wellington could fund lawyers and spokespeople to speak on their behalf. Corruption is rife in politics, and ever since the city of Dubbo has become smaller, than its more popular suburb of DubVegas, it has swarmed over the north of the Central West. Normal means have been exhausted, more violent means are not working, we are stuck with appealing to the people and those same people have disappeared. We have become outnumbered and outmatched."

Jiemba had been duped. The light was fading in the silo as night arrived outside. Small floodlights attached to generators were slowly being lit to provide both heat and something to see the sadness surrounding them. Jiemba was running it all over in his head. He had been set up all along. He had been used to do something that he had believed would help him, something that he could never have achieved. Those he sought were being protected by those who had been helping him. Price had played him so well, and he had got everything that he had wanted while Jiemba was turned into more of an outcast. No, these people were outcasts, Jiemba had become the villain.

"Docker!!!" a voice called out from high up in the silo. There were apparently look outs all over the place. "Viper's gang is here."

"Viper?" Jiemba questioned.

"An old friend of yours, goes by the name of Selena," Docker replied angrily.

"How did they know how to find us?" Josh asked. "We have been hidden here for so long."

"Another coincidence Jonathan," Docker growled at the group. "I think not. Turn out your pockets." Docker ordered Jiemba. Jiemba wanted to punch the man for throwing it all back on him. He didn't have anything on him except a wallet and phone, which he threw heavily onto the table.

"Where did you get the phone?" Docker asked, Jiemba could tell the man's rage was building. "You don't have to answer, I already know. Spartan gave it to you didn't they. Probably straight from Price's hand himself." Docker smashed it on the table. "Are you still working for them or just plain stupid?"

Jiemba did not reply, he could not argue with the accusations that were placed towards him.

"It's ok for the moment," Josh replied, visibly shaking. "They can't get into this place, but we can still get out if we need to." Attempts at opening the rollers and external doors could already be heard with no success. The roars of the motorcycles could be heard getting louder and louder.

"Docker!!" the sentry's voice called out again. "We have a huge problem."

"What?" Docker yelled back.

"Run!!!" the man yelled instead, not willing to provide an answer or without time to do so, before disappearing back onto the side of the building. People on the ground floor had already been startled and were busy trying to get away from the perimeter.

"Will, Gum, start getting everybody towards the pipes," Uncle Lou ordered softly.

"We can't move the sick and injured," Jonathan added.

"We won't have to," Docker said to the group. "There is no way they can get in."

A heart pounding thud suddenly impacted on the outside of the silo. Long stuck grime fell freely along with some stone work which had already been crumbling away from the walls.

"What was that?" Josh asked in confusion.

"Will, Gum, go now," Uncle Lou ordered more persistently. "Now." A second thud followed the first, followed by another and then another. People inside the silo staggered as each sound rocked the silo's foundations. Finally a whole section of wall collapsed as another blow was delivered to the outside. Concrete buckled, casting rocks and dust in every direction. Jiemba hoped that everyone was clear but he couldn't see through the dirty mist. Whatever had caused the breach had pulled back only to strike through again a second later. More of the wall collapsed; fractures and cracks appearing all over the remaining walls. No sooner had the breach been widened chaos flowed through from outside. The jostling roar of dirtbike motors filled and echoed around the inner chamber of the silo. Bike after bike jumped through, splitting into multiple groups. Some of them pursued the homeless wrecks which fled before them while others sped towards the exits to either open them for more attackers to arrive from outside, or to cutoff the escapers completely.

"What is that thing?" Josh asked, pointing at the machine that had caused the initial hole in the wall.

"They call it a Gear machine," Jiemba explained as the massive robot like device cleared debris from the path it had created.

"We can't fight that thing," Docker announced, before sharing a defeated sigh. "I am done with fighting anyway." He walked over to where those who were still in the beds quaked with fear at the noise which was erupting around them, they could not see what was coming towards them as they were still hidden. "You all need to get away. I will buy you some time. I won't leave these people alone."

"I will stay with you," Jonathan declared following him.

"You are not a fighter," Docker argued.

"I am," he responded, "we just fight differently."

"It is useless to run," a voice, which Jiemba suspected was Price, boomed over a loud speaker. More doors were opening. What Docker said earlier was clear to Jiemba now. The bikers and Spartan group were working together and swarming over what could be the last remaining resistance to their ideas for social harmony.

"Jonah and Joanna, help get Uncle Lou out of here," Jiemba ordered.

"What are you going to do?" Joanna yelled. It was hard to hear her over the noise which surrounded them.

"I am going to try and buy some time, hopefully we can get more out of here," Jiemba replied. Without looking back he sprinted over the hill and down into the melee. Bikes tore dirt and grit in every direction. People screamed as they were pursued, tripping and stumbling as they tried to flee. They fought off their attackers as they came closer, failing in their attempts as they were knocked brutally to the ground. Many of the homeless fell to the ground or cowered in corners, hopeless in their efforts to escape. One bike was chasing a young Sudanese man in front of Jiemba. Jiemba was not weighing up who needed him more than others, he was just acting. The Sudanese man saw Jiemba approaching and suddenly surged forward with greater energy. Jiemba was going to get to him before the pursuer would. The young man made it past Jiemba with only seconds to spare. Jiemba threw an arm out, clotheslining the driver and knocking them to the ground.

"Get out of here," Jiemba bellowed and the man ran to follow the others. Jiemba could see Jonah and Joanna helping Uncle Lou to get to the massive pipe with no bars. In the entrance of that pipe Jiemba could also see Will and Gum urging others to go through, fighting off anybody who would try to stop them.

Jiemba turned back to see Docker and Jonathan standing defiantly with a handful of others who were defending those who could not do so themselves.

"Don't worry about us," Docker barked at Jiemba noticing that he was being watched. "Get the others out of here." He didn't acknowledge the demand except for turning and obeying. He trudged down the hill until he made it to the bottom. A whole bunch had made it to the pipes while others were in the process of doing so. Some had already been captured and could be seen being dragged towards the many vehicles that had appeared outside the opening and inside the silo through the roller doors that had been opened. Jiemba made it to a spot where he felt he could be the most help. He grabbed at bikers who had pinned some of the homeless people of Wellington, and sent them flying without remorse into walls or back towards the other assailants. He knocked down and rescued, three, four, six, almost a dozen. Wave after wave came and he found he was caught up in the brawl. More came straight at him in an attempt to take down the biggest threat to their success.

"Take him down," Price's voice bellowed again. Jiemba followed the voice and saw the man that he had worked with. Price stood with a mouthpiece in his hand near one of the always white vehicles. There was no doubt Price knew that it was Jiemba he was directing people towards. Beside him Jiemba could see the slender shape of Selena, wearing a Spartan uniform rather than the jumpsuit she was last seen in. Jiemba felt hurt just looking at her. "And get those others up here," Price directed others, drawing Jiemba's attention away immediately. A mighty explosion saw the large Gear machine finally break through completely to land hard inside the silo. Jiemba took down another cyclist but found himself faltering. He felt like he had to make an impossible decision just like he had done at the mission. This time it was to save those who were already escaping, or rescue those who were being taken away. No matter which way he decided he would let someone down.

Not again. He crunched his eyes together as if the action would help him make this decision. His senses heightened as he focused on logic. Where could he make the most difference? What could he do that no one else could? His muscles tensed, his teeth clenched, his smell was blocked by the combination of petrol fumes mixed with dirt which clung to his sweat stained body. He could hear the sound of bikes, and some of them were somehow getting louder.

He opened his eyes assuming that a bike was coming towards him again, but none threatened him. The throbbing rhythmic pulsation of a louder engine ricocheted off the interior walls, however, the bike that was causing the disturbing resonance was not even in the building yet. A mighty roar and crash saw another motorcycle erupt into the fray. It looked more expensive and far more impressive than the others as it spun in the dirt, doing circle after circle and spraying shrapnel in all direction. The commotion it caused made everyone cease what they were doing. It made no sense. Why would the other bikers be worried about this rider?

Unless they weren't with him.

The rider stopped suddenly, sweeping a hand through the Driza-Bone jacket he wore. The dust settled around him as he turned to look in Jiemba's direction.

"Sorry I am late," the man said as he pulled up the rim of the dark Akubra that he wore; revealing a large moustache and a mischievous grin. "I have been looking for you everywhere."

"Dennis?" Jiemba announced with alarm. "How did?"

"Now is not the time," Dennis shook his head. "I am assuming that these guys aren't friends of yours. You take the big one, I will help out the others where I can." He ripped at the throttle spitting more dirt into the air as his wheels spun powerfully. Jiemba watched as Dennis sped towards the other riders in the silo, and was shocked when his friend pulled out a whip which he spun wildly overhead. The whip spat out time after time, clipping rider after rider and sending them to crumple on the ground.

"Get up and run," Jiemba bellowed at them, hoping they would listen before they could be captured again.

"That is enough from you," a mechanical voice filled the air. Jiemba reflexively jumped to the side as a large robotic hand slammed into the ground where he had stood only moments before. The Gear machine had entered the fight and was focused on Jiemba. Another hand slammed forward but again Jiemba leaped out of harm's way. This time he spied the cockpit.

"Of course it would be you in that thing, Rogers," Jiemba snapped back. Jiemba knew that he had to distract this machine to allow everyone else time to escape, knowing that it was Rogers who drove it only made him want to do it even more. Jiemba wanted to just run in and start pummelling the machine but that was not going to help everybody else.

"Running away again," the mechanised voice of Rogers followed him. "The only thing you have ever been useful for has been leading us right here. But after today you will once again realise just how useless you really are, all while I am living it up on some beach far from this dump."

"Figures that you would be the only one scared enough to hide behind a machine," Jiemba replied. "Everyone out here at least is brave enough to fight me man to man. Cowardice suits you."

"I was wrong about you," Rogers spat, "you won't be worried about how useless you are. You will be too busy being dead." Jiemba could hear the pistons and gears pump and grind as the machine cranked up its speed. Blow after blow followed Jiemba as he dodged each as they came. They came close as Jiemba wasn't overly fast, but Rogers' recklessness was doing him no favours. One of the blades that the machine used to lift things was being used to slice at the ground in Jiemba's wake. The floor was cut to shreds resembling a tilled crop as it came after him. Jiemba managed to create some space between himself and the machine and regather near the escape pipe.

"Do those people need help?" Dennis yelled as he skidded to a halt next to Jiemba. "I have rescued all I can from the riders." He was looking up to where Docker and Jonathan were being overrun.

"They are protecting others," Jiemba said with a shake of his head, accepting yet another failure. "We can't save all of them this time. Not with other pressing issues."

"I will trust your judgement on that. It seems like it is time to go then," Dennis spoke urgently, "but if we don't seal this pipe they will just follow us."

"I will sort that out," Jiemba told his friend, "make sure the others are safe." Dennis flicked a switch on his bike and without a second thought drove it down into the pipe with a deafening roar. Jiemba watched as many of the Spartan vehicles had left, full of captives. The downed cyclists were regrouping; if they were to get into the pipe they would catch the others in moments. Jiemba couldn't just stand in the way, they would all get by him way too easily. He watched as both Price and Selena turned away from the scene, barking orders as they returned to the van and left.

Jiemba looked back at Rogers in his massive Gear machine. He then moved over to a large boulder of concrete which lay nearby.

"Hey Rogers," Jiemba yelled. "Catch this." Jiemba strained with all his might and dug his fingers into the outside of the concrete. He struggled for a grip for a moment but then found it moments later with a large smile on his face. He held it aloft, hauled it back over his head, and then launched it towards Rogers as hard as he could. The machine was too slow to move and took the blow straight in the chest underneath the canopy of the driver. The machine was flung hard into the wall, causing more destruction to the interior of the silo. With a mighty crunch another section of wall collapsed.

"Is that all you've got?" Rogers bellowed. It took a moment for the machine to recover. In that moment Jiemba had made his way over to the entrance of the pipe. The machine recovered quickly and picked up a portion of concrete that was almost triple the size of the one Jiemba had hauled. The man was too dumb to think about what he was doing. Electricity sparked from its circuits and the hydraulics crackled under the strain. Rogers was going to do what Jiemba had intended, even if he destroyed the machine in the process. The concrete was held aloft and then thrown like a baseball pitch. Rogers was completely accurate, but Jiemba wasn't going to hang around to see just how accurate. He turned and sprinted back down the dark entrance to the tunnel, following the throb of Dennis' bike engine for direction. The light which was present slowly fled as the concrete ball moved closer towards him.

Slam!

Jiemba had to keep running. The tunnel entrance collapsing under the earth shaking impact all around him. Jiemba realised that he was suddenly afraid. He doubted that he would survive if the silos were to collapse down on top of him, regardless how strong he might be. The pipe shattered into the flowing combination of water and mud, crushing the small plants that had grown in the torrid environment. Jiemba jumped clear and landed in a puddle which covered his legs. The pipe was completely dark. A moment went by before Jiemba walked back. The concrete ball had not only blocked the pipe but it caused it to cave in. A ground shaking shudder continued for a few moments. No one would be following them from that direction. He placed a hand on the rubble, hoping that Docker and the others would be safe.

At least a small group had managed to escape. But how much time had Jiemba bought them?

Chapter 17 – The passage

It was like a warzone.

The pipe was old, possibly built at the same time as the silo many, many years before. It didn't just run a couple of metres to meet a drain or stormwater runoff system. It crept slowly downwards until it met the river, just above where the Bell and Macquarie Rivers met. The pipe had been forgotten about a long time ago. It had been a refuge for nothing but plants that had overgrown its circumference and now only exit. A combination of ivy and moss crept up the sides of the tunnel, firmly growing in all directions before hanging down in curtains from the roof. The pipe was not just concrete. It was a building, worn spots along the walls revealing bricks that had been used to create the structure years ago.

As Jiemba made it to the exit he realised how terrible the situation was. Night had fallen all along the river's edge. There were only a couple hundred people who had managed to flee from the assault in the silo sanctuary. They were all strewn about finding shelter amongst the multiple gum and willow trees at the water's flank. A torrent of rain spewed down from above the canopy of the trees, flashes of lightning occasionally illuminating the tops of those tallest. Many sat about staring into the darkness unable to accept what had just happened. Countless others were busy nursing injuries that were carried by themselves or others. Some were badly wounded, having been beaten badly by the pursuers or crushed by the debris that had been flung into that once safe place by the massive Gear machine. No one met Jiemba's eye as he walked between the moaning and crying mob.

"Jiemba come here," a voice called out to him. A massive motorcycle was sitting quietly, acting as a barricade to the small group that had gathered beyond it. The clearing a little further along was only just big enough for them all to stand, but yet they all sat.

"I can't believe this," Jiemba muttered to himself, still loud enough for the others in the group to hear. He shook his head as finally someone looked at him. Josh shook his head as well, but somehow managed a smile.

"This has been coming for a while," the boy said. "You just had to be standing in the right spot to see it."

"I didn't see any of this, clearly I was in the wrong spot," Jiemba shook his head again as he reprimanded himself. "I allowed this to happen. By ignoring this I made it worse."

"I don't know how it can get much worse," Gum, the young Sudanese man spoke for the first time. "We were helping those people because we had the ability to do so. Now that power has been taken away."

"Yeah," his friend Will added, "at least we could hide out before. There is no going back, and how long can we stay down at this river before they find us? There is no where else we can go, and even if we could many of these people aren't able to move."

"Sounds bad," Dennis finally spoke up. "Jiemba, what are we going to do?" The others, including Uncle Lou who had yet to speak, all looked towards him for an answer.

"I just said I was the problem here," Jiemba said startled, "there is no way that anybody here should be listening to me for any reason."

"I heard you," Dennis said with a smug look, the rain trickling from the brow of his hat and the edges of his jacket. He looked like some wild bush tucker man, though far more focused. Jiemba was sure that he was taller than Jiemba remembered. "I have seen what you are physically up against, and I can see what is happening at this moment. Problems, all problems, without a doubt. So what are the solutions?" The heads either looked at the ground or back towards Jiemba.

"Look, Dennis, I appreciate your help from earlier. But this is way too big for us. I don't have time to explain, if I did you wouldn't believe me," Jiemba replied.

"You would be surprised, but, I don't need to know," Dennis spoke softly so the others not near the group couldn't hear him, silently urging Jiemba to do the same. Ever the teacher, Jiemba thought. "All I need is for you to tell me what you need."

"I have done some dumb things," Jiemba shook his head with a quiver. "Some terrible things. If you knew . . ."

"It would change nothing," Dennis interrupted. "Look, I didn't come looking for a fight. It wasn't by chance that I just happened to be driving through Wellington. I was looking for you. That was my only goal. I actually figured it would take longer, but seeing that massive machine stroll down the main street sort of forced my attention in this direction. I don't know what happened to you after that night at Burrendong. I am sure you could tell me some stories, just like I could share some of mine. But, I had to make sure that you were okay. I would have searched for as long as possible. No matter what. You were the laughing cheerful member of the group, the one who could light up a room with a smile and bring down the house with your laugh. I had a feeling that there was something else that you weren't telling us. I knew that you wouldn't tell anybody. I am just sorry that I couldn't do anything to help."

"I don't think anyone could," Jiemba replied sadly. "Not then anyway, and I am not sure anyone can now."

"You have to let people try," Dennis told him. "I know that, despite what you think in your darkest hour, that people who are close will not give up on you. They would take the hit, no matter how frequent or how much it hurt, just for the chance that something would change. There have been countless times in my career as a teacher where this has been proved. You want to be liked, you want students to be successful and then to remember you when they are at their highest moment. But you put even more effort into those who don't like you. You can be the most hated person by the student and by their family, to the point where everyone involved will say things that attack your character and try to confirm a perspective that you have no value, and that despite all the energy that you committed that it was all your fault. It hurts, but then a little voice inside tells you that they are wrong, and the only proof you need is that you tried. It is harder to believe if you did nothing. I have had to deal with something similar lately, the whole story can wait for another time, but I know that there are no lost causes. Even if there was it wouldn't be this, for the simple fact that you are here, and you are trying to make a difference."

"You really think that he can help us?" Gum asked, looking at Jiemba who had just stared at his feet the whole time.

"I know he can," Dennis replied with a smile. "There is no doubt in my mind. There is no one I would trust more, because everything he has ever done has come from a good place. Sometimes you can do the wrong thing for the right reasons. Jiemba has shown me that frequently. Once I saw him wave down a police car while he was driving in the other direction. The car in front of Jiemba had a man who was beating his girlfriend as he was driving, the car swerved all over the road. The police followed and pulled them both over, the man who was doing the beating was taken in to custody, the girl was helped in that moment."

"I wanted to do far worse to that guy," Jiemba added.

"And I know you could have done so," Dennis confirmed, "but the problem was also that Jiemba was driving without a licence. He didn't know at the time, he had lost his points somewhere along the way. He suspected it but wasn't sure. When they took his details he was charged and suspended. A choice made for the benefit of others."

"That was an easy choice," Jiemba argued.

"There are none of those," Uncle Lou finally spoke up.

"If they are easy it isn't really a choice," Dennis said nodding towards the older man.

"But there are so many things to think of," Jiemba was still not convinced, "I will miss something. It won't work. I can't plan for things that are outside of my control."

"You have done that before as well," Dennis continued. "2015, Emus vs Lions, cross city derby in the grand final. Jiemba is the most energetic guy at our club, usually building up everybody else before a game. 'You can do it' he would say, 'you've got this'. Everyone felt better, everyone were ten feet taller because they knew that Jiemba thought they could make a difference. The last night after training, Jiemba did not laugh and get merry with everyone, not straight away at least. Jiemba is not someone who chooses to read or write for recreation either. On that night though he wrote down every name of every player on the other team, even reserve grade players just in case they played. He expected them to make fun of him or straight up insult him. It wouldn't be an attack on how well he played, because he was good and they knew it. The abuse would be more personal. So, not willing to allow anyone to bring him down when others were depending on him so much, he wrote five comebacks next to every opposition player so that he could hit straight back and lose nothing. All unique, all as a reply never as a sentence starter."

"Really?" Will laughed. Jiemba just nodded, drawing a small chuckle from the others.

"I also remember a couple of Christmases ago," Dennis continued, "Jiemba went out and fed a big group of people in Orange. He made contact with several businesses in town, as well as a bunch of people who were willing to help out, and went out for a couple of weekends and gave out a free feed. It was up to you if you wanted to come or not, but it was targeted for people in need. Hundreds took up the offer, and were also given more food in the form of meat or hampers that would go a long way at home. Jiemba stayed around the whole time, talking to everyone, inviting groups like the local police force and mental health or support, so that they could walk and talk together. It was a big deal, even if Jiemba undersells it. It may seem like an easy idea but no one had done that before, or successfully since. No one thinks about community like Jiemba does. Some people didn't like it but I tell you, it made waves."

"The hardest choice is not picking between what is right and what is wrong," Uncle Lou spoke up after listening with great interest. "The hardest choice is choosing between what is right and something else that is right." Dennis nodded, loving the gem that the older man had dropped. "You rarely make a wrong choice my boy, just sometimes there was a choice which was better. But when you do anything people see you. The only person who has not been able to see all of this, is you. No matter what you do Jiemba, whether you do it all or nothing, it always makes the most impact."

"But we have no power here," Gum repeated his earlier thought. "We have six guys who are trying to make a difference, plus two more if you include those younger cousins." Jonah and Joanna could be seen and heard moving with encouragement through the forlorn group of homeless people. "How do we get it back? We have nothing. No resources, no place to hide or come up with a plan, we have nothing."

"That's not true," Jiemba finally said. He looked up for the first time, suddenly a spark glinted in his eye. His head spun towards Joanna, who, seemingly feeling his gaze upon her, turned back towards him. The fierce determination that Jiemba saw there was all he needed. "And all those things would be simply useless unless you have people who can use them."

"Yeah, but," Will countered. "We don't have many people who can do anything."

"We have enough," Jiemba said. "An avalanche can start from a snowflake, you can start a community with only two different people coming together."

"That doesn't make much sense," Josh was not convinced by the statement.

"Maybe not, but what about these for ideas?" He gathered the small group around, telling them their roles and what he wanted to do. He didn't want to risk anybody else but himself, but he conceded the idea that if he walked in alone then he could easily be outmanoeuvred. Someone would get hurt to either spite or stop him. Everyone agreed that the idea could work, even though it was a long shot.

"There is nothing left but to fight back. We cannot wait any longer. It is now or never. Everyone in?" Jiemba asked when he was finished. The others nodded. "There are two problems that we have at this point. The first is that my phone was destroyed along with my contacts. I can't call in the cavalry."

"Leave that to me," Dennis nodded confidently. Jiemba stared blankly at him wondering what brought on such confidence. Jiemba expected his friend to start flailing limbs awkwardly as he was put on the spot. "Just . . . trust me. I have my methods." He stood up, collected his gear and made to leave the group. He turned for a second and looked straight at Jiemba. "Whatever you decide to do back yourself. Don't doubt. Your heart has always been the strongest bit of you, and even though things have changed, in many ways, I still believe that to be the case." With a swirl of his jacket he was gone.

"The other problem?" Josh asked, redirecting as water welled at the corners of Jiemba's eyes.

"The people," Jiemba added, finding his voice with only the tinniest of quivers. "This plan is going to need them, and they will be put in harms' way. Adrenaline and thoughts of justice or revenge will only get you so far."

"I think I have a way," Uncle Lou put a hand on Jiemba's shoulder.

"Really?" Jiemba questioned his elder. "I can't wait to find out what that is." There was a hint of sarcasm.

"You doubt me now," Uncle Lou remonstrated his nephew, "but believe me by the time I am done it is going to change your life."

Everyone was wet. Not just because it was raining, hard, and not just the exposed parts of their bodies either. Those few who had taken up the call to fight back against Spartan and the criminals they employed had wholeheartedly followed Uncle Lou and Jiemba, promising to do whatever was required of them. After leaving the rest of the group, who were being looked after by the young Will and some able bodied people to assist those that remained, the problem became that the path moved from the side of the river and into the river itself. In some parts they were only as deep as their shins, but others they were as deep as their chests. This was fine for Jiemba but he was bigger than most. He deliberately stayed at the back of the pack to help those struggling to swim or even to keep their heads above the water.

Uncle Lou was surprisingly nimble in the water. He took Josh, Gum, and Jonah with him, and a small handful of others, as they went on ahead. Uncle Lou hadn't precisely outlined where they were going, even if he had the night hid almost everything from view. He did mention a couple of landmarks near the water's edge where Jiemba must turn so that he and the others could find the location.

Joanna was with Jiemba as well. She lead a small group of girls who were assisting him with those who couldn't swim, but their almost constant calming support to whoever needed it combined with their scary scolding if you were not doing what you were asked, was of enormous comfort to Jiemba. There were parts of the river where Jiemba had to hold some individuals up over his own head just so they could manage better. He thought nothing of it; until the one instance when he slipped on a rock under the water and was completely submerged. Those that he had carried plummeted into the water as Jiemba floundered about. He kicked hard off the stone beneath, launching out of the water to land firmly on the bank a couple of metres up from the river. He turned to see what had happened to the few he had carried and was greeted by a wave from Joanna and her girls who had assisted them immediately after.

"Not my proudest moment," Jiemba volunteered.

"Everyone has one sometimes," Joanna smiled back, "besides you jumped out of the water from the bottom. Probably the first time someone has ever done that." Jiemba nodded, feeling like he was getting away a little too easy. "Good thing the girls were here to save you." There it was. Jiemba nodded with a smile.

"You are absolutely right," Jiemba agreed.

Jiemba followed the landmarks as instructed, taking longer than he had anticipated. It would only be a few hours until the dawn, and that was when Jiemba had decided to put his plans into action.

"There should be a hidden creek here," Jiemba fumbled about in the flowing water. The overhanging reeds were mostly solid but as he searched he found a section where it separated.

"We had better be there soon," Joanna called out to him, "or all these people will be frozen to death or drowned. Won't be much good then." Jiemba agreed. He could see that those nearest to him were shivering as they slowly crept forward waist deep in the cold water. The rain had stopped but they were waterlogged through to their bones. They had endured so much already he wondered how much more they could take. When you had hit rock bottom the only option was to go up, because the alternative was something that he could not bare to think about. That was where he had been, but he could also feel a change within him.

Light could be seen far ahead as they made their way through the plants that fought each other at the water's edge. Despite the colder months setting in the native flora still thrived in the area. It was not tropical in Wellington, but it stood somewhere in the climatic crossroads between dry, wet, and subtropical. Jiemba saw the glow of yellow wattle hang down from taller bushes, felt the bristles of vibrant red bottlebrush, and smelt the fragrance of the eucalypt trees as cold morning dew penetrated the veins upon their leaves. Jiemba found that he was connecting with everything around him on a deeper level than he had ever done before. He could hear the buzz of insects all around him, the birds that shuffled in the trees searching for a meal for breakfast, and the animals that fled due to the commotion this foreign group of people made. The sounds these animals created and the reaction that the land had to them, scratching of leaves and the rush of branches as they were swatted aside, became louder the more the group went back inland away from the water. He couldn't feel the cold, nor was he affected by the flow of the water as he pushed through as easy as he walked on land.

Jiemba, however, could hear and feel the suffering of the people around him. No longer was he worrying about himself, no longer was he concerned about his future. All of his thoughts belonged to them. He found that he was thinking of solutions for them. As they had walked on in almost silence to avoid detection, even as they left the city and moved into the bush, Jiemba found himself back inside his head. The voice was not negative, it was helpful. Jiemba found himself thinking of solutions, not for what they were about to do now, but for when this was all over and the threat that Spartan presented had been removed. His mind found faults with his plans, but asked the questions how and why and what to enable him to get around obstacles. He reflected on things that he had done before that had worked that he could instantly apply to these people, but also how he could make those things better. Everytime he came up with a solution he realised that he could apply the same thinking to his own life. The dark spots in his mind suddenly lit up, filling the space occupied by problems with solutions instead. He felt himself walking with more purpose, his drive became stronger as the will of those around him waned.

The light became brighter in front of him, not filling the still dark sky but instead being more focused closer to the ground, shimmering along the water before jumping forward to stab at his eyes. The vegetation became more dense around them before suddenly it disappeared entirely. They unexpectedly came upon the entrance of a cave where the only way to enter was via the water. Jiemba imagined that if you came upon the spot when searching on the land you would walk straight by, never knowing that it had been there in the first place. Light from somewhere deep inside flicked and fluttered along the cave walls. There was not much clearance for Jiemba as he continued to walk through knee deep water.

Jiemba assumed that he was somewhere near the base of the mountain range that skirted Wellington. Underground caves were something that Wellington was known for, and surprisingly Jiemba found that he was recalling the knowledge as he walked. He was never a good student and names didn't stick easily for him. Small figures seemed to stalk him from the tunnel's walls. Drawings appeared all along the length of the tunnel, carved using stone or brushed using paints from the earth. Jiemba had never witnessed such a sight.

"Are these ancient drawings etched up here?" he asked quietly, even his breath created an echo despite the small group filling the interior.

"They sure are," Joanna responded. She was pressed up beside him, staring in wonderment just as Jiemba was; eyes darting between each image. "But these must have been done a very long time ago. Look. There are some basic shapes of people, Aboriginal of course, and they are doing a whole range of things. Hunting, gathering, and building mostly. But look at the animals. There are kangaroos, emu and possum. They are easy. But if that one there," she pointed to a small figure next to a man on the cave wall. She turned and pointed to others as she explained. "If that little one there is a wombat, then what is that one? It is the same drawing, but it is bigger, way bigger than the man next to it."

"So a big wombat," Jiemba offered, half laughing, but then stopped. "I remember seeing a big wombat at the Wellington Caves last time I was there. Assuming that whoever drew these didn't just draw a few wombats out of scale, that could be a Diprotodon."

"It could be," Joanna nodded. Her eyes sparkled as her thirst for knowledge grew, reflecting from the light at the end of the cave and water below her. "And if that is a Diprotodon, then these other animals could be from the same spot. Look. A giant snake, that is

Wonambi, the lion looking thing is a Thylacaleo, and that last one. Well that is you."

"What?" Jiemba chuckled.

"Megalania," she answered, "the giant goanna that used to roam around here. You are the only giant goanna I know." She ended by slapping him in the stomach where his own painted image of a goanna was exposed through a partially ripped shirt.

"You seem to know a lot about this," Jiemba said continuing to pay attention to all the images.

"Yeah, well," she started looking all sheepish as she analysed each image that they slowly passed. "People who assume that I am stupid will always be surprised. On the flip though, if the only museum in town is the Wellington Caves, guess where you go for every excursion at school? Eventually even if you are dumb you should still have some things sink in." Jiemba looked over at her as she stared back at him.

Then he dunked her under the water.

She came back up spluttering.

"What the heck was that for?" she asked.

"I thought you wanted something," Jiemba laughed loudly at her. "It couldn't have been sympathy, because I came from the same place and moved on. So I decided to give you a wakeup call. Hopefully the cold water brought you back to your senses, so you can use that brain you were just bragging about."

"You wet my hair," she growled at him, "and I was mostly dry before." She tried to keep staring at him but eventually started laughing along with him. "At least there is a warm fire up ahead."

"Really?" Jiemba asked, finally calming down.

"You can't feel that?" she asked. "The heat is filling this whole tunnel. I was actually starting to sweat before you saturated me."

They had been slowly creeping forward at the end of a long line throughout the length of the water tunnel. It would have only been about twenty metres long, maybe thirty. As they came towards the end Jiemba could see and hear more. They came into a cavern that reminded Jiemba of an igloo. At its centre was a mass of large wood that was burning ferociously, crackling loudly as light and heat filled the room. The ceiling had multiple chimney-like holes that were releasing the smoke into an outside area, somehow removing all of it as it had not flowed down into the tunnel where they had just come from; ensuring that the cave drawings were protected. There were no paintings inside the cavern but there were still many images etched into the walls. Many of the people that had made the journey filled the room. The new arrivals that were lined up in front of Jiemba welcomed the warmth from the fire with hands stretched out towards it. The rest of the room's occupants stood along the outside walls, talking to each other with renewed vigour. Making sure they spoke to each other. Only a few stood by themselves, but they stood with a fierce look of determination planted on their faces.

They also had something else. Each of them had markings on the exposed parts of their bodies. The Aboriginal men had red hand prints and animals painted or dragged extensively. Arms, legs and chest they were covered. The women were the same, although they had yellow and white paint. The other occupants who were not Aboriginal also had markings. Short lines on the foreheads, nose and cheeks. Small symbols showing respect that they were friends, even if they weren't family or those who belonged to the land. It didn't matter. These people were not concerned by what they wore, rather wearing it like a badge of pride.

The group flowed through the space towards the only other entrance to the room, which was on the far side of the fire. Darkness returned as they entered but there was something far more mysterious. When they had walked a few steps and rounded a few bends in the tunnel the light vanished. It was replaced by the look of millions of tiny stars above them.

"Are we outside?" one of the others in front of Jiemba asked out loud in amazement.

"No," replied another. "We haven't left the cave."

"They are glow worms," a third person chimed in. They were heading back towards where Jiemba had just come from. This man was also freshly painted. "This place is amazing." He said with a massive smile as he continued on his way. Jiemba shuffled slowly forward. He was aware that it was only Joanna and himself going slow. As much as his excuse was that he didn't want to run into the person in front of him accidently in the dark, and as a result crush them, he was quite content to just relax in this space. It made no sense why all these people who have had everything taken away from them, who then got hunted down and fled for their lives, before walking for kilometres through a river at the dead of night during a storm, should have any reason to be happy.

But they were. They were all happy. So was Jiemba. The pressure was still there, but somehow in that moment it wasn't.

"What is that noise?" Joanna asked. Slowly the sound of small drips of water that had accompanied the silence were replaced by something else. Music and chanting bounced along the walls as light once more returned. Jiemba could hear many sounds, most of them familiar. He heard the sounds of clapping sticks as he and Joanna walked along. These were accompanied by the didgeridoo, more than one to Jiemba's ear, some drums, and also some singing. When they came to the last turn once more were they greeted by the flickering of fire. The room they came into was enormous. The last few people stood before them but the rest had left back down the tunnel. Jiemba stopped, his head swirling as he took the whole sight in. They were forced to walk through smoke as soon as they entered. Two young men were waving large fronds at the fire which was covered in eucalypt branches. Jiemba walked through last, though everyone before him must have done the same. The cave that opened up before them after the smoke was astounding. It was an enormous chamber with stalactites, stalagmites and an abundance of glittering curtains of mineral filled rock seeping down from the ceiling. Gum accompanied by some other people of African descent played drums and danced enthusiastically as Jiemba and Joanna started heading up stairs carved from rock at one side of the room. Some other youths, who were still old enough to be out of school, held clapping sticks as they stomped through the grit on the floor. They chanted as they continued, being led by a much older man who knew every word perfectly in the language that he sang it. Jonah and Josh sat amongst rocks as they continued their climb. Josh had a long didgeridoo which sounded so melodious, while Jonah's was far shorter and was belting out a much deeper tone. The sound they made somehow resonated deep within his bones, filling his cells and penetrating his soul. The acoustics within the chamber made the notes repeat over themselves many times before they dissipated, giving the sensation that there were far more performers than were actually present. A shiver ran down his spine as he made it to the top of the cavern. Stairs led down the far side where the last person was heading down to join the others by the fire.

Uncle Lou stood at the highest point of the cavern, smiling deeply at both Joanna and Jiemba as they drew closer. He beckoned them to come closer and stand beside him. To do so they had to walk around a huge hole in the ground. It had a diameter of only a couple of metres but was still the focus of the platform. Uncle Lou was holding a large stick in one hand. In one motion he brought it across his body to crack into a large hollow log which rested against the cave wall. The beat echoed along the walls, the signal for all other music and movement to cease. The others present stopped playing, dancing and singing immediately. The music took a few more moments more before it disappeared hauntingly into the depths of the cave beyond.

"Welcome Joanna and Jiemba," Uncle Lou said as silence resumed. Despite the echo which had been present before, Uncle Lou's voice maintained its singular sound. "This place is an ancient site for the local Wiradjuri people. It has been passed down in secret from generation to generation, some people unworthy of knowing its location due to their intent to use it for their own purposes." Uncle Lou moved towards some rocks behind him as he spoke. Each of the rocks had bowls carved into their surface, each filled with Ochre of three different colours. He beckoned Joanna towards him first, as he did so an elderly woman stepped forward and waited without a whisper at his side. "This has been a sanctuary in times of war, in times of great hardship, or in times of great need. For millennia this cave has been used to ensure the survival of the people of this land, but from the point of no return they have exited from these halls stronger than ever before." He continued to speak as he started the next stage of what he was doing. He had moved Joanna over towards where the yellow and white Ochre was situated. The elderly Aboriginal woman followed her, delicately collecting whole handfuls of the special soil before beginning to smear it on Joanna's arms. Uncle Lou proceeded to talk as slowly Joanna was covered. "What changed when they were in the caves? They had less food, they were faced with water which was barely drinkable, they were forced into solitude with no sunlight or fresh air. How then did they emerge stronger? They drew strength from the earth, from the land around them. Before you is the only known Ochre well in existence. To make Ochre you usually have to complete a process of mixing the earth and water in exact amounts to turn it into a fine paste. In this cave that process occurs naturally. Underground springs of the purest water force the Ochre from the walls of this pit, heating up its contents like a hot spring or an ancient tar pit, churning it constantly. The strength that causes such natural phenomena is transferred into the Ochre, and thus does so again when it is worn by you. It brings out the strength of the individual from deep inside and holds it against the Ochre within the skin, thus making the individual stronger." The elderly woman was taking great care as she attended to Joanna. She wiped some Ochre on the face of Joanna, along the bridge of her nose, across her forehead, against her neck. "Strength doesn't just come in a physical sense though. It is strength of mind also which gives you wisdom, your strength of conviction which presents you with courage, your sense of justice which gives you purpose and a mastery of all three which gives you power." The woman had finished with Joanna, Uncle Lou immediately beckoned her to stand. She had tears rolling down her eyes, Jiemba could feel just how much this all meant to her. She bowed her head and moved off to the side.

"This place also funnels your strength with the land, with nature and the animals and people that live upon it. You draw strength from them past, present and the emerging," Uncle Lou looked at Jiemba, but instead of beckoning him forward the old man just sat.

"Before I share with you some of the strength of the earth. I want to share a story that you may not have heard," the older man continued. "An old story tells us that long ago a creature that we call the Rainbow Serpent, which created the land and life along with it, creating a diversity of people just like it shares a spectrum of its light. The Rainbow Serpent looked after the people with its enormous power, but power so great can also be terrible. After some time the people became complacent. They did not look after the land like they should have, they did not look after themselves. The Rainbow Serpent became enraged and unleashed its destructive force on the people. They were done for, they had made mistakes and it would be the end of them. Then, a mighty goanna rose up and defended the people. It protected the people from the fury and dangers, before chasing the Rainbow Serpent back into the sea. There the goanna stayed, at the water's edge, waiting for the return of the Rainbow Serpent."

"Sort of mimics real life don't you think," Gum spoke as everyone took the story in.

"The lady with the snake helmet, who just happens to be working for Spartan, all of whom are trying to destroy the people of our town," Jonah added.

"Then megalania over here, the giant goanna," Joanna added thumping an arm, unfelt, into Jiemba's ribs. "Ready to rise up and save the people."

"We cannot mix reality with belief," Uncle Lou interrupted, "that leads to arrogance and destruction. Instead we learn lessons from them, regardless of how much the tales parallel with our lives. Now Jiemba, come forth and I will rub this Ochre on you. The rest of you must prepare." Jiemba had no idea what Uncle Lou was talking about, but he assumed the others did, as they quickly turned and walked away. Joanna followed swiftly behind.

"Uncle Lou," Jiemba asked when everyone had left. "I have a serious question that I need to ask you before you cover me in Ochre."

"What is it Jiemba?" Uncle Lou replied feeling the heaviness of what he had told the young man, stacked on top of what he had been through.

"Well, I was just thinking," Jiemba started sheepishly. "I already have marks on my body that will probably never leave me, from when we did the ceremony last time. I understand the story you just told, and why you shared it. I am ready to lead this group, knowing what I must do and what may be lost."

"Go on," Uncle Lou waited for the serious question to come.

"I think it would be better if I was just covered in Ochre, from top to bottom, every bit of me, over my jeans, my ripped shirt, everything. Every bit of me should look like a movement coming at them." Uncle Lou was shocked. It was not how he imagined this chat going.

"Jiemba," Uncle Lou had no words. "It has never been done."

"Let's do it," Jiemba said with a laugh. "What else have we got to lose?" Jiemba didn't want to wait for an answer. He was so eager that he fought the urge to leap in at the first instance. He knew that he must be respectful, and completing his desire without permission would be anything but. Uncle Lou seemed to ponder the notion for a moment as he stroked his boney chin. Eventually he smiled, nodding in Jiemba's direction. Having received the approval he had requested, Jiemba jumped willingly into the Ochre well. He made sure that he was close enough to the side to latch on just in case it sucked him under. At first it felt like thick mud, but then it felt like quick sand. His legs were quickly devoured by the Ochre, his waist swallowed down a moment later. Jiemba clung to the side as his chest was submerged, further he sank until he was down to his neck. A big red gash of Ochre splashed across his face as he clenched hard and pulled hard against the forces that dragged him down. He could feel his muscles tense hard and the strain on the rest of his body. Then, slowly but surely, he felt his body rise back up. Moments later he was free on the outside, his Uncle giving him a curious look at how he had reappeared from the well.

"Probably should not allow anyone to do that again," Jiemba suggested to the older man. The pressure and steam which had bubbled up around him would almost certainly be too much for another person to endure. He also felt like Uncle Lou may have bent a rule to allow him to perform such an action.

"You're probably right," Uncle Lou admitted as he gestured at his young relative to follow him. "I know that talks are not your thing, big speeches and the like. The closest you have come was at half time during one of your games. You were pretty angry at the time, and the words were somehow inspiring despite every second one being a swear word or inaudible."

"You aren't wrong," Jiemba said. He felt like Ochre was dripping off him but didn't move to stop the flow. However it eventually settled would be how it would stay.

"So I thought I would help you out," Uncle Lou told him as he guided Jiemba back through the now empty space. The Ochre well left behind them and the dimly lit corridors of the glow worms all around them. "I thought of something more appropriate. This has been mostly forgotten, but what you are about to see is something that helps reduce anxiety and build self-belief. It provides strength to your soul while building resilience to anything that comes towards you." Jiemba suddenly felt the whole atmosphere shift. The tunnel filled with a mighty roar and the ground shook as something took shape in the igloo like room that Jiemba had entered into first. "Do not call it a war dance because it is not. We don't war here. There were never fences that kept people out in the old days, that is a new invention. Our tribes were all about welcoming, gathering together and building relationships. This dance is about all of us here, and everyone else who will join us, coming together no matter what background or belief you may possess, to be the change that needs to happen. Love, not war, has the power to make Wellington a place where people are united.”

He walked out into something that he could not describe. He had had to stand in front of a New Zealand Maori Haka once, as he prepared to play a New Zealand team when he had been on a rugby tour during his youth. This was like ten times louder than that and a hundred times more intense. Everyone in the room was taking part in some way. They were either involved in the dance covered in Ochre, or standing at the side cheering the whole thing on. Jiemba felt that the room was going to fall down around them as the dancers became more frenzied, the cheers shaking the foundation of the earth itself. Every ounce of everybodies effort was enthusiastically sharing the purpose they felt deep in their hearts. The skinniest person was suddenly a beserker, filled with energy beyond what their body could normally be capable of producing. Even the fire at the centre of the room was dancing to the rhythm of the wild fever that pulsated around it.

“Marramarra,” Uncle Lou added as the eagerness and exhilaration overcame the room. “Make. Create. Do.”

Jiemba felt every muscle of his body twitch with excitement.

This was it, this was the moment.

No one would stop them.

“Follow me,” he yelled violently into the room.

The next instant they all cheered, and then every single one of them followed.

Chapter 18 – The Bigger Man

"Gumbo is on the line again," one of the operators called out. Price waved a hand towards the man who had said it, motioning for him to cut the line and end the phone call. Price would not speak to the police officer. He stood in the massive surveillance room deep within the Spartan headquarters. It was situated far below ground, deeper than any other area in the complex. It was effectively a panic room the way it was built, more likened to a bunker or bomb shelter. Price was surrounded by state of the art equipment being operated by the best hackers, tech experts and surveillance specialists the country could offer.

Yet still he was unhappy.

He wanted to pace the room, wanted to yell at someone for a result that had not been achieved, but that would not be best for business. It would reveal how he truly felt and display that he may not actually be in complete control. Besides he could clearly see that there was nothing they could do. Any outburst he made would only make them question him, and at this moment he needed all of them loyal and ready to do what needed to be done.

Each of the screens in front of him, besides him and also above him, showed an image from somewhere within Wellington. He mostly ignored the screens off to his right as they only displayed a video image from the corners of New Wellington. He had security occupying that area like always, and apart from his own people there was no other movement from that area. Unfortunately there was no movement on any of the other cameras either. Nothing he didn't already expect anyway. He could see that the people he had left up at the old silo were still there. Some were busy arguing with local police while the rest were helping to fix a terrible accident that had occurred. The story, the lie, had been that one of his Gear Machines had been the victim of some mechanical failure, causing it to careen out of control and crash into the side of the massive stone building. He had also allowed the word 'sabotage' be spread, convincing those that listened that he was not just dealing with innocent people, but that many were willing to be violent and destructive. Thus they must be removed.

He had sent a crane, a tech crew, and his fire and rescue team to help fix the problem. None of them were needed. Most of them were only required to draw attention away from the other crew he had inside the silos, removing the last of the vagabonds, drifters and beggars that had been captured during the night. When he deemed it to be appropriate, and there was no trace of wrongdoing on his behalf, he would simply request the whole lot to come back to base, the Gear machine would all of a sudden function normally and, apart from a patch job that would be required to fix the silo, everything would return to normal. The people of New Wellington would foot the bill for the reconstruction, and they would be happy to do so, because after today they would all be free of the filth that had been allowed to hang around Wellington for so long. But that reality hadn't arrived.

Yet.

He knew the last of those who would oppose his ideals were still out in the streets, they had nowhere else to go, now that their hiding spot had been discovered and destroyed. They had also had their muscle and voice removed when Spartan had captured both Jonathan Mires and Shane Docker. The people were leaderless, leaving the only thing left to do being to round them up. But so far none had been found. Price estimated that there would be no more than a couple of hundred that had escaped from him the evening before, and he also assumed that half of that number were injured or ill; like so many of those that they had already taken in. The fight was gone in them, the conflict was over.

So where were they?

Then there was that other group. What was his name? Judge. The man had come alongside only a few others with demands and accusations. What he had said was all true but Price had him removed from the outside perimeter nonetheless, without confirming anything the man had said. Price had expected a threat from the man as he was sent on his way, but he had received nothing but a smile and a wave. It was another wildcard in the mix. He had already had his fill of that with Jiemba. It would eventually make no consequence.

"Sir, we have movement," one of the operators flagged his attention. Some of the cameras weren't showing the best images. The sun was only just rising and apart from the normal bright light that struck the devices they were also being impacted by the glare from the road. The storm that had blown over from the night before had left the roads wet and the rays of sunlight bounced, seeming to enhance that brightness straight down the lens. None the less there was a small group of people moving in the shadows out onto the roads. They were not trying to hide and keep to the hidden parts of the streets, instead walking boldly straight down the middle.

"There are others on this camera sir," another operator called out, pointing out more on another screen. Price squinted as he saw more appear at a different location. Hands started to go up as more and more operators discovered people walking without care through the streets.

"We have a presence in New Wellington," another called out. Price rubbed a palm over his brow as he took in all the information. He was glad there was movement, but he had hoped it wouldn't have come all at once. It didn't matter as he had the resources to deal with them. It just made his group more visible than he would like.

"Okay listen up," Price took charge and the room took notice. "I want all those already out in the streets to move in on those who are alone. Discover whether they are people that we want removed or those who are just going out for a morning walk. Remove the dissidents, and reassure the others. We have teams ready to go for the larger groups, identify those groups and eliminate the threat. Bring them in immediately. Any larger groups notify me and I will release a suitable force to deal with it. Once the transports leave the hangar area I want the building locked down." He received words and nods of compliance. "Continue this as new targets are identified, notify me on my headpiece if anything else comes up." He left the room after taking a transmitter connected to ear pieces and a microphone. For the first time in a while he felt like there was something he didn't have control over and he didn't like it. Price went to get ready for any other eventuality.

Jiemba waited until he saw the last of the vehicles leave from Spartan headquarters. He didn't have a phone or communication device to tell the others that it had started, but he was also grateful for that. He hated to micromanage people, and the point of the entire job they were doing was to have trust in each other. Jiemba knew his role just like the others knew theirs. It was time to act.

Jiemba pulled himself free of his hiding place beneath the bridge that connected the old and new versions of Wellington. He looked, and felt, like the troll from old fantasy tales. He jumped onto the bridge from where he had been hiding just below in the bushes. The red Ochre he had been dipped in had stuck hard to Jiemba, staining blood red and suggesting he was a creature of far more malice. He walked alone for the moment. Past the stadium and on towards Spartan with the sun at his back. Jiemba cast an eye towards a camera nearby, knowing he had been seen. He only had a couple more moments where he would be alone, and he ran through the plan in his head. Just like that night Dennis had talked about, he had many of them. Plans existed from A through to Z, and then there were still some more.

The headquarters were completely locked down. The front gate with the razor wire bar at the top was closed, and the hangar doors were shut with an addition that Jiemba hadn't seen before. There was a trench that ran around the edge of the building, and a wide bridge which he realised had always been lowered. Made of lead or some other metal it had folded up to form another barricade and remove vehicle access to the building.

The familiar sound of motor cycles erupted from the nearby streets. Jiemba looked around, not denying that he searched for Selena amongst the group. She wasn't there, but nor did he assume she would be. The large collection of bikes congregated along the street, barring his access. They waited for him to make a move but he did not.

Another booming thump of an engine roared to laugh from back along the bridge. It was accompanied by a stereo which belted out some song that Jiemba hadn't heard before. The bike in the lead was followed by a handful of others. Jiemba smiled as Justin led the charge. He stopped only metres away from his friend and gave him a wink as he swept long strands of his hair out of his face. Riding without a helmet, surely he wouldn't have gotten away with that in Orange.

"Hey mate, what's happening? You alright," Justin Rhymer, the man known as Justice, asked him as if there were no cares in the world.

"I'm alright, you?" Jiemba replied back with a grin.

"Yeah, I'm good man, good," Justin nodded. "Anyway are these hounds bothering you? I mean, I would be happy to move them for you. I could be like, your cavalry. You know?"

"I don't want to put you out," Jiemba shrugged. The seriousness of the morning had somehow lifted slightly.

"Nah man, I would love to help you out," Justin answered. He revved his engine so that it thundered in the middle of the street. He gave Jiemba some sort of salute with his hand, his middle two fingers and thumb wrapped as his pinky and index pointed towards him. He turned his handles and did a burnout in the middle of the street, cheering as he spun. The smell of burning rubber filled the air.

"Whoooh," Justin screamed, barely audible above the sound of his own bike. "Chase the sun my friend." His bike shot out and instantly sped towards the group that blocked Jiemba's path. Justin's companions followed in his wake. They were only metres away from the other group. Justin's hair fluttered in the breeze as he charged, his unbuttoned shirt exposing his chest for everyone to see the muscles below. He seemed to be in ecstasy as he rode. His opponents seemed to waver as he came at them, some gunning their own engines in a show of defiance. At the last moment Justin took on the line at an angle. His bike was so heavy that the smaller dirt bikes had no chance of blocking his way. He slammed into the first couple, forcing a hole in the middle and sending some of the riders flying. He then turned and sped down the rest. Pulling his guitar free of a holder at the bike's side he started whipping it around with one hand and pummelling some of the others. His companions pulled out their own weapons and set about clearing the group. A moment later the street was clear, left with those riders who were beaten and bloodied moaning on the bitumen. Jiemba walked on.

The situation with the bikes, which continued to blow up around him, was not his concern. He walked towards the gate of Spartan headquarters. He touched and heard a spark. Electrified. Jiemba had felt nothing. He grabbed the bars on the fence and started pulling. The electricity flowed through his fingers. He was sure it would be a high voltage but it just made him laugh. Jiemba giggled the whole time he moved. He pulled the gate back towards the road, snapping wire and poles as he moved. Eventually the hinge snapped at the gate's side, ceasing the flow of electricity and allowing the whole thing to swing back without resistance. He slammed it back against the fence, before doing the same thing with the other gate. He walked forward unopposed. A red light spun at the top of the headquarters. He knew that if he got inside he would be met with a sizeable force.

There was no if though. This was not a siege, it was an inevitability. Jiemba had come to grips with how strong he had become. He did his best to look intimidating, hoping that all those inside were scared of his approach as they watched on from behind the surveillance cameras. The trench was about as deep as a person, a problem for anybody trying to get across quickly as it was at least a metre wide. Jiemba lent over full stretch and grabbed the top of the bridge which had been pulled up. He felt like his feet were stable enough although he was unbalanced. He wrapped his fingers around the edge of the bridge and started to pull. It was more difficult than the gate, causing Jiemba to flex and tense more so. He gritted his teeth as he started to pull. The bridge was heavy and Jiemba felt locked into place. It seemed hopeless.

So Jiemba just tried harder.

Jiemba pulled hard with as much effort as he could muster. Nothing happened at first but then he started to feel it in his fingers. Little by little the metal started to give, crunching as the locks holding it in place broke, followed by the mechanisms that had forced it into place to begin with. When Jiemba had pulled it half way down he took a step back to get a better grip. Then he slammed it into the ground. The concrete shattered with the force, and Jiemba found himself taking a deep breath. He shook it off.

"Hopefully this one is easier," he said out loud as he looked at the massive hangar doors. He looked for a spot where he could get a grip. There weren't many. He decided that he would probably have to make some for himself. Then the massive doors opened. Just as he was about to slam his fists into the iron. "Why couldn't they have done that before?" Jiemba asked himself, chuckling again.

"That will do," a familiar voice said to him as the gates opened completely. Price stood in front of him with an entourage of dozens. Each with a weapon held in their hands. Most had tasers while a couple, closer to Price, had guns. As Jiemba looked around the interior he could see that they weren't just on the floor but also littered amongst the ladders and walkways that spread throughout the area.

"Finally realised that you weren't going to stop me," Jiemba replied as he took it all in. "Only took me to break your fence, and your bridge. I reckon it will probably take you longer to fully give in though." Price flicked his eyes around the defences around him.

"From where I stand I don't have to back down at all," Price held his hands aloft showcasing what was at his disposal. "But I also hold all the cards. You were always so easy to manipulate Jiemba. It was a shame you chose to side with the people who are destroying this community. We could have continued to use you."

"I won't be used anymore," Jiemba replied. "Besides, people don't destroy community, they ARE community, and, when they realise how strong that makes them, when they are united they can do anything."

"And yet here you stand, alone, once more like you always were. And always will be," Price laughed. "It makes you vulnerable. No matter how strong you think you are you will always have a weakness." Price moved a hand to his ear, opening a communication line to his security bunker. "Patch me through to the silo," Price ordered, before turning his attention back to Jiemba. "I don't need to be as strong as you to bring you down. I just need the right leverage." Price sniggered and returned his hand to his ear. "What?" Price asked, trying to hide his anger. "What do you mean? Then try someone else. All of them? What?"

"You see," Jiemba replied for him, "you assume that I am alone because I am here by myself. You will instead find that you won't be able to contact your people up at the silo, and soon you won't be able to make any connection with anyone outside of this facility. What you need to realise, like I have had to, is that no matter where I go, no matter what I am doing or who I am with, I am never alone. My friends, family and the support they give me, is always with me no matter where I am or how far apart we are. You assume that even now I am here acting by myself. But you are wrong."

"But you are also wrong in one other way, in a way that will be your undoing," Jiemba also offered.

There was more than a hint of annoyance in Price's voice as he only just held his cool. "I am always one to listen to feedback," Price even managed a smile. "Enlighten me."

"You assume," Jiemba said, a tear fell down his face as he remembered JayDee and the lessons that he told him. "And when you assume, you deny yourself any opportunity to find out the truth of who someone really is, relying on stereotypes or poorly formed preconceptions which only disrespect those who you are focused."

"Never assume," Jiemba said finally.

"Thank you," Price said with a nod of his head. "Thank you so much, Jiemba. I will make sure I never do that again. From this moment on I will take on what you have told me. Someone who comes before me covered in mud, who hides in the gutters, with no home or possessions. I will aspire to be just like you." Price smiled and turned around, walking through the first line of those who stood behind him.

"Kill him," Price said.

Jiemba reacted as he would have before, as any normal person would have. He cowered behind his hands as the guns started firing and all those present lunged into motion. Jiemba felt the bullets slap against his shirt, splattering some of the red Ochre which hung there. His shirt ripped, as did the jeans he still wore, but the bullets felt no different to if he was being poked by a child. Why fore then was he cowering?

Jiemba charged headlong into the line. Watching as Price disappeared behind the group and the throng of people pressed forward. Jiemba wasn't just aimlessly moving. He targeted all those people who had guns in their hands. One by one he pursued them, removing the guns from them, crushing the weapons, then disabling those who had fired. Stupidly they continued to fire upon him as he entered the melee, many other security personnel felt the sting of the bullets instead of Jiemba. He was like a bull in a china shop. He terrorised anything that moved until he was convinced that there was no more lethal danger around him. Staring up at the roof he saw the few who had been firing up there. He used the crushed weapons as projectiles, launching them to knock out those who had been threatening him from a distance. He had only knocked down a dozen or two, but the crowd was overwhelming even for him.

The sound of a trumpet being blown from behind him alerted Jiemba to the presence of more arrivals. "Sorry I bailed on you," Justin called out. He had been the person blowing the trumpet. Jiemba shouldn't have been surprised that the musician was able to play multiple instruments. "I needed more reinforcements." A small group of bikers rode in behind him. Judge's Court were the leaders, along with Dennis in his outfit. Each rider carrying one other on the back of their bikes. Judge had Jonah, while Gary McShaun, the executioner, had some giant maroon jersey wearing man riding on the back of his. Jonah and many of the others that Jiemba had handpicked were responsible for causing a scene all over town to draw out the vehicles. Where vision would suggest they were alone they were actually supported by several others.

"This is Billy," Gary said, "he wants to help." Jiemba nodded, watching as Easter, the Jury, arrived carrying Joanna and Justin had Josh riding with him. Gum and Will were riding with some of the others.

"We have to end this now," Billy called out. He was representing the ideas of the people. Jiemba saw Judge staring at him.

"Tell us what we need to know," Judge said, all of their engines purred quietly, waiting the command to jump back into action. Jiemba didn't have to pretend, he knew what had to be done.

"Listen up then," Jiemba started, pointing in different directions as he spoke to everybody in turn. Spartan personnel weren't standing by waiting for Jiemba to reveal their secrets. They were remobilising into a defensive structure ready to oppose them. "Judge, you will find your old man in a small vault if you go through those doors, down a few flights of corridors, and then into some secure rooms. I don't know what else is down there." Jiemba received a nod. "Easter, Joanna is a wiz with computers, she told me. I need you to get her down to the lower levels. There is an elevator but it is secured, so you will have to take the long way round. There is a surveillance bunker, but there are a bunch of people down there. You might need some more help."

"I will be enough," Easter replied defiantly, receiving a small smirk from Joanna.

"Okay," Jiemba ignored the rebuff. "Justin, through those doors are the holding rooms. If you get in there you will be able to release everyone who has been taken in over the last few days. If you can get them out that makes this whole process easier, plus we might get some support from those inside."

"I will help you," Josh agreed, "A friendly face to those people might help."

"Gary, I need you to clear a way," Jiemba told him. "I will help you."

"It will be my pleasure," Gary, the executioner, replied.

"No killing," Jiemba demanded.

"Well, that is less fun," Gary complained. He was fixed with a glare from Judge. "Fine, no killing,"

"Let's go then," Jiemba yelled. The screech as tyres squealed back into life was defeaning. Judge's Court and the few extra riders ressembled a cavalry charge of old. Jiemba turned to Dennis. "Is it sorted?"

"The silo is secured, plus I called in some help," Dennis nodded as he rolled his bike casually to one side and parked it out of harm's way. The fighting had already commenced from within. "Looks like the only thing left to do is to clear out the riff raff." He pulled a whip clear from his side and looked at Jiemba. "Are you ready?"

"I was born for this," Jiemba replied. "It just took me a while to figure it out. By the way . . . a whip. That is like the worst weapon to take into a gun fight."

"Wait until you see it in action," Dennis replied, before charging into the fray.

All members of Judge's Court sped into the fight. They did not get off their motorcycles like Dennis had done, instead using them as a battering ram to get to where they immediately needed to go. Spartan personnel tried to lash out as they sped past but most jumped clear to avoid being hit. Judge was the first to reach his destination. The front of his bike had a reinforced bar which he slammed into the doors that Jiemba had told him to head towards. They splintered as they smashed back against the brickwork. Judge continued riding with Jonah still holding on tightly behind him. The corridor was empty apart from the sound of the bike rebounding down into the lower halls. The sound that came back revealed a small amount of Spartans hiding down below.

"Have you got any weapons there?" Judge asked his young friend.

"No," came back Jonah's reply. "All I have is my didge."

"Well that isn't a weapon, and I don't really want to break it," Judge nodded. "Did you know my old man?"

"I did," Jonah answered, "he was one of the nicest old blokes I ever knew. I learned a lot from him. He gave a lot to others without ever asking for something in return." Judge seemed to ponder that for a moment.

"Can you play that thing?" Judge asked.

"Sure can," Jonah said proudly.

"Play something for the old man. And hang on." Jonah sat back down and pressed his legs hard into the seat for balance. He aimed his didgeridoo down at the ground and then blew as hard as he could. Despite playing on the back of a bike in the middle of an epic battle Jonah maintained the calmness in his breathing and played a tune that was profound. The combination of engine and didgeridoo against the solid walls and floor resonated everywhere. It was like the bike was riding with an electric charge all around it. The melody itself almost becoming the destructive force ready to overwhelm any opposition. They turned a corner, after slowing down for a moment, and were greeted by a score of Spartans.

"Hold on," Judge said out loud. Jonah continued playing. With his father so close Judge unleashed his fury on the people who had held his body captive. He opened the throttle and charged. He wasn't aiming for any of them, but he also didn't care if he hit them. Some were struck out of his way, others fled before him, some became speed humps down the hall way. When they made it to the end Jonah finished his song and Judge looked back at those he had just run over. His gaze dared them to follow, none took up the challenge. Judge and Jonah were left alone. Judge finally parked his bike, and found the door he needed. He opened it, beckoning Jonah to follow him. The pair walked slowly into the cold room. It took no time at all to find where the old man was located. He had been there for weeks but Judge still wished to see him no matter the condition. To Judge's surprise the old man looked okay despite what had happened. Judge even chose to believe that he was smiling.

"Do we need to get back to the fight?" Jonah asked. Judge shook his head slowly.

"Be my guest," Judge said, "take my bike if you would like. I will be staying right here."

"Do you mind if I stay with you?" Jonah asked.

"No," Judge said with another shake of his head and a smile, "in fact I would welcome the company."

"So are you actually good with computers?" Easter asked Joanna as they continued down another flight of stairs.

"I am okay," Joanna suggested. "Not as good as Jiemba made out. If I was not useful Jiemba wouldn't have let me come along though, so I had to tell him something."

"Even, if it is dangerous?" Easter asked.

"I can look after myself," Joanna replied. It was less than a snap but there was a hint of defiance in her tone.

"I believe you can," Easter replied with a smile. "You might have to in a minute. Joanna, as strong as I know you are, please leave most of this to me." It wasn't an argument. They had almost arrived to the bottom of the stairs. The elevator was next to them but red lights flashing all over it suggested it could not be used. The bunker stood before them as did several guards.

"You aren't allowed here," one shouted at Easter as she bounced her way towards him.

"I know," she replied. She quickly flicked one leg up to kick him across the face, leaving a blood filled gash as he fell to the ground. In the next step she planted her foot and kicked her other leg straight up to catch the next guard in the chin. He dropped instantly to the floor alongside his companion, both out cold.

"Whoah," Joanna remarked with gleeful astonishment. "You can take all of them. I am just happy to watch you." Easter removed a key card from the pocket of one of the guards and pressed against the panel to open the door. She smiled at Joanna for the remark. As the door opened she was punched hard in the face.

"Easter," Joanna yelled. She jumped forward to attack whoever had done the damage but was immediately thrown back against the wall.

"Leave her alone, Viper," Easter yelled as she flipped back to her feet. A bruise was developing on her face as blood trickled down her cheek.

"Long time, Python," Viper said as she walked out from the doorway.

"Python?" Joanna repeated as she got up from the ground rubbing her side. "How many names do you have?"

"A few, but that isn't important right now," Easter answered. She waited for Joanna to move slowly towards her before adopting a defensive stance in front of the girl. "But I don't go by that name anymore."

"That's right," Viper said mockingly. "What are you known as now? Jury wasn't it, what an odd name. So what does that mean, people's fate are in your hands? You have the last decision perhaps? You were able to make those decisions before."

"I made no decisions when I was a Fang," Easter replied, "it was a prison where we were used for our skills and abilities with nothing to show for it. I traded up, while you just sold out. What are you now, assassin for hire, a mercenary for a price? You can do better Selena."

"You know nothing about it," Selena spat back. She sprang forward, throwing a punch towards Easter and following up with a sweeping leg. Easter dodged both, ending her evasion by performing a backwards cartwheel. Easter then took her opening, returning a punch quickly followed by a round house kick. The punch was blocked but Selena caught all of the kick.

"I have heard from others about what you have been doing here, and seeing some of it first hand," Easter replied. "Getting close to people to betray them is a low act, even for you."

"Where did you hear that?" Selena asked, her hands which were held as a guard over her face dropping slightly.

"I made a new friend, a good guy who probably has more trust than he has sense," Easter replied. "He had it bad and then confided in you. Then you stabbed him in the back."

"Jiemba?" Selena asked with confusion. "Jiemba told you that."

"He did," Easter replied, still ready to fight. "He told us that he felt like he had found someone who could understand him, someone that he was prepared to talk to. But it turned out you were just trying to use him." Selena took a breath, her hands dropped completely.

"He is here, isn't he?" she asked.

"Jiemba is going to tear this place apart," Joanna answered instead.

"I believe you," Selena replied. She looked at the both of them for a moment, then she dropped her head. "The password is Leonidas, all capitals," Selena added as she walked over towards the elevator. She pulled a key card and the door swept open. "Tell Jiemba that it wasn't a lie." The doors shut and Selena was gone.

"Well that was fun," Justin swept his hair aside as the last body hit the floor. He, alongside a couple of others, had stormed the prison cells, most of his shirt was now ripped revealing more of his chest than before. Every guard that had stood in his way had been dispatched, lying unconscious on the floor. Despite looking like an unassuming minstrel the man was deadly. None were dead, as they had all been ordered to keep them alive, but when they eventually woke up many of the Spartan personnel would have injuries which would not heal for a very long time. "I thought that would have been a lot harder."

"It would have been," one prisoner called out. "But just before you arrived a big group of them went out another way."

"That isn't very chivalrous of them," Justin remarked, shaking his head in annoyance.

"Docker is that you?" Josh called out as he ran forward from the back of the group. "Are you alright?"

"Yes it is me," Docker replied. "And no they weren't running away, they were heading out to join the fight. Let me tell you, if that group is out there then you are going to need more help."

"Are you willing my good man?" Justin laughed as he found the keys and opened the cell.

"Absolutely," came the reply.

The hangar was in turmoil. A storm built from rage, confusion and release thrashed within the walls. The man known as the executioner from Judge's Court was built for the name. He swept in on his bike knocking countless down with his approach. Then, surrounded by a large number, he sprang from his bike seat and set to work. His dreadlocks bobbed in time with each blow he delivered, his warped smile creating angst from all around him. Every now and then Jiemba noticed the man pause, turning away from creating more serious harm despite his primal instinct. The man who had accompanied him was also busy, but he was gathering far less attention. For him to be more useful he would need to be part of a much larger group as he was individually outmatched by all the Spartan staff that surrounded him.

Jiemba found that he was blocking his companions from more serious harm. They were still only a few against many. Dennis was a destructive force. He went to town with his whip, knocking dozens from their feet with each wave of his weapon; the sound was terrifying as it cracked and echoed within the space. He needed no assistance as the Spartan force felt his wraith, but he pursued none as they fled before him.

The group had no end destination. They were causing as much chaos so that the others could infiltrate the space as best they could. Jiemba was on the look-out for three individuals as he pressed forward against the throng. For personal reasons he wanted to seek out Rogers and Selena, not knowing how his emotions would drive him if he should encounter them. Jiemba knew, however, that Price was his main target. Capturing that man would mean an almost immediate cease of activity.

Jiemba, however, could not find Price anywhere. Jiemba doubted the man was too far away. He suspected that Price had an instinct for survival but doubted that was not at the expense of what he had created here.

"If we don't find those in charge soon this is going to get out of hand quickly," Dennis called over to Jiemba. Jiemba could see what he meant. The ones who were not engaged in the fighting were communicating with somebody else, probably calling in reinforcements, and some of the others were getting into vehicles. If they managed to escape it would draw out the whole thing, with the possibility of making it worse. The fighting continued. Jiemba could do this all day without getting tired, but there was more at stake than just him.

"Look," Billy yelled out. "Out those doors. Reinforcements have arrived." Jiemba followed where he was pointing, still inside the facility. He didn't know about reinforcements but a great number of people fled out into the melee. Some, he noticed led by Docker, surged into the fight immediately causing damage. Others led by Josh and supported by Jonathan were slowly making their way towards the exit in an attempt to escape. They were not alone. Justin was wielding a large iron pole that he had pulled from somewhere, swinging it wildly at any who attempted to stop the group from leaving. More Spartan personnel flooded from more doors at all positions of the complex.

"To me," Billy roared out, and Jiemba watched as the released townspeople flooded towards him. A maelstrom was spinning from their position, an unstoppable force that whirled through the security force. The relentless passion for change overcoming any that stood against Billy and Docker, with Gary the executioner adding his own glee filled presence. Jiemba heard engines roar to life as vehicles were suddenly occupied. He ignored these as he kept searching for the faces he needed in the crowd.

Suddenly he found one.

Selena walked slowly out from one of the side doors. She was across the hangar but Jiemba still felt that their eyes met. She didn't look like she was preparing to fight him, or anybody else. She wasn't hurrying to leave, although she was avoiding all the trouble that she had helped create. The look in her eye was not one of scorn, hatred or rage at what he was doing. Instead she wore a mask of sadness. Her movements drooped, her head hung on her petite shoulders, and as much as she met his gaze Jiemba could tell that all she wanted to do was to look away. Their gaze held on one another. Jiemba's heart sank, his feelings all twisted. She had done so many bad things, but she had connected with him on a deeper level. He had thought that at least. What was he going to do?

"Jiemba look out!" Dennis bellowed at him. Jiemba had not been aware of what had been happening around him as he focused entirely on Selena. He was struck, hard, on the side of his body and tackled to the concrete with a painful amount of force. A giant foot slammed into the ground right where he had stood only seconds before, producing a crater to appear in the polished floor.

"That hurt," Dennis said as he helped his friend to his feet.

"You're telling me," Jiemba replied. The collision appearing to have hurt both of them.

"Hasn't happened for a while," Dennis continued, "I wasn't sure it would happen again to be honest."

"I know the feeling," Jiemba agreed. "You've changed man. You're so strong. I mean you were strongish before, but now . . ."

"You too mate," Dennis responded. Nodding too much so that it had become awkward. Their focus turned to a Gear machine which had become active. It was separating the remaining crowd, everyone scurried as it moved.

"I love these things," Rogers was once again in control of the big machine. "Can't wait to finish this." Jiemba shook his head, he had heard it all before.

"Is this bloke a friend of yours?" Dennis asked, jumping out of the way as another foot was slammed down towards them.

"Does he look like a friend of mine?" Jiemba answered. Dennis tilted his head as if the idea of someone trying to destroy Jiemba actually being a friend wasn't actually too farfetched. "We aren't friends," Jiemba confirmed. "I actually really hate this guy."

"Say no more," Dennis waved off the notion. "I have already disabled one of these things today, another shouldn't be too hard, even if this one is moving." Jiemba assumed that Dennis was talking about the other that had been present at the silo. Dennis had previously taken on the part of the plan that secured all those that had been left at the old sandstone building. He had also said he would bring in some reinforcements. Not in the sense of fighters, but others who could actually bring this whole situation to an end. Right on time, sirens could be heard in the distance. More than one, and more than one type. Jiemba could not ask Dennis if these were his reinforcements as he was already battling with Rogers. He dodged each blow from foot or clawed hand as they sought to slam and stomp him into the ground. The forks once more being used as blades, clanging off concrete as each attempt to slice at Dennis was dodged. Dennis was using his whip like a grapple line as he tried to climb up the massive device. In his other hand he was wielding some sword-like weapon which flicked between driving fire around its edge to surging crackling electricity.

Thump!

Jiemba felt a blow to the side of his face. His body turned with his cheek that had been struck and he again fell to the ground. Jiemba was quickly on his feet, spiralling to get out of the way of a follow-up blow should it come.

"You have been a thorn for too long Jiemba," Price roared at him. Jiemba noticed how the Spartan security director had managed to knock him from his feet. The smaller exoskeleton-like Gear machine was wrapped around Price's body. The frame appeared to be strapped tight to his spine, following the outer lines of his shoulders but also shielding his face. It had its own metallic legs, and apart from its own arms, which wrapped around Price's, it had smaller blades that could only lift a pallet rather than a shipping container, and clawed hands to assist with moving objects. Jiemba hoped that the designer had not wanted these things to be used as combat weapons, despite how they were currently being used.

"No more talking," Jiemba replied, he had heard enough. The giant battle that Dennis was engaged in with Rogers crushed its way through the space which was quickly becoming vacant as everyone fled lest they get crushed. Jiemba ignored that as he began one of his own. He flashed forward, throwing a punch towards Price's upper chest. The blow was blocked, with the arm spinning away that had done so, before another came flying straight back at him. Jiemba was struck again, staggering back only a few steps.

"How are you controlling that thing?" Jiemba groaned as he regained a strong footing.

"It takes intellect and determination, something in which you lack," Price spat back at him. "My mind and body control this at the same time. It is strapped to my spine and linked to my brain. My desires put into action before you can react. The purpose to avoid harm to the user, but it is equally effective when dealing out justice."

"You have no sense of the word," Jiemba shot back. He leaped into action. Planning his second and third strike as he prepared to launch his first. He was knocked from his feet before he made contact, glanced in the shoulder by one of the claws before being pumped twice by the hands. Jiemba hit the deck, rolling quickly as a fork cut down at him from above.

"You and your friend will not win this," Price told him. "And when we are done with the two of you, we will finish what we started with everyone else in this miserable town." Price went back on the offensive. Each arm slamming down at Jiemba like some form of enraged mechanical octopus, except he had more arms. Jiemba rolled out of the way at each strike. Large holes appearing all over the floor showing how much power was being put through each blow. Eventually they started connecting, close combat ensuing between the two as blow after blow struck hard on the other.

"Hey Dennis which creature has more legs than an octopus?" Jiemba yelled out, trying to distract himself.

"Is this really the time?" Dennis called out as he struck his sword down into one of the mechanical forks on the giant Gear machine. He was clearly making Rogers mad as he continued to leap from place to place on the giant machine.

"I just want to know," Jiemba dodged again.

"There was a recent discovery of an ancient octopus like creature, it had ten legs," Dennis told him as he jumped towards another arm, driving his fist down on the flat part before going to work again with his sword, which was once again spouting flame. "They named it after a president I think. But if you want a different creature, there are heaps of bugs, insects and arachnids. Perhaps even prawns."

"That's it," Jiemba yelled. "I'm fighting a prawn." This only enraged Price further. He connected with Jiemba before grabbing at him with both claws. Jiemba was hoisted into the air, both blades aimed at his chest as he hung in the air. Price punched Jiemba before slashing at him. One blade cut at Jiemba, creating a small cut. It was the first time Jiemba had seen his own blood for months.

"I am no prawn," bellowed Price. "I am the director of Spartan, like Leonidas himself I have seen your challenge and strength, and I have risen to meet it. Adapting this device to my needs I have power greater than yours. I tire of your voice." He stabbed at Jiemba again, creating a slightly deeper gash. Jiemba yelped with the blow. "You are worthless. Just like these people. Just like this town. I will destroy you all. You will be forgotten, as none of you ever mattered. They have lost the right to live in this place."

"They have the right to live however they choose," Jiemba snapped back, "they need guidance, not a cage."

"I am no longer offering a cage," Price roared. "Thanks to your meddling I will ensure that they have a small room, a few feet below the surface of the earth where they can't bother anybody anymore. Not just the violent ones, or the stupid ones, but all of them, regardless of age, gender or circumstance. And I will enjoy doing it." The blades had pierced Jiemba's shoulders, both working together to hold him aloft, feet dangling down towards the floor.

"No . . .," Jiemba squeaked, before releasing a louder version in defiance. "NO!" His eyes were slammed shut. He could feel pain as Price sustained his striking blows, leaving gash after gash in Jiemba's chest; each normally enough to damage a truck and leave a gaping hole. Jiemba felt every muscle of his body clench to resist the barrage. The goanna hidden below his red Ochre covered chest started to glow. Once faded white it now burned gold, cracking the Ochre all over his body, like an ancient being emerging from radiant amber. Jiemba felt a power he had not ever felt, more than muscle, more than rage. It flowed from deep inside and it filled him.

"I am not worthless," Jiemba roared. "I AM JIEMBA, AND I WILL HIDE NO MORE!" He reached up grabbing the blades that dug into his shoulders, holding him aloft in the air. He grappled at the metal and tore them from his body, tearing his flesh but dropping him to the floor. The blades came at him again. He let them strike, then he grabbed them with his hands before bending and shattering them. He then marched forward, tearing apart Price's other mechanical arms, flinging them to the far ends of the hangar before grappling the man himself. His body flailed to remove itself from the rest of his mechanical body. An electric spark shot out in a last ditch effort to get rid of Jiemba. Jiemba just took the shock before driving Price's mechanical body into the concrete floor below. Price gasped as the frame punctured his body, disabling him as blood crept onto the floor.

"Jiemba, help," Dennis called out. Jiemba turned to see Dennis still fighting Rogers.

"You will both die," Rogers screamed, pumping the hydraulics as hard as he could. The Gear machine had lost one of its arms but it was rampaging just as dangerously. It swept a giant fork towards them only just missing Dennis. The giant Gear machine retreated, Rogers cackling his delight at the destruction he was causing. "I don't get paid enough," he crowed, "Lucky this is fun. Dodge this one scum." The Gear machine hauled free one of the storage containers that had been stacked up high. Using the arms it had left, it dragged it clear and then hurled it towards the pair.

"Run," Dennis called out as he lurched back towards Jiemba.

"No more running," Jiemba snarled. He could still feel the strength flow through him. He marched forward watching as the container came closer. It was as big as a single car garage. Jiemba felt no fear or concern by what would happen. It was only metres away when he flexed his arms. He then swung a punch as hard as he could into the centre of the container. His fist remained where it had struck the solid metal, the rest of the container bending around the point. It split in half, wrapping itself around him. Everyone was quiet as it came to a halt, then Jiemba kicked it free, sending it sliding along the ground with an ear piercing grating noise. It struck one of the building walls triggering the whole structure to shake. The Gear machine that Rogers controlled stepped unevenly as well.

"I have an idea," Dennis yelled as another container was casually grabbed from its storage spot up high. "I am going to need you to distract it while I go in close."

"No problem," Jiemba replied with a smile. Dennis pulled free his whip and charged towards the giant hydraulic robot. "Come here big boy," Jiemba yelled, taunting Rogers. Jiemba did not have to try hard to get his attention. Another container was thrown and dodged, skidding noisily on the ground to slam into vehicles that had been parked, destroying them instantly.

"Get closer," Dennis yelled, "I am going to need you in a second." Jiemba obeyed. He closed the gap quickly as Dennis finally arrived at the feet of the machine. The whip came free and slapped against one of the legs of the Gear machine. It struck hard leaving a mark, but stayed attached. Perhaps there was something else hidden in the tip. Quickly Dennis started running around its base, wrapping the length of the whip around both feet. Jiemba realised finally what he was doing. He needed more time though.

"Come on Rogers," Jiemba called out. "I won't even move this time." Jiemba crossed his arms as the bully of Spartan sneered down at him. He couldn't resist. One more container came clear. Jiemba was too close to avoid it. He lifted it directly above Jiemba's head, who watched as each piston and cog spluttered under the effort, before driving it straight down. Jiemba crouched low before sweeping one powerful arm in an attempted uppercut. He slapped at the container with his fist, sending it sailing into another portion of the headquarters; metal clattered and iron tore as the container fell back to the floor with an earth shaking thud.

"Now Jiemba," Dennis called. Jiemba looked to see that the whip had been completely wrapped around the machine's legs like a lasso around a rouge calf or stallion at a rodeo. The machine teetered as Dennis pulled with all his might. It wouldn't take much more.

Jiemba sprinted the last few metres. Slamming full body into the machine. It wobbled out of control, Rogers roaring from the canopy. It fell hard into the tower which held the remainder of the containers. The remaining machine arms reached out like a person trying to stop itself from falling. It clung to anything within reach, dragging everything down with it.

"Time to move," Dennis called out. He pressed a button on the grip of his whip. The strap immediately detached from where it had been wrapped and retracted. Jiemba would not say anything bad about the tool ever again. The container tower buckled under the stress, screaming as its metal frame detached and crumbled to the floor. The immediate area was clear of people who had all managed to escape during the fight. The tower collapsed down and out, its size meaning that it would spread its destruction almost to the hangar doors.

"Price," Jiemba yelled, the realisation that the director in his crippled form would not be clear of ground zero. Jiemba sprinted towards him, feeling the shadow of items falling behind him. He flung himself to the side of the man as the crashing overcame them both. Price could not escape. Jiemba flung his body over him and braced. The foundations below the headquarters shook as each container and metal beam struck the ground, taking huge divots in the fracturing concrete. The rumble continued, until there was no visible way to see what had happened as dust was thrown into the air. Fragments of debris continued to fall for a few moments, until the only sound apart from those coughing from the dirtied air was silence.

The crowd that had gathered outside, consisting of emergency services, town's people and those who had been involved, watched on with breathless wonder at what would happen next. Dennis, who had cleared the falling debris by mere metres, was first to break the silence.

"Jiemba," he called out as he made his way towards his friend's last known location. Dennis easily shifted junk as he searched. Others held their breath helplessly as he began his search. It looked hopeless, with Dennis calling out over and over. Most of the buildings upper levels had remained intact with only minor damage in comparison to the wrecked mass which once was the hangar floor. Suddenly there was a low crash as metal was shifted and tiny bolts and screws sprinkled noisily around the floor. Jiemba stood tall, with gasps of elation from many, dragging the broken shape of Price out along behind him.

Thunderous applause erupted as Jiemba walked to the headquarters exterior. Dennis awaited him, as did a full squad of police officers in riot gear.

"Why did you come back for me?" Price spluttered as Jiemba rested him carefully on the ground. "Why didn't you let me die?" Jiemba didn't want to talk to the man. He felt that he should but that would have to wait. The presence he had felt inside him causing him to have such strength was slowly draining away. The glowing goanna disappeared, back to hide among the flaking Ochre on his chest, and Jiemba's rage slowly subsided.

"There was a time when I may not have come back for you," Jiemba answered, as he contemplated his reasons. "But a good friend told me that someone had to be the bigger man, and help those people who needed it, no matter who they are or what they may have done."

"So you are the bigger man Jiemba?" Dennis asked.

"Someday I hope to be," Jiemba replied. "But for now I am just a man, who happens to be big. Trying my best."

Chapter 19 – The clean up

"Yep, move those people over there," Senior Constable George Scott, affectionately known as Gumbo, had been busy for the whole morning and it didn't seem likely to stop any time soon. He had been so active, not only with Wellington but also with what had been happening in other areas around the Central West and Westopolis in recent weeks. It was not like he had been inactive before that. He had been doing everything he could for the town that he loved, impeded at every step by the upstart Spartan Security operation which had sought to undermine him at every turn. When he had received the anonymous call that today Spartan would crumble, plus a directive from area command in Orange to be in charge of securing Wellington, he had almost cried he had been so happy. His force, along with extras he had gathered quickly from the surrounding areas, had been directly responsible for the apprehension of the small dirt bike gang that had tormented the city for months. As the sun had risen he had been in place to support the people who had gathered, surprisingly for this reason, as they awaited more aggression. They were bait for a moment, but Gumbo's force had been swift and he had impounded their vehicles before swiftly transporting the attackers off to a processing facility set up outside one of the state run detention facilities on the outskirts of Wellington. Police paddy wagons and carriers had been busy all morning. His force had also taken several Spartan security personnel who had been wrongfully holding townspeople, who had been sick, injured, with some close to dying, against their will in one of the town's silos. The whole scene was disgusting, but Gumbo felt just as responsible. Despite having his hands tied, metaphorically speaking, he had allowed this to occur. It had only doubled his resolve.

"I don't want to see them yet," Gumbo responded to someone else who needed his assistance. Now in the aftermath he was coordinating the response for the whole town. Spartan headquarters was abandoned and destroyed. The staff had been collected and held for questioning. The streets looked like a triage unit had been set up on the outskirts of some foreign conflict, the once pristine newly established residence that was known as New Wellington now anything but. Some tents held federal police who had been called in to help with the process, others held first aid who were treating those in need and providing food for those that were hungry. Good thing there was a lot of it because everyone seemed to be in need. After being spoken to, many had been allowed to return home, and for some of those people it had been the first time in weeks that they had been able to do so. The Spartan threat was no more.

"Sir," one of Gumbo's officers beckoned him over to the side of an ambulance. "One group was able to get inside and find others that were injured amongst the rubble." Although it was a welcome relief Gumbo was still on the defensive.

"I didn't authorise anyone to go in there yet," Gumbo reprimanded, "that whole place could come down at any moment."

"We don't need your permission to render assistance," one of the paramedics responded. Gumbo acknowledged the claim. He smiled at the paramedic. This was a day where he would already have countless piles of paperwork to push through, one more sheet wouldn't matter, especially for the safety of anyone who had been involved. The paramedic, who Gumbo noticed had striking red hair underneath her paramedics cap continued. "We needed a blowtorch to get one of them out. The other is probably going to need a mechanic before he goes to hospital, that machine is buried deep in his skin. I wouldn't be surprised if it has penetrated his bones."

Gumbo glanced at the pair the woman was talking about. He knew who they were. Price, the former director of Spartan, lay in an unconscious state having finally succumbed to the pain he had endured. His offsider, Rogers, looked like he had been burned to within an inch of his life. They were a sorry pair, but that wouldn't stop Gumbo from making their lives far worse.

"Whatever needs to be done, do it," Gumbo said nodding his head. "Good work officer, you and your people. Take one of my men with you when you leave. I want to talk to both of these men once they are fit to do so."

"As you wish," the paramedic smiled at him. She pulled her cap tighter down around her memorable red hair before setting about her next task. Gumbo was promptly pulled aside again for his next thing. The wind swept up around them, making an already cool morning that much colder. A helicopter had flown down from the mountains from somewhere beyond. Gumbo knew who flew it. The massive GreenCorp name and logo planted all along its side. It landed in the middle of the street, the engines groaning as it came to a stop; the whirling blades making a threatening chopping sound as they slowed as well.

"What does he want?" Gumbo asked himself. Two officers flanked his side as he made his way over to the spot it had landed. Jumbo noticed that the man known as Jiemba was sitting nearby, with a small group who were busy reassuring community members who were rightly upset. It would be his next task to talk to the man and his group. He needed to be forceful with the young man, though he doubted he would charge him with anything. By all accounts he had been responsible for Spartan's downfall. That act alone was enough to convict him for a long time, but Gumbo would probably end up thanking him. Besides, Gumbo's young friend Jonah and his cousin Joanna had provided him with multiple copies of electronic files showing what the Spartan group had been doing since their arrival. Attempts by the company to purge all data had been countered by the young girl and a friend of hers. Joanna would not reveal the name of the friend, who also appeared to have left the area along with several others before Gumbo's arrival, but the information alone was all the proof he needed to end Price's career, and that was before he went through the countless victim accounts that his team was busy acquiring.

"Mister Green," Gumbo forced a smile as he met the new arrivals. "As much as I would love to have your company I don't think this is the time or place."

"You are absolutely right," Mister Green responded. He wore his long hair back in a ponytail and stroked his beard as he took in the scene. He wore a black and white suit, but that was common. "You and your people are doing a great job. I was so saddened to hear that there were people that would act so deplorably within the proximity of Westopolis. Luckily, we have you and your team to help resolve this. At GreenCorp we are striving to build a brighter future for everyone. It breaks my heart to know what these people have been going through, and that others thought that there was nothing wrong with it. I am equally upset that GreenCorp machinery was used for such sinister means."

"Thank you Mr Green," Gumbo twigged. "How did you know about this already?"

"I would like to say that I have my ways," Mr Green grabbed Gumbo by the arm warmly and started walking with him away from the helicopter. "But as you can see beyond the rabble there are news crews here reporting this already. I understand that you are hard pressed and you may not have noticed." Gumbo turned to one of his team who had accompanied him and nodded towards the media, who having seen the helicopter were busy pushing their way through the crowd. Gumbo knew his police team could keep them at bay for the time being.

"I didn't come to get in your way officer," Mr Green continued. "I have only come to offer my assistance. If you need anything at all to help you today, or over the next few weeks. You need only to ask. I am here to serve the people of this country, particularly those of the

Central West who are so close to Westopolis, with anything . . . anything, they need at all. You ask, and I will provide."

"Thank you Mr Green," that is a very generous offer.

"I know that you can't talk right now," Mr Green continued. "You and I will talk later. But for the moment I am going to stay out of your way, and probably help with your media problem over there." Gumbo didn't want to say thank you again, and he really didn't have the time to deal with GreenCorp at the moment. Gumbo let the man wander as he marched back to deal with something else. Mr Green looked around, appearing to analyse everything that had happened before him. He turned suddenly, his piercing gaze landing on Jiemba. Mr Green was confident however he walked, but he appeared like he swayed to some tune as he casually made his way over to the group.

"What is your name my friend?" Mr Green asked Jiemba. The big man stood out, particularly as he had refused to clean himself up. Fragments of red Ochre still littered throughout his dense beard.

"Jiemba," came the reply.

"I thought so," Mr Green smiled at the answer. "You are the one they are talking about on the news. A man of mysterious strength, overcoming adversity to free the people of the tyranny that had engulfed the town. You are quite the hero."

"I am no hero," Jiemba replied, showing the slightest hint of embarrassment. "I was just there to help when I was needed."

"Quite so," Mr Green smiled at him. "Nevertheless, I would be very happy if you could visit me in Westopolis at some point in the near future. All of you are welcome in fact." He extended the invitation to the entire group that were listening. "You can all explore my facilities with a guided tour organised by me personally."

"Thanks Mr Green," Jiemba responded politely. "I think for the next little while I will be busy enough around here."

"Are you a Wellington boy?" Mr Green enquired with interest.

"No," Jiemba shook his head. "But I think that I will be hanging around the town until everyone gets back on their feet, including me."

"I am sure the people would be lucky to have your support," Mr Green acknowledged. "Anytime that you want to see me you have an open invite though. I want to talk to you about many things. You and your Wrangler friend wherever he is." Mr Green didn't wait for a response as he turned and walked away. "One of my people will give you my personal details, but for now I better help out the best way I know how. Perhaps our paths will cross again before too long. I look forward to it in fact." Mr Green smiled as he walked towards the cameras. The mob of media were the only noise that could be heard as they enveloped the rich entrepreneur. In a moment he was gone.

"So," Josh asked, standing next to Jiemba. "You are planning to stay in Wellington for a while?"

"Yep," Jiemba responded happily.

"I have a couple of rooms that I can lend," Josh offered. "Some people will probably still need one or two, but you are welcome to have one."

"Thanks Josh," Jiemba patted him on the back. "I would be very happy to hang out with you a bit longer." Josh smiled but then shrugged that off, perhaps thinking it wasn't cool to show such emotions.

"So, how long are you thinking you will hang around with us anyway then?" the young man continued. "A week? A month?" Jiemba thought about the comment for a while. He knew he should probably go home, he knew he should probably see his family. He also knew that they didn't need him like these people did.

"For as long as it takes," Jiemba replied.

Because he needed them too.

Epilogue

It had been six weeks.

In that time, much had happened.

Since the fall of Spartan, the town of Wellington had changed so much. There was no longer an 'us' and 'them'. The title of New Wellington was never used or spoken about. Those people who had resided there had changed as well. Those who had wanted that title and believed in what Spartan had been doing had left. New arrivals had taken their place and adopted the culture of the town rather than where they resided. Many of those who had built there had had no idea what had been happening as Spartan had ensured that news was not spread widely. Afterwards, many had apologised for the image that they had presented and many took initiatives to be more involved and to give back to everyone, not only those on one side of the river.

The town itself had sprung to life. Even stronger, like a phoenix rising from the ashes, focusing on the future rather than the past. What had befallen them all had been terrible, but this community had the strength to overcome anything. With the persuasion of Mr Green, the state government had reinstated a local council to help in supporting the people of Wellington. This action had been quick and unprecedented. No longer were other cities responsible for them, they had their own destiny in their hands.

The head of that council was none other than Jonathan Mires. Every idea he had put forward was adopted with amazing success. He worked in consultation with everybody, so that everyone had a say in the direction of their town. He worked alongside the police force and other agencies to ensure that the law was still respected and that crime remained low in an attempt to work through the issues before they became bigger. Initiatives were taken on by many, pride starting to flow back from every street. He would not let there be an excuse that people would be turned away if they were searching for help. He had multiple plans and processes on standby for just such an occasion.

The former Spartan headquarters had been cleared and rebuilt. It was now the Wellington response unit, looking after any concerns within the city, run by the town's people and aided by the government. Mr Green had paid for its refurbishment, and those of other facilities like the run down fire department and police station, but he also had conditions that went along with the money. They had to be usable for everyone. Many of the rooms within, which had been used for detention, had been transformed into spaces where you could learn. The building was being developed into both a TAFE and PCYC building with inbuilt sporting areas such as basketball and tennis facilities. Officer Gumbo was seen there frequently with anyone who was willing to take him on in a game, regardless if he should have been on duty or not.

Mr Green also paid the rent for all businesses for the next six months so they could get back on their feet. He didn't want to be paid back, but he did want people to be working for themselves after that time. He even assisted in the development of more infrastructure.

The town was thriving, but so was the community.

Uncle Lou, along with Josh, were taking on the task of building a historical centre, showcasing the history of the Wellington area and the people who had lived there for so long. It took up a huge space, and apart from displays and information for everyone to learn from there were also areas where people could come together to celebrate. Dances could be learned and stories shared. Jiemba frequented it almost every day with a smile during its construction. Many of these initiatives seemed like bandaid solutions. They weren't going to last all that long. But underneath the issues of community and culture were being dealt with successfully. Hopefully the bandaids wouldn't be needed before too long. Then perhaps Jiemba could go home, but until then he would help in any way he could.

A small group was gathering at Jiemba's residence. He had lived with Josh for only about a week before he had moved out. Judge had offered Jiemba JayDee's old property, as long as he rebuilt it and looked after the land properly. Jiemba had reluctantly accepted for the short term. The house was slowly coming to shape and would take on a very similar footprint to what it had before. In the meantime Jiemba had spent every night sleeping under stars. He enjoyed the solitude, and was busy spending time studying the constellations which glittered above him; those of his culture and their stories, as well as those where science could explain more to him. The conversation that he had with himself had become far more welcoming and he was developing a love for time spent alone.

"It is taking a while," Judge told Jiemba as they stood by the side of the river. The group stood in the exact spot where Jiemba had floated ashore months before. Jiemba felt sorry for the man he had been when he washed up, but that was also a part of who he was.

"I have been busy," Jiemba responded, cocking an eyebrow at the other man. Judge was wearing a suit, as were the other members of Judge's Court who were assembled. Justin looked roguishly handsome, while Easter was beautiful in her dark slim dress with matching large hat. Neither of them looked like they could beat you up. Gary on the other hand looked angry just to be in the suit, no doubt he would rip it off, probably literally, the moment he left, or the moment that Judge would allow him. A combination of others walked down the hill from the unfinished cottage, many of them familiar faces.

Judge walked past Jiemba, crunching his polished black boots in the rocks on the bank. His feet then clomped on a wooden platform that led to the water's edge. Jiemba had been busy. He had built and rebuilt many things, with some assistance from Jonah and Joanna who had both become his apprentices as he taught them a trade. A small jetty stuck out into the river, built into it was a railing so you couldn't fall, but also a bench so you could relax. Jiemba had used it for fishing, though he had so far been unlucky in catching anything.

The bridge near the mission was fixed. It had been more cosmetic as its wooden foundations were strong. Jiemba had also added some seats and an allocated fire pit area, while reattaching a rope swing and some other equipment to be used. The area had slowly been coming back to life and the mission was being rebuilt. Shane Docker was in charge of the rebuild, with his mate Billy and another lady called Renee. The mission was being transformed into a refuge and rehab centre. There was a waiting list already, and most of them were people from the area who wanted to be a bigger part of what was happening.

"You have done well," Judge said to Jiemba once he reached the end. Jiemba had walked with him along the jetty which was wide enough for both of them and then some. He had a task which he had reluctantly accepted.

"Good morning," Jiemba started the proceedings as soon as everyone had gathered. "I would like to thank you all for coming this morning." Jiemba could already feel his throat stiffen and his chest compress. "My name is Jiemba and I have been given the honour of talking to you all today. We have gathered here for the funeral of a great man. I knew him as JayDee, although many of you knew him as something else. Out of respect I will not share his name, although I only recently found out what that was." A small laugh greeted Jiemba for that remark, but he continued on. "He was friend, family, mentor, and father. But for me he was saviour. When I was given this job I was reluctant. I knew the man at the end of his life, and during that time he revealed very little about himself. I thought that would stop me from talking about him, but as I thought about what I would say today I realise that I wasn't hindered at all. I could guess at what he had done right during his life, and I could presume of what he had done wrong. But one of the things he imposed upon me is that none of that matters. He could have been a celebrity, he could have been imprisoned a hundred times. In either sense he was still just like any of us, and at his worst he would still deserve a second, third, or fiftieth chance. While I didn't know the man, I believe I know what he stood for. If we take lessons from that, then I believe we will come to know even more about him as well as strive to live up to his message. Honesty, strength, and belief. The willingness to persevere even though it might seem too hard. A friend of mine told me that there is no such thing as a lost cause. I would have been wasting my breath in telling JayDee that because he knew." Dennis was in the crowd. Not dressed as the Wrangler, but in mourning just like everybody else. Dennis smiled as Jiemba continued.

"Today we say farewell to someone who meant a great deal to us," Jiemba continued. "But in return we acknowledge that a great spirit has been released into the world for everyone to enjoy. Whenever that voice is telling you to give up JayDee will be there to offer you a different point of view, and whenever you hear the rev of a motorcycle engine just know that he is riding right alongside you."

"Thanks for giving me the second chance I didn't think I deserved," Jiemba finished. Judge patted him warmly on the shoulder before turning away. He waved an arm, which was a signal to his crew. Hundreds of motorcycle engines roared from the roadside above, many more echoed through the bush surrounding them. Even a tractor added to the cacophony. Jiemba smiled. The sound stopped. Judge pulled the lid from a small pot and gently poured the ashes into the river.

Silence followed for what seemed like an eternity, broken only by the sound of Judge crunching back through the small stones at the river's edge and back towards the house. The others followed solemnly, a large procession leaving Jiemba standing alone on the Jetty. He watched as the last flakes of ash dashed on the breeze before diving into the land or the water.

"That was beautiful mate," Dennis said as he clomped up to Jiemba's side. "I am sure he would have been proud. I am proud of you for what you have achieved here."

"Thanks," Jiemba said quietly. The tranquillity around them stretched comfortably. Eventually Jiemba was the one to talk first.

"So," Jiemba started, "you have been trying to contact me."

"Yep," Dennis admitted, nodding his head. "It is partly why I am here. Obviously I am here for you, but I am also here because I need you."

Jiemba shook his head, but then he smiled. He had been purposely avoiding phone calls from everyone. He had bought a new phone. He had contacted his parents, finding out that Uncle Lou had contacted them weeks before, and he had tied up many lose ends. He had then told Dennis only to contact him if he really needed him. But then he had decided not to answer his calls anyway. Jiemba felt his work was just too busy, and the people here needed him first. "Who needs my help?"

"Do you still have that contact for Mr Green?" Dennis asked.

"GreenCorp?" Jiemba said in shock. Dennis nodded.

"We need to go, now," Dennis declared.

"And I have some friends that I want you to meet."

This story is a work of fiction inspired by true people and real stories. All details are written in the most respectful of ways and after talking to professionals and community leaders. If reading this has raised questions about mental health in yourself or someone you know or love, there is support available.

Contact lifeline on 131114

Books by the author:

Following the Leader
Creek Crew: Kingdom of the Creek
Warriors of Westopolis: The Wrangler
Warriors of Westopolis: The Bigger Man

About the author:
Drew is a qualified primary school teacher who resides in the city of Orange, within the Central West of New South Wales in Australia. He is a lover of sports, media, reading and exploring whatever the world has to offer. Drew shares his time between working as a teacher, spending time with his family, and, on rare occasions, writing. Drew can be found on social media platforms including Facebook.

www.facebook.com/drewbaleauthor